Bless Me, Father

STORIES OF CATHOLIC CHILDHOOD

Edited by

Amber Coverdale Sumrall

and Patrice Vecchione

A PLUME BOOK

Acknowledgments

We wish to thank our agent, Charlotte Cecil Raymond, and our editor, Rosemary Ahern. To the contributors of this book we send armfuls of spiritual bouquets.

PLUME
Published by the Penguin Group
Penguin Books USA Inc., 375 Hudson Street,
New York, New York 10014, U.S.A.
Penguin Books Ltd, 27 Wrights Lane,
London W8 5TZ, England
Penguin Books Australia Ltd, Ringwood,
Victoria, Australia
Penguin Books Canada Ltd, 10 Alcorn Avenue,
Toronto, Ontario, Canada M4V 3B2
Penguin Books (N.Z.) Ltd, 182–190 Wairau Road,
Auckland 10, New Zealand

Penguin Books Ltd, Registered Offices:
Harmondsworth, Middlesex, England

First published by Plume, an imprint of Dutton Signet,
a division of Penguin Books USA Inc.

First Printing, November, 1994
10 9 8 7 6 5 4 3 2 1

LIBRARY OF CONGRESS CATALOGING-IN-PUBLICATION DATA

Bless me, father : stories of Catholic childhood / edited by Amber Coverdale Sumrall and Patrice Vecchione.
p. cm.
ISBN 0-452-27154-1
1. Short stories, American—Catholic authors. 2. Catholics—United States—Fiction.
3. Children—United States—Fiction.
I. Sumrall, Amber Coverdale. II. Vecchione, Patrice.
PS647.C4B57 1994
810.8'09222—dc20 94-15605
CIP

Printed in the United States of America
Set in Sabon
Designed by Leonard Telesca

MICHAEL DORRIS
"Martyrs"

"There were fine-print rules governing almost everything: the recitation of the names (in proper sequence) 'Jesus, Mary, and Joseph' was good for a 300 day commutation of one's eventual Purgatory sentence, *but only if they were vocalized.* Simply *thinking* a rote litany gained one no time at all."

RITA WILLIAMS
"The Mathematics of the Moon"

"Mt. St. Gertrude's Academy for Girls sits on the butte like a penitentiary for the criminally female. . . . The sisters are right to be suspicious of my contriteness. I am guilty. My sin springs from that most original of Original Sins. I covet knowledge. I want to understand why they flourish while my family, descendants of Geronimo and the black pioneers, die meekly, like roadkill on the interstate."

TONY ARDIZZONE
"Baseball Fever"

"Because just as the game has its men in black who call the balls and strikes, the fairs and fouls, the safes and outs, so my life had its crew of women dressed in black hoods, floor-length black robes cinched by beads, and oversized white bow ties. The Sisters of Charity, to whom I was delivered at age six by my well-meaning parents for instruction and the salvation of my eternal soul."

MAUREEN HOWARD
"Role Model"

"I was a sinner from the start. . . . My soul was always in question and to launch my spiritual life I mucked up my First Holy Communion. I broke my fast, but I didn't have the guts to go through with the ceremony. I could not take the body and blood of Christ into my mouth now fouled by orange juice."

AMBER COVERDALE SUMRALL is the co-editor of *Touching Fire: Erotic Writings by Women, Women of the 14th Moon: Writing on Menopause,* and other anthologies. PATRICE VECCHIONE is a poet and the editor of three books. Together they edited *Catholic Girls* (Plume). They live in Santa Cruz, California.

We dedicate this book to our
guardian angels for never giving up.

Contents

Preface

One inspiration for *Bless Me, Father* occurred just as we were leaving on a book tour for *Catholic Girls,* when it came to our attention that one of our fifty-four contributors was a man. Just after the book's publication, we received a telephone call from a contributor who we had believed was a woman, telling us that she was a man. Imagine our surprise! Throughout history women have had to pose as men in order to be published. This turn of gender made us realize there were bound to be many Catholic boys out there eager to tell their stories. And judging from the number of submissions by men, we were right.

But certainly, the true inspiration for this book came long before that, harking back to our own childhoods and memories of Catholic girls and boys together. In *Bless Me, Father* you will find stories that give voice to a variety of childhood experiences particular to growing up within the Church and to the turmoil these experiences create. The primal fear of God and "Mother" Church with which we were indoctrinated is a pervasive force throughout this book, along with the ramifications of guilt, shame, the imperative for absolution, and ultimately, the necessity for rebellion. The stories and poems in *Bless Me, Father* are sublime, awe-inspiring, and bold. Their spirited words are laced with humor and spunk. Each contributor gives testimony to the truth of our connected childhoods, a truth we have carried with us, a small flame burning. The stories and poems range in subject from a young boy's first confession, when he begs God's forgiveness for what he believes is his sin of adultery, to the apparition of a girl's Aunt Lucy, which she sees emblazoned on the side of a building; from a girl's terrifying discovery of her best friend's stigmata to a catechism teacher's obsession with Satan; from a boy's circumcision at age twelve to a girl's attempt to secure a back-alley abortion.

Bless Me, Father is divided into three sections, beginning with "Days of Black and White," stories and poems about young children attempting to make sense of religion, their first confession and communion, the world of good and evil. They are questioning the appearance of things, wondering what lies beneath the surface. The writings in the second section, "Wings," explore benevolence, magic, and the child's desire for flight. These are stories of transformation. The selections in "Wild Heart," the last section, are heady, rambunctious, full of sexual confusion and desire. These works resound with a longing for freedom and an awareness of the impending responsibilities of adulthood.

We have not only survived our Catholic childhoods, but have been transformed by the fortitude of an inner fire that was in fact lit by the Church. We have translated the longing for truth, beauty, reverence, and ritual. With the embers of rebellion smoldering, we rise up in defiance of the creed of silence and speak our holiest words.

Silence never brought us anything.
—Audre Lorde

PART ONE

Days of Black and White

The first step . . . shall be to lose the way.
—GALWAY KINNELL

LOUISE ERDRICH

Fooling God

I must become small and hide where he cannot reach.
I must become dull and heavy as an iron pot.
I must be tireless as rust and bold as roots
growing through the locks on doors
and crumbling the cinderblocks
of the foundations of his everlasting throne.
I must be strange as pity so he'll believe me.
I must be terrible and brush my hair
so that he finds me attractive.
Perhaps if I invoke Clare, the patron saint of television.
Perhaps if I become the images
passing through the cells of a woman's brain.

I must become very large and block his sight.
I must be sharp and impetuous as knives.
I must insert myself into the bark of his apple trees,
and cleave the bones of his cows. I must be the marrow
that he drinks into his cloud-wet body.
I must be careful and laugh when he laughs.
I must turn down the covers and guide him in.
I must fashion his children out of playdough, blue, pink, green.
I must pull them from between my legs
and set them before the television.

I must hide my memory in a mustard grain
so that he'll search for it over time until time is gone.
I must lose myself in the world's regard and disparagement.
I must remain this person and be no trouble.
None at all. So he'll forget.
I'll collect dust out of reach,
a single dish from a set, a flower made of felt,
a tablet the wrong shape to choke on.

I must become essential and file everything
under my own system,
so we can lose him and his proofs and adherents.
I must be a doubter in a city of belief
that hails his signs (the great footprints
long as limousines, the rough print on the wall).
On the pavement where his house begins
fainting women kneel. I'm not among them
although they polish the brass tongues of his lions
with their own tongues
and taste the everlasting life.

MARY GRACE VAZQUEZ

Jesus Loves You

"Mama, Mama, wake up! It's time for school, Mama." Little Alice tugged at her mother's sheets. "Mama," she said urgently.

Alice's mother rolled over in bed with a big sigh. "What are you doing, baby, it's still nighttime." Alice's mother reached for the lamp at the bedside and looked at the clock. "It's only four o'clock in the morning." She took a close look at Alice and began to laugh.

"What's funny, Mama?" Alice asked.

"Baby, look at you. You're all dressed up for school and it's only four o'clock."

"What time does school start, Mama? I don't want to be late. Sister Helen said we can't be late for school."

Alice's mother got out of bed and took her by the hand. "Come on, Alice, you have plenty of time. You won't be late for your first day. I want you to put your nightie back on and go back to bed and dream about your first day of school. Okay?" Alice looked unsure, but she knew that her mama knew what was best for her. Her mama always said that: *Alice, drink all your milk, I know what's best for you. When you grow up you don't have to drink your milk if you don't want to, but right now I know what's best for you.*

Alice took off her pink dress with the small roses all over it and very carefully put it on the chair next to her bed. She took off her soft white slip, her pink panties and her pink socks with the white lace around the edge and put them next to her dress. She hadn't put on her shiny black patent-leather shoes yet, so she gave them a little pat as she bent down to pick up the nightie she had thrown on the floor in her haste to get dressed. She put her nightie back on and jumped into bed. "Mama, don't forget to wake me up, okay?" Alice's mother tucked her in, gave her a kiss and told her to go to sleep. She would not forget at all. Alice closed her eyes and dreamed that Sister Helen was reading a story to her about Baby Jesus.

Since her new school was only two blocks away, Alice and her mother walked there. Alice was going to be in the first grade and she was very excited. She knew she would like school. She already knew how to write. Her mama had taught her how to print her name, address and telephone number. Alice's mama had said she was a fast learner and very smart for her age. Yes, she knew she would like first grade very much, even though she wasn't very sure about Sister Helen.

Sister Helen was a little scary to Alice. She had met her after church on Sunday. Sister Helen was very tall and had big round glasses and a very loud voice. "So, Alice, you will be in my class," Sister Helen had said to her. "I like little girls who behave themselves and say their prayers every night." Then Sister Helen had leaned over and patted her on the head. "We're going to get along just fine, aren't we, Alice?" she had asked.

"Yes, 'ster," Alice had said in a tiny voice.

"Alice, we can begin with you calling me *Sister* Helen. Not 'ster. 'Ster is not a word. It is *Sister.* Can you say that to me?"

Alice's mouth had gone dry. "Ye-ye-yes, *Sister.*"

"Very good, Alice. I'll see you in class on Monday. And don't be late."

Alice and her mama could already hear the other children in the playground laughing and shouting. "Alice, do you want me to stay with you until the bell rings?"

"No, Mama." Alice was horrified that her mama could even think of staying with her. "You go home now, and I'll play on the swings until it's time to go into school. Look, Mama," Alice cried out, tugging on her mama's arm and pointing. "There's 'ster Helen. I mean *Sis-ter.* Hi, *Sis-ter* Helen." Alice waved. Sister Helen gave a short wave and then turned her attention to a little boy with Band-Aids on both knees, who was pushing another little boy. Alice watched as Sister Helen came up behind the boy with the Band-Aids and gave him a slight hit on the back of his head. Alice looked at her mother with wide brown eyes. "Oh, Mama, will *Sis-ter* Helen hit me?" Her mama never hit Alice. She always tried to talk with her instead whenever she did anything wrong.

"Alice, if Sister Helen ever hits you, I want you to tell me. But I think you'll be a good girl and everything will be just fine."

The school bell rang, making both Alice and her mama jump. "Mama, that scared me, but next time the bell rings, I won't be scared. I have to go now." She gave her mama a hug as she stooped down to brush back Little Alice's black curls with her hand.

"Alice, please get in line now." Sister Helen walked over to Alice and her mother. "Good-bye, Mrs. Maldonado." Alice's mother knew she had been dismissed and that Alice was now in the hands of the Sisters of the Sacred Heart of Jesus.

Alice and the other children were herded into their new school. "All right, children," Sister Helen said, "I want you all to hang up your sweaters and jackets on the hooks with your name on them." She steered them in the direction of the coatroom.

The children, all twenty of them, rushed into the coatroom, causing a major jam of small bodies pushing and shoving. The boys found their way to the head of the coatroom right away, but then stood there, looking perplexed. In their haste to push the girls aside and find their names, they had managed to push themselves into the farthest end of the coatroom, not even glancing at their names. The girls, all fourteen of them, found their hooks right away. Except for Alice, who stood there with her little pink sweater in her hand, looking as hard as she could at all the hooks. *Mary, Carol, Michelle, Pauline, Anna Jane* . . . and then her heart leaped. There it was: *Alice*. Her very own hook. Just as she was about to put her pink sweater on the hook, the boys, all six of them, decided to try again. One of them threw his coat onto Alice's hook.

"That's my hook," Alice said to the boy in a very determined voice.

"Now it's mine, crybaby," the boy, whose name was Johnny,

said, giving her a push. Just as Alice was going to take his jacket off her hook, Sister Helen gave Johnny a cuff on the head.

"Johnny, that's twice today," Sister Helen said. "If I have to speak to you one more time, you are going to have to sit under the table over there." Sister Helen pointed to a large oak table in the front of the classroom. "Now find your hook, hang up your jacket and go find a desk. Alice, hang up your sweater and go sit down."

The rest of the children had already taken their seats. Sister Helen walked to the head of the class, looking at each child, her arms folded under her cape. Alice thought Sister Helen looked very scary and she didn't dare move. Some of the children were turning around and whispering. Sister Helen brought her arms out from under her cape and in her very long fingers was a ruler. *Crack!* went the ruler on top of Carol's desk. Carol yelped and then there was complete silence. All eyes in the room, all the blue eyes, the brown eyes and the hazel eyes, were riveted on Sister Helen and the ruler.

"You see, children," Sister Helen explained, "this ruler is my helper. If you do something wrong . . ." *Crack!* Sister Helen brought the ruler down hard on Carol's desk once more. Once more, Carol yelped. Sister Helen then looked straight at Johnny and cracked the ruler on Carol's desk again. This time Carol did not yelp. Carol threw up on Sister Helen's shiny black shoe.

Sister Helen looked down as Carol's lumpy breakfast slid off her shoe onto the floor. Sister Helen groaned. "Welcome to first grade, children. I see it's going to be a long year." Sister Helen then pulled a great big white handkerchief out of the side of her black skirt, bent down and began to clean up Carol's breakfast.

After Carol's breakfast had been sufficiently cleaned off the floor and Sister Helen's shoe, Alice watched as Sister Helen pointed a long gnarly finger at Carol and said to her, none too gently, "Go see Sister Bernadette in the office across the hall. She is the nurse, and for goodness' sake, Carol, stop crying. Jesus does not like little children who cry and throw up."

Alice watched Carol leave the room still crying, whether Jesus liked it or not. She had seen Carol crying in church during Mass last Sunday and guessed that Carol just cried a lot, though she didn't know why.

Alice gave a little jump as she realized that Sister Helen was now standing right next to her. "I am passing out paper, children, and I want you all to take your pencils and print your names clearly on the first line of the paper. You are not to go off the line and you are to print in your very best *penmanship*. You all know what penmanship is, don't you?" Sister Helen asked, looking from Alice to Michelle and then picking up her ruler from Carol's empty desk.

"Yes, Sister Helen," a very hesitant class answered in semi-unison.

Sister Helen then looked straight at Alice and asked, "Alice, what is penmanship?"

Alice's brown eyes got very round. She sat up straight in her chair and said, "It's . . . it's . . . it's making your name on a piece of paper, 'ster Helen." As soon as Alice said *'ster* she knew she was in trouble. Sister Helen put her face close to Alice's and said, "Alice, I think I told you on Sunday to say *Sis-ter,* not *'ster.* 'Ster is not a word." Sister Helen stood up again and looked around the room. "Everyone say, 'Sister Helen of the Holy Cross.' That is my name and I want it said clearly." The children responded with a very jumbled "Sister Helen of the Holy Cross."

"Very good, children," Sister Helen said. "Now, print your name. I will come to each of you and check your work. All the best papers will get gold stars."

Alice wanted a gold star, and she knew how to print her name. Her mama had taught her how to print it when she was four and a half. She picked up her pencil, looked quickly around the room to make sure the other children had started to write, and then began to print ALICE MALDONADO. Her name was long, but she knew she could print it. She had written it at home many times before. When she was finished, she felt proud. Her name looked good and she hadn't gone off the line even once. Alice put her pencil down and waited. The whole class waited.

Sister Helen walked up and down each row of desks, slapping her ruler on the palm of her hand and glancing quickly at each child's work, her long black rosary beads rattling against her leg with each step she took, like a half-full jar of jellybeans. Alice was fascinated with Sister Helen's rosary beads. She had never seen rosary beads the size of jellybeans before. When Sister Helen passed Alice's desk, her rosary beads were so close that

Alice was tempted to reach out and touch them. Sister Helen stopped in front of Carol's empty desk again and finally spoke.

"All the children who used their right hand to print their name, raise your right hand." Alice began to raise her right hand, but then realized she had used her other hand to write her name with. She put her hand on her desk.

"Very good, children," Sister Helen said. "Jesus loves you. That is the correct way to print. Always with your right hand. All of you will get gold stars. Now put your hands down, and all the children who used your left hand to print, raise your left hand."

Alice put her hand up, looked around and saw that hers was the only hand in the air. She didn't know what to do. Johnny, who was sitting right behind her whispered, "Alice, you don't get a gold star. Alice, you're bad." Alice decided right then and there that Johnny was not a nice boy, and was just about to say so when Sister Helen came and stood by her desk again. Alice could feel Sister Helen's black skirt rub up against her arm. It was not soft like her own pink dress. She had an urge to scratch her arm where Sister Helen's black skirt had touched it, but she didn't dare put her hand down yet.

"Alice, put your hand down, pick up your pencil in your right hand and print your name. You must never print with your left hand. It is not correct and it does not make Jesus happy."

By the end of the first day of school, Little Alice was very happy to see her mama come to pick her up. "How was your first day of school, baby?" her mama asked as they began to walk home.

Alice burst into tears. "Oh, Mama, Sister Helen of the Holy Cross was mean and Johnny was a bad boy and Carol threw up and I never ever want to print my name again." Alice sniffed and wiped her nose on her sleeve.

"Alice, here's a hankie. Don't wipe your nose on your dress." Her mama handed her a white handkerchief as they waited at the corner to cross the street. "Now, I'm sure it wasn't all that bad. When we get home, I'll give you a snack and you can tell me all about it."

When they got home, Alice's mama gave her some Oreo cookies and a tall glass of cold milk. It was her favorite snack.

"Now, Alice," Mrs. Maldonado said, sitting down at the table, "tell me what happened at school today."

Alice put down her glass and wiped her milk mustache with the back of her hand. "Mama," she began, sounding like she was going to cry again, "I didn't get a gold star and Sister Helen said Jesus doesn't love me." Alice's voice cracked and she began to sob. "Mama, I really, really *really* wanted a gold star."

Alice's mama pulled her chair up right next to Alice. "Why didn't you get a gold star, baby?"

"Sister Helen said I have to use my right hand to print my name." Alice raised her right hand to show her mama. "And I tried and tried but I kept going off the line and it looked funny and Sister Helen said it was the messiest name she had ever seen." Alice was sniffling and hiccoughing now. "She made me print it the whole day and everybody else got to go to recess and play on the swings and sing a new song and I just had to print my name all day long. Sister Helen said I'll never get a gold star until I can print my name with my right hand. She said printing with your left hand is evil and I have to use my right hand. That's why it's called your right hand, because it's the *right* one to use, but I tried and tried and it just works better with my left hand. But if I use my left hand"—Little Alice looked at her hand—"Jesus will never love me." She dissolved into tears again. "Mama, I hate school. I don't have to go back tomorrow, do I? I'll stay home with you, okay?" Alice looked at her mama with big wet eyes.

"No, Alice, it's not okay. You'll have to go back. But I want you to know that Jesus does love you, even if you write with your left hand. I write with my left hand, and don't you think Jesus loves me?" Alice's mama looked at her and waited for her to nod. "And Mr. Cataldo next door can't use either of his hands because of his arthritis, but don't you think Jesus loves him anyway?" Again, Alice nodded. "Now, we'll practice printing with your right hand every night before bedtime until you can print your name without going off the line."

"But Mama, why do I have to print with my right hand?"

"Because it will make Sister Helen very happy and then she'll give you a gold star." Alice's mama got up from the table and went to the kitchen drawer. She pulled out some paper and a pencil. "Here, you can start as soon as you finish your snack."

Alice pouted, but she took the pencil and started to make a shaky A. Maybe if she worked really hard, she could get a gold star.

The next morning when Mrs. Maldonado's alarm went off, there was no Little Alice waiting by the side of her bed in a pink dress, lace socks and shiny black patent-leather shoes, all ready to go to school. Instead, Alice was fast asleep, dreaming that big gold stars were falling from the sky and she was running after them. Just as she was about to catch one with her left hand, she heard Sister Helen calling. "Alice, use your right hand. Your right hand, Alice. Alice, Alice . . ."

"Alice, Alice, wake up, Alice." Alice's mama was standing by her bed, gently shaking her. "Alice, go brush your teeth and get ready for school. I'll go fix your breakfast."

Alice slid off her bed and padded into the bathroom. She stood in front of the sink, looking at her red toothbrush. Alice remembered the crack of Sister Helen's ruler on Carol's desk, and the way Johnny had teased her when she didn't get a gold star. Alice let out a big sigh and slowly reached for her toothbrush with her right hand.

KAY HOGAN

The El Train

The train roared throughout the city, weaving its way through tall buildings like a giant roller coaster. A magic carpet. Kathleen loved the ride, loved being with her mother, loved the places they saw.

"She's only six," her mother said with a smile to the collector as she shoved Kathleen ahead of her. I'm almost nine, Kathleen thought, squeezing herself small. Her mother's lie left her feeling exposed, and she felt her cheeks flush. Even though money was scarce, she still hated having to be part of a lie and ran ahead up the big steel stairs. The air and the light never ceased to delight her and, looking down at the moving city, the people and cars, she felt free. She and the family generally used the subway to travel around the city—the subway, dungeonlike, cold and damp, with people cold and damp. But the "El," which ran overhead along Third Avenue, was a different world altogether—fast, airy, free.

She peered down at the tracks, searching for the third rail. "If you ever fall," her brother had warned, "you'll fry like an egg sunny side up." She shivered and knew that when the train came she would be careful, very careful.

"Glory be to God," her mother screamed. "Another pervert. Sweet Jesus, they're all over the place." The scene was familiar; the man stood with his zipper down, exposed and—smiling.

"Filthy pig," her mother yelled. "Don't look, Kathleen, don't look!"

"I won't, Ma. I won't," but sometimes she did.

The man, completely unperturbed, waved, zippered up and boarded the train. They got into another car while her mother kept talking to everyone in general and no one in particular, finally resting her eyes on a small, thin woman near her. "Bloody blackguards, they are. Dirty filthy things. The devil is in them."

"Who?" the woman asked.

"The perverts that stand around on the platforms."

"Oh really? You mean they expose themselves in the open?"

"Glory be to God, woman, they're all over the place. God will strike them dead the way they carry on. And smiling he was when the train swooshed by. I tell you there's no place left for a decent woman. All men, they're all after the same thing, you know what I mean, but outside, my God, outside!"

Kathleen smiled and crossed over to watch the buildings and the world flash by outside. She thought about "the leg" and hoped her mother would meet people all the way downtown and not remember to talk about it.

What fun, riding past people's lives, peering in windows and whizzing by. Some smiled; others glared, upset by the intrusion; and still others stared blankly, pretending that a train was not roaring by their windows. She watched the clotheslines strewn across yards, the laundry waving in the breeze like colored flags. You could tell a lot about people just by their laundry, she thought. Poverty showed—underwear with holes and gray threadbare towels, while the rich had no lines at all. They didn't need any.

The lines disappeared. Parks and trees jutted out in welcome relief to the gray world of buildings, and she thought of her park, St. Mary's, her one oasis. There she would roll down the hill, hugging the grass to her, and even later, when her mother yelled about the dirt on her, she didn't care, she could still smell the grass, and it made their own dark apartment seem brighter. Silky wartime banners rustled in the wind, and she thought she saw the kids on the street smile up at the train. "Eighty-sixth Street," someone yelled, and like the changing of the guard, waves of people left, waves came in.

"This is Yorkville," her mother said. "Lot of German people

live here. They are supposed to be cheap with the dollar, I hear," her mother whispered. "By the way, what are you?"

"Polish."

"Ah, good people, good people. I like the Polish and they're strong in the faith, have good shrines too."

Too soon, too soon, Kathleen thought. She knew the routines, her mother's definiteness about everybody and everything. But please, not "the leg," although once she starts on the shrines, it could be too late.

"Yes, the Polish shrines are pretty, but St. Lucy's is my favorite, just like Lourdes, miracles all over the place."

"Ma, what station are we at?"

"Oh, it's the Italian section. Never let you out of bed is what I heard. It's no wonder they have so many kids." She was talking in her secret voice, the kind used when somebody was going to get a baby.

"And how many have you?" the woman asked.

"I have five sons besides my daughter."

"Well, that's quite a family. I have four, but I lost two at birth. Have you lost any?"

"No. None."

"Ma, what about Phillip?"

"Hush, child, hush."

Just then two heavyset black nuns came in with a collection plate. Praying and humming, the Negro nuns went through the cars.

"Anything for the Lord's work?"

"They're fake," her mother declared. True, Kathleen had never seen a black nun before and they seemed so happy, compared to the nuns in school. But still, she couldn't envision these women whipping their robes off in the ladies' room and sashaying down the platform, counting their money. "Yes, they are phonies," her mother repeated.

She watched her mother's face and, although her mother still chattered nervously and laughed a lot, a sadness crept over her. Her mother refused to talk about Phillip but her Aunt Margaret sometimes did. "He was brain-damaged. God took him, thank the Lord. Nobody's fault. It just happened. Nobody's fault." That's when they started moving around to different shrines.

Everything was worse after that; her father drank more, and the arguments grew harsher and louder.

Her mother began talking to the woman again, a total stranger, about the drinking and all about her father. At the hospital she would talk for hours with the nurses and doctors about the same thing—strange, when at home, with relatives or with the women on the corner, how different she was, talking about how hard the men worked and if some of them took a little drink once in a while, well, that was no harm. "You have no breeding if you talk to strangers about your family," she said often.

The ride didn't seem like much fun anymore. She would be at the hospital soon and, although her mother denied it, she knew this was another one-way trip to the hospital, but not back home. She remembered getting ready this morning. Her Aunt Margaret and her Cousin Mary were there, dear Aunt Margaret, always there for the good as well as the sad times.

"Give us the underwear," her mother had said to her Cousin Mary. "And the socks, too."

Kathleen liked her cousin but sometimes envied her, her neatly pressed look and that Chinese laundry smell, clean and starchy. Little things bothered her, too—Mary's sharp new pencils and the way Mary lingered on the double cones they bought. Kathleen devoured hers quickly, while Mary licked slowly. There would always be more for her. Mary knew that. Still, Kathleen squirmed in the seat and wondered if Mary was cold going home without her underwear.

"We'll never get a decent bed if she doesn't have decent underwear," her mother had whispered in a low voice to Aunt Margaret, but Kathleen heard and knew she was headed for another hopital stay.

"Such a pretty little girl," the woman said.

"Why, thank you. Sit up, Kathleen, stop slouching. Yes, she's come a long way."

Oh, here it comes, Kathleen thought, moving around nervously, trying to hide, but "her friend" could no longer be hidden.

When had she started thinking of her leg as something outside herself? Maybe because everyone talked about "the leg" as something separate, not a part of her, it had made her dissociate herself from it as well.

"How's the leg?" Mrs. McNulty or Mrs. O'Connor or Mrs. Reilly would ask.

"Fine, just fine. It's all taken care of."

She saw the woman stare down and wished her mother would stop talking, but she went on. "She used to have a problem, a small problem, with the leg, but we took her to the shrine at St. Lucy's, Allerton Avenue. Have you ever been there? I tell you there's miracles all over the place. Just like at Lourdes it is. The water comes down and we collect it in bottles and then at home we rub it to the leg. Well, between the water—it's special you know—the prayers, and a few operations, the leg is fine, just fine."

The way the doctors treated her—every operation, they brought her into their class, showing the interns the last mistake, turning and twisting "the leg." It wasn't that a clubfoot was any big deal. She thought about Mamie Hennigan. Now, that was a sad case, a Mongoloid confined to the apartment for the rest of her life. Or how about Peggy Breslin, another neighbor; she had polio and might never walk again. No, other kids were a lot worse off. A clubfoot was no big deal.

"Why, Aunt Margaret? What happened to Phillip?"

"Ah, Kathleen, he was a beautiful baby, just beautiful. He held him back. That's what did it, you know. The intern was afraid and held the baby back. Oh, the screams of your poor mother. I hear them yet. Well, he was never right, not really. It wasn't her fault, but your father—well, you know men, he wanted everything just right. God took him. Just as well."

She remembered the white wreath on the door, the small coffin in the living room. Kathleen stared at her mother, at the hands, tired and worn from use.

"What station are we at, Kathleen?"

"Seventy-fourth, Ma; not much longer."

"Sure I can see as good as the next. Just the dimness of the lights on these trains."

Her mother needed glasses, borrowed her father's whenever the *Daily News* had a scandal or juicy trial going. "Those dang doctors want to put glasses on everyone. Want to make money and destroy the looks as well. Do you really have to wear those?" she said to the woman.

"Well, they help me see."

"I'm not one for venturing an opinion, mind you, but I'd think about flinging them out."

"Yes, but, well, I'll think it over."

The poor woman, Kathleen thought, she was no match for Ma. She began to look forward to their stop at Nedick's. They always went there before the hospital. She imagined the coffee and orange juice smells, and hoped they could get hot dogs, too. Maybe this time, she thought, maybe he'll come and see me. She didn't know how she really felt about her father—frightened mostly. Even if he came, she didn't know what they would say to each other. Still, she remembered all those times staring into the corridor, willing him to be there. Maybe next time.

Music filled the train and a group of young boys burst in dancing. They were only about Kathleen's age, some a little younger, and they laughed and danced up and down the aisle. Her mother clapped and stamped her feet in happy appreciation.

"You're fine lads, you surely are," and she reached over and hugged the smallest of the group, a boy about five. "You're a fine broth of a lad, you are." She reached into her purse and Kathleen thought, Oh no, there goes our trip to Nedicks. Pressing the money into the boy's hand, her mother hugged him one last time. "There, give us one more step, just one more."

"Good-bye and God bless," her mother called to the woman as the train came to Fifty-ninth, their stop.

"Nice meeting you," Kathleen said and then her mother grabbed her and pulled her along to the door. The woman wouldn't get a chance for one last look at "the leg."

They walked toward the hospital, Kathleen trailing behind her mother.

Maybe they'll guess right this time, Kathleen thought.

"I hope the clinic won't be crowded."

Maybe it will be fine and somebody will say it doesn't make any difference; it never did.

"He'll be mad if I'm late getting home. If I'm late and he has to go work without his dinner, he'll be mad."

Maybe she'll find more money in the bottom of her pocketbook. Yes, she will, she always does.

"It's not my fault, Kathleen, you know it's not my fault."

I know, Ma. I know.

AMBER COVERDALE SUMRALL

First Day of School, 1951

Knees locked, arms hugged to body, the girl holds
her shiny lunchpail with its thermos of milk.
Her white uniform blouse, buttoned at the collar,
tucks into a cocoa-brown jumper. Her mother has tied
a polka-dot ribbon around the girl's short curly hair
and crouches now, behind the lens that will capture
her daughter in this place and time.

A cross glows above the tan stucco doorway.
Her mother wants this in the photograph.
Hold still, she says.
The girl's tongue pushes against her cheek.
There is a trace of a smile. She is remembering
the black spider, big as her fist, that lives
in the ivy outside the living room window.
How it appears only to her.

She looks down at her new red shoes. Magic, like Dorothy's.
Her grandmother bought them instead of the brown oxfords.
These shoes will lift her over the fear, over the shyness.
Look at the camera, her mother is saying.
Don't move.
Dreams gather like curtains behind the girl's eyes.

I would fly through decades to wrap this child in my arms,
show her the path to the creek, its smooth marbled stones.
I would whisper of wind in redwoods, the great horned owl.
Promise hundreds of spiders in silken webs.
I would tell how all these things and more
already dwell in her, constant as her breath.

RUDOLFO ANAYA

Excerpt from Bless Me Ultima

There is a time in the last few days of summer when the ripeness of autumn fills the air, and time is quiet and mellow. I lived that time fully, strangely aware of a new world opening up and taking shape for me. In the mornings, before it was too hot, Ultima and I walked in the hills of the llano, gathering the wild herbs and roots for her medicines. We roamed the entire countryside and up and down the river. I carried a small shovel with which to dig, and she carried a gunny sack in which to gather our magic harvest.

"¡Ay!" she would cry when she spotted a plant or root she needed, "what luck we are in today to find la yerba del manso!"

Then she would lead me to the plant her owl-eyes had found and ask me to observe where the plant grew and how its leaves looked. "Now touch it," she would say. The leaves were smooth and light green.

For Ultima, even the plants had a spirit, and before I dug she made me speak to the plant and tell it why we pulled it from its home in the earth. "You that grow well here in the arroyo by the dampness of the river, we lift you to make good medicine," Ultima intoned softly and I found myself repeating after her. Then I would carefully dig out the plant, taking care not to let the steel of the shovel touch the tender roots. Of all the plants we gathered none was endowed with so much magic as the yerba del manso. It could cure burns, sores, piles, colic in babies, bleeding dysentery and even rheumatism. I knew this plant from long ago because my mother, who was surely not a curandera, often used it.

Ultima's soft hands would carefully lift the plant and examine it. She would take a pinch and taste its quality. Then she took the same pinch and put it into a little black bag tied to a sash around her waist. She told me that the dry contents of the bag contained a pinch of every plant she had ever gathered since she began her training as a curandera many years ago.

"Long ago," she would smile, "long before you were a dream, long before the train came to Las Pasturas, before the Lunas came to the valley, before the great Coronado built his bridge—" Then her voice would trail off and my thoughts would be lost in the labyrinth of a time and history I did not know.

We wandered on and found some orégano, and we gathered plenty because this was not only a cure for coughs and fever but a spice my mother used for beans and meat. We were also lucky to find some oshá, because this plant grows better in the mountains. It is like la yerba del manso, a cure for everything. It cures coughs or colds, cuts and bruises, rheumatism and stomach troubles, and my father once said the old sheepherders used it to keep poisonous snakes away from their bedrolls by sprinkling them with oshá powder. It was with a mixture of oshá that Ultima washed my face and arms and feet the night Lupito was killed.

In the hills Ultima was happy. There was a nobility to her walk that lent a grace to the small figure. I watched her carefully and imitated her walk, and when I did I found that I was no longer lost in the enormous landscape of hills and sky. I was a very important part of the teeming life of the llano and the river.

"¡Mira! Qué suerte, tunas," Ultima cried with joy and pointed to the ripe-red prickly pears of the nopal. "Run and gather some and we will eat them in the shade by the river." I ran to the cactus and gathered a shovelful of the succulent, seedy pears. Then we sat in the shade of the álamos of the river and peeled the tunas very carefully because even on their skin they have fuzz spots that make your fingers and tongue itch. We sat and ate and felt refreshed.

The river was silent and brooding. The *presence* was watching over us. I wondered about Lupito's soul.

"It is almost time to go to my uncles' farms in El Puerto and gather the harvest," I said.

"Ay," Ultima nodded and looked to the south.

"Do you know my uncles, the Lunas?" I asked.

"Of course, child," she replied, "your grandfather and I are old friends. I know his sons. I lived in El Puerto, many years ago—"

"Ultima," I asked, "why are they so strange and quiet? And why are my father's people so loud and wild?"

She answered. "It is the blood of the Lunas to be quiet, for only a quiet man can learn the secrets of the earth that are necessary for planting—They are quiet like the moon—And it is the blood of the Márez to be wild, like the ocean from which they take their name, and the spaces of the llano that have become their home."

I waited, then said, "Now we have come to live near the river, and yet near the llano. I love them both, and yet I am of neither. I wonder which life I will choose?"

"Ay, hijito," she chuckled, "do not trouble yourself with those thoughts. You have plenty of time to find yourself—"

"But I am growing," I said, "every day I grow older—"

"True," she replied softly. She understood that as I grew I would have to choose to be my mother's priest or my father's son.

We were silent for a long time, lost in memories that the murmur of the mourning wind carried across the treetops. Cotton from the trees drifted lazily in the heavy air. The silence spoke, not with harsh sounds, but softly to the rhythm of our blood.

"What is it?" I asked, for I was still afraid.

"It is the *presence* of the river," Ultima answered.

I held my breath and looked at the giant, gnarled cottonwood trees that surrounded us. Somewhere a bird cried, and up on the hill the tinkling sound of a cowbell rang. The *presence* was immense, lifeless, yet throbbing with its secret message.

"Can it speak?" I asked and drew closer to Ultima.

"If you listen carefully—" she whispered.

"Can you speak to it?" I asked, and the whirling, haunting sound touched us.

"Ay, my child." Ultima smiled and touched my head. "You want to know so much—"

And the *presence* was gone.

"Come, it is time to start homeward." She rose and with the sack over her shoulder hobbled up the hill. I followed. I knew that if she did not answer my question that part of life was not yet ready to reveal itself to me. But I was no longer afraid of the *presence* of the river.

We circled homeward. On the way back we found some manzanilla. Ultima told me that when my brother León was born his mollera was sunken in, and that she had cured him with manzanilla.

She spoke to me of the common herbs and medicines we shared with the Indians of the Río del Norte. She spoke of the ancient medicines of other tribes, the Aztecas, Mayas, and even of those in the old, old country, the Moors. But I did not listen, I was thinking of my brothers León, and Andrew, and Eugene.

When we arrived home we put the plants on the roof of the chicken shed to dry in the white sun. I placed small rocks on them so the wind wouldn't blow them away. There were some plants that Ultima could not obtain in the llano or the river, but many people came to seek cures from her and they brought in exchange other herbs and roots. Especially prized were those plants that were from the mountains.

When we had finished we went in to eat. The hot beans flavored with chicos and green chile were muy sabrosos. I was so hungry that I ate three whole tortillas. My mother was a good cook and we were happy as we ate. Ultima told her of the orégano we found and that pleased her.

"The time of the harvest is here," she said, "it is time to go to my brothers' farms. Juan has sent word that they are expecting us."

Every autumn we made a pilgrimage to El Puerto where my grandfather and uncles lived. There we helped gather the harvest and brought my mother's share home with us.

"He says there is much corn, and ay, such sweet corn my brothers raise!" she went on. "And there is plenty of red chile for making ristras, and fruit, ay! The apples of the Lunas are known throughout the state!" My mother was very proud of her brothers, and when she started talking she went on and on. Ultima nodded courteously but I slipped out of the kitchen.

The day was warm at noonday, not lazy and droning like July but mellow with late August. I went to Jasón's house and we played together all afternoon. We talked about Lupito's death, but I did not tell Jasón what I had seen. Then I went to the river and cut the tall, green alfalfa that grew wild and carried the bundle home so that I would have a few days of food laid in for the rabbits.

Late in the afternoon my father came whistling up the goat path, striding home from the flaming-orange sun, and we ran to meet him. "Cabritos!" he called, "cabroncitos!" And he swung Theresa and Deborah on his shoulders while I walked beside him carrying his lunch pail.

After supper we always prayed the rosary. The dishes were quickly done, then we gathered in the sala where my mother kept her altar. My mother had a beautiful statue of la Virgen de Guadalupe. It was nearly two feet high. She was dressed in a long, flowing blue gown, and she stood on the horned moon. About her feet were the winged heads of angels, the babes of Limbo. She wore a crown on her head because she was the queen of heaven. There was no one I loved more than the Virgin.

We all knew the story of how the Virgin had presented herself to the little Indian boy in Mexico and about the miracles she had wrought. My mother said the Virgin was the saint of our land, and although there were many other good saints, I loved none as dearly as the Virgin. It was hard to say the rosary because you had to kneel for as long as the prayers lasted, but I did not mind because while my mother prayed I fastened my eyes on the statue of the Virgin until I thought that I was looking at a real person, the mother of God, the last relief of all sinners.

God was not always forgiving. He made laws to follow and if you broke them you were punished. The Virgin always forgave.

God had power. He spoke and the thunder echoed through the skies.

The Virgin was full of a quiet, peaceful love.

My mother lit the candles for the brown madonna and we knelt. "I believe in God the Father almighty—" she began.

He created you. He could strike you dead. God moved the hands that killed Lupito.

"Hail Mary, full of grace—"

But He was a giant man, and she was a woman. She could go to Him and ask Him to forgive you. Her voice was sweet and gentle and with the help of her Son they could persuade the powerful Father to change His mind.

On one of the Virgin's feet there was a place where the plaster had chipped and exposed the pure-white plaster. Her soul was without blemish. She had been born without sin. The rest of us were born steeped in sin, the sin of our fathers that Baptism and Confirmation began to wash away. But it was not until Communion—it was not until we finally took God into our mouth and swallowed Him—that we were free of that sin and free of the punishment of hell.

My mother and Ultima sang some prayers, part of a novena we had promised for the safe delivery of my brothers. It was sad to hear their plaintive voices in that candlelit room. And when the praying was finally done my mother arose and kissed the Virgin's feet, then blew out the candles. We walked out of la sala rubbing our stiff knees. The candlewick smoke lingered like incense in the dark room.

I trudged up the steps to my room. The song of Ultima's owl quickly brought sleep, and my dreams.

Virgen de Guadalupe, I heard my mother cry, return my sons to me.

Your sons will return safely, a gentle voice answered.

Mother of God, make my fourth son a priest.

And I saw the Virgin draped in the gown of night standing on the bright, horned moon of autumn and she was in mourning for the fourth son.

"Mother of God!" I screamed in the dark; then I felt Ultima's hand on my forehead and I could sleep again.

GIGI MARINO

The Miracle of St. Anthony

Her house was a shrine. Ceramic angels, saints, rosary beads, Madonnas, prayer books, vials of holy water, ratty palms twisted into crosses, and lovely, tragic airbrushed portraits of Christ hung or stood on every wall, shelf, and table. Holy reassurances were necessary, as if by virtue of their presence we were one step closer to grace.

For most of my childhood, I wore a scapular—a sacramental necklace of sorts—to ward off sin. The scapulars the church handed out every feast day had two tiny felt pictures of Our Lady of Mt. Carmel encased in a plastic covering, one in the front and one in the back, which bit both into my chest and back, but I didn't mind the suffering. In school we recognized each other by our attention to devotion, the way our scapulars showed through turtlenecks and T-shirts.

Grandma was even more devoted. At night, after washing our arms and faces in an enamel basin in the kitchen, we entered into the ritual of undressing for bed. I stripped down to my cotton T-shirt quickly, always removing the scapular last and placing it gently on her dresser in front of the Pietà. But Grandma's religious medallions were like armor. She'd take off her dress, next her slip, then remove her scapular, worn thin with age, the picture of the Virgin so faded that I thought Grandma must have worn it in Italy at the turn of the century when she was my age. She unclasped her Madonna necklace. Then came the undoing of the heavy medals she kept pinned on her bra, next to her heart—a benevolent Christ in pewter, another Virgin in bronze, Mother and Child on a silver locket. Sometimes she kept a house key there too, and almost always a wad of sweaty bills. I'd sit cross-legged on her bed, studying her naked walnut-colored skin, and wonder if I would have to do this when I got old, carry so much weight next to my heart where no one could see it, except God.

At her house, we prayed the rosary several times a day. Whenever I stayed with her, she woke me early in the morning, wrapped my hair in a babushka, and demanded I go to the seven A.M. mass, where a weary priest—any priest, they all performed the same automated motion of serving the sacrament—gave communion to a few broken immigrant women who lived for the afterlife.

But for all Grandma's goodness and piety, she had her own particular brand of justice and morality. Forgiveness may have been God's domain, but in the presence of sin, she took it upon herself to pass judgment and administer suitable punishment. And not just ordinary punishment, like a swift smack across the backside, but something more psychological, penalties that depended on deprivation. When I once refused to eat a bowl of boiled dandelion greens, she said, "If you hungry enough, you eat anything." Four hours later, I did. When my father lost his clothing business in 1968, she had the thousand dollars he needed to avoid bankruptcy but wouldn't lend it to him because he gambled: horses, dogs, craps, cards, the whole gamut. And once when my grandfather stumbled home staggering drunk, she locked him in the chicken coop for three days, though she dutifully brought him meals.

We were all sinners, weak, susceptible to the devil's trickery. Grandma talked about the evil one so often I believed he dwelt in the same house, following us, mimicking, snorting, laughing. Often Grandma would say, "Dat bad man got me again. I lose my timble and get so mad I swear. Now I pray." So, we knelt each night with our glow-in-the-dark rosary to pray for strength to keep the devil away.

A statue of St. Anthony, set on a shelf above her bed, hovered over us. Wearing humble brown robes, cradling Baby Jesus in his right arm, and holding a bunch of white lilies in the other.

Anthony towered nearly three feet high. I favored him; Grandma told me he especially looked out for small children. She was sure St. Anthony was present the day my sister, Mary, was hit by a car and left miraculously unhurt. That day Grandma had held our hands as we stood in front of the church. Mary bolted away and ran across the road, brushed against a passing car, and rolled like a tumbleweed. In memory, I see Anthony lifting her above the road on a dusty little cloud.

I liked St. Francis too, but doubted his ability to understand my problems since he had spent so much time out in the woods convening with animals and not small children. So, I prayed often to St. Anthony's statue, though Grandma told me that this statue wasn't the saint, just the way a picture of someone you love wasn't that someone. Just a picture. What Grandma didn't know was that I saw the life-size statues in church move. Nothing dramatic, a wink here, a flutter of the Virgin's fingers there, and once, St. Joseph shifted on his walking staff.

I knew they weren't just statues, though I couldn't tell this to anyone. Grandma herself had once told me that when she worked as a cleaning girl for rich people, she was dusting a picture of the Virgin Mary when it began to shed tears behind the glass. Saints and virgins were capable of anything.

One bitter winter day, when I was ten, I passed through Grandma's bedroom and saw Anthony's eyes move. I left the room and returned quickly. Everything was the same. Grandma was in the adjoining kitchen cooking, and all the windows were steamed, some frosted, etched in ice. The room was filled with diffuse white light. Anthony beamed. Beautiful and mute. I fixed on the statue and played a staring game. I moved my head, but not my body, shifting side to side like a Balinese dancer. He moved, he didn't move, he moved. After fifteen minutes, I convinced myself that I was not alone. Anthony was making an appearance just for me.

The spirit of St. Anthony *was* in the statue, I reasoned, and I was going to find him. I had read all of the pamphlets the nuns had given us on Our Lady of Fátima appearing to children and was convinced that if I believed and prayed hard enough I could summon a saint. I wanted to be holy, so holy that I would be divinely protected. My mom would stop drinking, and the next time my dad raised his arm to hit me, he'd be pushed back by an invisible force field.

Anthony, I knew, was my answer.

I approached the statue slowly. Reverently, I reached out to pat his bald head. It seemed warm. I stood back for a moment and saw a slight, but glowing, halo. This was the only sign I needed to believe that this was my miracle.

His head was already loose, so the plaster gave way easily when I pried it off with the spoon I'd slipped into my back pocket on one of my trips to the kitchen. I expected a wisp of white smoke to rise, like a genie in a bottle, and materialize before me. I waited, but nothing happened. I quickly realized I had made a terrible mistake. Not only was his body disappointingly hollow, but an obscene wire stuck out from the plaster head. In the process of trying to find the holy spirit in the hollow statue, I had chipped off pieces of plaster from Anthony's neck. No matter how hard I tried, I couldn't get the head to sit naturally on his shoulders. It slumped to one side, looking exactly as it was. Decapitated.

Utter dread displaced my spiritual curiosity. My usually deft fingers were numb and fumbling. I felt a click in the base of my own neck when I realized what I had done: beheaded my favorite saint. I had broken it. And even worse than Anthony being mad at me, I knew Grandma would be too.

I found an ancient bottle of Lepage's glue in the closet and attempted surgery. Trembling, I smeared the gummy amber stuff on his neck, but the head obeyed gravity and remained cocked at a painful angle. I tried then to bolster it by wedging bits of paper between the head and neck. Mid-operation, almost as if Grandma could smell my mounting fear, she walked in. She was tiny, maybe five feet, and fierce. Thick white hair whipped into a bun, a dark wrinkled face, deep black eyes. And even after seventy years in America, she still spoke with a heavy Neapolitan accent.

"Watch you doin' there?" she asked.

I didn't look at her. "Nothing. It just broke. I was trying to find the holy spirit, and it broke."

"Who tole you touch Antony? The bad man tell you?"

"No, Grandma, it was an accident."

"You lie. The bad man tell you."

"No, I was just playing." Then I wondered if the devil hadn't told me to take off St. Anthony's head. No matter. I was still guilty. And very scared.

"You did very bad thing. This is sin."

I wasn't sure if the sin was my lying or breaking the statue. Religious artifacts were sacred, and Grandma forbade us to throw away anything bearing a holy image. Dispensable things, like old palms and tattered postcards of Our Lady of Guadalupe and Fátima, had to be burned. Grandma never explained why incineration of the sacrosanct was not a sin. Once a year, we just gathered our palms quietly and burned them without question in Grandma's little brick furnace out back.

"You sin and you gonta get punished," Grandma said as she grabbed my wrist. Her grasp was surprisingly strong, and she pulled me off the bed and into the kitchen.

She wouldn't hit me. She never did.

"You a goin' in the cold room," she said, still holding on to me.

The cold room was just that. It had once been a porch and was now a spare bedroom with no insulation and no heat. The linoleum floor was always chilly, and the walls were thin. Grandma kept a stand-up freezer there, hardly necessary in the winter. There were also an iron bed, a few chests of drawers, and stacks of pots and pans. One naked light bulb hung from the ceiling.

"No, please don't, Grandma."

I started crying. She told me to stop. I protested louder. "I won't touch it again, I promise. I'm really sorry."

"You learn a lesson," she said as she dragged me into the cold room. She let go of my wrist, and I ran after her, but she slammed the door shut before I could escape. She bolted the door. I was barefoot, and my feet stung from the cold. I screamed after her to let me out. The skeleton key clicked in the lock. I looked around the room. In some places, the light blue wallpaper had separated from the wall, and when the wind blew, the paper shivered and trembled. I tried the window, but it was painted shut. Every time I begged, "Let me out," Grandma told me I had been bad.

I pounded against the door until my fists were red and puffy. I wasn't sure if Grandma was even still in the kitchen. She stopped answering my cries. I gave up too and huddled between stiff sheets trying to keep warm. My crying lessened to whimpering. Fifteen or twenty minutes later, I got up and went back to the door.

"Grandma," I said as calmly as possible, "I have to go to the bathroom."

"You lying," I heard her say, muffled, through the door.

"No I'm not, and I really have to go. Now."

"You lying," she insisted, "you not getting out."

Again we started the back-and-forth begging-and-screaming match. Again Grandma became silent. She stopped answering me. I knelt down and looked through the crack underneath the door. I couldn't see her feet. The kitchen was empty. She'd probably gone to watch *The Dick Van Dyke Show.*

I did have to go to the bathroom, and the more I thought about it, the worse the urge became. I was getting stomach cramps and yelled again to Grandma but heard no reply. I prayed to Anthony, crossed my legs, clenched my teeth, rolled up fetus-like on the bed, but I couldn't will the sensation away. The cramps kept getting worse. I knew I had to relieve myself.

Staggering, I rummaged through the pots and pans until I found an aluminum pie tin that seemed suitable. I looked around the room to see if anyone was watching before I pulled down my pants. I placed the flimsy tin on the floor, squatted over it, and shit in it. The air was so cold that immediately steam rose up out of the pie tin. I stood for a while over it, not sure what to do or where to go next. With my pants around my ankles, I waddled across the room and milled through another drawer and searched for a toilet-paper substitute. A crinkled old envelope was the best I could find. Once I got my pants back up, I felt relief, then a new panic, a terrible and deep shame. Shitting like a dog in a pie tin was worse than breaking the statue. This was base and low, worse even than the filthiest people Grandma talked about. I was even more desperate for escape now and to get out before Grandma discovered my new sin.

Wind rocked the room, the wallpaper twitched, thin panes of glass wobbled. I imagined the room breathing and laughing at me. I focused on the window, my only escape. I searched again and found a rusty butter knife in one of the drawers. Frantically, I poked at the seal of paint around the window. After several minutes, I was able to shake the window open. The sidewalk was just a few feet below me. I didn't have much of a plan. My frenzy was fueled by fear. I had just done a very bad thing.

I set the pie tin on the window ledge and jumped out. Outside the sky was still light, though dusk was fast approaching. I prayed again, this time so that no one would see what I was carrying. I thought about emptying the tin into the creek behind the house, but I was afraid Grandma would see me from the living room window. I quickly found a sturdy stick, dug a shallow hole in the garden, and buried the contents. I waited until there were no cars passing by in the alley. Then I scuttled down the sidewalk in the front of the house. I crumpled up the pie tin and stuck it deep in the garbage can.

I was hot with humiliation, numb to the cold. I didn't know whether I had committed a sin or not, but my guilt was great. I ran back to the open window, put my hands on the ledge, pulled myself up, crawled through, and closed it behind me. By now I felt a strange calm. I pulled the string that turned on the light bulb and sat on the bed directly below it as still as I could be, trying to imagine myself disappearing into the yellow-white glow. I sat straight up, hands in my lap, feet not quite touching the floor. I held my breath and counted the seconds I could go without breathing. I convinced myself that if I made no movement, I *could* be invisible.

A little while after nightfall, I finally heard the bolt unlocking. Grandma shuffled into the room, clasping rosary beads between her gnarled fingers. "You sorry now?" she asked.

"Yes."

"You apologize to Antony?"

"Yes."

"You suffer?"

"Yes."

"You din't hafta go to d' bathroom, did you?"

"No."

"What else?"

"I pray to God to give me strength not to lie anymore." I bit the soft flesh inside my mouth until I tasted the tinny blood.

"O.K. Good. You be a good girl now. Come eat, I saved you some supper."

I followed her into the kitchen. I prayed, broke bread, and ate silently. The next day she reached into her dress and handed me a bill to buy an Orange Crush at Milicia's corner store. I thanked her and brought back the change. We didn't talk about the night before, and I never told anyone that Grandma had locked me in the cold room. I wanted to believe she was the most pious woman I knew.

MAUREEN SEATON

An Ordinary Mass

Everything holy seemed sad.
Impossible karma,
wheels spinning death,
resurrection, death.
Purple white purple white,
ending in a garden of blood,
Peter's ear on the ground,
all that betrayal. "The world
is bad," the priest would say
so we waited for death to save us.

Things you find in heaven:
Angels, of course,
wings and choir robes, each
with perfect pitch.
Everyone in heaven is perfect,
everyone's soul visible,
stainless, you can put your hand
right through it, it feels
hot and prickly.
The Apostles walk around
on clean feet. Women
stand straight as trees.

You can bring your toys
to heaven, and Jesus
will play with you. "The good

die young," the priest would say,
and "Satan loves a sinner,"
catching us between eternities
of boredom and brimstone.
"Per omnia saecula saeculorum."
Imagine the word: Forever.

The little red bells
in my prayer book delight me.
The words that go with the bells
take me from my body:
Elevate, sacred, adoration.

First we break his bones,
then we devour him. Or
we break his bones, dip him
in his blood, devour him.
Later we drink the blood too.
Sometimes the blood is red,
sometimes gold.

When the altar boy rings the bells,
I feel Jesus enter my heart.
There are no lasers yet,
but Mass is full of secrets and light
and Jesus gets into me somehow.
I faint from kneeling up straight
on an empty stomach.
Tucked in bed, I wait
for the holes in my hands
to bloom like roses,
the blood to run across the sheets
and change my life.

JOHN VAN KIRK

Sin

The church smelled faintly of incense and melting candlewax, but the dark confessional held the perfume of the woman in the tight green jacket and green hat who had gone in before Henry. It seemed a long time after he pulled the heavy curtain closed that the door behind the screen slid back, and when it did, Henry began with the usual list of petty offenses: stolen cookies, spiteful thoughts, cruel words. Then, at the end, he forced it out in a hoarse whisper: "and . . . uh . . . I, uh . . . made sperm, Father."

"You what?" Father Jerome asked from the other side of the screen.

"I . . ." Henry couldn't believe he was going to have to say it again, wasn't sure whether the priest had simply not heard or had not understood. "I made sperm." He didn't know any other way of saying it to a priest.

"You mean you pulled yourself off?"

Father Jerome was the most distant and taciturn of the priests at Immaculate Conception. He was liked by the students though, the altar boys especially, because he said the fastest mass—when he had the seven o'clock mass, it was nearly always over by seven-twenty, and Henry had heard that he had once completed it in thirteen minutes. He made no attempt to converse with his altar boys as the other priests did, never cracked a joke or tried to draw you out, spoke only when he had to; if you missed a response he would just fill it in himself and go on, never counseling you about it afterwards. He also drank the most wine during the mass of all the priests, emptying the cruet and using almost none of the water. Henry had confessed to him before, and found him as terse and efficient there as in his sermons—no wasted words, no wasted time. Now Henry was confused and frightened. The unfamiliar phrase that Father Jerome had just used seemed in its awkward descriptiveness even more vulgar and embarrassing than the phrases Henry had heard from his young friends: *jerk off, beat off,* phrases which he had been afraid to use in the confessional. Nobody said *pull off.* He felt ashamed now not only for himself but for the priest as well. Was this what he had come to confess, *pulling himself off?*

"Yes, Father."

"Anything else?"

"No, Father."

There was a pause.

"For this . . . ," the priest prompted Henry.

Henry did not catch the cue.

"For this . . . ," the priest said again, his voice gently urgent. And Henry remembered.

"For this and all my sins I am heartily sorry. . . ."

Now Henry waited for the serious words he had coming to him. His eyes had grown used to the dark, and he could make out the shadowy silhouette of the priest. A faint red glow moved up from the lower left corner of the screen, grew suddenly bright near the center, then descended again in a smooth arc. Father Jerome was smoking a cigarette.

"This . . . this is a terrible temptation . . . a terrible sin," the priest began. "Our Lord is very severe with us on this, very severe, very . . . severe. You must resist this temptation with all your strength. You must fight against the flesh. This is a . . . a dangerous thing . . . It is . . . It is—" He broke off, took another long puff on the cigarette. "For your penance say five Our Fathers and thirteen Hail Marys." Father Jerome mumbled the absolution and slid the door shut with a soft *shunk.*

In a daze, Henry walked to the altar rail, knelt before the side altar with the statue of the beautiful Virgin in pale blue robes, and said the prayers quickly, sure that the others in the church would measure the gravity of his sins by the length of time he spent at his penance. He noticed that a lot of the little red-and-blue glass cups in the tiered wrought-iron votive-candle stand were empty; the altar boys for the morning's eight o'clock mass must have slipped out without replacing them. Henry considered going into the sacristy, putting on a black cassock, and filling them, but decided that it wasn't his worry, that he would as likely get in trouble for entering the sacristy out of turn as be praised for his initiative.

Leaving the church by the side door where the bike rack was, he felt at ease; confession and penance had brought relief, and he rode home feeling lighter than he had felt earlier, riding to the church.

The lightness lasted through dinner. Later, locked in the bathroom, he tried to master the terrible temptation, tried, in a vaguely scientific way, to understand this confusing mechanism of his body, to find a point at which he could stop between the first feeling good and the sudden, sinful flow. He failed, with a soft twitch and shudder, and found himself with a mortal sin on his soul between Saturday confession and Sunday mass, which he was supposed to serve.

The night passed slowly. Henry felt awkward and unworthy praying, certain that confession was the only way he could purify himself, and terribly aware that he wouldn't have the opportunity to confess for several days at least. And in the morning he would be expected to take communion; altar boys always took communion; it was automatic. But to take communion in his sinful condition would be an act of utter disregard for everything holy, would compound his already serious sin into something unfathomably vile, horrifying, unthinkable. He must not take it; he must bow his head in shame no matter what anybody thought, must refuse the host. He dreamt that he was sent down the dark stairs of the sacristy to the storage room below, where old broken statues reached at him from the shadows, and stacked fifty-gallon drums of air-raid water tumbled toward him. He tried to get clear, but his legs tangled in the skirt of the cassock, huge and heavy, gray with ashes, that seemed to envelop him.

In the morning he bicycled again to church. His mother had washed and pressed the red cassock and white surplice that he was to wear for the nine o'clock mass, wicking out the candlewax stains with layers of grocery-bag paper and the iron, spray-starching the surplice until it was stiff as posterboard. Henry held them out from him on their wooden hanger as he pedaled up the hills, and they streamed out behind him like a bright banner in the May morning. Yellow sunlight fell in shafts into the usually gloomy sacristy; the sanctuary was sweet with the smell of cut flowers, and Henry saw that the altar vases were filled with the long thick stems of yellow irises so open and exposed that it seemed almost shameful to look at them. The lean and muscular Christ brooded on his cross above and behind the intricate gold tabernacle, sunlight playing on his chiseled wooden thighs.

Henry had a start when he saw Father Jerome, but the priest showed no sign that he had recognized Henry's voice from the afternoon before. Still, priests were trained to show no sign; that meant nothing; Henry had recognized his voice; why wouldn't he have recognized Henry's?

"Who's serving with you?" Father Jerome asked.

"Roger MacIntyre; he's still getting dressed," Henry said.

The priest nodded, picked up a cigarette from the ashtray on the table beside him, took a long puff, and then slowly exhaled through his nose. He put the cigarette carefully back in the ashtray and began to put his vestments on; his lips buzzed softly as he sped through the prayers. The white-and-gold chasuble was adorned with an embroidered radiant Christ, arms half raised, wounded palms held out. A ruby heart, crowned with gold and encircled with thorns, floated in the air before the figure's white-cloaked chest.

Father Jerome took a final puff on his cigarette just as Roger arrived; then he crushed it in the ashtray, nodded to the boys, and they headed out into the sanctuary. Henry and Roger gave their responses in unison through the entrance and what for Henry was perhaps the most heartfelt *confiteor* of his life. The first reading was from St. Peter, and began with an exhortation to "abstain from the passions of the flesh that wage war against the soul." A wave of pure terror swept through Henry's body. He heard little after this; the gospel was a blur, and Father Jerome's sermon came and went almost before Henry realized it. The next thing he was clearly aware of was Roger hissing at him, and he looked up to see Father Jerome raising the host. Henry snatched at the quadruple bell, clanking it against the altar step on the first ring. Father Jerome went on as if nothing had happened, but Roger looked at Henry as if he were stupid and clumsy, and Henry felt as if all the eyes in the church must be on him; he could almost feel the congregation's hot breath on the back of his neck.

And then, before he had fully recovered from that embarrassment, Father Jerome was bending before him with the host held out.

"*Corpus Christi,*" Father Jerome said.

He couldn't refuse it. "*Amen,*" he said, and opened his mouth, laying his tongue on his lower lip to receive, and be forever branded by, the consecrated wafer. It was stale and dry and quickly turned gluey, and as he held the paten at the altar rail while the priest distributed communion, he worked his tongue to clear the roof of his mouth. He could feel his heart beating, knew that his face had flushed red. Worse, he felt a hurt somewhere in his stomach, the blackening of his soul as sensible to him as a bellyache. Fear of public shame had triumphed over his sense of private guilt, and now his sin was compounded, so shameful that he wasn't sure he would even be able to confess it. A fraud in his red-and-white robes, an abomination before the Lord, Henry went through the motions of the rest of the mass, never missing a cue, recovering somehow his poise. As usual, Father Jerome left no wine in the cruet, and lit a cigarette as soon as he was back in the sacristy. He said nothing to the boys.

"I thought you fell asleep or something," Roger said to Henry as they were hanging up their cassocks and surplices in the altar boys' closet. "What happened?"

"I don't know," Henry said. "I guess I must have been thinking about something else. See you tomorrow."

Henry, riding home, brooded on the fate of his soul, his certain condemnation to hell if he should die before he could get absolution. And he could not imagine confessing a sin of this magnitude. He coasted down the long hills in the fresh spring air, his collar unbuttoned and his tie streaming out behind him, trying to think when was the next time a general absolution might be given. The scent of wild azaleas and hothouse roses filled the air as he passed the Hudson Street greenhouses, white as chalk under the bluest sky the neighborhood had seen since the previous October. The sky in Henry's heart was black, sleet streamed out of it, stinging the back of his neck as he huddled, shivering, at the muddy edge of a crack in the earth. Below him coursed the burning lava flow of hell, and he could feel himself sliding toward it.

THOM TAMMARO

Eternity

Take a tiny bird—say a wren or sparrow. Then take a mountain, as large as any in the world—say Everest. Think of that bird finding its way to the highest peak of that mountain once a year—say spring—for the sole purpose of sharpening its beak, which it does by drawing it back and forth across the craggy peak until the beak's edge is sharp as a surgeon's scalpel. Now when that mountain has worn down to the size of a pebble a child could hold in its palm—that, we were told, constitutes one second of eternity. And there are an infinite number of seconds in eternity, just as there are an infinite number of days in eternity. And remember: if you think you have found the largest number in the world, just add one to it. The same goes for eternity: if you think you know how many seconds or days there are in eternity, just add one. Now you begin to grasp eternity.

Now take a seven-year-old child, a second grader on the verge of receiving his First Communion, and tell him this story on the same afternoon the great concept of Sin is introduced and planted in his psyche. All done, of course, for the sake of illustrating to him how long he will have to spend in the afterlife in the bowels of Hell, should he choose the path of Sin. A path always paved, we know, by the consequences of choice. One always has choice, remember. One always chooses his own path to walk down.

Late one afternoon, you might find this boy walking home

along his old neighborhood streets, gazing into the treetops, scanning the telephone wires and rooftops, searching for the tiny bird whose trilling pierces the spring air. When the boy is deep into night's sleep, if you looked closely, you might notice how his lips flutter and tremble the way the thin tail feathers of a tiny bird flutter lighting out for its first journey and rendezvous with a mountaintop. You might notice how the boy's lips open and a little cry comes forth, rushes against the night air, disappears, is lost in the darkness.

MAUREEN HOWARD

Role Model

I mistrust confessions. They seem from the vantage point of my Catholic training to suggest an easy road to redemption. Confessions and absolutions in the old religious doses were a staple of my childhood and, like cod-liver oil, were administered to clean out the system. At seven, having reached the age of reason, I was prepared to confess and receive Holy Communion. The first-grade Sister rehearsed the class. Like brainless automatons we were made to recite the set words of a model sinner over and over: "I stole one apple. I answered my father back twice. I lied to my mother. I forgot my prayers." When the real hour was upon us the simple boy in our class, whose head lolled to one side, took his turn in the confessional and announced in a loud uninflected voice: "I stole one apple. I answered my father back twice. I lied to my mother. I forgot my prayers." We were shocked. Our teacher flapped across the aisle and pulled him out from the darkened booth where he defiled the sacrament. Poor dope. If God couldn't forgive him his witless transgressions, how could He hear my intentional and real sins.

And I was a sinner from the start, never one of the good girls the nuns fussed over. My soul as always in question and to launch my spiritual life I mucked up my First Holy Communion. I broke my fast, but I didn't have the guts to go through with the ceremony. I could not take the body and blood of Christ into my mouth now fouled by orange juice.

The scene that morning in our kitchen is full of clues, and like the famous marriage contract of Van Eyck, can be taken as a portrait of our particular bourgeois style. White napkins, polished silver, a florist's box, a glass of pulpy fresh orange juice all denoting an event. Indeed, it would have to be a holiday, for one of my mother's precepts in the thirties was that only the rich indulged in orange juice. When we drank it at all it was by the thimbleful and here was a whole glass of pure gold squeezed, no doubt, for my father or brother on this special day. Alone in the kitchen, greedy, forgetting my spiritual obligation, I drank it down and immediately my crime was apparent. My white dotted-swiss dress hung up over the ironing board. My lace mantilla lay gently folded in a puff of tissue paper: it was finer than the veils the parish girls would wear (always, always finer, the single tedious note of our supposed distinction). My white gloves buttoned at the wrists with pearls. These clothes would never be worn. I picked up a grapefruit knife and tried to commit suicide. With a good deal of wailing I sawed at my wrists until they looked as though I had been clawed by a mean tabby cat, then plunged the harmless curved blade at my breast. Why, given the orange juice, was the grapefruit knife there at all? Grapefruit with a maraschino cherry—that was for later, for a Communion breakfast. After church Grandma Burns, Aunt Margaret from next door, my dashing Aunt Helen and Grandma Kearns, the *very* Catholic cousins of my mother who hovered nervously over our religious life—all would assemble in our dining room with presents for me, a little gold medal, crystal rosary beads, a white prayerbook. I had spoiled this day for my family: that seemed as important as my spiritual disgrace. The grapefruit went back to the refrigerator uncut. My finery fit for a child bride was packed away. I was not good: that idea was set in my mind. It was not disfiguring like a purple birthmark: not-being-good was my general complexion, like the freckles that stained my arms and legs. Whenever I felt—or feel now—that I am virtuous, something is immediately suspect. My religious periods have been genuine only as dramatic exercises. My Girl Scout honors (thirty-five badges and a curved bar) were earned when the tasks and the goodwill of the campfire were already too simple for me. Too many instances . . . whenever I am particularly kind, nurse the sick, give to the poor, I make sure I get the credit, then hate myself for claiming high marks. After the invasion of Cambodia in 1969 I rushed to the campus in Santa Barbara to hold hands in a phalanx against the State Police who were sent to close down the university: a good cause but I was sanctimonious, conscious of myself as a moral success. My spiritual self-aggrandizement is bad but not yet fatal. There is something decidedly clownish about my transgressions: they seem either careless, like the drink of orange juice protesting the idea that I had reached the age of reason, or so theatrical, like the suicide attempt, that my darkest intentions are rendered venial.

The nuns never tired of the apocryphal tale of Napoleon, that black-hearted man: when asked on Saint Helena to name the happiest day of his life, he replied: neither his victory at Austerlitz nor his coronation, but the day of his First Holy Communion. I received Communion in disgrace on an ordinary Sunday in some distant parish, wearing my winter coat and hat, filing up to the strange altar with children who did not know my name. I felt, too dramatically, that my soul was ill-fated. It was going to be uphill all the way.

DAVID KOWALCZYK

Sinner

Hell. For eight-year-old Jesse, the very thought of Hell was hell. He was terrified to think, say, or do anything that could possibly damn him. Yet he couldn't stop doing these things. The crucifix on the back wall of Holy Martyrs Church, ten steps past the font of holy water, terrified him. The broken Christ, battered, bloody, head sprouting thorns, made him retch. God allowed his own son, who'd never lusted for Mary Magdalene, to be tortured. What awaited Jesse, who lied to his teachers, disobeyed his parents, and stole from his sister? Jesse wanted to hide. Hide from the devil, hide from God, just plain hide.

In third grade, while taking classes to prepare for First Holy Communion, he learned about confession. Confession, the magic turning sinners into saints and sending devils to Heaven. Jesse couldn't wait to make his first confession.

But Jesse wasn't exactly sure what was and wasn't a sin. Words like adultery and masturbation meant nothing to him. In fact, just about everything about the sixth commandment made no sense at all. They should throw this commandment out.

The frail old nun who taught Jesse's communion class was probably an expert on the sixth commandment. One day, Jesse could no longer control his curiosity. He raised his hand.

"Yes, Jesse, what is it?" she asked.

"Sister Felicia," Jesse said slowly, "I've been wondering about something lately."

"I'm glad to hear that, Jesse. God loves us when we wonder about the sacred mysteries of his creation."

"Well, Sister," he said, "I was wondering if you could tell me what adultery is."

Her face flushed. She paused a few seconds, then said, "Adultery is when you do things you shouldn't do with your private parts." Before Jesse could ask another question, she began discussing why bearing false witness could be either a mortal or a venial sin.

Jesse scratched his head, lost. He waved his hand. Sister Felicia couldn't, or wouldn't, see him. His arm ached, his muscles throbbed, but his hand kept waving at her.

She finally noticed him. "What is it?"

"What are your private parts?"

She took a deep breath, rolled her eyes heavenward, then said very quietly and very quickly, "The parts of you in your underpants. If you must ask other questions concerning the sixth commandment, I suggest you ask your parents. We have more important matters to discuss."

Jesse couldn't ask his parents. His mother would say, "Ask your father," and his father would say, "Not now. I'm too busy." After several sleepless nights, Jesse decided that should a nuclear bomb fall on Ossuary, or an earthquake swallow up the town, he wanted to be absolutely sure he had no sins on his soul. Far better to confess everything and anything that might be sinful.

Confession at Holy Martyrs was Russian roulette. In the confessional waited either jovial, breezy Father Cybulski, or Father Kolb, with radioactive breath and a voice like a rusty chain. Father Kolb was the pastor of Holy Martyrs. Short, stout, balding, bottlecaps for eyes, Father Kolb started to smoke three packs of Camels a day after his request to fill the vacancy at his boyhood parish in Buffalo was denied and he was sent instead to this predominantly Polish parish whose congregation consisted of small-town factory workers and rural dairy farmers. Father Kolb felt edgy at Holy Martyrs. Unwanted and unappreciated. Or so people said.

Whatever the reason, Jesse had seen young girls step out from the confessional with tears rolling down their cheeks, had seen grown men exit with hands trembling and faces whiter than dried bone. Jesse's older sister said Father Kolb's confessions lasted forever. Endless questions about your most intimate thoughts. Threats to yank out your fingernails with a pair of pliers if he thought you were hiding something from him. Lectures about the tortures of Hell and how not one person in a thousand was truly worthy to enter the gates of Heaven. To make the agony complete, he'd assign a huge penance, sometimes five rosaries.

Jesse couldn't wait to have his soul washed clean of sin. But the cramped, cold confessional had to be the loneliest place on earth. Jesse snuck into the confessional early one morning before anyone was in church. When he closed the door, he smelled sin in the air, heard sin peeling from the walls. The booth was blacker than a coal bin. He stayed for about thirty seconds before terror drove him out the door.

As he entered the church, Jesse dipped his hand in the font of holy water, made the sign of the cross, then rushed past the crucifix, turning his face from the wounded Jesus, only to sneak a quick backwards glance and murmur, "Sorry, Jesus."

He slid into a pew close to the confessional. The green lights above the doors of the sinners' booths were on, meaning the booths were empty. The white light above the middle booth was also on, meaning the priest was now hearing confessions. If it was Father Kolb, Jesse would skip out of church and return at two, since whichever priest heard morning confession *never* heard confession in the afternoon. Jesse tapped the boy in the pew in front of him on the shoulder.

"Psst! Hey, Eugene!" he whispered. Eugene Peczkowski was a tall, blond, chubby boy whose stepmother bought all his clothes two sizes too big so he wouldn't outgrow them too quickly. His eyelids drooped unnaturally. He looked about to die. Always.

"Eugene! Were you here when the priest went into the confessional? Who is it?"

"I just got here but I think it's Father Cybulski. Yeah, I'm pretty sure it's Father Cybulski. All I could see was the back of his head."

"Father Cybulski! Thank God!"

"Yeah. Thank God."

"Whattaya waitin' for? Go first, Eugene. You were here before I was."

"You go first. I'm not sure I remember all my sins. I wish they'd let us bring a list in there."

"You couldn't read it. There's no light. I'll go first, then. Father Cybulski's always nice."

Jesse stepped slowly into the confessional. The door closed. He knelt down on the padded kneeler. Knelt and waited, in the silent darkness.

The wooden panel between the priest's and the sinner's booth slid back slowly, and a screen covered by a black cotton cloth was between Jesse and the priest. Some wall of secrecy, thought Jesse. What stopped a priest from matching a voice with a person's face?

The panel's opening signaled for the confession to begin. Jesse hesitated. Something was wrong. He smelled smoke in the confessional—cigarette smoke. His heart pounding, he leapt up, but fumbled with the doorknob.

"Where do you think you're going?" the voice rasped. Jesse's worst fears came true. Behind the screen lurked Father Kolb.

"I . . . I gotta go to the bathroom, Father."

"Get back here! Kneel down! You'll have plenty of time for the bathroom after you make your confession."

"Yes, Father." Jesse knelt. His bladder was ready to explode. His heart was pounding so loud it made his ears ache.

"Well? What are you waiting for? Begin your confession!"

"Uh . . . umm . . . Bless me, Father. I have sinned. My last confession was eight years ago."

"What do you mean, your last confession was eight years ago? Did you make a confession while in the cradle?"

"No, Father. I mean, I'm eight years old, and I never made confession before."

"Didn't you listen to Sister Felicia during class? You're supposed to say, This is my first confession. Now continue."

"Yes, Father. I disobeyed my parents fifty times."

"Fifty times?"

"Since I was a baby. I'm eight years old. That's not too bad, is it?"

"No, I'd say it's less than average for a boy your age."

"I lied twenty times."

"Just twenty times?"

"Well, twenty-two, I think. But Sister Felicia said if it was a number higher than ten, to just round it off to the nearest five."

"She did, did she?"

"She said we'd go nuts if we tried to figure out exactly how many times we committed each sin. According to her, most people sinned from the moment they were born, and we'd all committed sins we didn't remember."

"I may have to have a word or two with Sister Felicia. But tell me—who did you lie to?"

"My teachers at school, mostly."

"And why was that?"

"Because they wouldn't understand if I told them the truth. They'd just get mad at me and I'd get terrible grades on my report card. So I figured it was better to lie."

"You go to public school, don't you?"

"Yes, Father."

"I see. I'm sure you wouldn't have that problem if you went to Holy Martyrs. Go on."

"I stole a cookie from my little sister."

"What sort of boy steals cookies from his little sister?" Suddenly, the smell of cigarettes on the priest's breath grew very strong.

"I was hungry, Father."

"Well, you're truly sorry for that sin, aren't you? And you'll never do it again, will you?"

"Yes, Father."

"Yes? Don't you learn from your mistakes?"

"No, Father . . ."

"No?" the voice rasped. "Then why do you even bother going to confession? You know where your soul will spend eternity?"

"Probably in Hell, Father. Yes, I'm sorry I took my sister's cookie. That's what I meant when I said yes. No, I'll never do it again."

"Did you make restitution to her?"

"What's restitution?"

"Paying back what you stole. Did you ever give your sister another cookie?"

"No, Father. It's better that she never finds out about the cookie. She's little, but she's got a temper, and she bites."

"Well, then try to be extra nice to her for a little while."

"All right, Father." A minute passed in silence.

"What are you waiting for?" asked the priest.

"I don't have any more sins," said Jesse.

"Are you sure you remembered *all* of your sins?"

"Yes, Father." Jesse suddenly pictured a bolt of lightning hurtling down from the cloudless sky and striking him dead as he walked home from church. "Well, there's another thing, but I'm not sure if it's a sin or not. It might be hearsay."

"You mean heresy?"

"Yeah, that's it."

"Well, what did you do? Out with it, boy. I can't tell if it's a sin or not unless I know what you did."

"I did the sacraments of Baptism, Confirmation, Holy Orders, and Extreme Uncle. I mean, Extreme Unction."

"You did, did you? And when did you do this?"

"A few weeks ago."

"You certainly are the youngest person to receive Holy Orders I've ever met."

"You don't understand. It wasn't me. I didn't get the sacraments. I *gave* them."

"Oh? And who did you give them to?"

"My goldfish."

"Your what? You mean you baptized your goldfish?"

"Yes, Father. He looked like he was dying. I wanted to make sure he went to Heaven. Well, at first I was just going to baptize him. I was going to call him Daryle Lamonica in honor of the quarterback. But I really wanted him to go to Heaven, and I figured naming him after you would help."

"You named him Father Kolb?"

"Yes, Father."' There was silence in the confessional before the priest spoke.

"I'm very touched. No one has ever named a goldfish after me before."

"That's why I gave him all those sacraments. I figured that if he was named after you, he'd have to go through everything you had."

"I see. You know, it's not a sin to baptize a goldfish."

"It isn't?"

"No."

"So I wouldn't have burned in Hell forever if I forgot to tell you this?"

Father Kolb chuckled. "No. But I'm sure glad you told me. I don't know how you managed to perform the sacraments, but it's not a good idea to imitate the holy rites of the Church."

"It isn't?"

"No. You see, the goldfish wasn't going to Heaven, whether he was baptized or not."

"Why not?"

"Animals just . . . die, that's all. Their bodies decompose."

"They don't go to Purgatory or Limbo, like the dead babies in Africa who never get baptized?"

"No. The dead babies who aren't baptized are another story. They have souls. Goldfish do not."

"Well, after I flushed him down the toilet, where did he go, then?"

"Probably into the sewer."

"I'm going to be sick."

"Well, then, let's finish this quickly. For your penance, say five Our Fathers, five Hail Marys, and. . . ."

The thought of his Father Kolb floating around the sewer made Jesse so upset he almost forgot all about adultery. Then the lightning bolt flashed through his mind once again.

"Wait! I forgot! I committed adultery eighty-seven times!" he shouted.

There was another long silence before Father Kolb spoke. "Tell me, my son. Just how did you manage to commit adultery eighty-seven times? This is a feat many men dream of, but few actually accomplish."

Jesse was startled. Adultery didn't sound like a sin. It sounded like hitting forty home runs in one season. He still didn't have the slightest idea of what it was, other than that it had something to do with his private parts. All he'd ever done with his private parts was pee.

"Well, Father, before I went to kindergarten I would pee outside sometimes. My mother would yell at me. 'Why are you peeing on that tree? Do you think you're a dog? Go inside and use the toilet!' I liked to give the trees a drink. I never knew it was a sin until first communion class. Else I never would have done it, even once. Honest."

"Have your parents talked to you about the birds and the bees?"

"No, Father."

Another chuckle from Father Kolb. "I thought not," he said. "Well when they feel you are old enough to understand, they will. In the meantime, don't worry about committing adultery. If you're not old enough to be married, you're not old enough to commit adultery. Now then. Is there anything else you've forgotten, before I move on to the next confession?"

"No, Father."

"You're sure, now?"

"Yes, Father."

"Go in peace! And don't forget your penance. Five Our Fathers, five Hail Marys, and five Glory Be's. Oh . . . and try to follow your mother's advice. Use the toilet rather than the nearest tree when you have to relieve yourself."

Jesse opened the confessional door and let out a long sigh. He walked back to his pew, knelt down, and began to say his penance.

"Did Cybulski take it easy on you? Huh?" interrupted the eager Eugene.

Jesse looked at Eugene, then looked at the crucifix in the back of the church. For some reason, Christ didn't seem quite so bloody, quite so broken, quite so weary as he had before. Confession did indeed work miracles, thought Jesse. The miracle of knowing you were forgiven.

VIKI RADDEN

Shalanda the Reading Girl

I remember that day. I was standing in front of the whole class of those big boys. I was wearing my new pink dress and my new white patent leather shoes and even though my petticoat was itching me, that day was still the best day I ever had in my whole life. It was last year when I was in second grade and it was in May and it was almost my eighth birthday. Sister Mary Catherine and Mother Superior, they both said to me after I got done reading out loud to those big boys in high school: we're so proud of you. Mommy and Daddy, they said the same thing too, but they always tell me I'm smart. They say: Shalanda, you can do anything you want to do.

Sometimes Daddy says to me, Shalanda don't show off to those other kids in your class just cause you can read better than anybody else in the whole second grade. But I don't show off, 'specially not in class 'cause that might make my best friend Eva feel bad. I never go around saying *I can read better than you.* But it's true. I can read better than someone in high school even. And maybe that day I read to those big kids, I did show off. But just a little.

Sister Mary Catherine, last week after we took our reading test, she stood in front of the class with me and she put her arm around my shoulder and then she said to the class, "Shalanda has the reading level of someone in their first year of college." Everybody said, "Ooohhh," like I just won a prize or something. I like Sister Mary Catherine because she's tall and when I grow up I want to be tall. She has white white teeth that always show because she smiles a lot. Her habit feels scratchy like when my cat licks me on the hand, but she smells like peaches. Every day after we eat lunch she washes her hands and then she puts on peach hand lotion.

Mother Superior says, "Shalanda, where did a little black girl learn to read like that?"

That's what everybody always says. I told her what I always say, "My mom taught me when I was three." Sometimes I like to brag about my mom, even though Daddy says it's not a good thing to brag. Sometimes I like to tell people, "My mom's a genius." Genius. I learned that word because I heard Sister Mary Catherine say it to our class after we took those tests to see how smart we are. She said, "Class, there's one child in this room who's a genius." She never said my name, but everybody jerked their heads around and looked at me. Everybody knew.

I can't help it that they all knew she was talking about me. I'm used to it. Everyone's always talking about me. There goes Shalanda. She's the only black girl in the whole school and how'd she get so smart? Someone is always paying attention to me and everything I do. So I'm always trying to be good. Except when I have to beat kids up. 'Cause sometimes they call me names. And no matter what, I never lose a fight.

Kids started calling me names when I first came to this school. One day in first grade a boy with yellow hair called me a name I never heard before. I went home and I asked my mom, "Mommy, what's a nigger?"

"Where did you hear that word?"

"A boy at school said it to me."

Mommy said, "Why don't you sit down?" and I sat down and then she told me why some people like to say that bad word and why some white people don't like us because our skin is brown and their skin is white. At first I couldn't understand it but now I do. That's why I get into fights when kids call me that "N" word. But now, everybody knows, if they use the "N" word to me, I'm going to beat them up on the playground at lunch. After the kids got to know me, nobody ever said that to me anymore, 'specially since I'm practically the smartest girl in the whole school.

That's why it was fun to read to those big boys in high school. Sister Mary Catherine asked me if I wanted to read to the boys who were leaving the school because they were getting too big to go there anymore. I told her yes because I like to read out loud, and those big boys, sometimes they think they're so tough and they think I'm nothing but a little black girl but I don't worry about them because I'm smart and I can read better than them and they're eighteen and I'm only eight.

I walked upstairs with Sister Mary Catherine and Mother Superior cause that's where the big kids' school is. I could hear my petticoat going *swish swish swish* as I walked up the stairs. It was scratchy on my legs, but mom said it was a special day so I had to dress up. Mom washed my hair and pressed it and curled it and tied pink ribbons in it all over. And she bought me new patent leather shoes.

When we walked in the room, those boys were just sitting at their desks and they were looking at me like I was not even a real girl, like I was a make believe girl. I stood at the front of the class and Sister Mary Catherine and Mother Superior stood in the corner. I was scared and my stomach felt funny but I was happy.

And those boys, they just sat there looking at me with their eyes all big and surprised while I read to them. I read them a story about Indians, but then one boy, he said to me, "We don't believe you're really reading. You just memorized it." Then all the other boys in the class, they started the same thing. They couldn't believe I could really read that good. So then their teacher said to them, "O.K. then, you boys. You choose something for Shalanda to read. Choose the hardest thing you can find to read in the whole room."

Then one boy with red hair, he walked to the front of the room and took a purple reader from the SRA folder. Everybody said yeah, that's a good one, cause everybody knows purple is the hardest. Then I took the reader from him and everybody in the room got real quiet. I started reading, "George Washington was one of the most significant military leaders of the Revolutionary War."

Those boys all said, "I can't believe it, a little black girl reading like that."

Sister Mary Catherine ran up to me and hugged me and she

looked at those big boys and said, "You don't believe it? You'd better believe it."

That day in the cafeteria I spilled ketchup down the front of my new dress, and then on the way home I was so happy I was skipping all the way and when I cut through the lawn at the library I fell and got a big grass stain on the bottom part of my dress but when I got home my mom looked at me and I could tell she was happy and even though I had ketchup and grass smeared all over my new dress, she still looked at me and she smiled and said, "Shalanda, I'm so proud of you."

ELLEN TREEN

Enlightenment

On the second ring my father answers the telephone, something that as the only male in a five-female family, he usually considers beneath his dignity. Not that the telephone is often at issue; it seldom rings twice before one of us four kids grabs it, racing down the front and back stairways, around the hall from the kitchen, or through the living room. We make a final lunge into the sunroom, where the telephone sits on a maple desk.

But nothing is as usual, not since the cold Sunday two weeks ago when my mother drove out of here like snow blowing across frozen cement, leaving a hush behind her. She left right after mass, to go to Cleveland, she said, to visit Agatha, which is probably true. She and Agatha have been friends since music school and they still get together once or twice a year for a symphony or a play. It's not the where of her going that makes it hard for us to budge, even to answer the telephone, it's the why of it, the suddenness, like someone jumping up from the chess board in midgame. We are the pieces waiting to be moved, for the game to go on.

"Hullo," says my father, chopping off the word as though he has few to spare and every syllable counts.

My father ignores any question about what is happening, when one of us has the nerve to ask. No one knows whether he doesn't hear or just won't answer. He never talks much, but sometimes both my parents are quiet, too quiet, and the silence spreads through the family until we are all mute and might as well be blindfolded too. Then I feel as though I am playing a new game without knowing the rules. Rules that everyone else knows and won't explain until you bump into one. Then you know.

"Yes, this is Martin Healy," my father says, angry as though he has been dragged from an important chore. In fact, he was just standing here in the middle of the sunroom as still as a frozen post, looking out at the snow. There was a fresh fall last night but today the sun is shining, putting a hard sparkle on everything. When the phone rang I expected him to say, "Ruthie . . ." ordering me to answer it, even though I am stretched out on the window seat, reading. There is a whole wall of books in this room and it is my secret goal to read them all before I am eighteen, probably right here on this window seat. In a tall house of high walls and cold shadows it is the one cozy spot; on two sides French windows let in the sun and swing open in a strong wind. There used to be matching doors but one day I came home for lunch and found them replaced by a plaster archway. "Your father remodels by surprise," was all my mother said, but not really joking. No more than when he tore off the side porch and had the dining room painted a dark, gloomy blue while she was on a retreat.

"Yes," my father says, "put her on." When I realize he is accepting charges I know it has to be my mother calling. I hold my book absolutely still, but the print wobbles; I am stunned. After only six days, my novena is being answered. Someone must have found out, I think, but I don't know how. I have been reading the prayers by flashlight, rushing to the part where you put in your request, and sitting up in the dark to say the rosary, so I won't fall asleep. This novena is a hard one: a rosary every day for six weeks, and you have to finish it even if your request is answered before the end, out of gratitude. The harder it is the more likely God is to listen.

"Fine," my father says after a pause and his fingers drop to the maple desktop, stand there like a teepee. The desk is Mother's, where she drones through endless phone calls, arranging potlucks for the Catholic Women's Club, her head bobbing like a golden apple in the sun. When I look up from my book, she winks one gray eye at me while talking into the phone. "Your meat loaf is wonderful, Elida," she'll say, making her face into a horror mask. "Too bad I have five promised. How about a dessert?" Then she hangs up and describes Elida's meat loaf. "Shapeless and tasteless," she'll say, and we laugh until we choke.

"The girls are okay," my father says without moving a muscle. He gazes through the rows of immaculate windowpanes. Washing them is the punishment most often inflicted upon us by my mother. I know my sisters are praying, too, although they would never admit it any more than I would. But we have made it on time to mass every day before school, the way we're supposed to, not just dashing in for the gospel or final prayers like we usually do. Otherwise we are like cloistered nuns, our prayers are more private than time in the bathroom, where we congregate to talk things over.

"Do you want to talk to them?" my father asks. By now even Liz has guessed it is a collect from Mother and she bounces around the desk hugging the cat, squeezing it so its tail hangs like a bottle brush. "Poor Mopsy," says Fran, tiptoeing down the hall from the kitchen. Kate comes as far as the landing of the front stairs, where she has a view of the sunroom, and stands next to the statue of St. Anthony, Mother's pet saint. He helps her find all the stuff she misplaces, and she never passes him without a touch or a pat, no matter how many times she flies up and down the stairs. Kate shakes out her hair like a movie star, wanting us to think sixteen is too old to need anyone.

"I want to talk to Mommy," Liz begs, jiggling and jumping, bumping into the desk, until my father's hand clamps down on her shoulder, pressing out all the fidgets. Liz doesn't yell or anything; she just looks up at him, her brown eyes floating in those easy baby tears. Mother's voice would be sharp, warning, "Watch it, Martin, you're hurting her," making him snatch his hand back, quick and surprised. Liz has to wriggle away by herself and Mopsy gets loose in the struggle.

My father clears his throat. "Well, I hope you're enjoying your visit," he says. He sounds like he's strangling and I look up expecting to see a red face. But he is pale, the way he is on Sundays when he doesn't shave until just before noon mass. Later, when he takes us out for dinner, his heavy shadow will be grown back to normal. This will be the third Sunday dinner at the Bay Hotel and no one is looking forward to it anymore.

His long upper lip pulls down like a tight bedspread. "How much do you need?" he asks and I hold my breath but he just listens, then says: "I'll see about it." He asks about Agatha and her kids, and then looks up at the ceiling and I can tell the conversation is just hanging there, neither of them talking. "Say, Irene," he finally says in a brand-new voice, "as long as you're in Cleveland why don't you price those tweed overcoats at Halle's?"

Kate groans, and clicks her tongue against her teeth loudly so she sounds like a clogged drain, shaking her head at him hopelessly. During the first week I tried to talk to her. "They won't get divorced," I said. "Catholics don't get divorced."

"No, but they can separate," she said. "Remember the Kendricks?" After Mr. Kendrick moved to Detroit, Mrs. Kendrick and the kids moved out near the beach and no one sees them anymore. It was what Kate said that started me on my novena, even though Father Gregory said we should never tell God what to give us. Never ask for bicycles or new ice skates or good weather; instead we should pray for enlightenment because God knows best what we need.

Kate glares at my father, but his attention is on Liz, who is hopping up and down, urgently, as though she needs to go to the bathroom. "Well, you have a child here who needs to talk to you," he says, and hands over the telephone.

"Hi, Mommy," Liz yells. "You know what Mopsy did?" She begins one of her long boring stories about the cat, but no one laughs or tells her to shut up. Probably my mother is smiling and nodding on her end of the telephone. In the living room, my father is flapping the pages of the newspaper.

Kate moves into the archway, leaning into the curve, her eyes as dark and unreadable as my father's. She smooths her gray plaid skirt down over her flat stomach, and rearranges her rose-colored sweater while I watch, envying the way she looks, so blended and unwrinkled. Mother says it is because Kate is tall that she looks perfect in her clothes, and I shouldn't envy her because it's God's gift to her. Envy is one of the seven deadly sins and we all have our own gifts. So far I am the short one in the family except for Liz, but she is still practically a baby. Fran is a year younger than I am, but already she is taller. Watching Kate reminds me of the new skirt I got for Janey's Valentine party next week. It's too long and I'm afraid Mother won't be home in time to shorten it. If Janey weren't my best friend I would forget the party. I thought about asking her mom to help me with my skirt but I would have had to tell her why. Every day I rush home from school hoping to find things are back to normal.

"My turn," Kate says, wrestling the phone away from Liz, cutting her off before she can start another cat story or even say good-bye. Liz picks up Mopsy and carries her to the kitchen. In a minute I hear the refrigerator close. If Mother were here she would be yelling at Liz, telling her not to feed Mopsy anything. Liz loves to watch that cap lap up milk.

Kate is saying "yes" and "no" and "unh-uh," blending it all into a murmur. As though no one could guess she's answering Mother's questions, letting her know that the house is a mess, no matter how much Dad yells. That Mrs. Krusip ended up doing nothing but the laundry on her cleaning day. That Fran isn't staying on her diet and I had to stay after school for three days in a row. She probably isn't saying that she won't talk to Dad and refuses to do anything except take care of Liz.

She goes on and on, holding the phone with both hands, her voice so low that close as I am, I can catch only a few words. She twists around and stabs a look at me but I am not listening, any more than when she has those long, private talks with Mother in her bedroom. If I come near, they stop talking and just look, waiting for me to leave. Once, when Mother was crying, Kate began kicking the striped armchair, hard, with her penny loafers, while Mother screamed at her to stop.

I see Fran going down the hallway, past the sunroom to the living room, her head bowed, long braids trailing down her back. She is planning to be a nun so she practices the walk. It makes me mad that she won't even look at me. Usually we are close but for two weeks she's been saying nothing but "Poor Daddy," and following him everywhere. When I asked her if he talked to her, explained anything, she closed her eyes and shook her head. She acts like she understands everything without being told anything.

"Okay," Kate is whispering now. "Bye." I think she is going

to hang up without giving me a turn, but she holds the receiver against her chest and gives me a stern look.

"Ruthie," she says, "don't you want to talk to Mom?"

"Sure I do!" Sitting up, I answer fast, to cover a sudden reluctance, and Kate hands me the phone. She curves herself back into the arch and lays her head on the narrow frame, looking down at the flowers in the carpet. An attack of shyness almost overcomes me and I have to force the words.

"Hi, Mom," I say.

"Hello, honey," she says and the sound of her voice sets up a clamor for her presence in me, so sharp, so unexpected that I almost gasp. "How are you?" she asks and the very familiarity of her tone makes the distance unbearable. Tears spurt up, stinging my eyes, swelling my throat, and I rush into a swallowing battle against them and I don't think I can talk. Then I hear a croaking little voice, unrecognizable, out of control. "Why did you leave? I started a rosary novena for you to come back and I haven't missed a night. Are you ever coming home?"

The snow might have drifted inside, it is so still. A snort, a sound of unmitigated disgust comes from Kate as she peels herself off the wall and floats up the stairway on a great sigh of contempt. It is clear I have made a serious mistake; a point is scored against me in a game I don't understand.

"I didn't know anyone cared," my mother sighs, her voice thinning as though she has moved away from the phone. "Another week or so. I can't explain."

She sounds too tired to talk, as though she is sick or needs something, but I don't know what it is, or what to say. If I could, I would take back what I said, especially the part about the novena. Now it will never work. Father Gregory is right. I should pray for enlightenment. I wonder if I can change my request or if I have to start all over. Mother asks if I'm okay, if anything is wrong. She waits, listening, but the space around me is too large and open, too quiet for me to admit my shameful needs, tell her about Janey, ask her about my skirt.

"Everything is okay," I tell her, hoping she will guess it is not.

"I'm glad to hear it," she says.

When I hang up the phone, I go into the living room walking slowly, expecting questions, wondering what I should say. My father lowers his paper and looks at me, wearing his expression that is no expression at all. He leans back in his chair. Beside him, Fran sits cross-legged on the floor coloring a picture. I can only see the top of her head, the white line parting her auburn hair. It stays quiet so I go through the room, on up the front stairs and down the hall to the open door of Kate's room. She is brushing her hair, but then she lays her brush on the bureau and stares at me in her mirror. After a long time she turns around and comes toward me and I think she is going to say something but she doesn't, so I leave and go down the back stairs into the kitchen. It looks empty until I see the spilled milk leading to where Liz is hiding under the kitchen table with Mopsy. Pushing through the swinging door, I walk down the hall to the sunroom and flop back down on the window seat. At last I am learning the rules. Soon I will understand the game.

KRISTINA MCGRATH

Under the Table

Right now I'm under the table hiding. People say I color pretty good and even well and no one's ever going to make me go outside these lines.

I watch my mother's brown laced shoes with slanted heels, bent at the tips of her toes. Rounded, they ratatat across the floor, from here to there so quick, I can't keep up or speak.

This is not my house. I'm in the very residence of Miss Mary Louise Sims and her little sister, Anne Cecile, who are, and I'm telling the truth, 100 years of age, and 89.

Right now they're asleep, side by side, in their mechanical beds with silver wheels deep in Ali Baba carpets, in the dayroom papered pink, because it's ohsopleasant, says Mrs. Guntherman, who moved in and put them there to spare us all the steps, smack in the middle of the parlor, which is what Miss Mary Louise calls it. Why am I sleeping in the parlor? she'd like to know that at least fifty times a day. My guests will think it strange.

That's me, kind of, the guest. I visit at a distance from under the mahogany and think it strange. Sun's good for your blood, says Mrs. Guntherman, and pats their beds when they complain.

Shy and made of tinsel, they sniff the air and give a little shiver. Like fish out of water, Mum says to herself. She shakes her head and sighs. Her heavy eyelids close and flutter open. Then lifting her skirt above the knees, she breaks into a tiny run up steps, her feet softly drumming ratatat. In the folds of her skirt she sneaks down evidence of their rooms upstairs and pats it into their hands: a doily sachet in the shape of a human face stuffed with crumpled petals; a red Excelsior Diary from 1882 (which all it says is Very Pleasant Day, Pleasant Day, Stormy Day, Very Pleasant Day, and that's the way it was in Pittsburgh, honest to God, in 1882); one whole hatbox of china rosettes of no purpose on earth whatsoever, except they exist and were made by their father who spent a lifetime shaping them, baking them, which is not the worst a man can do, my mother says, rosettes. Then she puts everything back into tissue while the ladies smile into space, and sleep.

Lordy, says Miss Anne Cecile. Oh Lordy, help me, Mrs. Hallissey. My mother, Mrs. Hallissey, cranks the bed and the bed cranks up. She bends over the body of Miss Anne Cecile, wraps an arm around the back of her neck, the arm of Miss Anne Cecile, it hangs there, surprised, like a starched ribbon. Hold tight, Mum says, fishing her out from under slipped sheets, sliding her arms under Miss Anne Cecile's white dolly head knees, little tender eggs, then heaves, the body of Miss Anne Cecile, placing it by the window in a chair with clawed feet. It will walk away with Miss Anne Cecile very soon.

The only traveling they ever do is from being lifted by my mother from one spot of the bed to another (Miss Mary Louise) or to the window (she prefers it, Miss Cecile).

My mother's body is stranded in the sun like a schoolgirl, lost in the huge parlor. Her fingers scissor a clump of housedress when tiny Miss Mary Louise, drowning in waves of sheets made sharp from knuckles and knees, raises her hand from under the covers, pokes up her head with white ruffled feathers for hair, narrows the already narrow slits of her eyes, and points her crooked finger at me every time I'm here, What's that? What is she doing in my residence?

My mother, let me tell you, is proud enough to answer, Why that's my little girl, that's Lulie Hallissey, my daughter. Don't you remember?

And that's the only reason why I come here in the first place. Because I know I get to hear my mother say such a nice thing about me right in front of my face. Yessiree Bob, that's my little girl. And I can't help but know I'm guilty of that.

Lordy, says Miss Mary Louise who has my name. Mum fetches the bed pan; I study the dust that speckles the air. Dust is from the old ones, the quiet ones, it's their ancient feathers, it comes from the down on their cheeks, from the tops of their heads and the backs of their knees. So that's dust. It's from baby ones, the noisy ones, it's the down on my arms, it's my feathers falling from the backs of my knees.

I lie here, flat on my back under the table, counting Mummy's sorrows. And even in the sorrow, I can't keep up. Sorrow of the pork bone, sorrow of the brown banana, broken yolk, sorrow in the track of the worm in the soft peach that I pitch to the ceiling, Holy Moses, and she will catch it and eat it, the sorrow of the meal is hers. Umm Umm, she says, nothing wrong with it, stony bread.

That's why I make sure she gets her orange juice. Only if you are a kid or a grandpap are you allowed one itty glass a day because that's all Mummy has the money for. It hurts to drink it, so I chase at her heels, I hate juice, I tell her. I set it on the bathroom sink, on the bureau, in her flat shoe, just to let her know I'm serious, until finally she says all right. All right child, my sweetest baby, and drinks the juice.

I can afford to do without a lot of things because I am a strong, healthy girl in Our Lord, because my scapular verifies my apostleship in league with the Sacred Heart of Jesus bow your head, and because I have the body of boy. Besides, it's my sacred duty to get to heaven. Everyone in heaven is a famous person. My mother will be famous someday. In my mind I always go to Purgatory. But I am in the line that gets to God, and someday I will matter. And I know it is my sacred duty to sing songs, to protect my books from snow and rain because books like songs are sacred. Work is sacred. Knickknacks are sacred. And the rules. It's the worst sin in the world not to hear the rules or your true vocation, like nun nun nun late at night in your ear. Already I know I have to be a nun, not that I want to, because nearly every last dumb girl has to be one, wear black nightgowns, get plenty of soap, because everybody knows soap is the thing to give them and they will always take it, the nuns.

Sacred duty, says Mum. And I learn what that means from under the table at other houses. Last month when the oven blew up on her arm, she went out working at Mrs. Halloran's house with one arm tucked behind her back because work is the thing you do and get done. Burnt arm or no, Mrs. Halloran's mattresses need air.

I run through Shadyside streets to Mrs. Halloran's at lunch hour and climb the stairs to the stripped rooms upstairs, determined to be her other arm, and together we flip them over. And right then and there she teaches me how to make hospital corners on beds because it makes the world much nicer. There now, isn't that nice? she says, tucking in the sheet, giving it a sharp final tug. Doesn't that make the world much nicer? She looks up at me then from the tucked corner of the bed and I see that it is her, with eyes a papery blue and overlarge like heaven, and I see there is a movie star in the dark waves of her hair, behind her glasses, in the full turns of her skirt, where she hides her hands, though I see.

Nicked by walls, by the flaws in the woodwork, by floorboard nails hidden in the colors of the varnish, bitten red from bleach and smoking buckets of hot gray water that warm my face, they twist the colored clothes, wring mops. They spread me back and send me off. Because of what I see, I do not need a single thing to eat or soothe me. They hush me down. They are God's. They rest at the center of my silence. They send me off, into an urgent need, into another, not myself, whose hands are soft now and pudgy and will not take a single thing too easily.

Let's go, says Mummy. I'm hiding under the dining room table again because Mrs. Halloran's children have come home for lunch. What gets me here is shame; just because my mother cleans their floors suddenly I am the daughter of Mrs. Hallissey the cleaning lady and this is not true; I am the daughter of my mother, Anna. She takes me by the hand and turns me to her in the hallway. You have to have spirit where your job's concerned; work is like religion, she says, Sure you don't know God, but like the song says, the Spirit moves you anyhow. Keep your chin up, child, you have a beautiful face. God gave us English, use it and speak up. And against my will, I am raised high when I see her face, suddenly I believe in everything, in birdsong, in shine of the linoleum, in conversation. So what's new at your private school, I ask the children. Then slump my eyes at them.

Now my brother Eddy and me bring home the gambling boys. We linger by the ironing board, begging her with shut eyes to show her muscle. We're betting quarters that she can ring the bell at Kennywood and get us cigars or win us a turquoise teapot. After a lot of pleading, she blushes, she rolls her sleeve and there it is, all white and bluey. We hoot and holler and smack our foreheads.

Because of Mummy's work, we live among pictures of Rolling Rock horses, paintings of Paris ladies, centerpieces on the blond buffet, and rows of books, their edges gilded lavender and blue. Our flowered drapes are tailor-made because of the kindness of our landlord. Once a month he huffs and waddles in, everything fine everything fine, he nods and nods and listens to any sorrow we might have like rain in the cellar. Then his redheaded girlfriend, Dearie, tall and French in a black beret, takes it all down in a steno pad and smiles at me like we were related. I rush to the door when Dearie comes in, I am nearly tumbled into her long black skirt, though I have absolutely everything I need, which you probably already know if you've ever tried to give me anything.

Once a year we wash the house within height, and every other month, the windows; we plant peach, pine and apple trees; set bricks on the diagonal, completing a garden; Mummy fixes the back door, she fiddles with the screws and teaches me hammers and drivers and brads; every summer we haul the glider from the cellar and set out the pillows, ooph, we sit down; she jumps up, she wipes the stairs and window sills; she cooks us a good dinner; Go lie down, she tells us, you're straining.

Then she bakes the cookies. I sell them for the babies. Babies in alleys or India, with no mother and no father, they are screaming in their beds, they are missing parts of their faces, they have no windows or relations, and never even heard of Jesus. I want to bring one home and raise it myself, give it little hoops and stew. I hate stew.

Then she helps me decorate my collection can with flowers because it's extra nice to do it that way. Now I can go to the best places she says, the Salon de Beauté, the expensive butcher's, and ask, Will you give a nickel for the babies? Then I bite my hand until they do. If you give a nickel you can get the babies their very own bowl, the word of our Lord, and a doctor, all for a nickel, I tell the people.

If I'm not busy buying babies, I'm hiding from Russia. At Mercy School we are filing off to the cellar for air raid drills, we are falling with shut eyes under our desks. We cannot look out the window, we will melt. We will be alive tomorrow; that is only a rumor. And all we really want in this world is to go home and die with our mothers, to kiss them one last time.

But you must not love your mother more than God, they tell me. You must sacrifice your mother to the cross. And though you were dashed onto earth with her, heaven is your one and only home.

I'm always just about to lose everything I have on earth, but I never do because I whisper to the holy men. People like Jesus come to see me past midnight. I get old old old with laces on my head, loiter under pictures of the Sacred Heart, and I sleep with the Infant of Prague.

I put my arm around its five-inch body, place its crowned head on my pillow. Once when its starched lace sleeves or neck ruff cut my hand, I woke up bleeding and swore it was the stigmata; I prayed that it was. Now Mummy forbids me to sleep with the Infant of Prague one more night. My bed's already crowded with angels and sometimes I see the tiny smoky face of Jesus or the crown of thorns floating headless on the wall. Underneath my bed I keep my collection of laminated holy cards from Sister Magdalena and a flashlight. St. Christina and St. Joan in orange and silver flames, handsome Sebastian with the arrows in his side. All of the saints have locked themselves in their rooms. They are lying under their beds in the darkness. They wear the bristles of animals under their plain soft dresses, and smile.

Meanwhile, Get some sun, says Mum. But I stay put in a heap of crayons, paper, lavender and turquoise books under the table. I love the tales of Davy Crockett whose cradle was a snapping turtle, and I love Joe Magarac, the Steel Man, who melted himself to save others. I love Paul Bunyan, covered wagons, rabbit pictures, Zorro, and kittens who wear britches. All of my heroes are either men or baby animals, except for the Blessed Mother who is my best friend.

XOXOXOXOXOXOXOXOXOXOXOXOXOXOXOX

Dear Blessed Mother

I love you Blessed Mother I love you I do so Please do not cry becosea I love You and Please do not feall sad becosea I will sheer You up with sacrifices and hugs and kisses for You and Your Sweet Jesuses.

XOXOXOXOXOXOXOXOXOXOXOXOXOXOXOX

Sun, my mother says.

On a windless day, my mum and I hang laundry, bing bing bing in magnificent order. Hush hush hush on the line, like a string of sounds we didn't say. The sheet. This is very big. Mummy disappears into it, taking its great width across her body. Her chin comes back, holding it. Her spread arms work and diminish it. Scattering myself at its edges near the grass, desperate to catch what never falls, I land on my bent toes. I leap toward the sound of it, Here, let me help.

Today I have done everything wrong and she has done it over, talking me through it. Nicely, she says, Like this, Bing bing bing, Towels together, Panties together, Shirts by the shoulder all together, Two pins each. I dumped the lugged bushel of wet things on the line, while she swept black water in the cellar; Hey surprise, and in my hurry, all cockeyed, bedlam on the line, fever in the heart. What's next?

Why not get some sun, she says. Your daddy's on his way. But I never want to go. Because.

What's the matter, says Dad, Got cotton in your ears? I said, Your mum's malarkey. No buts.

Wildcat of the Dad roars up to the curb, and when the Chrysler door swings open, his voice rolls out like a big fat whale. We jump in quick before he gets out and into our kitchen. His voice struts like a marching band with his big talk in the front carseat, with his twenty reasons why he's late or wasn't here yesterday. My older sister Helen gets red in the face, tightens her fists, You're a liar, she says, and then he sings. He thinks he is the only one there. He talks to the windshield how we must never disobey or tell lies, especially to your father, the one he is pretending to be. Your daddy's gonna give you a lickin', he says of some other man he lost. We shrug our shoulders and throw our eyes to heaven. Your old daddy, he says, knows what he's talking about. I said your mum's malarkey.

We shiver in sunlight; we long for the road when the wind takes over. Somewhere in us, we recognize our father's voice from the phone calls in the middle of the night. Tell your mother she's a bitch. And somewhere in us we remember the phone calls from "that poor lady again," Mummy says. Where's your dad? she wants to know—and our mother takes the phone and tells her, Hush, it will be all right, I'll tell him to call you. It is hazy here where heat and sunlight ripple the windshield. We are still idling at the curb, shivering to go fast. When will Daddy start this car?

We roar past Natali's neat red brick at the corner; its kingdom of trimmed hedges and sloping lawn is the last familiar we see. We roar through Shadyside, then East Liberty streets, past blurry porches in a tangle of speed and stoplights. We roar into the otherwise unseen, past storefronts along Liberty Avenue, into the darker light of Bloomfield, its houses smaller, tighter, in rows with no porches, into secret alleys. He has no money for ice cream. Your daddy just made a car payment; no dough for ice cream, maybe cherry pop. Daddy has to go see a man about a horse. We wait as long as we can in sunlight in the back of the car. Our feet are hot. Our eyes are sore from sunshine. Heat simmers up from the black tarred lot of Bernie's First and Last Chance.

I said your mum's malarkey, he comes back singing. She never did give you kids enough vegetables.

I hide under tables, where I get my information. My mother, Mrs. Hallissey, bends over the body of Miss Anne Cecile whose eyes rise up from her sleep and flutter open, Yes dear, dear Mrs. Hallissey, she says and smiles at Mummy's kiss on the cheek. Miss Mary Louise Sims raises her hand from its faraway place in the sheets and pats the air in a fragile goodbye. It is silent in the residence of Miss Mary Louise Sims and her little sister, Anne Cecile. They are losing her again; they are giving her back; Mrs. Hallissey is slipping from them like the thin nightgowns from their shoulders. Mummy's brown laced shoes ratatat through the parlor as she gives everything a final tug at the end of the day. They are losing her again but she is what I have.

I know in the palms of my hands, in my fingers, and legs, this slim hold I have on her in the days of her running, and so I run. There is motion all around me in the course of our days. But there is something still underneath the days, under the running of our feet, something tucked in the scent of our clothes, in what is folded and put away. Underneath in shadow lies a fragile permanence. It is like the way light falls but still tells the colors of her clothes; and there is a moment in our running, Hey Sweetheart, she says, and pokes her head like sunset under the table, Let's go home.

Where you are, already I am.

CHRISTOPHER BUCKLEY

Days of Black and White

Still, they come back clearly,
unfocused and myopic as they were—
the cold eye of the CBS insignia zooming
out of the dark as we opened
the Sylvania's console doors,
or each Monday, the catechism responses
like dark brick layered down the page—
all the arbitrary and two-dimensional vision
of those days . . .
                                        The rush of it all
was thick and impossible to penetrate
as that marine layer of fog we wandered
our way through to class each day,
our checkered uniform shirts blue/gray
as the chafed, wind-dull winter sea
where the rote and repetition of the hours
were out-shouted by the waves.
                                                                        One day,
the nun marched a bunch of boys
from the blacktop and tether ball,
the skull and crossbones of her habit
waving over a sun-slick field where we were
to trace out a diamond and wear away the weeds—
this portion of the world, we were told, was ours

and no one else could interfere. So we felt
no sea change churning then beneath the oblique
surface of the times, or especially in our sleep-
walking blood . . .

The parents liked Ike,
the House Un-American Activities Committee
had made movies safe, and the Church flaunted
its Index of forbidden books. Our lives
came under the tutelage of nuns whose grasp
of the world was manifest in the thunderbolt
spearing St. Theresa's ecstatic heart,
in the sanctuary defiler struck down and burning
on the spot, or in the boy who, smuggling
a communion wafer home and floating it
on water, poked it with a fork to find blood . . .
These were the true uses of the mind
and so far as we knew formed the shining
perspective of the soul against darkness
in this life.

And though we suspected
most of what we'd heard was far from fact,
we understood it when the black & white photo
of the Crab Nebula in our 8th grade text
was described as a cloud of light the color
of rose petals appearing in the peasant's serape
as he stood beneath the Virgin of Guadalupe—
that scene on the Dry Cleaning calendar
with its gold and starry border tacked
to the coat room in back of class.

We had no idea
this would be the end of things as we knew
or would ever know them. That spring,
we were squared off final period across
the linoleum tiles, forced to count out
Fox Trot and Waltz. We wore clip-on ties
and the poplin suits our mothers bought
almost proudly at J. C. Penney's; girls balanced
in heels and dresses of unnatural gold,
or minty green, dresses so stiff with starch
and petticoats, they rustled like newspapers

with the least spin or twirl.
We'd been aching
to get at them all year, but now at arm's length
and half the time in gloves—and even when we were
allowed some Rock & Roll to head off a shuffled anarchy
or stomped rebellion—we were joyless, awkward
in our scuffed and embarrassed shoes . . .
True,
Alan Shepard had been hurled headlong
into space, but Sputnik was now years old—
fewer mysteries were explained by a saint's
sudden levitation above the assembled masses in Peru.
Now, we had Kennedy and were going for the moon;
the world was shrinking into its last three-quarters-size prints
taken with our Kodak Star Mites the night of graduation:
girls in their armored dresses, boy in business suits
with the pervasive evidence of safety razors—
constellations of small red stars on cheek and chin—
photos snapped walking out of the auditorium,
eyes wide a last time—into the flash—aspiring
to what we knew would be the future where our hair
could be slicked back with Brylcreem or held aloft
by lacquered waves of spray.
I remember
staying up that night, the test pattern's wheel
and one note, and how, as it was turned off,
the picture shrank to a dot of light tunneling
into the tube. The last image that came
to mind as I drifted off on the davenport
was of Parents Night during my first year
in the school where I'd just spent most my life . . .
The old School House stood next to the new
stucco rooms, and it was used as theater and stage;
the nuns had organized a Minstrel Show.
Looking out the windows into that spring sky,
stars stood out like little pats of butter
on the deep and comfortable blue, and because
this was the 50s and no one was thinking
of anyone but themselves, and because we were
brought up to do precisely as we were told,

the older boys delivered jokes out front
while, with the whole of the 2nd grade,
I waited in the back in overalls and kerchief,
in black-face with white gardening gloves
on my hands, to be called out
dancing and smiling for the final number.

TONY ARDIZZONE

Baseball Fever

Because just as the game has its men in black who call the balls and strikes, the fairs and fouls, the safes and outs, so my life had its crew of women dressed in black hoods, floor-length black robes cinched by beads, and oversized white bow ties. The Sisters of Christian Charity, to whom I was delivered at age six by my well-meaning parents for instruction and the salvation of my eternal soul. Imagine the toughest Marlboro cowboy driving the naive calf from its mother's shadow and then roping it, tying off its hooves, drawing out from the Pentecostal flames of the campfire the red-hot brands of Guilt and Fear, and then burning the calf's hide while it writhes and squeals like one of the Three Little Piggies being devoured by the Big Bad Wolf and you have a fairly accurate picture of my life's early religious education.

I believed them when they said that what they were doing was for our own good. I believed them when they collected our monthly tuition envelopes and said it was our parents' highest duty, the very least our folks could do.

I believed them when they taught us that Protestants were misguided (led by a doubting lunatic, they refused to worship the Virgin or believe in Confession, the nuns would hiss), that Jews were worldly (they were looking for a material king, Heaven on earth), that all atheists and agnostics were eternally damned (their downfall was their senseless egotism). After we were introduced to world geography I learned there were Muslims, Hindus, Buddhists, pagans, naked backward heathens—a myriad of wrong-minded religions and ways—popping off the inflated plastic globe with souls as starving for God's True Word as the broom-thin children with outstretched hands pictured in the ads for CARE.

My parents told me only to do as I was told. To learn, to obey, not to waste all the advantages I had. After all, they continually reminded me, I was the first of their families to be born into this great country. I carried the weight of expectation of all the Bacigalupos, all the Paradisos. So I'd better not screw up.

My mother took me with her to Mass every Sunday. She was partial to rear, side-aisle pews, where she'd kneel and say several rosaries, ignoring everything else that went on except Holy Communion, which she'd receive with so much reverence and humility that I'd worry she'd levitate and never return to her normal self. After each Mass we'd light a candle beneath the statue of the sad-eyed Madonna. "For special intentions," my ma would always say, then pat her always-pregnant stomach.

My father hit the pews with us on Christmas Eve and Easter Sunday, the only times other than weddings or funerals he ever wore a tie. He'd watch everyone and everything, turning like a top, now and then sucking his teeth, and didn't seem to know when to kneel or stand or cross himself. He never said any of the Latin responses. He never cracked a hymnbook and sang. He never stood and followed my mother in the line for Holy Communion. "I eat my own bread," he'd whisper as she'd try to pull him after her into the aisle. Then he'd add loudly, "Lucia, don't argue."

I didn't argue either. I concluded I'd eat my own bread too when I was old enough. In the meantime I'd be a good kid and not waste their hard-earned tuition money and learn and try to please my ma.

So I learned. Not that the earth is flat or that the four humors govern physical size and personality, but that way up in the sky is Heaven, a supposedly wonderful place full of clouds thick enough to stand on, saucers of light behind everyone's head, God's magnificent throne, and twenty-four-hours-a-day genuflecting.

I could think of several places I'd rather spend eternity (Wrigley Field, Lincoln Park Zoo, Riverview, any playground with monkey bars and unbroken swings, even the old sofa in front of Aunt Lena's black-and-white TV), but the Sisters told us our choices were Heaven, Hell, or Purgatory—no substitutions. Hell and Purgatory were made up of fires so hot you got a headache just thinking about them. The heat was worse than a glowing waffle iron, the nuns reminded us every week, so intense that the flames boiled and bubbled the miserable marrow inside your bones. In Hell even the nails of your two little fingers screamed with agony. And you'd have to stay there with nothing to do but suffer for longer than any teacher was able to count. For more years than there are grains of sand on all of the world's shores and beaches, and that wouldn't even be the first hundredth of the first second of time, which would never move because it was eternal.

During some of these "Exactly How Bad Is Hell?" lectures, my little classmates actually peed their uniform skirts or regulation navy-blue parish pants, prompting Sister to put the gory details on hold and call for the janitor and his broom and pan and bucket of sawdust.

Thanks for clueing me in, I'd think as the janitor muttered to me how I should be ashamed, how I was a big second-grader. "Daniel," Sister told me, "try and sit still and perhaps your clothing will be dry by lunchtime." I nodded, then stared at my desktop. See, I was grateful. God punished bad people whether they knew about Hell or not, and Sister was giving me a lifetime of advanced warning. I'd grow up and be a very good person, I promised God. I figured you had to be really evil to end up in Hell. Hell was for people like Adolf Hitler.

But then the good Sisters pulled the old hidden-ball trick on us, and all of us smug little snotnoses were caught flatfooted, a mile off base. Because, the nuns informed us, even though we were barely able to cross Clark Street with the aid of a green light and two patrol boys, all of us had *already earned* Hell's hottest flames, all because of two people we hadn't even met.

Let's pencil in Adam and Eve, the moronic apple eaters. They had a fantastic thing going (the Garden of Eden, tons better than Heaven by the way the nuns described it), but then couldn't resist listening to the talking snake. They had to go and nibble the forbidden fruit, in the process blowing the game for the rest of us.

So God punished not only dumb Eve and Adam but everyone else who came from their apple seeds. Which meant *everybody*, from the Chinese with their chopsticks to the Eskimos in their igloos to the Australians with their crazy boomerangs. The sin boomeranged throughout the ages. Which meant we were all brothers and sisters (momentary confusion and panic: then who will I be able to marry when I grow up?), damned to the never-ending broiler, furnace, blazing hibachi of Hell.

It didn't seem fair to me. I thought hey, hold your horses, *I* wasn't there to resist the temptation. *I* didn't get to choose. If only I'd been there—man alive—that apple would've rotted on the tree! I might have *looked* at it once or twice, maybe nodded to the snake, thrown him a dead alley rat so I could watch him eat. I might have touched the apple with my fingertips, given it a little sniff. Maybe even put my lips, my tongue, my teeth . . .

I'd have eaten it too.

I realized then that I was one of the lucky souls. I knew the truth. Plus I had a bona fide Catholic baptism splashed across my forehead. For at least a week I did my chores around the house without my ma having to tell me twice.

She was right, I concluded. You should eat God's bread. Kneeling next to her in church, I'd think of little pagans exactly my age all over the world who'd never even heard of original sin. How, when they died, their tiny heathen hands and screaming fingernails would crackle like slices of bacon in my ma's cast-iron frying pan. I'll travel all over the world when I grow up, I thought. I'll carry a hundred canteens of holy water and baptize every pagan I meet, even if I have to wrestle them first down to the ground. "It's good for you, honest, no fooling," I'd tell them. They'd be grateful to me later on. They'd shake my hand and thank me when they saw me again up in Heaven.

The missionary life was extremely attractive to me. As long as you watched out for cannibals and Communists, and didn't step on or listen to talking snakes, going around sprinkling water on heathen foreheads seemed just about the surest way to keep your buns out of the incinerator.

The nuns cushioned the Fall of Humanity with another story, the Fall of the Angels. It seems that trillions of years before Paradise, some of God's finest archangels and seraphim were disobedient too. The Good Lord was on them in a millisecond.

Also he had legions of good archangels (my first lesson in the concept of a deep bench) waiting with drawn swords behind Him. The defeated lay at His ankles, gasping. God unplugged their halos, plucked their feathers, stripped them of their mighty wings. Then He stepped on a giant pedal that opened a yawning trapdoor in the clouds, and all of the militant angels tumbled down from the blue sky.

In that moment of eternity's early timelessness, it rained angels—it rained devils—and they plummeted through space with a moan: like falling meteors, comets, Skylabs, Cosmos 1402's, twisting in an everlasting sizzle as the eager tongues of Hell's waiting fires leapt past their cloven feet to their devil mouths and French-kissed them.

This was the creation of Hell. Wowee! we all thought.

Indirectly these stories also taught us a lot about this strange Being we called God. For one, he wasn't a father who took much sass. Also He didn't seem to give second chances. (We didn't get to the New Testament until third grade.) God was all-powerful and knew and saw everything, everywhere, always; and to top it off He was invisible. Ogres in the Brothers Grimm seemed more benign.

What choice did we have? We could hardly raise our trembling hands and ask Sister to tell us a different fairy tale. This, the stern women in black were teaching us, was for real. Each year for eight years the well-meaning Sisters of Christian Charity trotted out these horror stories, and each year for eight years I listened with increasing fear.

We were told that, as Adam swallowed, the lump of apple caught in his throat and remained there, a constant reminder of man's sinful, evil nature. We were told that the talking serpent still slithers through the world in the form of creeping communism. All we had to do was ask our fathers to read us the newspaper; President Ike was combating it every day. One of the statues in our classroom showed Mary stepping on the writhing serpent. "See?" the nun would say. It was all the proof we needed. Evil was in our throats, in our world, even under the foot of the Blessed Virgin. Evil was everywhere. After the flames kissed them, the evil angels escaped from Hell and worked their way up to the earth, where they walk our streets and alleys, always in disguise, always looking like normal people, always there behind a streetlight pole or the open door of a strange car, hoping to lead us into the darkness of despair, into temptation, occasions of sin, eternal everlasting damnation.

I should tell you that my number is 13, so you'll recognize me down on the field. Every team from high school on gladly allowed me to wear it. No one else wanted 13 but me. Because when baseball collided with Mickey's death and I was forced to abandon my dreams of becoming a missionary, I felt it was only right and proper that the rest of my playing days be spent in sheer defiance of misfortune.

Because the first of our line of Paradisos and Bacigalupos to be born into the nation of baseball earned his birthright and stepped right out of Paradise into the foul mouth of the wolf.

Because I believed the good Sisters when they said that at seven you tag the age of reason, that from the moment the candles on your birthday cake go out everything you do goes into the record book. Because at age eight I was involved in a very extraordinary, extremely tragic play. I wish I could say it was a bit part in a grammer-school production of *Macbeth* or *Hamlet.* It wasn't. It was purple-faced, bulging-eyes real.

I didn't want to be evil and re-earn Hell, but if you've got the genes of a natural-born ballplayer it's not easy to pass up a fat pitch.

So I went with the pitch that began my life as a ballplayer.

On the city's North Side, on a street named Olive, there was a solid neighborhood of working-class Irish and Germans and Poles, with a few Italian families like mine sprinkled here and there, like basil, for flavor. Everyone lived in gray or red brick two-flats. Upstairs lived the tenants, preferably old people who didn't smell and who treaded the hallway quietly. The front of every house had a porch that faced a tree. Everybody except the old people and the Meenans and the Jankowskis had a new baby every year or so. At first we babies stumbled around our tiny backyards, eating grass and twigs and pebbles too large to stick in our nostrils and crunchy paint chips from the wooden garages that opened into the *stay away from there, do you hear me!* alley, touching fingers through the tilted square gaps in our chain-link fences that separated us, careful not to trample our fathers' tomato plants. Then we were promoted to the front yards, where we were yelled at by everyone. Because the new open space turned us into a herd of stampeding buffalo, and everyone had just planted marigolds or snapdragons or new grass seed. Perhaps because they were trained to be dainty, the girls at once obeyed. But we boys had no control over our shoes. So we fled and graduated ourselves to the alley.

The girls stayed in the front yards because they said the alley wasn't clean. Really they were afraid of the rats you would see sometimes munching on the day's garbage that spilled out of the big oil drums each house kept alongside its alley gate. Humorless men from the rodent-control section of the city's board of health marched through every spring stapling signs to the telephone poles.

WARNING! THIS BLOCK HAS BEEN BAITED
WITH RED SQUILL AND WARFARIN

So we called ourselves the Rat Squill Warfarins and armed ourselves with fifth-grader Joey Petrovich's baseball bat, and the alley became our kingdom, our playground, our limestone-and-asphalt Garden of Eden.

We explored every inch of it, naming every garbage can (Blue Streak, Rusty, Triple Dent), garage door (Big Ben, Lucky Green, Smasharoo), backyard gate (Squeaky, Busted Man, Fort Comanche). In the front yards our sisters stepped around the nodding petunias and drew squares on the ratless sidewalk with pieces of colored chalk. They began wearing dresses, using barrettes and red rubber bands to hold back their long hair. From our knees in the alley we could hear them sing.

"I live on Ol-live!"

Over and over and over, until we thought we'd go mad.

"Ay lives on Ol-live!
Ee lives on Ol-live!
I live on Ol-live!
Oh lives on Ol-live!
Do YOU *live on Ol-live?"*

And they always sang *see wye see oh?* (can you come out?) when they called from the backyards to one another to come out to play. I'd hear my sisters Rosaria and Tina. I'd listen, tempted to open my mouth and sing *en wye* (not yet) or *eye ay ell double you* (in a little while). But we were Rat Squill Warfarins; our rules said you couldn't sing. Our voices might scare away the rats that we hunted with rocks and Joey's baseball bat.

Whenever it rained or when one of our fathers would unroll his green garden hose and soap down his car, the potholes in our alley would brim deliciously with water and our playground would become the Chain of Great Lakes. We would play Dams and Beavers, on our hands and knees, using stones and sticks and pieces of broken glass. We'd see which one of us had the biggest beaver's buck teeth. Then Joey Petrovich's dark eyes would twinkle and he'd play Dive Bomber and smash our dams with his bat.

HOMES, Frankie Biermann taught us. Huron, Ontario, Michigan, Erie, Superior. Frankie had blond hair and polio and a brace on one leg. When you asked him if he had polio he said, "Yeah, that's how come my middle leg's so short." Skeeter Egan, who always wore his hair in a flattop and who could run faster than Old Lady Misiak's alley cat, and whose twin sister Deirdre was the most beautiful girl in the world, said Superior was the best.

Then for a while it didn't rain, and everyone's father's car was clean, and everything had a name, and the rats had made themselves so scarce that we forgot all about them. Then Lenny Sakowicz, whose arm muscles were as hard as cue balls, got a baseball and a genuine autographed mitt, and we all begged our parents for mitts. After my father told me no, "Don't be stupid, Danilo, I'll slap you, don't even ask," I got the scissors from the pantry and cut out all the pictures of baseball gloves in the Sears and Montgomery Ward catalogs my mother kept in a drawer in the china cabinet, and every night I'd stick one with my spit to the bathroom mirror, where he'd see it the next morning when he shaved. Each morning when I woke to go to school I'd find my mitt floating in the toilet bowl. Dive Bomber, I'd think as I'd sink the bit of paper with my pee.

But enough of the other kids got gloves. Then Joey and Lenny created the Olive Street Alley League, and Frankie got a pencil and wrote all the rules down.

Hitters gitters was the first commandment. That included even the backyards of childless old people who owned fierce dogs. *Ricochets are fair in play* was commandment number two. Off a garage roof was foul. Off telephone wires, fair. Pitcher's hands, you're out of there. Break somebody's window and everybody runs, with the hitter responsible for picking up the bat. Joey and the big guys foresaw most, but not all, of the possibilities.

"This here's a league of line-drive sluggers," the big guys said.

"Line-drive sluggos," echoed all of us little guys, even Frankie Biermann, whose leg brace made it awful hard for him to run.

Mickey Meenan was a very quiet kid, and most of the time he was around you didn't even notice he was there. He was tall for a third-grader, gawky, spotted everywhere you could see with freckles, and he'd pick his earwax with his little finger or a stick and then stare at it for so long he made you ask him what was he going to do with it. "I dunno," he'd always say, and then he'd always eat it or wipe it on his pants legs and then start working on his other ear. All the kids thought he was spoiled because he was an only child. Really, we were jealous. Mickey had a hundred toys, none of them broken; a thousand comic books, not one page torn.

Other than Grace Jankowski, in our neighborhood of mostly Catholic families Mickey was the only only child. Even though he was Catholic, his parents sent him to the public school on Bryn Mawr. So he was doubly strange.

Mickey's father had a job with the city, sleeping in trucks parked along the street where they had big potholes or busted water pipes, and he'd let us gather inside his garage as he'd boast that his CAUTION MEN WORKING signs sweated more in summer than he did. He was a big man and always smoked a fat cigar, and he'd tell us how great it was to go up to Wisconsin to shoot birds, really blast them out of the sky, or blow little squirrels or bunny rabbits to smithereens, and then he'd take out his shotgun and put a finger to his lip and say, "Shhh, be vewy vewy quiet. I'm hunting wabbits." We'd clap our hands with glee. Then he'd tell us how he'd once been a professional boxer, though he quit before he got cauliflower ears. He'd let us look at his ears, and we'd beg him to do Elmer Fudd again, and he'd say he was pleased as punch we played with his kid, and then he'd grab Mickey and rub his head real hard with his knuckles. Mickey would say nothing, except his face got fire-truck red as he squirmed.

Sometimes we'd tease Mickey about eating earwax and being spoiled, until he invited all of us over to his house. Mrs. Meenan made a hundred oatmeal cookies and ten gallons of Wyler's lemonade, and Joey and Lenny swiped a bunch of comics, and Frankie fell on a couple of toys and broke them all to pieces, and Mr. Meenan laughed and laughed and stunk up the house with his cigar, and everybody but poor Mickey had a wonderful time.

It was an accident, and it happened before I could even drop the bat and run. Winky Winkler danced on second base. Mickey was playing the garage door just behind first. It was a Saturday in early April and we had planned a triple-header, and we were getting good because several of us had our timing down.

Because it was a league of line-drive sluggos.

The ball cracked off the bat and I started to drop it as I ran toward first base, but I heard a hollow squish and Mickey stood there by Lucky Green staring right at me with no expression on his face. Then the world stopped as his bulbs went dim and he fell to his knees. For half a second I thought it was just a joke; I thought that Mickey had suddenly been struck by a sense of humor, that he'd begin to pray in pig Latin or sing "I live on Ollive!" or crawl like a turtle toward the ball. I wanted him to pick the ball up because I knew I could beat his throw. I wanted him to stand. I wanted him to say *something*.

Because suddenly I was terribly afraid.

By the time we got to him he had fallen to his face. Then Lenny and Joey and the rest of the guys rolled him over. His face and neck were turning blue. His throat was trying to pronounce the letter *K*. His eyes looked backward into his head.

"You're all right, Meenan," everybody said.

"Right off his Adam's apple! Didja see it?"

"Wake him up."

"Get the smelling salts."

"You shoulda seen it! It looked like he was trying to eat the ball!"

"You're O.K., Meenan."

"Get up, sluggo."

"You killed him, 'Galupo. Honest to Jesus!"

"He ain't even breathing."

We got him under his armpits and tried to make him walk. "You're all right, Meenan." His feet dragged like a Raggedy Andy doll. "Honest, Danny, I bet you killed him." Some of the guys laughed, scared and nervous. Little Frankie Biermann looked like he was going to cry. Then somebody took off down the alley toward Mickey's house. "Take deep breaths, Meenan, you're O.K., you're O.K." He wasn't very heavy. His skin still felt warm. His head rolled on his chest like Mr. Sakowicz on Friday nights when the men from the foundry walked him home drunk.

Mrs. Meenan bawled over Mickey as she knelt on her front-yard grass. As we waited for the ambulance, I thought I could hear the trees above me whisper their name. "Meenan," the leaves in the wind whispered. Then somebody shouted, "Hey Danny, better make yourself scarce."

There are times when events overload your circuits, and inside you blow a fuse. Your head suddenly goes dark. Dad says, "Lucy, where the hell did I put that goddamn flashlight?" You help him as he walks down into the basement, thinking maybe you'll get lucky and see a rat, hearing the sudden roar of the furnace as it kicks in. The sound frightens you but you're with your dad. Yet he says nothing as he shines his flashlight, the only light in the world, on the gray fuse box.

"Say something to him, Francis."

"Get me a clean shirt. I have to shave."

"Again?"

"I can't go over there wearing this filthy shirt."

Supper, some soup and noodles, and nobody talked until Louise started to sniffle, then cry. Ma held Francis Junior and said, "Eat." Only the baby ate, one hand raised and wrapped in Ma's dark curly hair, the other holding her breast so she wouldn't pull it away. The rest of us sat around the table, not eating. Louie wiped his ears with the fist that held his spoon. Dominic poked his noddles with his fingertips. Gino stared up at the ceiling, making stupid sounds with his tongue, and Tina held her rubber doll just like Ma held Francis Junior. Rosaria's hands hid her face. I looked at them, their dark heads, then down at my soup, then at the little piece of bloodstained toilet paper Dad had clinging to his chin, then at the dish towel he wore over his immaculate white shirt.

Ma thought I was asleep when they came back from their visit to the Meenans that night. Everybody was in bed. She kissed the others, then touched my forehead with her hand, pressing the coolness of her palm against me for several moments. I couldn't understand why she didn't bend down to kiss me until the middle of the night, when sound-asleep Louie woke me by peeing out his misery against my leg.

She didn't kiss me, I thought, because my forehead now had the mark of Cain, and even in the darkness my own mother could see it.

I'll run away, I thought. I imagined myself as a hobo with a burnt-cork Halloween beard, a stick over my shoulder and all my belongings inside a red bandanna, riding the rails to the Wild West's unknown frontiers, my leg eternally wet with my brother's pee.

The next day I escaped, just before I could be taken to church. Ma was busy changing Francis Junior's diapers. Dad shaved in the bathroom. I scooted out the back door and ran to the Bryn Mawr El station, slipping under the turnstile and jumping on the first passing train, which happened to be going south. I was terrified when the cars dipped into the dark tunnel just beyond Fullerton. I thought the El was always elevated. I feared that God was sending me down to Hell. But then the ride leveled off. I rode that train until I was the only white person on board, then got off, somewhere on the South Side. I took the next train that stopped at the platform, riding north to Howard Street, the end of the line.

Then I went back south, plunging deeper, no longer afraid of the tunnel or of being the only white. People were friendly to me. "Where you going, boy?" they asked. "Say, you lost?" I pretended that I couldn't speak, pointing to my mouth and shaking my head no. "You must be one of them deaf-mutes." I nodded yes and smiled. An old woman gave me a stick of peppermint gum.

I rode back and forth most of that Sunday. I don't know why I finally went home. No one said a word to me about my absence. At my place at the kitchen table there was an empty plate, a fork, a spoon. My ma looked like she wanted to ask me where I'd been all day, but my father's silence made the house too heavy for her or anyone to talk.

And then I became so sick that the doctor had to quarantine the house. I didn't fall sick with scarlet fever because I'd murdered Mickey Meenan, though at the time I was convinced that was why. I fell ill because I inhaled streptococci in one of those El cars, and a legion of homeless scarlet-fever bees built a hive inside my heart. Then the bees' bubbling honey leaked into my bloodstream and fried my cheeks, my legs, my bones. My guts flamed. Everywhere I was aching hot. Thrashing on the sweat-soaked sheets of my parents' double bed, I boiled like a lobster inside the steaming pot of my skin.

The parish priest wouldn't come to the house to bless me because of the quarantine. My mother rinsed my forehead and chest with holy water she pilfered from the church vestibule. She filled the bedroom with a hundred red votive candles that flickered everywhere I could see, and then the room grew dozens of stand-by-themselves crucifixes, and three times each day my brothers and sisters knelt outside my closed door and recited the rosary and the Litany for the Dead. *Oh Lord, deliver them. We beseech Thee, hear us.* I ate ice cubes made of water and red wine. When I could I peed into a soup pot. My ma brought every vigil candle on the North Side into that room, and after each rosary and litany she cracked the door open and tiptoed in and had me kiss the feet, hands, side, and head of each of the crucifixes that stood behind the tiers of bouncing candles and hung on my sickroom's four walls.

You'd think I would have lain on my damp sheets praying for the eternal salvation of my wretched soul and for eternal rest for the dearly departed Mickey Meenan. You'd think the words *I'm so sorry, dearest God* would have been starters in the lineup on my lips. They weren't even on the team. My mind and soul sang a different cha-cha.

"My little sister Tina could've gotten out of the way of that liner, dear God. You know I ain't lying. So why couldn't You have let the spaz catch it? Or at least made him duck? A dog would've known enough to duck. You make the pigeons fly away when the ball goes near them. So how come it didn't work with Meenan? You can do *anything*, remember? You could've let it ricochet off his forehead. Given the kid a shiner. Busted his nose. Knocked out his two front teeth. Why'd You have to let me kill him? Our Father, Who art in Heaven, what You let happen couldn't have been worse! All right, so maybe You really needed him up there in Heaven for some strange and mysterious reason. In school Sister's all the time telling us that's the way You like to operate. But You could've killed him a million other ways! You could've let him catch rabies from one of the alley rats! Why me? What did I ever do? *What did I ever do?*"

While my family knelt in the hallway outside my door, respectfully slurring *the Lord is with thee* and *blessed is the fruit of thy womb.*

I thought a lot about Hell. I'd let my fever work itself up until I felt I was made of fire, and then I'd squint at the endless rows of candles. The flames would shimmy in their little cups and I'd see a dancing sea of red. I'd pretend it was a glimpse of Hell, and I was just outside, in one of Hell's waiting rooms, about to receive my punishment. I'd try to imagine eternity and begin to multiply two times two times two times two until the numbers melted in my brain. Sometime I'd pull myself to the bed's edge and reach out and stick my little finger into one of the flames. I'd try to hold my finger there, the multiplication tables hovering on my lips, but my arm always pulled my hand back. Then I'd feel my forehead for my mark of Cain, and lie back on my pillow, exhausted.

I'd play a game with the crucifixes. If I lay perfectly still there was always at least one Jesus whose hollow cheeks reflected the flames in a way that made His head move. I'd stare at that Jesus and ask Him questions.

"Are You happy hanging on Your cross?"

No, His head would shake.

"Is Meenan still alive?"

Again, no.

"Will I be well in time to make my First Holy Communion?"

No.

"Does anybody love me?"

No.

"When I die, will I go to Heaven?"

Always no, no, no.

"Then stay on Your old cross," I'd whisper, then feel terrible and cry until my tears made little puddles in my ears.

I'd think of baseballs, endlessly arcing in on me, my hands gripping the bat, my wrists snapping the sweet part against the lazy ball. I played more games in my head than convents have black shoes and stockings. In every one I always hit safe line drives that were at least fifty feet over every fielder's head, that sailed like kite strings through the air touching nothing, nothing, ever. Never old Adam's forbidden apple stuck in an innocent freckled kid's throat. No, my balls would always land with a magnificent splash in the middle of Lakes Huron, Ontario, Michigan, Erie, and Superior.

Only when the fat doctor came to probe me with his instruments would the room fill with blinding light. I imagined him as Satan's chief inspector trying to decide which boiler room I'd be sentenced to and how high to set the thermostat. "His fever hasn't broken yet," he'd say. "Let's give it some more time." Then he'd turn with a belch or a fart, and my ma would sigh and turn off the terrible light, then replace the spent candles, then call the little disciples to the hallway for the evening's rosary and litany, which was followed by another round of Sacred Wound kissing.

Meanwhile my former classmates shuffled through practice and then real Confession en route to their first-Sunday-in-May march up to the Eternal Bread Line. "So what if I miss making First Holy Spumoni?" I hissed at the flickering flames. I was sick of being sick and so jealous I wouldn't be with them that I wished none of them would have any fun. I prayed the monsignor would screw up and none of the Sacred Snacks would get consecrated. "No, no, no," said the Jesus with the moving head.

I pictured the church, glowing more greenly than kryptonite, as the priest topped each communicant's virgin tongue. I imagined their sin-free souls gleaming like my feet in the X-ray machine at Maury's Bargain Shoe Store. I saw the ribboned pews and kneelers. All the kids filling their chipmunk cheeks with Christ. Everyone afterward posing on the church steps for adorable snapshots. Then they'd all tumble like socks in a dryer into a hundred just-washed Fords and Chevys, happily driving home to hamburgers on the grill, reheated roast beef, pineapple-covered ham, white First Communion cake. And all of them, knowing why I, the little murderer nailed to the cross of scarlet fever, wasn't there.

By then I was able to sit up and not feel woozy, and that afternoon I held the wall and slid my feet to the window, then pushed apart the dusty drapes and pulled up one narrow yellow slat of the venetian blinds. I was able to gaze out on a sunny sliver of Olive Street, so I stayed there, dizzily holding on to the drapes, until Mr. Egan's pine-green Plymouth scraped its whitewalls against the curb and Skeeter bounded out of the back seat in his white suit and bow tie. Sanctifying grace beamed all over his face. He twirled his thick Communion candle like a baton. Then Deirdre slid from the car like an angel on Christmas morning. I cried then, if my body had enough liquid left in it to cry. I began knocking down the rows of crucifixes and blowing out the thousand candles. It felt like a cruel birthday party I hadn't been invited to, and since I couldn't blow out all the candles with one breath, I realized that I wouldn't get my wish.

Which wasn't that the liner had never left my bat, or if it had that it hadn't struck Mickey, or that Mickey could be resurrected. I was more selfish than that. My wish was that I could be *normal* again.

Because I'd seen what happened to the kids who weren't. The others ganged up on them like a school of pet-store piranhas. They took chunks out of you until you were barely alive. They tripped you whenever you tried to walk down their row. They stuck KICK ME I'M AN ASSHOLE signs on your back with chewing gum. They snotted out gobs of boogers on your seat, then hooted like hyenas when you sat in it. They hid Tootsie Rolls of dog shit in your desk. No one would sit with you in the lunchroom, mess around with you out on the playground, stand next to you when you waited in line.

So I blew out every one of the damn candles and kicked over the soup pot and then got up on a chair so I could take all the crucifixes down from the walls when my ma came in and screamed, "Francis, Gino, Dominic, Rosaria, Tina, Louie, Francis Junior! Thank God! Our prayers are answered! Danny's well!"

And, in a way, I was.

ALBERTO RÍOS

The Purpose of Altar Boys

Tonio told me at catechism
the big part of the eye
admits good, and the little
black part is for seeing
evil—his mother told him
who was a widow and so
an authority on such things.
That's why at night
the black part gets bigger.
That's why kids can't go out
at night, and at night
girls take off their clothes
and walk around their
bedrooms or jump on their
beds or wear only sandals
and stand in their windows.
I was the altar boy
who knew about these things,
whose mission on some Sundays
was to remind people of
the night before as they
knelt for Holy Communion.
To keep Christ from falling
I held the metal plate

under chins, while on the thick
red carpet of the altar
I dragged my feet
and waited for the precise
moment: plate to chin
I delivered without expression
the Holy Electric Shock,
the kind that produces
a really large swallowing
and makes people think.
I thought of it as justice.
But on other Sundays the fire
in my eyes was different,
my mission somehow changed.
I would hold the metal plate
a little too hard
against those certain same
nervous chins, and I
I would look
with authority down
the tops of white dresses.

BETTIANNE SHONEY SIEN

The Cold War

I don't believe Russia exists.

When I think of Russia I hear my mother shouting that if someone were at the neighbors' with a gun pointed to their heads, wouldn't we defend ourselves?

"But Mom, why would Russians point a gun at Allie Ziegler's head?"

"You're seven years old," my mother says, "what do you know about Russians?"

It's just that it has been snowing all week. It has to do with God and St. Norbert's Catholic Cemetery and how the ground is so stubbornly frozen that our dead uncle can't be buried.

"Russia's even colder," my mother says, "so be grateful you don't live there."

If Russia exists.

I breathe holes into the frost on the pane to watch the sky. I confuse flurries with stars and planets while my mother whacks sprouts off last summer's potatoes before throwing chunks of them into the soup pot.

It is eight o'clock. It has been snowing all week and has been night for hours. The house smells cold and the scraped ice I suck from my fingernails tastes sweet.

"Stop it," my mother says. "You know you can't see stars when it's snowing. Why don't you listen to me. Half the time those aren't even stars. It's the Russians, watching us. They can hear everything, too. Put your coat on if you're going to sit by the window."

Out the window I watch a million tiny Russian ballerinas plummet to the ground, while my mother mixes chicken fat into the soup pot.

I pull my mother's plaid woolen coat around me and play with the sharp beads I find loose in her pocket. I once thought they were glass, before I held one up to the sun and saw the plastic seam.

"What does it matter?" my mother said. "They're still pretty."

I had been sitting on her lap in the car, the frost like moss across the dashboard in front of me. The tip of my tongue stuck to the metal in the same moment that she warned, "Don't you dare lick that dash." She had given me the beads for comfort but the string broke as I wondered how long taste buds took to grow back.

It is eight o'clock; it has been snowing for months. My mother is a gray frayed dress with red hands.

I wish they would come, marching in their furry hats across Highway 12. They could blow like drifts from someplace that does not exist, past toy farms and humps of wrecked tractors in white fields. The children would stop with their rusted wooden sleds to watch as the soldiers knocked over the priest. The dogs would be too scared to bark, they would stand like they had been dipped in dry ice. The Sisters of St. Francis would excitedly chant the rosary, their faces triumphant with martyrdom.

My mother looks at the clock and strains to hear a car engine above the silence of the snow. She drops dry chicken bones into the soup. It is eight o'clock and I watch seamless snowflakes build hills across our farm and walls to hide us from our neighbors. Fog rises from the soup, and I think of the headless chicken that ran scarlet circles in the snow yesterday.

When the Russians point their guns at my hat, I will fold my hands as I have been instructed by the nuns, bow my head and tell the truth, "Nope, I do not believe in God."

Then will the soldiers take me back to Russia with them?

"You'll see when they come," my mother insists. "Look at the snowflakes," she says, "God made each one different."

But I have no proof, they always melt into my mitten before I can compare.

My mother says, "It's eight o'clock, how can it still only be eight o'clock?" She opens the door, tries to make out the road through the gray shield of the storm, then slams it against the invading flakes. She sits down at the oilcloth-covered table and picks walnuts loose from their cracked shells.

What if the Russians don't ask me if I believe in God? They might just line me up with all the others against the barn door and blast us.

What will happen then? With no God or heaven, and I'm not so sure about limbo either, though I like that limbo song on the radio. But I think they only allow babies.

So there I'll be in the snow bleeding with my family in stale hay and manure and the cows will be mooing, while the Russians climb the walls to Allie Ziegler's farm to point guns at their heads.

Soft bombs of snow will fall and our bodies will have to wait for the frost to end before we can be buried along with our dead uncle.

I uncurl a strand of paint from the windowsill and say, "Mom, the clock is unplugged."

"You and your snotty mouth," my mother says, "you do this on purpose to make me crazy."

MICHAEL DORRIS

Martyrs

I lived to die. At any moment, the Red Chinese might sweep across the Pacific, through California, ravaging the continent until they reached Kentucky and surrounded Holy Spirit Church while terrified, hymn-singing parishioners cowered bravely within.

I was well aware of the Communists' ultimate goal: the ciborium, full of spare Eucharists, locked behind the carved golden door in the alcove at the center of the altar. Host-defilement was known to be a major motivator for nonbelievers of all stripes, and it had to be anticipated as adjunct to any invasion. The protection of sacred wafers, however, presented a problem for Defenders of the Faith because it entailed a tricky stipulation: with the exception of priests, consecrated hosts could only be manipulated or touched by the tongues of post–First Holy Communion persons (in the state of grace, naturally), and, to complicate matters even further, but one tiny disk could be consumed per capita per day.

What was a Catholic boy to do when at last the polished mahogany doors were battered down and enemy soldiers charged past the imported Italian marble holy water fonts and up the center aisle? I projected the ensuing scene as a vision reminiscent of Donald Duck's avaricious uncle cavorting with wild abandon in his money vault, except in this instance Scrooge was a *Peking* duck and each silver dollar was transformed into a miniature Body of Christ.

How to forestall this abomination without, in the process, committing a Mortal Sin by swallowing multiple wafers? Did the end justify the means? Could omnipotent God make a rock so big He couldn't lift it? In 1950s Irish-American Catholicism, paradox abounded.

We debated such philosophical topics in grade school, pausing even in the cafeteria over our sloppy joes and Jell-O. Timing, it seemed, played a key role—always implicated by a delicate system of checks and balances. Even when the intention was good, if the act was bad it was still a Sin, whether one realized it or not. There were fine-print rules governing almost everything: the recitation of the names (in proper sequence) "Jesus, Mary, and Joseph" was good for a 300-day commutation of one's eventual Purgatory sentence, *but only if they were vocalized.* Simply *thinking* a rote litany gained one no time at all (unless Communists were listening and would torture your parents if they overheard the magic words; under such circumstances, it was provisionally okay to simply mouth an invocation of the Holy Family without sound—unless there was a *deaf* Communist present who could lip-read, in which case . . . and so on and so forth).

You could sin by omission and commission, by desiring to do something bad you didn't actually do, or by begrudging something good you did. The Ten Commandments, in their various interpretations and subclauses, pretty much excluded all but a tightrope of permitted behavior toward your family, teachers, associates, and self, and God never, ever blinked or looked away in indulgent amusement. When I was nine—two years into the Age of Reason and therefore eternally, cumulatively responsible for every transgression—confessing my sins and doing Penance twice weekly hardly seemed often enough, the list of slips and slides was that long.

There was, joyfully, one surefire escape hatch, one soul-bleaching rinse that erased even the most persistent stains. All was absolutely forgiven and forgotten in the event that—even if positively stuffed with unleavened bread, even having at one time or another given Scandal to a Protestant by making a joke about a nun, even with a record as a prideful, self-abusing Friday hamburger-user—I managed to be persecuted for my Faith and perish in the process. Martyrdom, that just-like-new Baptism of Blood, automatically canceled all debits.

Treasure Chest magazine and the *Junior Catholic Messenger* offered a weekly parade of historical and virtually contemporary child saints who earned their wings through suffering. Maria Goretti succumbed intact to a pornography-crazed handyman. St. Martin was roasted on a spit rather than worship false gods. Father Brébeuf watched benignly while Iroquois tormentors ate his heart. St. Peter, even after thrice denying that he so much as knew the Lord ("Jesus *who*?"), ascended to heaven without detour after having been crucified upside down. Beheaded saints-to-be politely carried their own skulls to the graveyard, blessed their executioners with their final breaths, eschewed every "This is your last chance to dance naked before a Golden Calf statue" offer of reprieve. The message was clear: the road to Heaven is filled with bamboo spikes, and the fastest route is to run barefoot.

Okay: I believed. I was ready. Test me. I wore a scratchy Scapular against my bare skin and caused a rash on my chest. I did without—you name it: chocolate, pie, *I Love Lucy*—during Lent. I self-castigated, I regretted. I unfavorably compared my innate miserableness to every anti-Catholic reprobate from Attila the Hun to Henry VIII. I knelt on pebbles, gladly. Along with the rest of my family, I boycotted *Your Hit Parade* on television when one of its stars, the famously Catholic Gisele MacKenzie, got a divorce. A year or so later, we collectively stopped speaking to an old friend when she paid admission to see the "condemned" film *The Moon Is Blue*. I put up with, accepted, denied, prepared myself for the day the Communists underestimated my resolve. I was so ready I became impatient, then disappointed, then bored. The moment of truth passed and I was left unscathed, yet I yearned to be scathed! It was like training and stretching before a race, then never hearing the gun go off.

In spite of my ambitions, unlike Dominic Savio, the preteen role model saint who uttered the fateful phrase, "Death Rather Than Sin," and then conveniently died, I lived into the complexity of adulthood. The innocent right-and-wrong view of the world I had been offered by Sister Stanislaus Kostka shaded into layered ambiguity. Once removed from the regimen of Catholic-approved textbooks, issues that had once seemed simply religious blurred into politics, psychology (as in paranoia), and ethnocentric or misogynist bias. Like Adam and Eve, who, after eating of the Tree of Knowledge, lost their comfortable digs in Paradise, I found myself awash in a permanent state of unsureness—an emotion for which I had no preparation.

The popular survivor-saints in my grade school pantheon were hard to imagine emulating. St. Francis of Assisi talked to animals—and they answered! St. Theresa didn't eat anything but a daily host. St. Ann, an aged primipara, produced the Mother of God, while in the next generation St. Joseph remained on the sidelines while his wife, ever a virgin, gave birth to God Himself.

Without the drama of martyrdom, normal longevity—unless one possessed magic powers—seemed positively dull, an endless succession of Canaan conferences, compromise, toil without glory, and boring, predictable imperfection. Real life didn't hold a candle to old-fashioned Catholic boyhood, which, for me, had a swashbuckling kick, a dizzy aura of danger and flamboyance and possibility—provided that it didn't last too long.

LINDA NEMEC FOSTER

The Martyrdom of St. Agatha

(after a painting by Bernardino Luini, ca. 1475–1532)

Third grade was filled
with such torment:
reading *Lives of the Saints*
and its tabloid renditions
of sacrifice and death.
Virgin martyrs making bones
into relics. Their gentle
hands adept at holding
lambs, doves, white roses.
Those symbols of purity
the young boys wanted.

Agatha was the first,
always the most intriguing.
Her smooth body mangled,
breasts ripped away.
The empty holes in her chest
appearing in an obscure painting
in some forgotten museum.

But in the picture she smiles
bemused, as if to say:
"why am I holding this plate

full of round flesh—
the breasts more alive now
than when they were a part of me?"

And who can answer her?
Not the priest locked
in his red vestments.
Not the nun shrouded
in her black silence.
Perhaps the thin boy
sitting behind you,
his hot breath aiming
for your neck.

PART TWO

Wings

. . . a bird who halting in her flight . . .
sings
knowing she has wings

—Libana

LUCILLE CLIFTON

Far Memory

excerpt from a poem in seven parts

1
convent

my knees recall the pockets
worn into the stone floor,
my hands, tracing against the wall
their original name, remember
the cold brush of brick, and the smell
of the brick powdery and wet
and the light finding its way in
through the high bars.

and also the sisters singing
at matins, their sweet music
the voice of the universe at peace
and the candles their light the light
at the beginning of creation
and the wonderful simplicity of prayer
smooth along the wooden beads
and certainly attended.

2

someone inside me remembers

that my knees must be hidden away
that my hair must be shorn
so that vanity will not test me
that my fingers are places of prayer
and are holy that my body is promised
to something more certain
than myself

A. MANETTE ANSAY

Blue Light Special

I wasn't afraid of anything until the summer I turned twelve, when Mrs. Spieth showed me the wrongness of my thoughts. That summer, I had terrible thoughts, thoughts to make Christ blush and turn his head from me in shame. I walked that first Thursday night five blocks beneath a razor-edged, shining moon which could, the priest had warned, become God's eye if He so wished, and I battled those crimson thoughts with every step. The air was cool; mosquitoes whined and danced. I walked quickly, hunched in my stepfather's sweater, which was huge and brown, too loosely knit, a gift to him from his ex-wife. Summer nights, in the dull, flat face of the Wisconsin chill, that sweater drooped over my skirt like a shield.

The parochial school kids got their summers free, but we publics were sent to special catechism classes each Thursday evening, from eight until ten. Mrs. Spieth taught our seventh grade. She held class in her home instead of at the church because she was ill with Parkinson's disease. Her sixteen-year-old daughter, Anastasia, served us grape juice and Ritz crackers at nine-fifteen. Anastasia was sullen, with a mole's long nose and wistful eyes. It was hissed behind the backs of hands that she let boys have their way. Mrs. Spieth's proud gaze clung to her like strong perfume, for Anastasia was a Miracle Child, born after seven miscarriages. Anastasia was the proof Mrs. Spieth offered us for the existence of God.

Mrs. Spieth was a brittle-boned woman with dry brown hair and eyes the color of sparrows. Everything shook on her as if she were resonating from an unseen but violent blow. Her hands she controlled by clenching them into fists, her feet she kept locked through the rungs of her chair, but her head trembled constantly no matter what she did, clattering her teeth together when she spoke. She told us during our first class, that crisp, clear June night as we solemnly chewed our crackers, that she'd seen Satan many times in her life.

There were nine of us there, all girls, except for Chipper Grassen, and we were in the living room, sitting cross-legged on the linoleum floor, the coolness of it numbing our buttocks. The room was bare except for a couch, where we were forbidden to sit, and the chair which supported Mrs. Spieth. A crucifix hung behind her. Twisted around it were braids of blessed palm fronds, dried, thick with dust.

Up until she said *Satan,* I hadn't paid much attention. I was lathering my body with daydreams of Chipper, blurring time, enticing sin. Oh, I went to Mass on Sundays, even when my mother was too tired to go with me. I made my confession once a month, I said my prayers. When my stepfather cooked meat on days of abstinence, I refused to taste it. But my mind was my own landscape, unaccountable to God or anyone. There I took pleasure, gulped it down, until Mrs. Spieth sniffed out the poison in that cup.

"The first time I saw him," she was saying, "I was lying awake in my bed. It was very late at night. Suddenly, I felt I wasn't alone, and I smelled a very bad smell. It was then that I saw Satan circling me in the form of a blue light." She awkwardly stroked the copper-colored medal, about the size of a penny, which hung from her neck by a string.

We looked at each other and tittered, embarrassed. This was more than we'd expected, more than we wanted to hear. It made something twist in our guts.

"Blue light special," I whispered to Jenny Nadolski, but something about the acoustics of the room, maybe all that linoleum, made it seem like I'd just shouted. Mrs. Spieth shook so wildly I thought she'd fall out of her chair. But her voice came low, gentle.

"My dear Amanda, you think I don't know what's going on

in your mind?" She spat as she spoke; I could see the droplets, falling slow-motion to the floor.

I shrugged. The room was dark, lit only by one feeble lamp that hung above her chair, and for this I was grateful because my blush remained my secret.

"If I projected your thoughts onto a screen, where everyone could see, wouldn't you be ashamed?"

No one tittered now.

"How about if I tell the class exactly what you were thinking? Because I know, and you know I know."

I did not say anything.

"Do you know I know, Amanda?"

"Yes," I whispered, convinced she did.

"Well, then," she said. "I will pray for you. Will you pray for me?"

I gulped and nodded. Poor Chipper Grassen was narrow-boned, nearsighted, and peppered with small dark moles; no girl in her right mind would even *want* to think about him in an impure way. Saturday afternoons we went sometimes to the movies, but I made him sit in the seat behind me so nobody would think we were together. And if he let his hand bump mine, reaching over my shoulder into the popcorn, I kept the popcorn all to myself until he told me, *Sorry.* A second wave of blushes scalded my face. Mrs. Spieth was talking about thought signifying intent, which meant that we would be held responsible for the actions our thoughts represented.

"You mean," Jenny said, "that if we think about, ah, murdering someone, we're murderers?"

Mrs. Spieth knew exactly what she meant.

"If you think about sexual intercourse, in God's eyes, you're no longer a virgin."

She beckoned to me after class, pulled me down to where she could breathe her musty breath into my ear. "There's nothing you can do that God won't forgive. You have a beautiful soul. Don't let it be lost." Her fingers shivered in my hair. No one had ever said before that any part of me was beautiful. The copper-colored medal blinked its shining eye.

The walk home was cold, ablaze with the light of the round-shouldered moon. Jenny came with me as far as Middle Avenue. Neither of us said much. At the end of our catechism classes last summer, Father Clardy had invited the girls from his sixth grade over to the rectory. He showed us a film about chastity, and made us each promise to keep our virtue. We all knew what he meant. Now Jenny turned to me and said, "I guess I'm still a virgin because I never imagine going all the way."

I'd imagined going all the way many times. The wind rose as she turned off onto Middle, and I wandered on through the darkness, my stepfather's sweater bloated behind me like a sail. I knew the moon couldn't hurt me, but I noticed a slight bluish tint about it like the blue in the white of a cow's wide eye. Blue light special. The irreverence of my words tripped me; I fell to my knees. *If the moon could be God's eye, perhaps it might be Satan's.* I got up and ran the last block home.

The next Thursday night I tucked myself into my stepfather's brown sweater and flew beneath the wink of moon to that cold linoleum floor. I hadn't known Christ lived in this world, that he appeared to holy young girls my age and caused the chipped eyes of statues to weep. Two sisters in Blue Hills, Alabama, awoke with the bloody stigmata in their palms. An old priest in Maryland was taken by St. Peter on a whirlwind tour of purgatory.

"It's a terrible place, purgatory," Mrs. Spieth quoted Peter to warn us. "Everything's dry as dust."

But Satan interested us more than dust or visions. He was the tall, chilling stranger, dressed in impeccable black. He had the smile that crushed hearts.

"All my life Satan has loved me," Mrs. Spieth said. "Does it surprise you that I say 'love'?" She paused to sip grape juice from a straw Anastasia pressed to her lips. "Remember that before he fell, he was God's most beloved angel. Satan remembers love."

The light bulb above her head flickered, spat, and died. The room hissed with a tremendous intake of breath; nobody moved. Mrs. Spieth's voice slipped like a canoe through our dark-watered fear.

"Ana, would you find a new light bulb? Under the kitchen sink, on the left."

Anastasia arose and stumbled between our bodies until she found the door. Light from the kitchen broke the dark. We could hear her heavy step, the creak of a cupboard door. Mrs. Spieth's shadow bobbled on the wall.

"I saw the face of Satan in my husband's wedding ring, just after Anastasia was born. I did not want to believe it. Finally I said, Ralph, take off your ring. I said, If you love me you'll do as I say. And he tried to take it off, but it stuck to his finger. Take it off! I said. I'll get you some butter. Why should I take it off? he asked, and I told him what I'd seen. He held his hand up to the light, but by then the face was gone. There's nothing in this ring, he said. Six months later he disappeared."

That such a thing could happen struck my heart with the force of a blow! For once, when my mother had warned me of sin, my stepfather put his hand on my knee and dared Satan to take us both. Nothing had happened; he lifted his hand as my mother stared into the air, and I'd chewed my lip with a relief that was only as keen as my disappointment.

Now I felt the beating of my heart as though I held it in my fist. Anastasia came back into the room, carrying the light bulb which shone white as a skull. She twisted it into the socket; brightness stung my eyes. Mrs. Spieth grasped the copper-colored medal at her throat.

"This is the blessed medal of St. Benedict," she said, as if it made no difference to her whether or not we had light, whether or not we believed her. "This alone keeps me from the power of Satan's love."

Chipper Grassen broke the spell.

"I'm going home," he said. He stood up and flashed a look at me, but I just scratched at a mosquito bite on my wrist. The back of his neck flushed dark; the moles there glistened, plump as raisins. He picked his way toward the door and nobody moved to widen his path. We listened to the scrape of his footsteps dwindling down the walk.

Anastasia shrugged. "His parents are just gonna send 'im right back."

Mrs. Spieth's hands and feet rattled with spasms. Then she smiled at her daughter. She smiled until Anastasia's face darkened beneath the bright eye of the lamp.

Silence stretched thin and white.

"Let us pray for his soul," Mrs. Spieth finally said.

I thought of Chipper wandering home through the dark, shivering under the distant dusky stars. I briefly wondered if he was angry with me, but that seemed so silly, so trivial in the face of the eternal salvation Mrs. Spieth held in her crimped, dry palm. I longed for the trembling embrace she sometimes gave me as I came through the door, as though she'd thought of me all week. "You are precious in God's eyes," she said, "believe me. I've seen through His eyes, and I know."

I felt an odd, sticky warmth on my wrist. Blood! I thought for a moment that, like the sisters, I'd been chosen. But it was only my mosquito bite, oozing where I had picked it.

Hail Mary, I said with the others. *Full of grace. The Lord is with thee.*

I fell in love with Mrs. Spieth.

Chipper Grassen figured it out. We walked to the movies one Saturday afternoon while my mother slept and my stepfather watched TV. In the spirit of my newfound Christian love, I told Chipper he could sit beside me if he promised not to talk. We found two seats way up front just as the theater filled with a musky darkness. I stared self-consciously at the previews, eating my popcorn and ignoring Chipper's elbow against my arm. Suddenly, he nudged the popcorn aside and wriggled his hand into mine like he was forcing his way through the small mouth of a jar. He would have kissed me; shocked, I spat full in his face. Bits of half-chewed popcorn clung to his cheeks like pasty tears.

"It's sin!" I said. "Your body is God's temple!"

Chipper wiped his face. "What's the matter with you?" he said. "You *believe* all that stuff she tells you?"

"Who?" I said, but Chipper wasn't fooled.

"You know who."

"No, I don't."

Chipper thrust his face into mine, shaking it wildly, his tongue hanging out.

"S-S-Satan is-s-s coming to get-t-t you!" he wailed, raising his arms like a ghost. The people behind us kicked our seats. I crawled over him into the aisle, stomping on his feet as I went. He charged after me and we exploded through the double doors into the wide, painful lights of the lobby. I bolted through the EXIT and ran down the sidewalk, Chipper's feet pounding behind me, closer, closer, until his hand just touched my shoulder. Then

I dropped to all fours, and he catapulted over me, skidding on his hands and knees across the concrete.

He was hurt, but he wouldn't admit it and quickly rolled to his feet. He flicked bits of gravel from his palms.

"You're crazy!" he shouted. "You're crazier than she is! You're crazier than even your ma!"

I backed away from him, starting to run.

"Amanda!" he yelled, but I took off and this time he didn't follow. I ran all the way back home.

My stepfather, Julian, was asleep on the living room couch in his underwear. The straps of his undershirt clung to his shoulders like ribbons. The elastic in his boxers sagged below his belly.

"Julie," I said. His nakedness made me squirm. Sometimes he'd stand too close to me, so close I could sense the parts of his body I couldn't see.

"Please, Julie."

He opened his eyes a little.

"Where's Mom?" I asked.

"In the bedroom," he said. "She's sleeping, don't bother her."

My mother was a clerk at the dime store around the corner. When she came home she was tired and needed to sleep. *I'm so depressed,* she'd say. She slept almost all the time, except when she had to go back to the dime store. Sometimes she fell asleep there, in the middle of what she was doing, and had to be taken home.

"I want to talk to Mom."

"You can sit down here and talk to me."

I didn't say anything and I didn't sit down.

"How was your date?"

"It wasn't a date. We had a fight."

"Uh-huh," Julian said. "What did you fight about?"

"Nothing."

"Old Chipster get fresh?"

I shrugged.

"Uh-huh," Julian said. "A boy ever kiss you yet?"

When I wouldn't answer, his eyelids lowered like the leaves of a dying plant.

I went into my bedroom and knelt by the bed, and I thought about Mrs. Spieth. I thought about her a lot that summer. Flush-faced, I told myself it was holy. Thursday nights, I found ways to brush against her, and the ache in my bones grew deep enough for me to believe I was blessed.

Always there was Anastasia. She answered the phone, took our cups into the kitchen, brought the small yellow pills that Mrs. Spieth sometimes needed for her nerves. How was I to prove my love? I'd close my eyes to think about Mrs. Spieth, but instead I'd confront Anastasia's wide body, her thick, moist lips, her mole's eyes.

Finally, I saw my chance. Anastasia was away on a date; Mrs. Spieth asked if somebody would mind assisting with a few small things that evening? My hand shot into the air. And so I was the one to hold the straw to her lips. I wrapped the shawl around her crow-thin shoulders, and turned out the light in the kitchen so the bulb above her head alone would shine.

Late as usual, Chipper slouched in and thumped to the linoleum, loose-boned as a doll. Mrs. Spieth called his mother if he didn't show up, and then his mother docked his allowance and made him work Saturdays for the ladies who cleaned the church. This particular night, Mrs. Spieth did not speak until he raised his head and nervously met her gaze.

"Tonight I have something for all of you," she said, looking just at him. "A gift."

She fumbled with the copper-colored medal at her throat. I stood behind her, my stomach pressed to the back of the chair, waiting for her instructions.

"Chipper," she said, ignoring me. "Go into the kitchen and in the drawer left of the sink, you'll see a candle and a match."

Chipper didn't move.

"I'll get them," I said jealously, but Mrs. Spieth's eyes were on Chipper. He got to his feet, then, and lurched over hands and stretched-out legs until he found his way into the kitchen.

"He doesn't care about this," I said, and I buttoned and unbuttoned Julian's brown sweater. "He doesn't believe in any of it."

Mrs. Spieth's lips twisted into a dark rose. "That will change," she said. She worked a white envelope from a pocket in her housecoat; she nodded to me, and I plucked it from her fist.

Inside were seven copper medals, just like the one she wore from her neck.

"Be careful with them, they're blessed," she said. "As long as you keep them on your person, Satan cannot harm you."

We each took one, fingered it uncertainly. When Chipper came back into the room the envelope was empty. He glanced at our medals, the envelope, confused.

"Light the candle," she told him.

When the match struck, she tugged the lamp cord from the wall, so Chipper had to find the wick by his own small light. His face looked like a rabbit's, drawn and hushed. He sat down, holding the candle in both hands.

"Does everyone have their medals?" she asked. We nodded, our shadows dark slashes on the walls, unrecognizable shapes. Only Chipper shook his head.

"I don't have a medal," he said.

"I'd like everyone here to think their most secret terrible thought, a thought so evil it could never be said aloud. Encourage that thought. Dwell on it. Allow it to rule your mind."

She bowed her head, and after looking around at each other, so did we. The flame danced wildly in Chipper's hands.

"Hey," he said softly.

"Your most terrible thought," she whispered. "Keep your medals close. Understand that Satan loves you more than anyone you have known."

I closed my eyes and let the pent-up poisons of the summer rain down on my soul. I stoked my secret fires of lust with bras and boys and Chipper's thin shoulders. But deep inside I sensed I was capable of more, something so horrible I hadn't known it could exist. It was then I opened my eyes on Julian. I saw his soft belly, the loose folds of his underclothes. He beckoned me closer; I obeyed. His lips parted, too close, and I shivered as his hands slid the brown sweater from my shoulders. *You ever kiss a boy?*

How could I have screamed with my hands pressed to my mouth? Chipper screamed too, thrusting the candle into the air like a sword, and the other girls screamed and in the tousled darkness I saw a flicker of blue above his head. The candle fell to the floor. Chipper fought his way between us and ran from the house. One of the faster-thinking girls stamped out the flame, and Mrs. Spieth, as if awaking from a dream, worked the plug back into the wall.

"Now do you understand?" she said.

Stunned in the glare like animals, we thought we understood.

Julian was sprawled on the couch when I got home. He wore only a bathrobe, open to the waist and belted loosely below his belly. The dark fur there was like an arrow pointing down. I pinched my St. Benedict medal between my fingers.

"Where's Mom?" I said, looking carefully away from him.

Julian jumped. "You're home early," he said.

"I need to talk to Mom."

"Talk to me. Sit down over here and tell me what's the matter."

"Where is she?"

"She's asleep. Don't go bothering her. Hey!"

I went down the hall and opened the door to their room. My mother was lying on top of the covers, fully dressed.

"Please," she said. "I'm so tired."

I sat on the edge of the bed. Julian stuck his head through the door.

"Come on," he said.

"Mom, look," I said, showing her the medal. "Mom, it's important."

"Amanda!" said Julian.

My mother rolled over on her stomach and started to cry. Julian lunged through the doorway, grabbed me by the arm.

"Mom!" I yelled.

"Please," she kept saying. "Please."

I kicked Julian hard in the shin and twisted away. His robe swung open and he made no move to close it. I knew that thing hanging smack between his legs had no right to exist in God's clean world.

"Jesus Christ, Amanda!" he said, and I held up the St. Benedict medal like a cross.

"Cover your shame before the eyes of God!" I screamed. Julian froze, bewildered, then fumbled with his robe. My mother raised her head. I walked past them, down the hall and into my bedroom. I threw off the brown sweater and lay down on the bed. Their voices rose, blended together, faded away, but I didn't care. That night I slept with one ear listening; waiting, beloved, the medal at my throat like a kiss.

BIRUTE PUTRIUS SEROTA

Lucy in the Sky

The souls for whom no one prays are especially dangerous. My Grandmother Marijona always said this. To her the very air was thick with souls. She made me pray for each dead member of my family. We'd name them and count them out on our fingers. I sometimes dreamt of a group of ancestors following me everywhere I went, commenting on my life like some Greek chorus.

When my grandfather died, I prayed and prayed for him. He was such a powerful presence in my life when he was alive, I didn't want him to be dangerous in his after-life. But when my Aunt Lucy was killed while crossing Western Avenue, I forgot to pray for her. I don't know why. Maybe it was because she was the "modern" aunt, the looney one, everyone said. The one who refused to speak Lithuanian at all times, the one who liked to drink and swear and to flirt with married men. They said she had a bad romance with one of the congealed bachelors who sit at the Sports Club most evenings. They said she had a broken heart because he wouldn't marry her. They said she got in trouble. It didn't turn out well. They said the drinking was just bravado to hide her hurt. They said she was drunk the night the car hit her. She never went in for church much and so I thought she didn't seem to need praying for, but that's where I was wrong. She needed it more than any of them. Her soul was lost. Not in the church way, but because she, more than any of us, had broken with the past. The long string of souls reaching back to the beginning. I always thought of them holding hands like a long string of children in the playground playing Red Rover. Lucy broke the chain of hands. No telling what that meant.

This wasn't apparent right away. In fact we all continued to lead our normal lives. We went to church on Sundays and all the holy days of obligation. I prayed for my dead family in heaven, naming all but Lucy on my fingers the way my grandmother had taught me. I continued to be the best student in my fifth-grade class at St. Casimir's School. All was well until May Day.

On May first we crowned the statue of the Virgin Mary with flowers. I was chosen for this honor. I was dressed like Mary in a long blue gown with a white long veil on my head. I felt like a pastel nun. I was at the head of a long procession of girls dropping rose petals and singing Mary songs: "O Mary we crown thee Queen of the May . . ." I was about to climb the ladder to put the flowers on the head of the statue when I had a strange thought. If Mary is the mother of God, why don't we call Joseph the father of God? Oh yeah, Immaculate Conception, the Virgin Birth. Well if Joseph isn't Jesus' father, and God really is his true Father, then why don't we call Mary God's wife? Then she would have a rightful place in the Trinity of Father, Son and Holy Ghost, only then it wouldn't be the mysterious triangle. It would be the square of God and Mrs. God on top and Jesus and the Holy Ghost on the bottom. Or maybe Mary is just God's daughter-in-law. All this confusing genealogy of the Divine was for some reason swimming around in my head as I placed the floral crown on the statue in the courtyard. I wished I could ask Sister Kunigunda about it or maybe even the handsome Father Dan, but I dared not. I remembered how they called Bad Irene a blasphemer for questioning the raising of Lazarus. She had merely asked if Lazarus had been green or moldy, or if he smelled bad after he had been raised from his grave. I thought it was an interesting question myself, but the nun didn't think so.

The question was never answered, but that didn't matter. Something bigger had happened. Someone had questioned. This was big. For me it was a moment of pure clarity. The idea of questioning became a secret obsession with me. A heady and powerful experience—to question that which was unquestionable: Dogma. It became a daily habit. A new way of looking at the world.

After the procession and after school, I went home as usual to do my homework. I was on my second page of long division when Connie O'Connor came over.

"Milda, come quick, there's a real live miracle happening in front of the Valentinases' house on Talman Street. Mary's appearing and she looks just like you did at the May procession today."

"Are you kidding me?"

"No lie, honest to God." Connie crossed her heart. "Hurry up before she disappears."

I was running down the street and again my mind started its new habit of questioning. Why is it that Mary always appears at all these miracles, I thought? How come we never saw Jesus or Joseph or any of the apostles at Lourdes or Fátima? As usual, there were no answers to the questions.

When I got to the Valentinases' house on Talman Street, I saw what looked like a patch of fog and I could see that something was glowing inside the fog. As I got closer I could see that there was a woman in blue robes in the clouds. Her head was turned the other way. I saw that she had her hands out in front of her in the traditional Holy Virgin pose. It all looked like an authentic miracle all right. I tried to move closer to get a better look. So many people had gathered there. Everyone was kneeling. I squeezed toward the house and I was about to kneel down when I saw the Virgin's face: It was my dead Aunt Lucy, the looney one who died last year.

"Hello, Milda, how's it going?" said the apparition.

"Aunt Lucy, what are you doing?" I was so startled and confused.

"I am waiting for Albinas Valentinas to come out of the house and declare his undying love for me," answered the spectral Lucy. "Right here in front of all these God-fearing people the way he used to declare it to me in the back seat of his Hudson." Milda looked around. No one seemed to have heard her.

"Why are you impersonating Mary? Everyone thinks you're the Virgin with those robes."

Aunt Lucy choked back a laugh. "That's a good one."

"But you're an impostor, Aunt Lucy," I whined.

"So? I got the idea from watching you do your impersonation this afternoon."

"But that was May Day," I protested.

"Well this is V-V Day. Victory for the Virgin." Aunt Lucy chortled. "Valentinas Day. Where is that bum, anyway?" Aunt Lucy looked around. "I had loved that lout for most of my short forty-six years on earth." Lucy was getting worked up. "Albinas Valentinas, the one I worshiped and adored, the one I lost my virginity to, the one who wouldn't help me get an abortion, the one who ran away, drank, hid from me. I'm back to torment him for as long as he tormented me. Look at him peeking out from behind his mother's lace curtains. Ha! He knows it's me. He's afraid to come out. He's making it in his pants, he's so frightened." The aura of light around Lucy was getting brighter. She blazed like some Old Testament prophet. Her anger seemed to be fueling her like propane in a lantern. The people gathered around oohed and aahed at the brightness of the light. Rosaries were pulled out of pockets and pocketbooks.

"Milda, go tell that miserable excuse of a man to come out here."

Reluctantly, I went inside the brick two-flat and found Albinas Valentinas cowering in the corner of the fussy living room.

"Wh-what is she doing here? Why doesn't she stay dead the way she's supposed to?" Albinas was chewing his mustache nervously. "What does she want?"

"She wants you to tell everyone you love her. You know, a declaration of love from you."

"To tell everyone I still love her. That's all she wants?" His face softened. "To think she took this love for me to her grave and beyond." He shook his head. He looked like a boy who would cry soon. "Now that is the power of love."

I wanted to say that it was the power of anger, of revenge, not love that was powering this return from the grave, but I kept quiet. Albinas pulled some paper out of a drawer and began to compose a love letter. His letters were thin and spidery like the hairs on his head. When he was finished he thrust it into my hands and told me to give it to Lucy quickly. I did as I was told.

I watched Aunt Lucy read the letter over several times. I wondered how much she knew about God and the workings of the world. Maybe she could answer all those burning questions that plagued me so.

"Ha, he says it was his mother's fault. She didn't want him to marry me. What a coward. He couldn't stand up to that ax of a mother. Did he think that this would be enough for me? Did he think that I bothered to come all the way from the other side of death for this puny little letter? I want a declaration of love that the whole neighborhood could see."

"Like a sign?"

"Bigger," she bellowed. "And tell him I'm not moving until I see it."

"O.K., Aunt Lucy, I'll tell him, but before I go in can you answer one question for me?"

"Maybe."

"What about the Virgin Birth? Did Mary really become pregnant without sex? Did God arrange to keep her pure for some reason?"

"Do you really think that God cares about the Virgin Birth?" Aunt Lucy laughed. "God doesn't care about that. God simply is."

"Is? That's all?"

"No, that's not all—that's everything."

"God doesn't care about the Virgin Birth? Are you sure?"

"God doesn't judge."

"No one judges?"

"I didn't say that. Your ancestors judge—and how they judge. A more resentful bunch you'll never find than the dead. Be careful."

So my grandmother was right about the power of ancestors, I thought.

A week went by and news of the apparition was spreading. My whole family came to see Aunt Lucy. My grandmother cried to see her. I couldn't tell if she was crying from happiness or sadness. My mother was shocked at first and then embarrassed. She kept telling Lucy to go away and vanish before anyone else recognized her. "I always knew you were different, Lucy, but I never expected *this,*" she said.

Grandmother had many questions about all of her family and friends who had "passed over to the other side," as she called it.

I realized that my grandmother knew more people who were dead than alive. She was the last of her generation still living in this neighborhood. Two school friends still lived in Lithuania, also isolated leftovers from a time now gone. They wrote occasional letters in a shaky handwriting. My grandmother read them with a magnifying glass. I sometimes saw her tears magnified as I watched her read with the glass close to her face. The news from Lithuania always seemed to be sad. I saw the longing in my grandmother's eyes to join the dead—a whole family, a tribe waiting for her to pass over.

One by one, people in the neighborhood began to recognize Lucy. Old friends and acquaintances dropped by to say hello. Some were shocked, others took it in stride, a few called Father Dan to investigate. They wanted to declare Lucy, the former local looney, a saint.

Father Dan explained that two miracles needed to happen in order for Lucy to be considered for sainthood. Things like miraculous healings or rosaries that changed from silver to gold, or strange lights or whirling discs in the sky. The usual saint requirements and a waiting period during which the Pope must declare her Blessed.

"Piece of cake," said Lucy when she heard the news. That afternoon as the neighborhood gathered to watch the appearance of one of their own potential saints, every silver filling in every person's mouth turned to gold.

"Rosaries, the priest said rosaries," I muttered under my breath, "not dental fillings."

"Don't be boring, Milda. You worry too much about the rules. Relax, you're too intense."

I tried to relax in school. I no longer listened to a thing the priest said in religion class. It all seemed irrelevant. God does not judge, God simply is, I would repeat to myself over and over. But one day Father Dan was droning on and on about the Virgin Birth again. It was one of his favorite subjects. He was explaining how Mary got pregnant the night of the Annunciation, when the angel whispered in her ear while she was sleeping. I thought of blowguns with sperm in them. Is there a way for sperm to get from the ear to down there, I wondered?

"God doesn't care about the Virgin Birth." I hadn't meant to stand up and say this but there I was blaspheming in front of the whole class.

"Where did you hear such a thing?" asked Father Dan.

"Lucy told me."

Father Dan looked around. "Lucy who?"

"Not here. Lucy in the sky, my Aunt Lucy."

The priest frowned.

Several days later, Father Dan was performing an exorcism. Sprinkling holy water and commanding Aunt Lucy to be gone from there with her minions from hell.

"Fat chance," said Aunt Lucy. "I ain't leaving till I get my declaration of love and if it doesn't come soon, I'll make life hell for one Albinas Valentinas."

Albinas came out the next day with placards, but it was not enough. The following day he had larger signs printed, but she still wasn't satisfied. He declared his love through bullhorns, but it was still not enough for Aunt Lucy. She wanted more, she wanted bigger. A love letter went up on the corner billboard, above the Sinclair station. It was still not enough. Albinas was frantic to show his love, but he was running out of ideas.

That night my dreams were tortured by large groups of ancestors watching my every move. I felt cowed by the intensity of their interest. I dreamt of long strands of DNA, like the trees of life, with all of my dead family attached in a chain. There was nowhere to hide, no one to confess to. This was beginning to feel more oppressive than the Church. I went to Lucy for help.

"Silly girl," said Lucy. "Your ancestors are there to help you, not just to judge you. Ask them for help when you need it. Honor them when your life goes well."

"How do I honor them?"

"Get some pictures, light a candle, say a prayer. It's elementary. Life is hard and quick but it's also sweet and simple. Relax, Milda, have some fun."

I went out and bought some candles, put up some pictures, started praying. My mother thought I was becoming strange. I sometimes saw Sister Kunigunda and Father Dan looking at me with suspicion. But in my grandmother's eyes, I was the family savior.

One night, after lighting my candles, I prayed for Aunt Lucy. I wanted her to get what she wanted. I fell asleep and dreamed of my dead grandfather. In the dream he was flying a plane and writing in the sky. It looked just like Albinas Valentinas' spidery handwriting. When I awoke, I decided this was an important dream and I went over to tell Albinas about it. He was overjoyed. He kissed me on both cheeks and ran out the door. I heard later that Albinas rented a skywriting airplane. It made a huge heart in the sky and in the heart it printed: "I Love Lucy" in big white puffy letters.

No one in the neighborhood paid any attention. Everyone thought it was an advertisement for the TV show of the same name. But Lucy was ecstatic. "There, he finally did it so the whole neighborhood could see he really loved me." She glowed warmly and faded away slowly with the letters in the sky. The last I saw of her she was smiling beatifically and blowing kisses to Albinas. He cried copious tears at her fading. He loved her far more in death than he ever had in life. He never did marry. He still spent time at the Sports Club with the other bachelors, only now he cried over his lost love, Lucy. He spent the rest of his days in lovesick mourning.

While I spent my nights trying hard to relax under the gaze of a new cosmology. Lucy never was declared Blessed, even though my grandmother's arthritis mysteriously vanished the day Lucy left. We both lit candles and prayed especially long and hard for the soul of my looney Aunt Lucy.

GARY SOTO

The Music at Home

Sometimes I stared at the marble-white Christ
On the nightstand. Monsignor Singleton
Had blessed Him in the rectory
And said good things about us when he learned
We kept holy water in a cupboard.
Sometimes I stared at the mirror nailed
To the closet door and tried to scare myself.
For a long time I believed the air inside jars was ill,
That if you didn't open them up slowly,
If you didn't hold them from your body,
You'd get sick. I thought a lot
About the jars when my mother and stepfather
Argued. Jim yelled that we were spoiled,
That we didn't pick up around the yard.
I thought about the jar, the evilness of air,
and tried to remember everything he said.
A tape recorder helped. When I was twelve
My brother's friend David and I saved enough money
To buy a cheap one from Long's Drugs.
The Beatles were popular. Still, their faces collapsed
Into an egg of light when they appeared
On Ed Sullivan—our stepfather had words
For men with long hair. Still, we saved our money.
We wanted to sing along to their records

To see what we sounded like. We sang
At his house because it was scary at mine.
Sometimes David and I would go inside for a ball or a mitt,
And Jim would shout from his chair,
What do you want? Other times we would look in
From the front window. We could see that he
Was drunk. His head was sinking into his chest,
Mouth open to gray teeth. David and I sang
At his house and laughed a lot because
We were louder than the Beatles. David wanted to be
All the Beatles. One day he was Ringo,
The next Paul, then John. I had to be George
Because David paid a dollar more
For the tape recorder. Later we
Didn't play records but sang into the microphone
Songs we learned at school. One time when
I took home the tape recorder,
Mom and Jim were arguing. I walked quickly
To my bedroom and closed the door. The mirror
Was scary at the edges. Christ was marble white
And hollow, an afternoon glow from the window
Fading at His feet. When I turned on
The tape recorder, David was singing
"I Want to Hold Your Hand." I rewound the tape
And recorded *My feet hurt.*
You don't give a shit. You'll never give
A shit. I work all day and your kids aren't happy with food.
You don't know a damn thing about my children
Mom said, *You don't know a damn thing*
About anything. You got rice on your face
You drunk fool. They said these things slowly
Because the battery was dying. I sat on
The edge of the bed and remembered
The air inside a closed jar. I couldn't understand them.
I played the argument over and over
Until their voices slurred to a crawl
And the tape recorder died on the word *face*. It took
Another battery to make David and me sing.

MARY ELLIS

Wings

If snow falls on the far field,
where travelers
spend the night,
I ask you, cranes,
to warm my child in your wings.

—"Mother's Song," Anonymous
Japanese (ca. 733)

Ever since his brother left for Vietnam, Bill had the same dream. Only it wasn't a dream so much as it was a sensation. It beat across the inside of his eyelids and he could see slits of sunlight as the white feathers expanded to soar on a current of air. He was underneath but he couldn't see anything except the feathers. The wind whistled in his ears and the feathers flapped against the bright yellow sunlight. He was being carried but Bill could not see where and he could not turn his head because it was held in a viselike, even painful grip. Then, when he was listening intently to the melodious whistling, it became shrill and he was suddenly dropped. His arms beat frantically against the wind but they were useless. He heard the sound of his own voice but it did not say what he had intended, what would have been natural. It did not say *Mama!* or *Help!* It said:

"Billy!"

His mother's voice cut through his fall.

"Here," she said, shaking his shoulder. He strained to open his eyes, recognizing that it was still night. He could see the outline of his mother but not the details of her face. She was waving something white in front of him.

"From your brother," she said before dropping it on the covers and disappearing from his room. He pulled an arm out from underneath the covers and groped for the white thing. A letter. Still shaking from his dream, Bill crawled out of bed and onto the floor to the night-light by the closet. He sleepily crossed his legs and ripped the top of the letter open with his thumb. Then he held the seemingly fragile paper under the dim yellow light to read.

Sept-68

Dear Billy Baboon (just kidding),

I know it's been awhile since I wrote to you. We're stuck in the compound this week. It's been hard to get some time alone here. Seems like when that happens, the guys want to play poker or do something. I told them tonight, though, I had to write to my little brother. How are you doing? How's Beans? I just got a letter from Mom so I know she's doing okay. Well, okay enough I guess.

I'm doing okay. Man, you should see the weather here! I'll never complain about another Wisconsin summer again. It gets hotter than hell here, and so muggy that I feel like I'm wet all the time. If you were here, you'd be running around bare-ass naked—except it wouldn't be allowed 'cause you'd be a running target. And not from the VC either. My sergeant says I shoot pretty good. I don't give a damn if I shoot good or not anymore. When I come home, I don't want to see another gun again. Even if I have to bust the ones we have over the old man's head just to get rid of them. And him too.

Did I tell you they call me Elvis Jr? My buddy, Marv, even painted it on my helmet. I don't know why they call me that, all my hair is shaved off. Did you hide all my albums like I told you to? If it looks like the old man is getting close to finding them, take them over to the Morriseaus'. Mrs. Morriseau will keep them for me.

I better go. Keep writing and let me know what's going on there. I'll write again in a bit—hopefully before they send us up to the DMZ—it's still a rumor though. Don't worry, I'll be back soon.

Love James

P.S. I sent Mom some money—don't tell the old man. He'll take it away from her and use it on a beer dream. I sent you some too. Keep it under your mattress, or better yet, hide it in the barn in case of emergencies.

Bill looked down at the two twenty-dollar bills that had slipped out and fallen to the floor while he read the letter. He picked them up and stared at them. He lifted his head, still in the trance of so much money for a nine-year-old boy, and gazed at the twin bed across from him. *James.* Bill's mother always called his brother "Jimmy," but Bill, looking at his brother's empty bed, had always called him "James." Like James Dean, another one of his brother's idols besides Elvis. Or St. James, although his brother was anything but a saint before he left. There was the good and the bad James, but the letters Bill had gotten so far seemed full of the good James.

Bill crawled back to the bed and hefted the mattress up, slipping the letter underneath to the other letters his brother had sent. This was the first time James had sent money though. He folded the bills in half and tucked them under his pillow. Tomorrow before school, he'd have to think about where in the barn to hide the money and the letters.

He climbed back into bed, pulling the covers up next to his chin. Feeling the coldness of the sheets at the spooky end of the bed, he bent his legs and curled his toes. Since James left, he worried about the safety of his feet so close to where *something* could reach up from underneath the bed and grab them. And no one, not his mother in her frantic few hours of peace, or his father in his Pabst-saturated slumber, would hear him like James.

He turned on his side so he could look again at his brother's bed, covered with a white crocheted spread and untouched now for five months. He thought about the letters lying underneath him, and the ghostly way his mother always brought these letters to him, in his sleep. As though they didn't exist in the daytime. As though his brother didn't exist except at night, a black inky voice on white paper.

The wind whispered through the pine boughs outside his window. He slowly dropped off to sleep again and waited for the feathers.

The next morning, he crept out of the house early, clutching a large blue Mason jar in his arms, and the letters and money stuffed inside his shirt. It was late October and he'd forgotten his jacket in his desperation to get to the barn and back before his parents woke up. By the time he reached the creaky old barn door, he was shaking violently from the freezing morning whip of fall temperatures. He put the money and the letters in the jar and buried it deep in a corner of the barn where he knew the loose hay would be untouched by his father. Peeking out of the barn door at the house to check for signs of life and seeing none, he streaked across the barnyard and slipped back into the house.

"Billy, why don't you want to go outside and play? It's not that cold!" Sister Agnes questioned him at the beginning of the morning recess.

"Nooo," he faltered, and, swallowing quickly, came up with an excuse. "I thought I'd practice my penmanship."

The excuse glided across his lips better than he thought, and Sister Agnes beamed with an approving smile.

"All right then."

He watched the long black skirt of her habit glide as smoothly as his excuse out of the door to the playground. He opened his notebook and began to write in his usual scrawly print.

Wednesday

Dear Elvis Jr (ha, ha),

I am doing okay to. I hid the money in the barn. Dad hasnt found your records. He has been pretti drunk. Mom and me found him on Saturday in the field sleeping. He ran over Beans to.

Bill stopped momentarily and stared out of the classroom window, the recent death of his dog causing beads of tears to escape. He wiped them away and continued to write.

I buryd him behind the barn. Do you use bombs? Will you teech me how to shoot befor you bust our guns? I am writing this at school. Its been pretti cold. But no snow. We are having turkey for thanks giving. Mom says becase your not here to get a goose. I am going to help Mom bake cookes. So we can send them to you.

He heard the wild laughter of many children fill the hallway outside the door.

Resess is over. I got to go.
Love Bill

He quickly stuffed the letter inside his desk as the room filled with third-graders.

"How's the penmanship?" Sister Agnes's voice loomed up behind him.

"Getting better," he answered in a small, tinny voice and tried to shrink himself farther down into his seat.

"That's good," she said, patting his shoulder, her long skirt brushing past him. He let out a long sigh, relief buoying him back up to his normal size.

When he got home from school, he'd ask his mother for an envelope and a stamp, painstakingly writing James's address in small letters so it didn't swamp the front of the envelope the way his writing usually did. Under his address though, in the top left-hand corner, he would write USA in big block letters, and he did the same under James's address with the words SOUTH VIETNAM. Then his mother would take the letter and it mysteriously disappeared until he saw her from the frosted bus windows in the morning thrust two letters (hers included) into the pale gray mailbox that said LUCAS on the side and jack the red flag up.

Every day as the bus rumbled down the gravel road toward town, he'd watch her dwindling figure walk tiredly up the long driveway saluted by red pines until the bus rounded the curve in the road and he could see her no more. She wore the same thing. An old pair of green rubber hunting boots over her slippers, a black-and-white plaid jacket that covered a housedress of faded blue polka dots, and her reddish brown hair still wound in foamy pink rollers that from a distance looked to Bill like newborn mice under the pale blue netting of her nylon scarf. The bus became hushed when he got on, and he fervently prayed every morning that she would wait until the bus rounded the curve before she began talking out loud to the pines as she walked back to the house. That she would keep her hands to her sides until then, before moving them through the cold air as if explaining *something,* as if to touch *someone* strolling beside her. Then it would start up.

"Hey Luuucasssss," Merton Schmidt would tauntingly croon, sometimes putting a finger up his nose. "Hey Puuccass! How come your mother's crazee and your dad's a stinkin' drunk? Maybe 'cause yr'all *Luc-asses* Hey! My brother says your brother *should* get a bullet between the ears jus' for bein' a dumb ass and enlistin'! But hey! He's a *Luc-ass,* right!" And Merton would laugh so loudly it resonated through the bus like several jackhammers.

Merton Schmidt was thirteen and supernaturally big for his age. So big that the other kids called him Shithouse Schmidt but never to his face unless they wanted to run for the rest of their tiny lives. Bill's brother even called Merton the "little Hun," but names didn't do Bill any good even though his hatred of Merton outdistanced even Bill's hatred of his father on some days. Bill kept his face pressed to the cold bus window and tried to keep the crying safely down in his stomach or Merton would be on him. He vainly struggled to picture his brother's face, but all he could see was his walking, talking mother in the driveway. He bit his trembling lower lip and gazed out of the window. He ran the same gauntlet of teasing every day.

One morning, after a particularly severe verbal beating from Merton, he turned his face to the window only to see the family's blue Chevy station wagon lodged into the ditch by the curve, and the upper torso of his father hanging out of the driver's window, a smiling haze over his unconscious face. The bus didn't stop.

"Hey Billy!" the bus driver yelled back, "I'll call somebody to haul him outta there when we get to town."

A grin broke across Merton's face and the shots from his mouth began all over again. Bill's nine-year-old heart split open with pain. He stayed huddled in the bus seat, his eyes barely level with the bottom of the window. But he continued to peer out of the window, watching a scattered group of crows circle above the pines and wishing desperately that he were one of them.

Thankfully, Merton rarely rode the bus home from school, catching a ride with his father, who worked at the feed store, instead. And Bill's mother did not walk down the driveway to greet him when the rattling black-and-orange bus brought him home.

Still, he trusted her more now. Bill ate his grayish brown oatmeal with an island of peanut butter in the middle and watched his mother's eyes drift to the kitchen window from where she leaned against the countertop and stared at the frozen fields and adjoining swamp and woods. He never forgot what he overheard their neighbor, Rosemary Morriseau, say to her husband, although Bill knew it was not meant harshly, just sadly.

"Poor Claire," Rosemary sighed quietly while she washed the supper dishes and her husband Ernie, polished his boots. Bill pretended to read a book in their living room. "She's three sheets to the wind most days."

He vaguely understood what the expression meant. But what constituted three sheets to the wind? Why not four or five? Or even one? What was a sheet in the wind, Bill pondered with childish bewilderment. A piece of white cloth that got whipped around, if the wind was strong enough that day, and sometimes tangled across the clotheslines. What did that have to do with being crazy?

On the weekends, she wandered through the house during the day, talking and talking, her tired and haunted face appearing in one of the windows every so often when Bill was outside playing. She used to hit him. And shake him until he thought his head would snap off, rolling across the floor like a bowling ball and crashing into the legs of the furniture. That changed after his brother left. When anger flushed her face, she kept her arms and fists locked to herself now, and just yelled at him. Even the yelling had tapered off. She had become, gradually, his ally.

He was being carried again. This time he could look down and the Chippewa River was a black wriggly cord in the landscape seeping beneath him and everything beside it was covered with snow. The whistling filled his head. The grip was not so tight now but it held him firmly. He spread his bare toes and wiggled them in the rushing wind. But it was not cold, it was *warm,* like maple syrup was warm after it settled on his hot pancakes. He spread out his arms to catch the same feeling as his toes. The whistling slowly took on a familiar tune, something he'd heard in the not-too-distant past. He could see his brother's face, his Brylcreemed hair, and dark, narrowed eyes. What was it? He listened harder. It was . . . "My Baby Does the Hanky-Panky"!

"James!" he shouted. It was his brother whistling "My Baby Does the Hanky-Panky." Bill laughed. He laughed and his heart felt whole. He laughed at the waves of wind pushing his hair off his face. And he began to sing . . .

"Shshsh. Wake up," she said, nudging his head. It was close to Christmas and another letter floated out of the darkness and onto his blanket. He blinked, trying to catch the dim outline of his mother. She caressed his forehead and then was gone. He almost fell out of bed in his sleepy but hurried effort to get to the night-light. Then he opened the letter, the whistling still echoing in his ears.

Nov-68

Hey Bill,

I can't believe it's going to be Christmas soon. It doesn't snow here although if you look hard enough at the mountains, you can see a little white—they're mostly purple and green though. I had a dream the other night that you and me were down at the river—I don't know—fishing or something. It was a good dream. I needed it cause it's been a bad week. Two of my best buddies, Rick and Marv, walked right into a land mine and were blown up. I wasn't far behind them. I hit the ground pretty fast and all I can remember is feeling like my ears were going to split. Something landed on my back and it turned out to be Rick's helmet. It also turned out that they didn't walk into it—Sarg says he saw the wire wiggling, and he yelled but it was too late. We found the guy dead too, just one fucking VC by himself. I'm still not feeling so good. I got some kind of shit growing on my toes too—Sarg says it's jungle rot—you know—like athlete's foot except it's worse over here. My feet look like Ma's bread dough. God I can't wait to come home.

Say, I'm sorry about Beans. Goddamn the old man. He's got to fucking destroy everything he touches. He should come over here and trade places with me. I'll bet he'd be one big chicken running through the rice paddies. You know why he's that way? Cause he's SCARED. I used to wonder about him, but since I've been in Nam, I've figured it out. He's fucking scared of everything, but he's really scared of Mom. Cause he knows she's better than he is. When I come home, he better watch out for me cause I'm gonna bust his fucking head.

I'm sorry I couldn't get you a Christmas present. But I sent along some money. I sent Mom some money too and told her to spend it on herself. Make sure she does it, okay? Thanks for the cookies, they were really good. My buddy Hank's sister sent him some cookies, but they were as hard as grenades. After I ate one, I felt like my stomach was gonna blow up too. We used the rest for target practice.

Pray for me. Some days I feel like I'm rotting. Probably cause it's my own damn fault. I guzzle booze over here as much as the old man when I get a chance to. I need to over here, to forget I'm here. Keep writing. The guys think your letters are great. Merry Christmas.

Love you, James

There were splotches in places, where the ink had run slightly. Bill traced a finger across the raised wrinkles in the paper where the splotches were. His brother had been crying. Bill shivered and looked up at the white winter moon framed in his window. Its light reflected off the snow-covered Norway pines next to the house and filled his room with its pale winter glow. He gazed at the moon, absently fingering the money James had sent, seventy-five dollars in all. Bill shivered again. His brother talked to him like he never had before. He talked to him like a *buddy* and not his little brother. He picked up the letter and held it up against the moonlight. It was written in late November, but he didn't know what day or time, and his brother was changing and he couldn't see or touch him.

Bill crawled back over to the bed and lifted the mattress, stashing the letter and money underneath until morning. Then he grabbed his notebook and pencil from where they lay on the floor at the foot of his bed and crawled back to the night-light. He would cheer his brother up.

Friday

Dear James Dean (ha, ha),

I had a dreem to. Just you and me and we was flying over the river. And you was singng to. And you had wings. But not chiken wings. Big wings. I saw Bunny at the store. She says hi you good lookng devil. Sister says my spellng is gettng beter. I have been playng with Angel. He is a good dog and Mrs Moriso says I can play with him all I want. But I cant bring him home becase you know. I am going to buy Mom some perfum for Christmas. We sent your presants out last week. Mom cut my hair. Now I dont have none to. My ears get cold. Can I have your red hat? I wont wreck it. I promise. I am writng this in the midle of the night. The moon is realy white. I member the foxs you showd me. Well its like that now. We got lots of snow. Me and Mom are going to church to pray for you. I will be good and pray doubly hard. I got to go to bed now.

Love from your brother,
Billy Baboon

P.S. I will pray for your buddys that got blown up to.

Bill folded the letter and placed it on top of his notebook so he wouldn't forget it in the morning. He climbed into bed, curling himself into a fetal position, and stared at the shadows on the wall made by the snow-laden pine boughs in the moonlight. Christmas was going to be extra hard without James. But he sent money and that would help some. Bill's father, John Lucas, had been drinking more and working less but for the past two weeks he had been gone most of the time, logging for the lumber mill in Olina. He would be back for Christmas, however. Bill pulled the covers up over his face and shut his eyes tightly to bring back the dream. But water squeaked through and he cried himself to sleep instead.

"What does he write when he writes to you?"

Bill looked up from his oatmeal. It was Saturday and he was in no hurry to eat his breakfast. His mother's face was hollow-looking and colorless as though she had not slept. She propped her elbows up on the table and rested her face in her hands.

"What does he write when he writes to you?" she repeated.

"Jus' letters," Bill mumbled. He swallowed another spoonful of oatmeal.

His mother sighed heavily.

"I know something isn't right. But he always says he's fine when he writes to me. And he sends so much *money.*"

Bill almost stopped his spoon in midair but caught himself and neatly guided it into his mouth. He felt the blanket of his mother's gaze cover him.

"Billy. Can I read the letters he sends to you? I promise I won't say anything."

Bill quietly placed his spoon on the table. He was hoping she wouldn't ask that. He looked up and silently scrutinized his mother's face. He watched for any sign, a false smile, or too many tears, or even one tear, that might signal her betrayal, signal her old anger that would pull him across the kitchen by his hair if he said no. There was nothing. Nothing but exhaustion so pure it rendered his mother a sagging shell and he thought he could almost see through her to the kitchen sink.

"I'll give 'em to you at lunch. But you gotta give 'em back before . . ."

But he didn't have to finish because his mother knew. She nodded, reaching out slowly to touch her small son's sand-colored hair. Bill's mouth fell open as he watched her arm extend itself toward him, toward his quivering face, and all he could see and feel was a thin finger of sunlight gently touch his head.

Pray for me.

He always thought of the Sacred Heart Church as a large brick cave. Except that it was dry, not damp, and the cavernous ceiling was covered with frescoes of trumpeting angels and the ascension of the Virgin Mary into Heaven, painted by the German immigrant artists who first settled Olina. It was surprisingly empty even for a Saturday afternoon. He tagged after his mother in the enormous hush of the empty church, trying to keep his bulky winter boots from thumping. There were two votive light stands on either side of the church, placed before the steps to the altar. Four rows of twelve short white candles, most of them unlit, filled the ornate wrought-iron stands. Each stand had a small iron box with a slit in it, for dimes. A dime to light one candle, one lit candle to pray for a beloved's soul, a piece of fire to keep the prayer alive.

As if by silent agreement, Bill and his mother parted ways at the top of the aisle, and she went to the votive stand on the left while Bill knelt at the one on the right. He heard the clink of her dime as she inserted it into the box. She took a long toothpick-sized piece of wood and held it in the flame of an already lit candle until it caught fire. Then she lit her own chosen candle. Bill listened to the low hum of her voice carry through the church as she began to chant the Hail Mary and Our Father. He waited until he was sure she was engrossed in prayer before pulling out a ten-dollar bill from his jeans pocket. He folded the bill into fourths and quickly tucked it through the slit in the box.

He glanced over at his mother. Her head was bent, and her voice, although wavery, didn't stop. He took one of the wooden sticks and held it in the flame of the only lit candle at his stand.

He let it burn while the words of Sister Agnes came to him. *These candles are for votive prayers. That means to pray or make a vow, usually for someone else but you can pray for your own soul. The flame of these candles means your prayer burns eternal.*

Eternal meant forever. He lifted his burning toothpick of wood and reached across to the back row of candles. He lit one, two, three . . . and finally all twelve in that row. Then, snuffing out his stick of wood because it burned too close to his fingers, he reached for and lit another stick. He lit the second row of twelve candles, then the third row, and finally, the fourth row of eleven. He snuffed out his stick and clasped his hands. He squeezed his eyes shut and thought of his brother and his brother's buddies, Rick and Marv. The whistling filled his head. He smiled. "My Baby Does the Hanky-Panky." His face burned and he stopped smiling. He tried to think of a prayer. But the formal prayers of the Church didn't mean anything to him. Then it came to him. He whispered the only thing he could think to say. *Come home, come home, come home, come home . . .*

"Billy, did you have to light all of them?"

He lifted his head, his face flushed red from the heat of the candles, the eternal flame of forty-nine candles blurred in his eyes. *Pray for me,* his brother had said.

"Mom," he answered. "James told me to."

The snowflakes skipped and skidded across the watery blue hood of the car on the way home. The sky was an ancient pearly gray and Bill felt strangely happy. His mother drove, not saying a word, but he could sense that she, too, felt the same as her small son. They had stopped at the drugstore in Olina before driving back out to the farm. She bought him a new shirt and a pair of jeans and a giant solid-chocolate Santa. It was as though she had read his mind when she gave the druggist, Bogey Johnson, a radiant smile and said, "Mr. Johnson, my son would like one of those Santas. Do you think we can oblige him?"

His mother hummed to herself. Bill bit into the fat arm of his Santa and watched the snow-covered field and woods go slowly by as the car crunched over the new snow. Then as the chocolate elbow was melting into the roof of his mouth and they were nearing the farm, his mother braked the car in a series of small jerks and finally stopped it on the shoulder of the road right after they'd cleared the curve. She pulled the packet of letters out of her Wrigley's Doublemint-perfumed purse and laid them on the seat between herself and Bill. The chocolate trickled down the back of his throat.

"Thank you, sweetheart, for letting me read those," she said. She shifted in the car seat so that she faced him. Her face sparkled like the new snow and for the first time that day he noticed that she had taken her pink rollers out. Her reddish brown hair was brushed and sprayed into full curls around her face. She could be, Bill realized, staring dumbfounded at his mother, very pretty.

"You know somethin'," she said matter-of-factly. "Jimmy is gonna come home. I feel it." She placed a clenched hand against her chest and repeated, "I *feel* it.

"You know somethin' else," she said almost gleefully, huddling down in the seat to look Bill in the face.

He shook his head, his eyes fixed on his illuminated mother. He absently bit off the tassel on his Santa's hat.

"*Things,*" she emphasized confidently, "are gonna get better. Hell, they can't get much worse. But you and me and Jimmy can run this farm and make it go. Don't you think so?"

Bill couldn't answer and quietly pushed his bitten-up Santa back into the bag. He cautiously looked back up at his mother. She didn't seem to notice his lack of response and had shifted forward in the car seat again. But her face was no longer jubilant, it was sad and tears ran down her face.

"You know I love you boys . . . very much. But," she said softly, looking through the windshield at their house in the distance nestled among the red pines, "if I'd have had wings, I would've been gone a long time ago."

Dec-68

Dear Bill,

I know this letter is coming pretty fast right after the last one but Sarg said there would be a special pick-up for holiday mail. It's raining and I'm writing this inside a tank. Remember how much I used to love the sound of rain on the roof? Except Beans always howled like he was dying or something when it rained. I'm sorry that I threw my boot at him that time and hit him in the head. Then he really started howling, remember? Anyway, it rains like it's going to flood here. Listening to it makes me kind of sleepy. I pretend sometimes, when we can't hear any shooting or bombing, or even when the jets (we call them warbirds) are gone for a little while, that I'm home. Or when that doesn't work, I pretend this is a real country. It is a real country but sometimes I feel like I'm floating just above the ground and I can't touch it. And other times, I feel like I'm in a doll house—cause American soldiers are so big, me included. The Vietnamese are the size of you, Bill. I'm a giant compared to them. I guess you could have joined the army with me after all (ha, ha).

We were cutting trail through some jungle near the DMZ two days ago, and I barely missed stepping into a pungee pit. The VC dig these holes, and then put bamboo spikes in the bottom. They cover the holes up with leaves and even buffalo shit so you can't see them. If you step in one, the spikes go right up through the bottom of your boots and up into your legs. It scared the shit out of me.

Don't tell Mom, but I caught some shrapnel in my arm. The medic just cleaned it up and gave me a shot of penicillin. It's not that bad. Is Mom okay? Her last letter was strange.

Thanks for your letter—it was great! And it got here pretty fast too. You can wear my hat and I don't care if you wreck it. I'm not going to wear it again anyway. Hey! I'm glad I don't have chicken wings—they'd never get me off the ground.

The other day I saw a really big bird flying over. Like a heron, only bigger. I asked one of the ARVNs what it was. (ARVN stands for Army of the Republic of Vietnam—one of the Vietnamese fighting on our side.) He said it was a crane and laughed at me. He said didn't you ever see a crane before? I guess we have them in Northern Wisconsin, but they usually stay in Southern Wisconsin. They're beautiful, Bill. I hope I see more of them. But they must get hit in the cross-fire and bombing. I wish I could have wings like a crane. Seeing that crane reminded me of the geese in the fall. I really missed seeing the geese this year.

Here's a picture of me. I look pretty dirty, but that's the way it is when we're out here. Thanks for the presents and the fruitcake. Well, little man, I've got to go. Give Mom a hug for me. Tell the old man to piss-off (just kidding—don't do it). Say hi to the Morriseaus if you see them.

Love James

Bill stared at the Polaroid of his brother under the night-light. He had his helmet on so Bill couldn't see how short his hair was, but the rest looked reasonably enough like James. Except his smile wasn't real. His mouth looked as though invisible fingers had taken his lips prisoner and pulled them sideways, the skin unnaturally tight underneath his nose. His eyes were sunken and dark, and it was clear that his brother had lost some weight. Besides the picture there was more money still, and Bill counted five ten-dollar bills. He leaned back against the wall. *Little man.* That's how he felt, as though when his brother left all the unspoken reasons for James's leaving suddenly descended upon Bill, and in his awareness of them, he became old.

It was a week past Christmas. Bill's father had come home, drank and slept through Christmas Eve and most of Christmas Day, getting up only to eat the holiday meal. It surprised Bill, covertly watching his father eat his turkey, how little he knew or cared about the tall, pasty-skinned man at the head of the table. His nine-year-old life had revolved so intensely lately around his daily struggle to survive at school, the strained wait for his brother's letters, the fields, the woods, the swamp, and the sky of their farm, and lastly, the fragile web of his mother's world, that he had forgotten to be cautious around the beer-reeking presence that he'd been avoiding, it seemed, since he was born. He silently ate a forkful of stuffing before catching his mother's eye. A small conspiratorial smile passed across her lips. Her dark eyes had lost their dull captive look and shined. *Things are gonna get better.* He glanced down again to the far end of the table where his father sat, and felt an unfamiliar stab of pity. James was thousands of miles away from them in a country that even Bill, in his enormous capacity for imagination, could not imagine but only carried with him in the word *Vietnam.* A country of purple mountains, man-made woodchuck holes that stabbed, wriggling barbed-wire bombs, a bird that flew bigger than a Canada goose, and hot metal that flew like a bird. Yet Bill knew it was his father, not his brother, who was in a strange country he'd never get out of; a country where only he thought as he did, and whose borders he broke through occasionally to hit his wife, to despise his sons.

Still, now that John Lucas was home for the holidays, Bill wondered how he was going to survive without his brother there to shield him, to shield her. But in his small head he knew, survive he must. James would come home. And James would tell the priest that what he preached at the Christmas mass was wrong. The loving brotherhood of man did not exist.

Sunday

Dear James,

Mom and me prayd for you. I ate alot of choclate at Christmas and got sick. Dad got fird and is home now. Me and Mom went sledding. She lost some of her curlers but did not get mad. She sat in front so I wouldnt get hit by snow. I am back at school. Sister says to look for Janury stars. Do you have stars over there? We saw a big white owl sittng on the fence by the barn. Mom says it is a snowi owl from canada. She says he came to visit us becase he ran out of food in canada. Mom cryd. She says you shoulda went to canada to. I said, mom, if they dont got any food, why should James go there.

Bill stopped. He could hear his mother shouting in the kitchen and the banging of pots and pans. His father's deep rumbling voice answered her. Bill tensed up. Then he heard a heavy thump. His mother shouted some more. Bill sighed.

Can they let you out earli?

Bill raised his pencil from the paper. Now he could hear his mother sobbing.

Please come home. I am scard. I like your picture. Can I have your helmit when you come home? Mr. Moriso says he will take me and you to show us the crans. He says they fly by lake superier. They say hi. If they let you out earli will you come home? I got to go to bed now.

Love Bill

He put his notebook down. His mother's crying was ebbing. Bill crawled back into bed and covered his ears against the muted notes of her sorrow. It was the middle of January, the middle of a freak midwinter thaw. The chickadees had broken into their spring song that day. Bill had opened his window to the unseasonably warm wind and it blew the ivory curtains into midnight dancers. He felt both elated and ashamed, having betrayed his fear to his brother. But as much as he wanted to destroy what he had written, he also felt sure that it would bring his brother home. Maybe, he thought, listening to the melting ice drip from the eaves, he could even persuade his mother to call the Army and tell them that James was needed at home. That he had made a mistake by enlisting.

Bill turned to lie on his right side. He tried not to think of tomorrow. Tomorrow was school. Tomorrow meant Merton. He stared at the dancing curtains. Their fluttering hypnotized his already tired eyes and, combined with the soothing plunk, plunk of the melting ice, made his eyes close. Tomorrow was not now.

The wings flapped, enclosing Bill for a few seconds and brushing his face and chest. They opened again, lifting upward against the surging wind, and he raised his eyes to see that the white wings spanned an enormous length from side to side. His bare legs swung back and forth and he was held this time by his shoulders. The air was heavy and moist. So moist that he felt slippery like a fish and as helpless as one, clutched in the talons of an eagle. But his shoulders felt no pain, just roped and secure. He dropped his head against his chest and looked below.

They were passing over the Morriseau farm with its two silos and big duck pond. The eighty-acre field behind their house was filled with little clouds of dust, each one exploding like spores from the head of a smashed puffball mushroom. Poof! Poof! Poof! they went. Little black specks were chaotically running through the field and every time a speck hit one of the clouds, it burst into flames, becoming a ball of fire. He could hear shouting and the deep pop and zing of rifles going off. The air became thick and choking with dust. Bill's small chest caved in and his lips quivered. He coughed hard and his hands jerked up toward his mouth.

Then the wings came together again, enclosing his small body in a cocoon of feathers. When they opened, he saw that the field was clear and a cloud of cowbirds dipped and circled beneath them. His chest cleared and he no longer felt like crying. He heard the high, clear notes of whistling and looked down. There was someone standing in the middle of the grassy field, waving and waving. The wings caught an upcurrent of air and they glided toward the far end of the field. They cruised its wide square edge before coming back around.

Bill cried out. It was James, wearing a dull green helmet that had **Elvis** painted in black letters on the side, and balancing a rifle across his shoulders. He dropped the rifle and waved with both hands.

"Hey Billy! Hey Billy Baboon! It's me! It's your brother!"

"Jaaaamess! Jaaamess!" Bill shouted but the wind took his voice and it disappeared in the rush of air between the feathers above him.

"Over there!" his brother shouted, and, picking up his rifle, pointed with it toward their own field. A single black speck was running over the brown plowed earth. The wings caught the cue and flapped harder. They closed the distance in a few seconds and swept lower. Bill screamed joyfully.

"Shithouse! You better run! You're up shit creek now!"

Merton was desperately running and tripping over the deep furrows in the field. Bill pulled his legs up to his chest and curled his toes. They dropped altitude and cruised right up behind Merton. Bill lowered his legs and hooked his feet under

Merton's arms. With legs suddenly as strong as steel cable, he lifted the squirming tonnage of a boy into the air twenty feet before dropping him.

"Don't hurt the little Hun! Jus' scare 'im!" he heard his brother shout.

Merton hit the soft plowed earth with a thump and a groan. But he got up and began running again, his head swiveling to pinpoint Bill's location. Bill whooped. Merton, his eyes rolling wildly, ran harder. Again, they came off a large current of air to level themselves behind the nemesis of Bill's days. This time Bill did not pick him up, but, with legs wound tight as springs against his chest, aimed and kicked, knocking Merton between the shoulder blades. Merton went down so hard he bit into the overturned field and ate dirt. He stayed down, breathing hard, grinding and spitting dirt. But he was not hurt, just scared. Bill stared at the sprawled-out boy as the wings lifted him back into the sky. Then as quickly as the desire for revenge had come, it had also gone, and they left the Lucas field with its cleaved and unplanted earth and returned to his brother standing almost perfectly camouflaged with his green jungle uniform in the middle of their neighbor's lush grassy field.

James had taken off his helmet and stood smiling broadly up at Bill. The wings, despite their massive size, lowered Bill until the bottoms of his feet touched his brother's shaved and bristly head. Bill could not speak. *This is not a dream. That's really my brother.* The wings didn't lower him any farther and they hovered while Bill's feet curled around and hugged his brother's head. A look of pain crossed his brother's face. James reached up and encircled Bill's ankles with his hands, kissing the bottoms of his little brother's feet.

"Man! It's really good to see you, Billy Baboon," his brother said softly. "Really good."

James released one of Bill's ankles and swept his arm in a semicircle around him.

"I dream about this place all the time . . . yeah, all the time. I told Ma I never wanted to see this place again and that I wasn't comin' back. I told her . . ." his brother stopped in a half-sob, half-yell, gripping Bill's ankle so tight it hurt, "that she didn't know a fucking thing! But she did know. She *does* know."

He kissed Bill's foot again.

"Don't ever leave here, Bill. You and me . . . we'll have some fun when I come home."

The wings flapped. Bill strained, stretching his legs as far as he could to touch his brother's head. But the wings lifted him higher and higher. His brother put his helmet back on and picked up his rifle. He wiped his face on his sleeve and stared up past Bill to the wings. James opened his mouth as if to say something but shut it again, raising his hand slightly while a deeply troubled look passed over his face.

"I gotta go. But don't worry. I love you, Billy! And Elvis," James said, pointing to his helmet, "loves you too!"

Bill watched James run from the field and disappear into the swamp on the edge. His heart beat against the wall of his chest. He heard the high notes of whistling echo from the swamp, and smiled through his tears. "My Baby Does the Hanky-Panky." He tried to cry out. Nothing. He listened to the lingering sound of whistling and then it struck him. If his brother had been down there, who was above him, carrying him?

He stretched his neck to look up, but all he saw was sunlight, bright yellow and blinding. The wings flapped, covering his face, tickling and brushing his cheeks. A high guttural call pierced the air around him. The wings swept forward and covered him for the last time, enveloping him with the more familiar feel of his sheets and blankets, and with the descending silence of dreamless sleep.

MAURA STANTON

John McCormack

The day was cool and gray and smelled of approaching rain. We wore sweaters even though it was August. We would have stayed inside to watch television that morning, except that our visiting uncle from Chicago sat in the big chair in the living room, smoking and staring at nothing. We were a little afraid of him, although he was kindly and gave us quarters when we bought him bags of popcorn or bottles of Pepsi at the store. He always had a glass of Pepsi beside him on the floor. He was supposed to be leaving in a few days. He was a plasterer, and there were some unfinished jobs waiting for him back in Chicago. He had been up north taking the "cure," he told us. "Cure for what?" we asked. "Booze," he had answered in a low voice. "But don't tell your mother I told you so."

We made cocoa in the spaghetti pot and sat around the picnic table in the back yard with our hot mugs, reading the new mystery books we had checked out of the library yesterday. Our oldest sister sat on the step, copying recipes from a thick *International Cookbook*. She had been reading cookbooks for a month and had a whole notebook full of recipes with ingredients we had never heard of before.

"How does this sound?" she would ask, interrupting us. "Norwegian Baked Herring."

"Awful."

"It's layers of herring and potatoes. I think it sounds good.

I've never tasted herring. Or how about this? Rice and Spinach Armenian."

"You don't like spinach," we told her. "You know you don't."

"I might, if it were cooked like this. I'd leave out the garlic, though."

We returned to our books. It was pleasant to look up occasionally to watch one of the cats roll in the mint that grew under the garage window or to listen to the piano next door. But after a while, when we began to get chilly, we went inside to refill our mugs and decided to read at the kitchen table.

Our brother Joe, who had been over at the archery range all morning, suddenly appeared at the screen door, panting. A misty rain had begun, but he stayed outside on the steps. There were droplets in his dark blond hair.

"Something's happened at the lake!"

"What?" we all asked at once. "On our side?"

"This side of the bridge," he said. "I don't know what it is. But there's lots of police cars. I'm going back."

He jumped down the steps. We heard his shoes pounding on the walk around the side of the house. Our oldest sister hastily dropped the dipper back into the cocoa, and turned off the burner.

"Let me get my sweater," she said.

"Hurry!" We edged into the dining room to wait for her, setting off a tinkle of glasses in the sideboard. Our uncle, his back to us, was standing over the record player in the living room, humming "tura-lura-lura" to himself. He was about to play our father's old Irish record again. We hard the click as he changed the speed to 78, and noted the shiny red bald spot on the back of his head. His hair always seemed greasy, the way it parted over the bald spot. Yet he took a shower every morning, and when he shaved, he left the bathroom door half open, so that we had all seen him patting his cheeks with blue after-shave lotion.

Two police cars had been driven across the grass to the edge of the lake. We saw that first. Then we saw the boat and the diver in the wet suit who was putting the oars in the oarlocks. A small crowd of people had gathered at a short distance from the black cars, mostly children in shorts, but there were a couple of mothers, too, and the old man who lived in the tiny, unpainted house down at the end of our alley. The surface of the lake was dark and absorbed the drops of light rain without ripples.

Joe waved at us as we hurried across the thick, wet grass.

"They're dragging the lake," he said anxiously when we reached his side. "Somebody drowned."

"Who?"

"A woman." He pointed to one of the police cars. A man was hunched in the back seat, his head turned away from us to look out at the lake. "That's her husband."

"Was she swimming?"

Joe shook his head. "It's awful," he said. "She jumped from the bridge."

"Jumped?"

We all turned to look at the concrete bridge which arched across the lake at its narrow neck. We were at the smaller, shallower end of the lake, but there were still "Danger" and "Deep Water" signs posted on the bridge pilings. We noticed how some of the cars crossing the bridge slowed down as they spotted the police cars on the shore.

"Why would she jump?" our brother Pat asked in a puzzled voice.

"To kill herself."

Pat stared at Joe, frowning. He ran his hand absently through his short, almost white hair. "Why?"

"She was unhappy, I guess." Joe looked out at the cold lake. "But I don't know how anyone could be that unhappy."

We watched the diver and one of the policemen row out toward the bridge. The diver attached his face mask and dropped silently into the water. He had a breathing tube, but it was hard to spot it on the dark surface. Occasionally his head emerged. Twice he climbed back into the rowboat, and the policeman poured something to drink from a thermos. The other policemen paced up and down the shore, rubbing their chilled hands together, sometimes listening to the static and strange bursts of talk on their radio, occasionally speaking in low voices to the man in the back seat, who would roll the window down and lean out.

We squatted down, trying to cover our bare legs with the tails of our sweaters. The light rain turned into a fine mist, and the bridge looked silvery and insubstantial. The trees in the little woods behind the archery range were obscured by fog. More mothers had arrived. Some had come to fetch their children, but had remained standing near other mothers, talking in subdued voices and glancing out at the boat. Our oldest sister had found a stump to sit on, a little away from the crowd. Joe plucked at his bowstring absently and in a while went to sit by himself under the willow tree.

"Let's go home," one of us said after an hour. "I'm hungry."

We stood up. Our legs were stiff from the damp. The grass had printed greenish lines into our knees.

"Pat!" we called.

He ignored us. He was staring intently out at the lake.

We started home without him, glancing back at the police cars once or twice. We planned to come back after lunch. On the other side of the park road, where the grass was smooth and cropped for baseball, we broke into a run. We were out of breath by the time we reached our yard. The inner door was open, and through the screen we could hear two voices singing "The Harp That Once Thro' Tara's Halls." One voice, sweet and far away, was spoiled by static and crackles. The other voice, loud but weak and interrupted by a hacking cough, was our uncle's. We stood outside by the blue spruce for a minute or two, listening in embarrassment.

Finally we entered the house. Our uncle did not even hear us at first. His head was tilted toward the ceiling, his eyes were closed, and his hand was wrapped around his throat as he sang, as if he were controlling the pitch by the pressure of his fingers.

The song came to an end. Our uncle opened his eyes during the shot band of static that followed and saw us as we crossed the living room.

He blinked and cleared his throat. "He was the best," he said to us thickly. "This old record doesn't do him justice."

"John McCormack?" we asked politely.

"John McCormack," he repeated. "I heard him sing once. That was at the ballroom of the Lakeshore Palace Hotel. It was at a banquet. All the men were wearing tuxedos, and all the women had on strapless gowns—I was a waiter. I never told you I was a waiter, did I?"

"No," we said as we backed shyly away from him, trying not to be rude.

"When he started to sing, I forgot I was supposed to be filling the water goblets. I just stood there, my mouth open. I felt it all the way up my spine, up and down every bone, in my skull—"

"Felt what?" one of us asked.

"I felt like I was dying, but it was so sweet. . . . he had the voice of an angel, a voice like the harp of an angel. I hope it's like that when I die; I hope the angels will sing 'Ireland, Mother Ireland' as beautifully as John McCormack."

"Somebody died at the lake," we said.

The vague, dreamy look on his face disappeared. "I know. One of the neighbors knocked at the door." He stood up heavily. "I need a walk. I suppose you're all going back there after lunch?"

We nodded.

"I'll go with you," he said as he headed toward the bathroom. "Your mother's at the store with the baby."

He came into the kitchen a few minutes later, and absently placed the John McCormack album on the table where we were making our sandwiches. He poured another Pepsi into his smudged glass. We stared at the album as we chewed. A brown castle had been sketched against the turquoise background, next to a portrait of John McCormack, who looked very handsome and foreign. He reminded us of our father in the old photographs on the mantel where he was wearing his army uniform and had a thick wave in his hair.

We did not like to be seen in public with our uncle, who walked stiffly, as if his legs hurt, and sang or hummed out loud even when he was passing a stranger on the sidewalk. His baggy trousers, splattered with paint around his cuffs, seemed about to fall down around his ankles. His black dress shoes were unpolished and worn at the heels. The back of his shirt was creased. The skin under his eyes was thick and swollen, his nose and cheeks reddened by broken veins. He always had a vacant, faraway look in his light blue eyes.

We were ashamed of our reluctance to be seen with him, however, and had never spoken of it to each other. We stayed close to his side as we crossed the park to the lake, pointing out interesting features of the neighborhood—the bus wye, the sycamore which had been split by lightning, the red ring of paint around a diseased elm, the archery range where Joe practiced with his bow and arrow, even the grove of trees in the distance where a man had exposed himself to some third-grade boys.

The rain had let up completely and the sun was coming out. The crowd had grown; now it was mostly adults, all of them silent, standing shoulder to shoulder as we came toward the shore of the lake. We recognized Mrs. Wagner, who lived across the alley; she was still in her nurse's uniform, standing on tiptoes in her white, rubber-soled shoes, trying to see over the heads in front of her. An ambulance had been parked next to the police cars. As we joined the crowd, we saw two policemen come around the side of the ambulance with a bundle. The doors were opened, then slammed shut. The crowd began moving apart.

Our oldest sister saw us and jumped off the stump, which must have given her an excellent view of what had happened.

"They found her," she said flatly. She tried to smooth her damp hair, which was beginning to dry in frizzy peaks.

"What did she look like?"

"I couldn't look after all. I only looked after they had her in the boat, covered up." She shivered. "But I saw her foot when they carried her out on shore."

"Where's Pat?" our uncle asked.

"Over there." Our oldest sister pointed to some bushes. "I think he's throwing up. I should have sent him home—" She frowned, thrusting her hands into the pockets of her shorts and turning away.

We looked out at the lake. The surface was scaled with silver now that the sun was out and a wind was rising. The ambulance and the police car with the husband in the back pulled silently away. The diver stood by the rowboat, smoking and talking to two policemen.

Pat came up beside us. There were deep circles under his eyes, and he was wheezing slightly.

"You better use your inhaler," our oldest sister said.

"I'm all right."

"What did you see?" we asked.

"Her hair was so long it was caught in the weeds. They had

to cut her free." He swallowed. "She was stiff. Her blouse was muddy."

Our uncle crossed himself.

Pat watched him closely. "Can you do that?"

"What?"

"Pray for her?"

Our uncle blinked. "Of course you can pray for her. For her soul."

"Isn't her soul in Hell?"

Our uncle glanced down at Pat, then gripped his shoulder. "Now who told you that? Only God knows about the soul."

Pat trembled. His lips were blue and bitten, and for the first time we realized that he had seen something that was going to haunt him—something that he could not describe to us in words. We did not know whether to be envious or relieved that we had not seen it, too. Our oldest sister's guarded face told us nothing.

"We need to light a candle for her soul," our uncle said, bending closer to Pat. "I lit a candle when John McCormack died. That was in 1945 before any of you were born. I'd been sent home from the war with a bullet in my thigh. That candle burned for weeks and when it was almost out, I lit two more from the same flame. I like to think that other candles were lit from my flame, for other souls, and that my flame is still burning somehow . . . or burned until John McCormack got out of Purgatory, the good man."

He brushed his hand across Pat's face, as if he had seen a tear which we had missed. "What do you say? Shall we go up to church and light a candle for this poor drowned lady?"

"Our new church doesn't have candles," we said.

"What? It's a Catholic church. Of course it has candles."

"We've never seen any candles," we said emphatically. "We go to mass every Sunday."

"There are candles," our oldest sister said. "In the vestibule on the far side, near the pamphlet table. It's the side we never go in—and they're way back in the corner."

"Let's go," our uncle said. "You can light the candle, Pat."

Pat nodded, and we started off across the grass, which smelled fresh and sharp as the sun dried the blades. Other people who had seen the drowned woman brought ashore were moving slowly across the park, too, or standing in small groups, talking quietly. As we passed one group of women, which included Mrs. Wagner in her white uniform, we looked secretly up at their faces, but their moving lips and eyelashes and slightly knitted foreheads did not tell us what we needed to know.

We climbed the hill to the church, pausing a few times to let our uncle catch his breath. His face grew red and congested. The exertion caused his hair to stick to his forehead in wet coils.

Our church was a modern building of yellow brick, with a squat bell tower and a curved facade. It was attached to the older, three-story grade school. A few cars were parked in the lot.

"They must be hearing confession," we told our uncle.

He looked up at the church. "What a pity. You don't have any stained-glass windows."

"The windows are colored glass," we said. "When the sun shines it turns all blue inside."

We led him to the nearest door, and held it open for him.

"Did you ever see Sacred Heart in Chicago?" he asked in a low voice. "When you go to mass at dawn, the whole church is as bleak as the inside of a mountain. You can't see the ceiling it's so high. Then the sun comes up—it pours through the center window, the Sacred Heart window, and you've never seen red that red. It's the color of wine or rubies or real, wet blood—" He coughed, glancing suddenly at Pat. "There's a gold canopy over the altar, too, and the candlesticks are massive silver. But the candles you light yourself are at the side altars."

We were inside the vestibule, a low, square room where a few metal folding chairs had been stacked against the wall. Another door, which our oldest sister opened, led into the church itself.

"The candles are on the other side," she said.

We dipped our hands into the aluminum holy water font as we entered. The water was cool and soft as we splashed it on our foreheads. The church was dim, for the sun was not hitting the blue windows this time of day. When we reached the center aisle, we genuflected. A large, abstract sculpture hung above the altar instead of the usual crucifix, and although we had gotten used to seeing it, we always felt a little funny when we crossed ourselves. Only two people were in line at the confession box on the left. The red light on the box at the right had already been turned off.

The vestibule on the other side of the church was shadowy, for the venetian blinds were shut. The pamphlet table was empty except for a few out-of-date copies of *The Catholic Messenger.* We looked curiously at the tiered metal rack in the corner. Each shelf contained little red glasses with white votive candles inside. A black box with a slot in the top was attached to the side of the rack.

"That's strange," our uncle said, fumbling with the change in his pocket. "None of them are lit." He handed a dime to Pat. "Put that in the box."

The dime made a hollow clink as Pat dropped it in the slot.

"Let's see if I've got any matches, now." Our uncle began going through his other pocket. He pulled out nail clippers, ticket stubs, the broken end of a pencil, crushed grains of popcorn, three finely wrinkled one-dollar bills, and finally produced a matchbook with softened edges.

He was lighting a match for Pat when the inner door of the church opened. Father North, one of the three parish priests, appeared before us in his long, black cassock. He had just come from hearing confessions, for the purple stole still hung around his neck. We felt our throats constrict. His face was stern as if he had been listening to terrible sins.

He looked at our little group and his face darkened.

"You're the new children in the parish, aren't you?" he asked briskly.

"Yes, Father," we whispered back.

"Who is this man?" he asked. "Are you children all right?"

We stared at him, not understanding.

His lip twitched impatiently. "Is this man bothering you?"

We looked at our uncle then, stunned and horrified at what Father North was suggesting. He stood there in front of Pat with a match burning down to his finger, his mouth open a little, a slightly dazed look on his face. The white lining of his pockets hung partly out.

"Please, Father," our oldest sister said in a voice that was high and shaky. "This is our uncle." And then, although we had never seen her touch anyone affectionately before, not even our father or mother, she put her arm around our uncle's shoulder.

"He's from Chicago," we said, all of us speaking at once for we saw that our uncle's face was beginning to redden in shame. "He's our favorite uncle. You should hear him sing. We've come up to light a candle."

"Fine," Father North said. "But I'd like to lock the doors. Confession is over."

"Do you lock the doors in this church, Father?" our uncle asked in a soft voice, his eyes on the floor.

"It's not safe to keep the doors open when no one is here—it's a sorry comment on the world, I'm afraid."

Our uncle nodded.

Our oldest sister moved away from him, then, dropping her arm self-consciously.

Our uncle handed the matchbook to Pat. "Be careful," he said hoarsely.

Pat lit a match above the long wick of a candle in the first tier. It caught immediately and made the dark red glass translucent. He made the sign of the cross and bowed his head. We watched him pray for the woman who had drowned herself.

Then we turned to go.

Father North cleared his throat. "I'd appreciate it if you'd blow the candle out before you leave."

"Blow it out?" Pat looked at our uncle in surprise.

Father North pointed to a small sign taped to the side of the candle rack.

"What grade will you be in, son?"

"Fourth," said Pat.

"Can you read the sign?"

Pat swallowed. " 'Please do not leave candles burning. Fire—' " He hesitated.

" 'Hazard'," Father North finished emphatically.

Pat looked at the candle flame. "I just lit it," he said, his voice quivering. "It's for a dead soul."

"Let it burn for a while, Father," our uncle asked in a voice so humble that we squirmed with embarrassment. "In most churches . . ." His voice trailed off inaudibly.

Father North pointed at Pat. "Please blow out your candle. What if the curtains caught on fire? I know you lit it for a soul. Very nice. But it's not the candle that counts, it's the prayer behind it."

"I always thought it was the candle, Father," our uncle said.

Father North shook his head. "It's only a pretty custom."

"But I've lit a lot of candles over the years," our uncle said, his voice trembling. "You mean my candles did no one any good?"

Father North hesitated. Then his somber face lit up with a smile, the first we had ever seen across his face. We could see the edges of his teeth. "If they did *you* good, that's fine. That's important, too."

"I thought I was helping the poor souls out of Purgatory."

A flicker of annoyance crossed Father North's face. "Only God decides about that." He tugged nervously at the stole hanging from his neck, and pulled a set of heavy keys from his pocket. He looked severely at Pat.

Pat bent over the flame. We all drew our breath in and held it down in our lungs a long time until our chests ached, as if we could keep the flame burning by not breathing. We wanted a miracle, and when Pat's weak mouthful of air caused the flame to brighten, instead of go out, we thought we had been granted our prayer.

"Blow harder," Father North said.

"He has asthma," our oldest sister said.

Pat closed his eyes, then spat at the candle. The flame disappeared with a hiss. We knew it was the sound of a soul slipping into darkness, a soul that might have lit her way to heaven by the light of Pat's candle. That was our fancy, at least, when we glanced into Pat's cold and vacant face as he brushed past us and ran out the door.

"Good-bye, Father," we said hastily, to cover Pat's violent departure and the gloom which had fallen over our uncle's face, sealing his lips.

"Tell your brother to come see me sometime when his heart isn't so hard," Father North said. "You seem like a nice family."

"Thank you, Father," we said.

We walked home beside our uncle. He did not hum or talk about John McCormack, and we were afraid to mention the singer now. Our uncle's ankles seemed to hurt, for he walked even more slowly and carefully than usual, and he stumbled in places where the sidewalk was uneven or badly cracked.

Later that night we got out the box of old black and white

photographs to show our uncle, who seemed despondent. We showed him pictures of ourselves at every age, in high chairs, in teeter-totters, in strollers, in matching dresses, in funny bonnets. When he held the photographs up to the light to see them better, we saw his ghostly fingers shining through the paper upon which our smiling faces had been, as we thought, permanently fixed.

Evangeline #8

years slide away   two four five
and the loneliness gradually simply annoys
like a rollerskate scar on your knee
when you are all dressed up or at the beach
loneliness on the girls' side of the church
loneliness when you go to the Baptist church
because your mother and your brothers never change
never dare to risk what you must
confess and confess every week
loneliness among the girls next door
down the block around the corner
you like them bald-
head nuns?   why they priest dont marry them?
dont they sweat in the summer?   can they wear
bathing suits?   you aint never seen no colored
nuns, right?   they aint got no colored, right?
loneliness in the words you know how to defend:
indulgence Extreme Unction catechumens
words you may never use
Immaculate Conception Trinity purgatory
at the family Thanksgiving Christmas Easter
mornings when all your kinship parades itself
against the dark stubborn defeated souls
rejoice not one of us out-of-doors

not one of us in jail crippled blind ragboned
in this politely unbrotherly city
alleluia
loneliness in your exemptions from school:
Ascension Thursday All Saints' Day St. Patrick
loneliness in your holy water
your rosary miraculous medal scapular holy cards . . .
then on your sixth first day of school
a boy steps through the invisible door
a family of boys colored and African-looking
like the martyrs of Uganda
you've never seen but imagine really dark
and you rejoice you share the mark though
you barely say hello
as your history moans
you share the mark

GIOVANNA (JANET) CAPONE

Gramma and Mrs. Carmichael

Every Sunday after church, Dad, my sisters, and I visit Gramma in the nursing home. When we first walk in, there are new green rugs everywhere. It smells like a carpet store. Nurses in white uniforms walk back and forth. They get into the elevator with us.

Dad pushes the yellow button. The silver doors slide closed, and we wait, staring at the glowing numbers above the door. We all rise to the third floor.

A few years ago, Gramma started losing her eyesight. Her diabetes got worse and finally she went blind altogether. After Grandpa died, she had to come here to live. Now every Sunday we visit her.

We reach the third floor. The doors slide open and suddenly an old man in a wheelchair is two feet in front of me on the other side of the door. He must be a hundred and fifty. His head is sagging. He's got no teeth and he's drooling. He's blabbing something that doesn't make sense and everyone is ignoring him, walking back and forth. Why did they leave him right outside the elevator so he's the first sight you see, bam! soon as the doors slide open? Where's his family? Don't they visit him? Maybe he went crazy and people decided forget it. Who wouldn't go crazy in a place like this?

I look at him and in that split second I think maybe I'll wait in the parking lot. I'll wait for Dad and Rosemarie and Theresa in the parking lot outside, except Dad is striding down the hall now and so are Rosemarie and Theresa and I wonder about whether or not to follow them before they slip too far away.

I'm the only one left in the elevator. The doors are about to slam shut on my head, so I step out and run after them. I wouldn't want to get lost in a place like this. I don't know my way back to the car.

I rush after them down the hall to Gramma's room and just before we get there I hear the sounds. The sounds start coming already.

"Mi mamma mi mamma mi mamma mi mamma oo!" I hear Gramma calling out. I hear these moans every Sunday. They go on for our entire visit. Unless someone asks Gramma a direct question, she'll moan the entire time we're there. "Mi mamma mi mamma mi mamma mi mamma!" If you ask her a direct question, she'll answer it, then she'll be quiet for a few minutes, and then she'll go back to her cries.

We turn the corner and enter her room. I see Gramma lying in bed, but she doesn't see me. The white sheets and bedspread twist around her. There are iron fences up on either side of the twin bed. I see Gramma, who looks so different than she used to when she lived with Grandpa in their house on 233rd Street. She looks so small now, all pale and bony, her blue veins visible through her skin. Her face is still soft and without wrinkles. I see Gramma and hear my father speaking Italian.

"Come sta Mamma? È Mario." Dad walks over to the twin bed and lowers one of the iron fences. Rosemarie, Theresa, and I walk in and stand at the foot of the bed.

"Come sta, Gramma," we all say.

"Here, you want to sit up?" Dad props another pillow behind her. "It's Mario, Ma." Gramma looks around and can't see him, can't see any of us from her opaque, blue eyes clouded with cataracts. "I'll tilt the bed so you can sit up. How about that?" Dad says, pressing a button on the wall that makes the bed hum as it shifts into place. Gramma is slowly lifted into position.

"Mi mamma mi mamma!" Her mouth stays slightly open when she stops to hear what Dad is saying, then she goes back to her moans: "Mi mamma mi mamma mi mamma!" I can see her teeth. They look just like Dad's teeth, and her mouth and chin look just like my Aunt Sophia's mouth and chin. I think about 233rd Street and visiting Gramma and Grandpa on Sunday. She'd give us Stella D'oro diabetic cookies and anisette biscotti. On Sundays, she would cook big meals. She'd feed me before anyone else. I'd get the first meatball. I'd tell her I was so hungry I couldn't wait, so she'd give me a saucer and fork. "Here Dolly, take a dis. I make meata ball." She calls everyone Dolly.

I'd take the meatball covered with gravy and wolf it down hungrily, running my fingers around the plate and licking the last delicious bits of sauce off my fingertips. I remember 233rd Street and Gramma in her old house while my father presses the button on the tape recorder just in time for Jerry Vale's voice to hit a high note and come crashing down with the cellos and violins at the end of "Torno a Surriento."

"Mi mamma mi mamma mi mamma mi mamma oo!" Gramma's crying continues over Jerry Vale's singing.

"All right," Dad says. "Listen to Jerry Vale now. You like this tape." Her mi mamma's stop for a few minutes as the next song blares out of the tape recorder and she listens.

In a corner of the room in a chair, Mrs. Carmichael is sitting completely still. She's so quiet today. Her skeleton body barely fills up the dark gray dress she's wearing. She must be a hundred years old. That's what the nurse said. She always has this little smile on her face. I glance at her from time to time. I read the name over her dresser: Mrs. Edith Carmichael. She's Gramma's roommate. The name over Gramma's dresser is: Mrs. Rosario Martimucci.

I sneak a peek at Mrs. Carmichael to see what she's doing and she says "Hello" in a very shaky voice, nodding her head at me. I quickly look away but it's too late because now she says, "Are we taking the boat ashore? I didn't bring my bathing suit. Are we going ashore?" I peek at her again and see her head tilted in that same questioning way she always does, waiting for my response. Maybe if I don't look at her, she won't ask me that question, the same question she asks me every Sunday. Maybe if I don't look at her today she won't assume we're in a conversation.

I force myself to look instead at the photographs on top of her dresser, the Carmichael family photos of years gone by. What happened to all those people? Where are they now? I think about a record playing in your head, a record that is your life, and the needle keeps skipping in one place, the same place again and again.

"Are we taking the boat ashore? I didn't bring my bathing suit and the water seems lovely, don't you think?" says Mrs. Carmichael. Rosemarie, Theresa, and I look at each other, rolling our eyes.

I think of the time the three of us stood in front of Mrs. Carmichael in our knee socks and Sunday dresses, shouting at her. We had just come from church. It was Palm Sunday and we had palms for Gramma and Mrs. Carmichael. We held the dry yellow stalks in our fists. They were long and pointy and beautiful.

We had palms, but we had no patience. We stood in front of Mrs. Carmichael and said the words we had often wanted to say: "We're not going ashore and you can't get your bathing suit because *we're not on a boat*!" We shouted the words all at once and looked at her to see her response. But Mrs. Carmichael sat there patiently, hands folded in her lap, the same little smile on her face. We stood there and waited for a response, but nothing happened.

Dad burst out laughing, watching us, and pretty soon the nurse wheeled the dinner trays in and Mrs. Carmichael got ready for her meal.

Later that day, Gramma showed us how to make canoes out of the palm leaves. We watched her weave with her fingers. She still knew how to make small canoes even though she was blind. Me and Rosemarie made a yellow boat for Mrs. Carmichael and left it on her dresser. I wonder if she ever noticed it.

I remember this as Jerry Vale's sole mio's fill the room and Dad is rummaging in a paper bag of anisette biscuits and diabetic cookies and Gramma is lying quietly on her bed, her eyes staring up.

"Come and help me," Mrs. Carmichael says all of a sudden. "Please come and help me." Her voice is so shaky. I swing my head to look at her and see her shrunken embryo body sitting upright in the chair, her gray dress hanging, hands folded neatly. Her feet are placed side by side in her black old lady shoes. "Come and help me," she says.

I glance back at the dresser and her photos and want to

scream at those people in the pictures, those ghosts who exist on film but never appear in the flesh. Why don't they visit her? How can they leave her like this, an old lady with no one to talk to?

Suddenly Dad is standing before Mrs. Carmichael, an anisette biscuit in his hand. He offers it to the old woman. "Here, you want a cookie?" he says, standing a few feet away, bending toward her and talking to her like she's a baby.

"Come and help me," she says in a small bird voice.

Dad repeats himself. "You want this cookie?" He leans toward her and I feel my face get hot.

"Don't talk to her like that," I yell. "She's not a baby!" My father laughs.

"Whadda you mean?" He leans forward, still offering her the cookie.

All of a sudden Mrs. Carmichael's eyes narrow. "Get away from me or I'll smack your face!" she says in a burst of hostility, and Dad jumps back, laughing and looking at us.

Me and my sisters roll our eyes. Dad pokes me with his elbow. "Ask her where her bathing suit is," he says.

I look at him in disgust. "Fa schifo!" comes to mind, but I don't say it. I heard my aunt calling my uncle that one time when they were fighting.

Behind us, I can hear Gramma murmuring. "Mi mamma mi mamma mi mamma mi, mi mamma mi." I think of the time I was with Dad in the hats section of Korvette's department store. He was trying on hats. He put on a ten-gallon white cowboy hat, looked at me, and became John Wayne, saying, "Bring the horses over the pass, podnuh," waving an invisible herd forward and laughing. I kept glancing around hoping nobody would see us. I remember my father standing in the livingroom one morning, tucking his shirt into his pants while conducting an invisible orchestra. He waved his arms in sweeping arcs like Toscanini conducting Beethoven. "Ta ta ta taaa! Ta ta ta taaa!" Is that any different from Mrs. Carmichael's endless boat ride? I wonder what will Dad be like at ninety-eight and will I visit him in a place like this?

He's back at Gramma's bedside now, going through a paper bag of food. Gramma is moaning as she hears him.

"Did you see Sophie last week? Did Sophie come by?" he says. Gramma immediately perks up, hearing my aunt's name.

"Sophia! Is she here? Sophia!"

"No, she's not," Dad says. "Here Ma, I brought you a banana." He holds a ripe banana out for her.

"Dov'è Sophie?" Gramma says. "Figlia, dove sei?"

"I don't know. Sta a casa. Here." He peels the banana for her. She eats it hungrily, like she does every Sunday when he brings a banana for her, a ripe banana, eaten in the middle of our visit. Dad said she needs it for her bowel movements. Every Sunday, the ripe banana.

"Where's a Sophie?" she says again, chewing.

"Sta a casa." Her blue eyes stare steadily forward as she swallows and listens to Dad. I wait to hear Gramma's next sentence, the sentence that always comes after someone mentions home. "Me too. I wanna go home too." Or just "Andiamo!" I wait to hear her say this and the answer my father always gives. "You're here now, you stay here. It's a niza place."

"Mi mamma mi, mi mamma mi, mi mamma mi." Gramma sinks back into her pillows, moaning and closing her eyes. The left side of her mouth settles into a stiff line.

Why does she call for her mother? Who was Gramma's mother? I never knew her. I remember the stories of Gramma, that she was an orphan by the time she was three. She was raised in an orphanage by the nuns in Naples. When she was seventeen she came to America to marry Salvatore, my grandfather. Grandpa was thirty-one, and working as a street sweeper. Aunt Sophie told us. One day she showed us his dark green work shirts on hangers in the back of the closet. There was black writing over one pocket. I remember the white bristles on Grandpa's face, how they were always rough and stickly. They felt like sandpaper against my cheek whenever he kissed me. Salvatore and Rosario Martimucci.

I think of the clay flower pot above the kitchen sink in their house on 233rd Street, Gramma's clay Madonna. Her hands were pressed together, head bent slightly in prayer. Her eyes were dreaming and half-closed. A blue and white shawl draped her shoulders. She was perched on the windowsill, the leaves of a big green plant growing from her back. Her face was peaceful and half asleep.

"Mi mamma mi mamma mi," the moans come again as Gramma sinks into her pillows, her eyes half-closed, her lips moving. She looks like the praying Madonna.

Dad stands up now, motioning to me and my sisters. "The girls are here," he says. "Come on, say hello to Gramma." He herds us closer to the bed. Rosemarie, the oldest, steps up first.

"Hi, Grandma," she says, "Come sta?" and Gramma's blue eyes open and stare forward.

"Who's a dis?" she says, taking my sister's hand.

"Rosemarie," my sister answers.

"Oh Rosa-maria!" Gramma calls out loudly. "Quant' è bella!" Dad immediately echoes her, singing out my sister's name in half English, half Italian.

"Rosa-maria! Quant' è bella Rosa-maria!"

From across the room, Mrs. Carmichael echoes him. "Rosamaria! Come and help me, Rosa-maria." We turn to look at her again. She's still sitting quietly in her chair, feet still placed side by side in her black old lady shoes, hands folded in her lap. Jerry Vale's voice is singing: "Mona Lisa, Mona Lisa, men have named her."

In a few minutes it's my turn to say hello. Dad ushers me closer to the bed. "Who's a dis?" Gramma says, as she takes my hand.

"Hi Gramma. It's Franny." I announce my name in a cheerful tone. Gramma's blue eyes stare in the direction of my voice.

"Hello, Dolly." She says "Quant' è bella!" like she always does. Her grandchildren are still beautiful even though she can't see us anymore. I look at the blue veins in her skin. Her mouth has settled into a flat, stiff line. Her eyes stare forward and her hair stands in gray wisps on top of her head. A year ago she was completely bald, the year she had a stroke and they shaved her head so they could operate. She wore a little cloth cap till her wisps of gray hair grew long enough to cover the scar. After that, her left arm and leg didn't work anymore and the left side of her mouth settled permanently into a flat, stiff line.

Staring at that line, I travel backward, before the stroke, before the nursing home. I'm in the house on 233rd Street, dusting the livingroom furniture. My sister Rosemarie is vacuuming. My mother is changing the sheets. In the kitchen we hear my Aunt Sophie's voice. "She can't take care of herself. She can't be left alone." We're in the house with the wine press in the cellar, anisette biscotti in the kitchen cabinet, and chocolate sundaes in the freezer. "She's incoherent. She talks gibberish," my aunt says to my father, irritated with Gramma.

In a second, I'm home and the yelling is going on, Ma and Dad talking. My mother is furious. "I raised five kids and nobody ever lifted a finger to help me, including you, goddammit! I'm not gonna take on any more dependents at this late date. It's your sister Sophie's responsibility, not mine!"

I see Gramma's face and try to think of something to say. "I won the sixth-grade spelling bee." Her hand is loosening its grip now and her eyes close. "Gramma, there were five classrooms of kids and I was the best speller." I hold her limp hand and look at my father. He doesn't know I won the spelling bee either. He's opening drawers and closet doors, seeing what's around, and doesn't hear me. My thoughts go back to the house on 233rd Street, the house with the wine press in the cellar and the praying Madonna on the windowsill. I picture Gramma walking through the rooms feeling for doorways and edges of tables, feeling for the telephone with the cards she puts in instead of dialing.

My aunt's voice is in my head: "She's incoherent. She talks nothing but gibberish." And my mother yells: "You're not gonna saddle me with her!" The tape recorder clicks and reverses itself and Jerry Vale shouts: "Volare! oh, oh! Cantare! oh oh oh oh!" My eyes fill up with tears. Why can't we take her home? I look at my father, who is going through the bag of cookies again. My little sister Theresa has been standing behind me waiting patiently for her turn to say hello. But Gramma is disappearing fast, sinking into her pillows, down, down, down, and the sounds start coming again. "Mi mamma mi, mi mamma mi, mi mamma mi." Is she calling for her mother, or the Madonna?

Who is Gramma's mother? No one knows. When Gramma was a girl, her mother died. Aunt Sophie used to tell us the story of Gramma's life. In Italy everyone was very poor. The families were big and there wasn't enough food for all the kids. Gramma's mother had fourteen babies. When she had the last one, she got sick and died. Gramma was three years old and went from aunt to aunt. Then she was given to strangers. If she didn't like them, she would run away, put her dresses on, one over the other, and run. She lived like that till she was ten, then she went to the Catholic orphanage for girls. I remember Aunt Sophie's voice telling the story: "She was dying to call somebody 'Mommy.' " Whenever Aunt Sophie would talk, we'd sit at the kitchen table and listen. One time, when she was telling us, she started to cry. I pictured a girl with three dresses on asking women on the street, "Would you adopt me? I have no mother."

In the orphanage, the nuns taught her to read and write. My aunt said she did beautiful hemstitching. They sang religious songs and prayed. Whenever a nun died, two girls had to sit vigil over the body all night. They would pray for the soul of the nun, sitting in vigil till her soul would float like a white feather up to heaven.

When she turned seventeen, Gramma came to America. She worked every day in a factory to pay back the man who paid for her passage. A year later, she married Grandpa.

Now my father is talking only Italian. He does this every Sunday at the end of our visit, so I know we'll go home soon. Every Sunday by the end of our visit, when Gramma won't stop moaning, he starts speaking only Italian. It calms her down.

"Ha mangiato la cena ieri sera?"

"Sì."

"E, che cosa ha mangiato?" and Gramma answers him, and my sisters and I sit at the foot of the bed, like we do every Sunday. We're bored because we don't understand. I won the spelling bee in English, but I don't know Italian. But sometimes I listen, and sometimes I think I know what they're saying. I hear the names of my aunts and uncles and cousins. Sophia, Anthony, Vinny. I hear names and I hear "casa." Gramma wants to go home, and Daddy talks her out of it or changes the subject. Their talking continues and I hear it again, casa, and Daddy continues talking, or changes the subject. He wrestles her, an alligator that eventually will give in.

On the other side of the room, Mrs. Carmichael is still sitting quietly. She doesn't understand Italian either. What does she think, hearing another language spoken in her room every Sunday? I picture Mrs. Carmichael in a boat. She's on a lake in the mountains, going ashore for her bathing suit. I hear my father and Gramma talking. I picture Gramma at the head of the table in her kitchen on 233rd Street. We're all gathered together. It's Sunday, and the lasagna is covered with tomato sauce and piled on every plate. The meatballs, braciole, and sausage are steaming in a glass dish.

Suddenly Dad is standing and moving toward the door.

"Ready to go?" he says to us girls. Rosemarie and Theresa slide off their chairs and follow after him. I get up too. We stand in the doorway for a minute.

"Bye Gramma," we say over our shoulders. "Ciao nonna!" But Dad comes up and makes the shhh! sign.

"Leave her alone," he whispers. "She's taking a nap." We look at her again and see her eyes half-closed. Her breathing is heavier, her hands folded over the blanket.

In the hallway, while we're waiting for the elevator, the same old man is sitting in a wheelchair, his head sagging. He's alone. Why is he still there and why is everybody ignoring him? Where's his family? At least Gramma gets visitors, at least she belongs to somebody. I feel sorry for the man in the wheelchair. It's not his fault no one comes to visit him. Whose fault is it? As the elevator doors slide open, I see the nurses leaning against the walls inside, waiting for their floors. I see the nurses and I hate them. What kind of nurses are they, leaving this man, somebody's father, sitting like this in full view of anyone who walks in? What kind of nurses are they, and who would ever want to be like them! Who would want this job? Where's his family? What kind of family are they? Someone should call them up. Someone should tell them off. Someone should scream at them and keep on screaming and screaming! I step into the elevator and the doors slide closed, sealing the old man from my sight.

In the car, driving home, I sit in the back by the window. I feel heavy, like I'm underwater. I always feel like this on the way home. Tears fill my eyes and I stare out the window, never turning my face. Someone might see me crying.

Dad is mentioning hamburgers and French fries and stopping at McDonald's on the way back. He says one day he'll open a McDonald's restaurant and everyone can work there. The whole family. Theresa can run the cash register, Rosemarie can make the shakes, I can flip the burgers, and Ma and the boys can be there too, taking orders or cooking. Maybe he'll call it

Martimucci's, instead of McDonald's. We can serve spaghetti and meatballs on the side.

"How about it?" he says, winking at me in the rearview mirror. I turn my face away. Sometimes it's the Lennon Sisters. He wants us girls to be a singing group, like the Lennon Sisters, to wear the same hairdos, the same exact gowns, and go on Ed Sullivan. We could sing every Sunday night, before Topo Gigio, the Italian mouse. The point is, the family will stay together. But how can he think about the future now? How can he think about anything when Gramma, his own mother, is lying in bed in that place? She's alone in the nursing home, with her bed sores and bedpan and nurses who can't speak Italian. What if she dies in there, as the dinner trays get stacked and the game shows are turned off and Mrs. Carmichael herself floats from one shore to the next, each of them unobserved by the other, or anyone else who might care?

PATRICIA BARONE

The Hideout

Rose was breathless from hurrying out of the kitchen with two ham on rye, three pickles, a Coke and a piece of cake before her mother could say, stay at the table for once. She grabbed a branch and eased herself down into her dugout—the best hideout yet. No one could see through the leaves of the two tall birches growing from the mossy hummocks. Her mother didn't really miss her . . . her mother. Once quick, even at the beginning of the summer, a flip of the pan, a flick of the towel. Now so slow. And hunched over sometimes—as if she had a pain. No. She ate her sandwich fast to leave no room, and thought of the poem she was writing—*a tall green weaving* . . . She couldn't remember the rest.

Around the white birches was a ring of saplings. She planned to lash them together, looping each with a strong nylon rope, to the larger trees. If she covered the branches with wild grapevines, no one would be able to find her. The second story needed two, at most four, boards across the top of the hummocks. She'd tied the saplings again, high as she could reach at five feet tall. *"A double two by four at twelve—she'll be a barn by twenty-four!"* Her ten-year-old twin brothers always teased her, till Mom spanked Martin. Now they didn't anymore, though Alex still puffed out his cheeks and his belly when grown-ups weren't around. And this morning her thirteen-year-old sister Meg—

who thought she was great because she was thin—said, "I told you those jeans wouldn't fit you anymore."

Fit. What fit? If something fit, it belonged to you. Sometimes in the bathroom, she stared at herself in the mirror. A pretty face, her mother said. But her face looked weird, like her features should belong to someone else. Sharp points at the top of her upper lip. Eyes tilted up above the cheekbones. If you looked in someone's eyes, you could see their soul. She used to think her soul was in the middle of her chest, just above her stomach. Her stomach was the whole problem. Lately, it always felt so empty. Other people didn't feel so hungry all the time, did they? Maybe other people's insides fit their outsides better. Maybe your soul didn't have to fit your body. She used to think it was small, round and white—like a communion wafer.

What if the soul didn't particularly like the body it got? What if it wanted to get out? But you couldn't do that unless you died, or used your astral body—like in an occult book. She didn't know how far she'd travel, but she wanted to get out of her body—only so much white blobby skin; like the farmer's cheese her mother used to make. A body took up too much space—what would it be like to be invisible? Then she'd only have thin thoughts . . . *a willow wall in my mind* . . . what comes next? Her special writing book was in the bedroom . . .

Invisible, she wouldn't have to slip in the back door and tiptoe past the kitchen. Her sister was there, helping their mother clean up after Father and his two seasonal workers. But before she reached the back stairs, Meg looked up from wiping the table and saw her. "How come Rose gets to play all morning and I have to work?"

"That you, Rose? Get in here and help us with the kitchen." Her mother had that look—her face might unravel if anyone pulled the invisible string at the corner of her mouth. And her feet went clump, clump, from the table to the stove to the sink.

"I bet she was trying to sneak to her room," Meg said, "for some more books. So she could disappear into one of her hideouts all afternoon."

Rose began lifting plates from the drainboard with a damp towel. Her fair hair was plastered to her forehead with sweat. They were probably hotter than other people in this corner of Washington County—because of being wedged between two hills and a long ridge—a drumlin, made by a glacier, her mother said once. Drumlin—such a beautiful word.

"We're boiling in our kettle," Rose said, but her mother was too busy to hear her. Boiling—she'd rather think about ice. "How come you never sit on the porch with us anymore," Rose said. "How come we never sit there and listen to you talk about glaciers anymore?"

"Glaciers!" Meg snickered. "You're so smart, you're dumb."

"Meg! No name-calling! That's not dumb—at least a glacier would be cool. Oh, Rosie, Rose . . ." Her mother gave a huge hissing sigh—like air out of a balloon. "If you'd do your chores without being asked maybe I'd have more time to sit with you . . ."

As Rose swept, she imagined the huge ice sheet, how it stopped right at the place where their front door was. Where they lived was historic, and backpackers—from as far away as Milwaukee—hiked on the trail the county made between her dad's corn and rye fields.

"We're really lucky," Rose said, "we live at the northernmost edge of the Wisconsin Kettle Moraine." Meggy groaned and said Rose was crazy, but under her breath, so their mother wouldn't hear. Rose didn't care. She was pretending she had really been there when the glacier melted, receded, leaving the land pocked, full of crevices. Then, thousands and thousands of years later, she was sitting right there in the covered wagon when Great-great-grandfather Meyer chose the most secret hollow for his farm.

"Rose, you've been polishing that same plate so long there's almost a hole in it. Woolgathering again!" The word reminded her that she'd hidden her book about precognition and levitation under the bed. Now it would be all covered with dust kittens like the pineapple diet book her sister found with the dust mop. She closed her eyes, gritted her teeth in a scowl. At least her mother had given Meg a scolding when she brought the book down. "Don't you know that everyone needs some privacy?" At least she sent Meg off to gather eggs with the boys before she said all that stuff about *sensible eating:* "There are no instant ways to lose weight, honey. There are no miracles." Her mother was always saying there were no miracles. Just when she loved her mother so much—like when she told Meggy to let her have privacy—her mother turned around and said something she always said like "Rose, the trouble with you is you believe everything you read."

The trouble with her mother was—now she only believed in getting her work done—chicken incubation, the rising price of chicken feed and chicken wire! Only the things that happened to her. And not a whole lot happened on their isolated triangle of land—down a four-mile lane off County Road XY and ten miles from Highway 41. ("Five hundred acres is a *small* farm?" asked their cousin from Milwaukee.)

Rose poked her broom as far under the china cabinet as it would go. A squeal—one of the cats! She got down on her stomach, reached back and pulled it out. She sat down on the floor with it, her back against the cabinet. "Mom, why are we one of the last farms left in the moraine area?"

"You have more questions than a hundred cats have kittens," her mother replied but with a sort of smile at the corner of her mouth. "Most of our neighbors lost their farms in the Great Depression."

Rose put the cat out the back door, and started sweeping again. She knew that already, she didn't know why she'd asked. Now they lived in a land depression. Depressing. Only two more days before a trip to West Bend or Menomonee Falls so she could go to the library while her mother shopped. For eight years now—since she was four years old—she had borrowed five books a week. That made 260 eight times, and that was—2,080, and if they'd only let her borrow more she'd get into *The Guinness Book of World Records. Yah, as the fat girl who reads the most!* Martin's mocking voice in her head.

This week all her books had been about unsolved mysteries of the universe because last week at St. Luke's during the sixth-grade summer religion class, Sister Marcy told them about the Glorified Body.

"Finish sweeping the kitchen and hall floors, *now,* Rose!" her mother said in her how-many-times-do-I-have-to-tell-you voice. Rose didn't mind. Her hands on the broom weren't solid, but, instead, were full of spinning little suns called atoms. Sister Marcy (so pretty, so kind), her bangs in moist curls above her glasses, held up a brick and said, "Anyone know what's in this brick?" Molly Kinder, who was helping her father build the foundation for their new barn, said, "Well, you get this brick-making machine, and you mix all this stuff together . . ." Molly didn't know what she was talking about, but she thought she knew all about bricks. Then Sister asked, "Anyone know what's in clay, in water, in sand, in mortar, in the fingers holding this brick, in the flesh, in the bone, in the cell, in the soul?"

"What's got into you, Rose?" This time her mother's voice had a hard edge. Rose stood over a mound of cereal flakes, dust, popcorn, and pipe tobacco. "Mooning again," said her mother. Rose was glad Alex wasn't there to split a gut laughing.

"Mooning means something else, Mom."

"I'd have to stop talking altogether to avoid all the double meanings you kids have." She took off her heavy slippers and, moving to her bedroom, unsnapped the top of her shorts. "Throw the wet towels down the chute, Rose, I have to go to the doctor this afternoon."

The doctor again. The yellow mongrel called Streak turned three times in the sweepings, and squatted heavily. The dumb old female dog *Sounds like witch, you silly bitch. Alex get out of my head!* was too fat and getting fatter. Rose poked the dog's rump with the end of her broom. Her coat *was* the color of piss on snow. It wasn't right to want to kick a dog. "Go away!" Rose shouted. "Get out!"

Her new book on parapsychology was under her religion textbook on the hall table. If only she knew how to do psychokinesis! Want the garbage in the Dumpster? Click your fingers and it's there! No more lugging big plastic smelly bags.

By the time the pickup truck rattled down the gravel lane, Rose had already read five pages in the "Mind Over Matter" chapter. She'd have to remember to ask Sister Marcy about some of this stuff. Sister Marcy said psychokinesis was proof that faith moved mountains.

Slowly, one foot after another on the creaky treads, Rose took her book up the back stairs and sat down in her very own slip-covered reading chair. But the letters on the page made her eyes tired. She looked up with the feeling someone was looking at her—but it was just her mother's eyes in the photograph, taken long ago—a five-year-old girl in a fussy dress, sitting on a round-faced young Grandma's lap. Her mother's eyes looking right at her, as if she could see her own little girl—ahead into the future. Grandma's eyebrows were raised and she'd cocked her head to one side and down—as if she were listening to something very close.

If Grandma and Mom could live back there in 1930 at the same time they lived right here in 1965, then everybody's life would be like those Chinese boxes in boxes. Smaller and smaller if you went back in time, and bigger when you went forward in time. If you open the *Now* box—there sits Rose at twelve! Open the boxes the other way, and it is then—so far back the family didn't even exist yet—when nothing was here but ice and snow!

The curtains over the dormer window—so perfectly immobile, they were frozen sunshine—all at once ice, the folds of the curtains like ridges from the creeping of a glacier. A shiver, and then she was warm, not too hot, but just right. She closed her eyes and saw the words, *Rose Meyer is created.*

I am. I really exist. I don't have to be, but I am. Here. I'm not written. I am. A miracle.

So. She was real, and this was her body. How could she have been so dumb. The religion books—they were true. Then the curtains lifted over a breeze, the ice dunes turned to gauze, and she decided to write down her thoughts in the unlined calico-covered book.

The only breeze got caught behind the bureau, and then it got so hot her fingers stuck to the pencil. So she lay down on the nubby chenille bedspread and closed her eyes. She woke in just a few minutes, or thought she did, feeling cool again, and she saw she was inside the glacier, in the waxy blue walls of an ice cave. Only the ice directly overhead was transparent, thinner, so she began to climb, kicking little toeholds in the ice walls, which yielded like rubbery, boiled Jell-O. All at once her head poked through. The glacier was moving, uncovering the earth. Slowly, slowly, the tip of their own valley showed, and the slope where her hideout was. She climbed out, hoisting her body up with both her arms, until she flopped, gasping, on the hill of snow. But as soon as she stood and took one step along the upper ridge, her foot went through the roof. Her own body, like a heavy heated brand, melted the ice, and she fell back down to the cave below. The cave was moving out from over her. Behind the glacier, she was left in the cairn, in the hollow it scraped, while far above and carried faster on the ice, her mother waved.

She woke several hours later to the creak, creak, creak of the porch swing, and the low voices of her parents. Had they spoken a little lower or a little louder, she would have let the sound continue, like a murmur below, or a tuneless song above. But the unusual quickness, almost a harrying note in her father's tone, made her stretch to listen. She crept to the window, leaned her arms on the sill.

"Well, is he absolutely sure?" demanded her father.

"Yes, and what really scares me—Mother had the same thing."

"Well, your mother's all right now . . ."

"It's not five years yet, it's four."

"Still . . ."

"It's the operation! I don't want them to take it all, and then I'm scared they won't *get* it all . . ." After that, her mother's words were garbled—as if she had buried her face, as if she were crying.

"I think we should go to Milwaukee and get a second opinion," her father said.

Rose slid to the floor, her legs straight out in front of her. The floor had something sticky—the sherbet she'd spilled last night, not wanting to eat dessert in front of the family. She looked at the large pink cabbage roses marching in crooked lines under the slanting dormer ceiling. It was strange how she didn't feel anything—not anything at all. She wouldn't think about her mother, she'd think about . . . Glorified Bodies. Those spinning little suns . . . we're all made up of spinning little suns . . . But what if they started spinning the wrong way . . . it was better to feel nothing. Nothing, nothing at all.

At supper her mother's skin was loose and bruised around her eyes. She curved her shoulders over her coffee, holding the cup like she was cold, her back looking bony, almost like Martin's. Could it be her mother had been getting smaller every week and she hadn't even noticed? Rose leaned her elbows on the table, and crossed her arms on her chest; her own arms were solid fat and they flattened her breasts sore for a month now, and puffy. (Fat is okay there and there only, Meg said.) Did Mom have too little fat there? Or too much? Is that why it happened?

She was careful not to look at her father when he said, "Kids, Mom and I are driving to Milwaukee tomorrow, and since we may decide to stay overnight, I've asked Grandma to stay with you. She doesn't like to drive, you'll have to miss religion class."

"Miss religion class, too bad!" Meg got a silly smirk on her face. "Why are you going to Milwaukee?" Rose almost kicked her under the table. If only she could send a burning thought wave into her stupid head, so she'd shut her trap.

"Oh, we haven't seen Uncle Jim and Aunt Margaret for a long time, and I need to look for a new combine . . ."

Rose looked up in time to see her mother open her mouth and close it again.

For the first time all summer, she didn't want to be alone. She could be with Grandma by herself because Meggy would run off with her friends as usual. Grandma was easy to be around because she did all the talking any time she got away from her farm and Uncle Al and Uncle Augie, who worked hard, ate hard, and fell asleep at eight after *Gunsmoke* reruns. The second floor of the hideout would just have to wait.

After they drove away, Grandma eased herself down into the spooled rocker, sighing, smoothing her apron. She looked up and caught Rose looking at her. "Rose," she said, propelling herself back out with three deep rocks, "if you'll help me get out your mama's ingredients and pans, I'll whomp up some bread for us." Though she weighed almost 200 pounds at seventy-five years old, Grandma had more energy than Mom, who was thin and only forty. Rose winced. But today Grandma was not quite so bouncy . . . did she know?

"Oh, isn't my hair funny?" Grandma put her hand on the skewered knob at the back of her head and waggled her bangs. For the first time, Rose realized that Grandma's white hair had a delicate green cast. "Rose, I read in this old beauty-tip book that hickory nut juice makes a good rinse to take out the yellow. Now look at me! I wouldn't have minded a little blue—but green!" She chuckled again. Rose tried to laugh with her, but sounded like she was clearing her throat. It was almost as if Grandma was very pleased to be a walking joke. It must be nice not to mind how you looked.

While the dough was rising, Grandma knitted and Rose opened her new book about Edgar Cayce. It was so quiet that she began to count the needle clicks against the tocks from the regulator clock on the landing. She had to read three pages again because she hadn't taken in a single word.

After what seemed a long while, Grandma rocked herself to her feet and went into the kitchen to lift the corner of the linen towel over the dough. Rose put down her book and trailed after her. "Looks like it's almost ready, but we'll give it another ten minutes." Lightly, she patted the towel back over the mound of dough, then put both hands on the table and looked at her. "Rose, you're awful quiet. Hungry? Or is something bothering you?"

Rose's eyes filled with tears. "I don't want to talk about it."

"Your mother?"

Rose nodded.

"The others know?" Shouts and scuffles from the fallow pasture—Alex and Martin playing baseball with their friends. Rose scornfully shook her head.

"Sit down, Rose. Well since you know your mom is sick, I think it's good for us to talk about it. Kind of take the mystery out of things if you know what I mean. Take the mystery out of the medical things so we can get to the real mystery."

Grandma got up, went to the refrigerator and came back with a glass of milk. She pulled a handful of her homemade peanut butter chocolate chip cookies from the jar, and put them on a plate. "You're a real smart girl, and I think you can understand what I'm going to tell you. There's a lot they can do nowadays. Your mom will have to have an operation, and then she'll have some treatments, and that will be hard—for her and all of us, but she'll get through it, and we will too. When I was sick, when I was taking my chemo treatments, I got a little puffy—just like this dough. But my soul swelled too and now I'm in my health again—because of something that happened to me when I was sick. It was like in the Bible when the Lord says we should fall like grains of wheat into the earth and die, and rise again—like good bread." Grandma pushed the heels of her palms into the dough, then up and over. The dough popped, then made a sucking sound over the trapped air.

"Grandma, I don't know what you're talking about!"

"Oh, honey, I'm going too fast, I'll slow down. And don't be sad. Remember, your mom could be like me."

"Four years ago," Rose said. It was hard to remember . . . a white bed . . . Grandma at the hospital? She held on to the thought: In four years her mother would have been sick four years ago.

When she was seated out on the porch swing with her iced tea, Grandma took Rose's hand. "I have my life and it's better than before because I have a secret." She put her glass on the porch rail, and lowered her voice. "I'm not afraid to die, because . . ." She got a wavery look in her pale blue eyes, and hesitated.

"You're not afraid to die," prompted Rose.

Then Grandma finished, all in a rush, "because I *did,* and it ain't so bad! Why it's—beautiful!"

Why she's crazy, Rose thought, a crazy old loon. But she shivered. Out-of-the-body travel, the books called it! Could it be the psychic books were true?

"It was right at the end of my operation. They told me later that my heart stopped, but to me it felt like I just slipped out of my body, easier than taking off a tight girdle, let me tell you. I floated on the ceiling and looked down to see this white-haired old lady with the Herman family chin sticking out from beneath a mask. I didn't recognize myself right away, I thought I was my own mother! You see I wasn't used to seeing myself so *round.* I know, dear, I'm very round. But, in a mirror, we all look *flat* to ourselves, you see. Then I noticed that, up there, I still had a body—arms, legs and so forth, but it was different, lighter—like a feather."

Did Grandma's soul have a better shape than her body? Rose was afraid she was going to laugh—the sort of laugh that comes in church during a long sermon. Then the feeling went away and she felt very still inside.

The two lines along Grandma's nose got deeper, and her cheeks looked heavy. She stopped the swing and looked right at Rose. "My mother and father, your great-grandparents, everyone I'd ever loved, was there, looking so happy and welcoming, but they kept their distance. Then I heard lots of bells—like Christmas Eve in August, each chime separate, the way sound travels when the air is very cold. I didn't feel cold, but warm and comfortable. I grew warmer and more comforted as this light, this person with a bright halo, moved toward me. And then I was moving toward the light as if through a dark barn, and then out the pasture door with the sky above me full of spinning starry rings. At last I came to rest, all full of peace and happiness at a sort of fence. The light was Jesus himself, and he put a question in my mind: How do you weigh your life? And I answered, not finished yet, not full."

"And that's why you didn't stay dead . . ."

Grandma blew her nose and wiped her eyes. "I'm sure of it—I was brought back so I could be here to tell you this."

"My mom—if she goes there, will she get to come back?"

"I can only tell you what I know, and I didn't know it until just now, but I've been kept here so I could tell you this." Grandma took her by each shoulder and looked right into her eyes. "I can only tell you what I know," she said, "here or there your mom is gonna live."

Here or there! Rose let herself fall forward off the swing, and she landed on her knees. Here or there! So! The message didn't have an ending, it opened like a tunnel, connecting here to there.

What if her mother didn't want to come back? What if they didn't send her? Maybe she'd come back because she wouldn't like it there alone! Rose threw her arms around her grandmother's waist and buried her head in her lap. "Weren't you afraid at first, when you came out of your body? Weren't you sorry!"

"Honey, I felt so sorry for my poor body! It looked like a beached whale. I felt fond of it, and a little panicky at first. 'Dear Lord,' I prayed, 'however will I get back in?' " She opened her knees and held Rose between them. Rose stared down into the valley of her grandmother's seersucker lap. "Honey, then the fear just went away, and I was back in my body. I felt sad—at being here instead of there—for just a moment, until I remembered. I was going to go out of this old body again. And at the same time I was going to take it with me. I was going to go home someday, but at the same time, I'm home already. It's a mystery."

Rose looked for a few seconds into Grandma's eyes. A little Rose in there, looking back. Then she looked down again. Grandma's apron was all wet, as if someone else had been crying.

"I can't say it so well in words," Grandma said, "do you understand just a little?" Rose raised her head. "Just let what I told you settle in," Grandma said, "go sit in one of your hideouts, now go—just run!"

She *never* ran, she was too heavy, but she had to run or burst—not to her hideout, it was too small. Down the steps in one jump, and across the lawn, her head down, her legs pumping. She could almost count the separate blades of grass, like jungle fronds—coarse and tough for the boys to play on—and then she was moving lightly over the bluegrass, each fine hair combed down around her mother's phlox. Everything was much slower than she'd thought—like the dream, like looking at your life from the back of a moving glacier. She raced down the driveway to the barn as if her legs would never stop, but she had time to see the goose unfurl its neck and hiss each gosling into line. Everything was so slow that all of her life happened at the same time. The spinning little suns of the Glorified Body—were all moving in slow motion!

Her legs felt like rubber as she took large leaping strides, pebbles spraying from her feet ahead of her into the barn. The baled hay was like a staircase, so she scrambled to the very top. Her heart thudded against her chest, and then it too fell back to its usual place. She sat down and looked up.

If the whole family would make a pyramid, like in the circus, and add the hired men and Grandma and the uncles, they still wouldn't be even one third the way to the skylight in the roof where Grandma's old patchwork quilt was nailed to the rafters to catch bird whiting. People were very small, and the ones on the bottom of the pyramid had to be very strong. No one could let go of the next person's ankles. Maybe the dead were like that, maybe they were still holding on . . .

Down below—the yellow dog, dragging her belly on the floor. Puppies. Can't see her anymore. Just her panting. Must have collapsed between two bales. So quiet. Just breathing. So quiet. A good place to wait.

JOHN AZRAK

Sister Barbara

Back to the wall, I can lay some spit on the Spal-deen and hope it makes the ball hop, or stroke it with the Sign of the Cross and let God throw it. I go for the Cross, mutter a Hail Mary, and wheel around. Donald's got me. He's on one knee, stickball bat shooting out of his side like he's off to the Crusades, and what I hear is "and lead us not into temptation. Amen." I might as well lob because I know my Johnny Podres curve will be heading for the neat row of two-families on the other side of the fence.

He lives only eight blocks from me, but I think it's too far for a best friend. I'm near the bottom of the hill that drops like the Cyclone at Coney and he's two blocks over the peak where the houses flatten out like his hair. It's Donald's idea that we meet halfway to walk to school.

Donald marks the spot and he says whoever gets there first has the edge for the day. Sometimes he sounds just like the nun who tells us we can chop years off Purgatory for every minute we're early for just about anything. So there I am struggling every morning to get up the hill, running when I think I got a chance, bookbag making potholes in my kneecap, butch stick dripping on my forehead, school tie wrapped around my neck, and there he is, strolling, touching up his hair, waiting for me with his arms crossed. "But I gotta go *uphill*," I complain. He shakes his head while I gasp for air. "When are you going to learn about life, Paul?" he says and I get this ache across my eyebrow.

So I plan these surprise attacks which mean getting up earlier, lying to my parents about serving an earlier Mass, missing breakfast, just to beat him. It's still dark and I can't see anything. I kinda tiptoe but fast up the hill when *zing*—a white arm flashes, a belt buckle shines, a white buck moves until, growing out of the black like in the Polaroid I took of him, there's Donald, the teeth coming in last, smiling, because I tried so hard and there's no sixth grader who'll ever beat *us*.

I follow Donald into his house and lean the stickball bat against the extra refrigerator on the porch. Donald's family has seconds of everything: T.V., phonograph, car, dog, Bible, toasters in different colors, garage. The Polaroid leans against a Kodak in the bookcase. Donald's their only kid but he sleeps in a bunk bed. They're really strange about it, like we are about keeping doubles of our favorite baseball cards in case we lose one. But they're not storing anything in the attic or underground in a fallout shelter.

Donald pops open two Cokes with the opener on the side of the refrigerator. The caps fall into the bin like I knew they would. I love watching Donald crack open those bottles and listening to the *clink*. If he ever jumped from a burning building, even one of those skyscrapers in Manhattan, he'd hit the net, I'm sure.

Even though I'm dog thirsty, I drink the Coke slow. When I finish, Donald's heading for our baseball report card on the wall. It's got everything—games won and lost, batting averages, home runs, RBIs, shutouts, earned run averages, errors, and his favorite, slugging percentage, which he made up so no one else can figure it.

Donald takes my empty bottle for the return carton as I start rubbing my temples. "Your slugging percentage fell off point six today, Paul," he says. "If you had singled in the third, driving in the runner on second, you would have gone up point two." Donald remembers plays from the game that I can't remember even after he tells me about them.

"That was a mean curve you threw me," I fake.

"No it wasn't. It was a fastball, down and away. I set you up with the curve."

Donald fills out the won and lost columns in red ink.

Donnie, I'm dying to say, you beating me all the time really hurts. I mean, my head really hurts but it's not really that, I mean I could do without it, it's just that everybody knows that it's the fags that are the crybabies and I don't want to be a fag I want to be your best friend forever like it's supposed to be. When we saw that Audie Murphy movie you said that's the way we gotta be even when we're surrounded and I'm tryin' but when am I gonna get like Audie Murphy, Donnie?

"Oh, yeah, the fastball. You had a good fastball today, Donald." Against me, Donald, you're Bob Feller.

Donald pitches the scrap paper into the wastebasket. He snaps the blue and red pens into place on the bulletin boards. "I have to go with my father to the office tomorrow afternoon, so let's play a doubleheader on Saturday, okay."

I nod. His father. His father makes me call Donnie Donald because Donald is going to be a doctor. "Meet you in the morning," Donald says.

I leave and a new game starts. I'm Donald coming over the rise, cool, movie-cool, hair standing up without any grease, first to arrive at our spot. I have the edge for the day that's just about over but I got it. I know what it feels like. I leap onto the spot, spring from it like a cat, and sail down the hill that will turn on me in the morning.

I start pacing around my room and try to stop going over and over in my mind my losses. I try making plans like lifting weights or serving time in a leper colony to get God on my side. My head aches so I can't do my homework and Donald's climbing all over me. Last year it was close but by the end of the fall he's smack at the top of the class and I'm just falling faster than the temperature.

I'm just no good at home. I'm wearing out my floor which is wearing out my parents. And, bolting dinner just when they want to start talking about it has got them worrying, I can tell, so when spring comes and there's all that extra light, I have to stay out. I take up golf, the neighborhood fag sport, but we live across the street from a links with holes in the fence Jackie

Gleason could get through, and I can play alone if I want. I start practicing late afternoons after leaving Donald, early weekend mornings before meeting him. I practice like I'm going to the Masters, study golf books snuck in school books, sneak behind the pro at the eighteenth while he gives lessons to old ladies in plaid skirts. I get weird in front of the mirror—"a regular Beau Brummel," my father says when he catches me—freezing all the parts of the swing until my arms hurt. But I don't shake Donald. I play two balls from the tee, go from tee to green as a twosome—like in *Topper* when you see the two balls on the fairway—giving Donald all the best lies so when I putt both balls out, I never feel I'm cheating. I keep both scores and circle the pars and there are times when I'm practicing in front of the mirror that I see him.

The day school closes Donald leaves for the summer house his parents just bought somewhere in the mountains. I feel lousy all over as I wave at the station wagon that has my one best friend piled in the back with the other stuff.

We start writing right away and soon we get ourselves a good game going counting everything—crossouts, spelling mistakes, missing commas, capitals, the number of words. The best, though, is the armies of saints we're adding to the J.M.J. at the top. Donald wins a big one when he sends in St. Ignatius of Loyola, soldier of Christ that he was.

Donald's got a lot more to say than I do so I start making things up to get more words. But I don't write about golf even after I win the Brooklyn Pee-Wees or about how ticked I am that he's got a second house.

Any chance Donald's going easy on me after a vacation in the mountains dies when I spot him standing like the bronze statue my mother got in Greece or Rome, at our corner, the morning we start seventh grade. "We may have been something last year but they ain't seen nothin' yet," he greets me.

"Right, Donald. Welcome back. I didn't think you were home yet." Donald skipping the first day of school is a bad joke but I'm trying to cover up for my first loss of the season.

Donald just smiles and as we walk he fills me in on the days since his last letter. He's walking like he's trying out for military school. I can't keep up and I know as I get paler, I'm lighting up his tan. We hit the school gates, first, as he says, by a country mile.

We're a bunch of jittery seventh graders when, who knows from where, a young nun slides down past the first row. We're the honors class, stuck together for six years, and the new nun always looks like the last. I can't believe my eyes which are rolling crazy in the sockets trying to keep up with her. The room buzzes who's this as she signs in. We're playing mystery guest without blindfolds. I catch Donald's frown. I know for a fact he doesn't like surprises.

Sister Barbara with bright red hair. Only a quarter moon is showing, but I'm sure I see hair bouncing around under the white hat and black veil. She bounces, she moves like a runner on the balls of her feet and then, I swear, I hear music. Sister Barbara makes the overgrown rosary beads sound like more than just marbles banging around in a tin can. They sing, it's crazy, and even the forty-eight layers of black swoosh around her like there's nothing to them.

She's smiling and everything's shining. Her teeth, her green eyes, the big jewel in her crucifix that's catching the morning light, the flashes of pink on her forehead filled with freckles. It's the first smile we've gotten before All Saints' Day. It knocks me for a loop.

"I am Sister Barbara. I shall be with you for the year," she says and the words come out like soft ice cream. "I hope we shall all be friends—good ones at that." She smiles again. "I know it's the end of the summer—and I love the summer—but I am excited to be here. Now, if it takes some of you a while to catch up, don't worry. I shall wait for you."

I slide back in my seat, back from the edge where I used to wait for the alarm screeching boys and girls this, boys and girls that, boys and girls buckle up it's school. It's warm, Sister Barbara's voice is warm, soothing. I feel weird, a tingle in the back of my neck, a church calm in my head, in the room. I'm hypnotized. She glides in, out, around. Maybe she is watching me like I'm watching her. She is watching only me and singing to me words I can't hear.

The class giggles, louder.

"Not with us yet, Paul?

"Paul, isn't it?" She smiles and I jump.

"Yes . . . yes, Sister." The class laughs. I sweat. I'm afraid they can hear my heart, my thoughts. We are supposed to say something about ourselves, something we consider important. All I can get out is my name. Donald speaks from notes, but finishes with him and me being best friends. I want another chance to make it up to him.

I apologize to Donald on the way home. He says that I was out of it all day. He asks if I don't think Sister Barbara's strange. "And whaddya think of that red hair," he groans. He's upset that we didn't get homework or a rah-rah speech about being the tops and winning one more for the monsignor.

"I guess so, Donald."

He doesn't look at me regular. He even seems nervous which is a first.

Donald does me in on the basketball court, worse than ever. Bigger in a T-shirt and shorts he roughs me up when I get close. I long for the safety of stickball and wonder why the hell I didn't fill out like him over the summer. "I hope you're going to get better," he says. "I expect us to run the parish team." Embarrassed, I promise him that I will. "And you know, Paul, if we're going to win scholarships to the same school, you'd better get those grades back up." My head starts right up, like one of those big centers is using it to practice dribbling. Donald's got these great plans for us, right through college, and they always sound as if they're coming out of our Baltimore Catechism.

The thing about guys like Audie Murphy is that they never really talk too much when they don't want to but they don't have to hide. So I stick it out longer at the dinner table, put more time in the family room, excusing myself silly when I get up to go to my room where, as soon as the door closes, I cave in. I have this trick, though. If I can lie still long enough I can cool out and if I can get *really* still, I can almost always have this dream:

Sister Barbara holds back. She holds back even while I am circling her on my knees; but I know she does not mean it. As the room darkens she pulls me up from the floor. The room is black, blacker than the chalkboard, except for this yellow light that bounces off the church steeple, comes in on a slant through the window, and lands on her desk. There are just two pins to pull to loosen the bonnet and the veil. I pull carefully and she smiles. The red hair rushes like Niagara Falls to the floor. It's a blanket of sparkling red, warm and smooth. I touch it, walk through it, like Moses parting the Red Sea but like the Egyptians I'm swallowed until there's only Sister Barbara, bonnet and veil back in place.

"Hold on one second, Paul. There seems to be a piece of chalk lodged next to the glory bead." We've talked so often in my dreams and though I've got spaghetti legs I'm feeling pretty easy on the inside. "There, that's it," Sister Barbara says, breathing on the chain until the dust flies. She rubs the chain on her sleeve like a jeweler. "I like things that shine. Do you?"

"Uh . . . yes, Sister."

"Good! I especially like eyes that shine because as it is said, the eyes are the windows of the soul."

"Yes, Sister." She's coming from deep left field.

"And your eyes, Paul, they are a pretty blue but I daresay, not very bright these days."

"No, Sister?"

"No. Is there something bothering you? Is there something you cannot even work out with your best friend?"

She should know me like I know her. "I can't talk to Donald, Sister. No, I can't."

"Oh, that is unfortunate. But I certainly know how *that* feels."

"I don't know, Sister Barbara. We've never not been best friends unless you count kindergarten. You know, Donald is just the best at everything."

"Which means you're not?"

She is going too fast. "Because some of my sisters have won teaching awards doesn't mean I'm not as good if *I* think I am—with all due respect to Mother Superior, of course. Follow?"

"Yes, Sister." I'm not sure.

"What Donald does, Donald does. What you do, you do. Concentration on what you're doing is the key. I must say you were not concentrating on the basket last evening."

"You like basketball, don't you, Sister?"

"I sure do. I love all sports, Paul, not just the winning—that's okay, of course—but the joy of the game, the beauty. When I shoot a basket, Paul, I imagine a glow around the rim, a faint glow, like a saint's halo that lights up when the ball falls through." She smiles and my heart races. "I love the morning dew that covers the freshly cut putting green." She winks but I know to stay quiet. "And when the ball cuts through the dew, making a brand-new path, made by you alone—oh!"

"I love golf, Sister?" I say practically falling over, so wound up I forget Donald's waiting on the street corner.

"I know. You won the Brooklyn Pee-Wees, didn't you. Congratulations." She smiles and for sure I'm going to melt right there in front of her. "I know your scholastic record. It is not hard to conclude that you are in a slump—a long one at that." *At that, at that,* I love the way she adds *at that.*

"Want to play?"

"Huh?"

"The gym is free. We shall just practice our shots, develop our concentration together. Give me about fifteen minutes to change. I shall get the key from the rector and meet you over there."

"That's it, Paul. Feel the seams in your hands—watch the ball spin on the way to the basket. Light up that hoop?" She laughs. Believe it! I begin hitting shots from way out, shots I don't even usually take. "Love the ball, Paul," Sister Barbara says, floating around the edge of the key, nailing pump shots like the Cooz, bouncing on the hardwood in sneakers, gym shorts, a t-shirt with the number 5 on the back, a number I can hardly make out beneath the flowing river of red hair.

I keep books by my pillow. When my head's okay, I study, thinking always that Sister Barbara is going over the same pages. The dream changes, comes easier, as I lie on the bed.

The hair falls from the bonnet to the number 5. She asks me to brush it, straight back, over and over, until my arms ache. When I know I can't pull again, she asks for one more. I pull, slowly back from the forehead, and the hair rises in threads of light.

"These are my favorite volumes of poetry," Sister Barbara says, handing me beat-up copies of Byron and Keats, guys who sound kinda faggy to me—I mean I've never really read a poem except in a card—but I don't say this to Sister Barbara. "I'd like to see you start a library, books you will be able to share with your friends and family when you get older."

The extra work I do with Sister Barbara after class bugs the hell out of Donald, but the poems she teaches me aren't bad, really. "Feel them," she's always telling me. "Don't fight them. A good one is as smooth as a finely carved Louisville Slugger."

My parents are more confused than ever. I'm not eating or sleeping much and when they hear me moving around at night they gotta think it's the old pacing. But really I have all this energy and when they go into shock over my report card, I think they finally relax.

"He's not eating; he must be in love." My father stands up one night at dinner, with a message from heaven. "Sure, sure, he has all the symptoms." My mother thanks the Lord for this number one sign of my good health. My sister, who's big time in high school, giggles like when she's with her boyfriend.

I never say anything so they spend most spring suppers trying to get the name out of me.

Donald loses his edge. Slow at first but then so fast it's like what was it. He's not losing to me but he's not really winning. I quit praying in between points, pitches. Sometimes I give him better games. But I'm always playing against myself.

In the late spring I feel real loose, loose enough to tell Donald about golf. I wanna teach him before he goes away for the summer. The headaches are gone. I spend more time doing the mighty things, as Sister Barbara calls them, like polishing my irons and watching them shine. I learn to regrip my clubs by replacing the rubber with cool leather. I chew Sister Barbara's ears off about it. Donald thinks I'm not his best friend anymore but I'm just beginning to really love him. I should've known it was coming when he goes out and finds a second best friend.

Sister Barbara leaves the tenth day of June in the morning like she said she would the first day of class. Okay, I admit it, I cry my way through most of the front nine, spraying the ball all over the place, in and out of the rough and water. But I bring it home all right, keeping my head down, eye on the ball, and seeing that little light around the lip of the cup.

GERALDINE CONNOLLY

The Linens of the Sisters of St. Vincent

The nuns at Benediction,
we are in the forbidden hall
rifling through their lingerie,
shrieking, tying their cotton slips
around our heads like turbans,
dancing in Mother Ildefonse's bloomers.

It is even better than looking at natives
in the old issues of *National Geographic*.
We are two tipsy corks in deep water
next to the honeycomb of cubicles
that hold these secret garments.

Giddy with rebellion, we release one after another
flapping into the clean winter air.
We send the brassiere of our fat cook, Sister Philomena,
out next to Father Ryan's underwear. We slingshot
Sister Charlotte's panties all the way

to the furthest limb of the high evergreen.
Exultant, we send one last garment out
and it flies, landing lonely, glowing
with the sad light of a beached trout.

And then we head up to our rooms
with the news that they, like us,
have skin under their robes,
flesh aside from their holy faces
and swim the insistent tides of the body.

SIMONE POIRIER-BURES

Blue Coat

"It was the bluest blue," I told my mother. "Like the sky in summer, when it's full of fat white clouds." My mother handed me two bowls of clam chowder to put on the table. My sister, Annette, stood at the counter cutting big slabs of bread from the double loaves and arranging them on a pink Melmac plate.

"You should have seen the way it made my eyes look. When I tried it on, my eyes looked bluer than blue, even with my glasses."

My mother handed me two more bowls of chowder. "Put the molasses on the table, too, for André."

I put an empty plate at my brother's place. André ate almost nothing but fried baloney and bread and molasses. Since this was a Friday in 1957, and we were Catholic, there would be no baloney for him tonight.

When we all sat down and began eating, I tried again. "It was so gorgeous," I crooned in my best dreamy, singsong voice. "It flares out in the middle, then narrows at the hem. It's called 'the balloon style,' you should have seen it."

"What's all this?" my father asked.

"She's got her eye on a coat," my mother said. I looked at my father hopefully, but all he said was, "Pass the bread and butter."

"I haven't had a new spring coat in years," I persisted. "Annette got a new one last year."

"My old one didn't fit me anymore!" Annette half shrieked, as if I had accused her of something shameful.

"Hurry up and eat your supper," my father told me. "We've got a big night ahead." I hadn't even started my chowder yet. All I could think of was the blue coat and the way it had made me look.

"Honestly, that girl never eats," my father grumbled. "She lives on hopes and cold water."

"Some other people don't know when to stop eating," my mother said, eyeing my father's big stomach. My father's face stiffened and turned a few shades deeper red than usual; the folds on his neck shook like a turkey wattle. "Don't start that again," he said.

Nobody said anything after that. The kitchen filled with slurping sounds. Claude chewed with his mouth open and my mother didn't tell him to close it. I decided that this wouldn't be a good time to tell her how much the coat cost.

Later, while I helped my father load the truck, I kept thinking about the coat. I hadn't had a new coat in ages. Even the old wool jacket I had on wasn't new when I got it. My mother had bought it from an ad in the *Chronicle-Herald,* making me promise never to tell anyone. "No one will know it's not brand-new if you don't tell them," she'd said. The sleeves hovered three inches above my wrists now, but the front still buttoned, so I wore it with my old dungarees when I helped my father. For school, I had a better coat that used to be Annette's.

My father was a wholesaler of confectionery. He had backed his half-ton truck partway into the basement and climbed into the rear cab to rearrange the cartons, putting the candy we sold most of near the doors so we could reach it more easily.

"I'll need six more boxes of chocolate bunnies," he called out, wheezing.

I knew exactly where to find them because every few weeks I straightened out all the candy shelves along the basement walls. When things drifted out of place my father sometimes got confused and ordered things he didn't need. When new shipments came, I unpacked the cartons and put the new boxes in the back to make sure we sold the old ones first.

I handed my father the bunnies. "How about jelly beans? We sold a lot of those last weekend."

He twisted his big body around to face me. "I have some here, but a few more boxes wouldn't hurt." His voice sounded like bones creaking. His face glowed dark red.

After we'd finished loading, my father said, "I don't know what I'd do without you, Nicole." Ever since his heart attack the year before, I had been going in the truck with him on Friday night and all day Saturday to help out, but I knew he meant more than that. Often when my parents quarreled they tried to get us kids to take sides. Sometimes I took my father's side, sometimes my mother's. At that point I didn't care whose side I was on. All I could think of was the beautiful blue coat that I would probably never own.

Our first stop was McDougal's Grocery on the corner of Oxford and Young. My father went in to take the order and I followed him. On Oxford Street I didn't have to sit in the truck and guard it like I did on Gottingen Street.

"I see you've got your good little helper with you," Mr. McDougal said to my father. Mr. McDougal's red hair curled around his face, and he smiled a lot.

"Go get Mr. McDougal two boxes of duck eggs, one of blackballs, and two cartons of potato chips," my father told me.

When I carried in all the boxes at once, Mr. McDougal grinned. "She's just as good as a boy," he said, his green eyes twinkling.

"She's better," my father said. "I'd much rather have her along than *both* her brothers." After a while I forgot about the blue coat.

On Monday morning, at recess, I asked my friend, Joanne: "Are you getting anything new for Easter?" We were shivering in the cold, but the nuns would never let us in before the bell, no matter how cold it got.

"A new skirt and blouse." Joanne had twelve brothers and sisters, and at Easter, Christmas, and just before school started in the fall, her mother ordered them all something new from the Simpson's catalog. "Are you?"

"I don't know. Probably." I thought: it won't be the blue coat, though. I fished out some candy duck eggs from my coat pocket and handed two to Joanne. One of the boxes had broken open during our Saturday rounds so my father said we could eat them.

"I really shouldn't take these," Joanne said, eyeing the eggs in her hand. "I gave up candy for Lent." She put the yellow one in her mouth and chewed it solemnly.

Over Joanne's shoulder I watched Carolyn and Diane talking in a small circle of girls. I imagined them telling each other about their new Easter outfits. Duncan McKenzie and Ronnie Solari, leaning against the school building a few feet away, were watching them, too.

Next to Duncan, with his pink and white complexion, Ronnie's olive skin looked more yellow-brown than ever. Though I tried not to, I remembered the dream I'd had a few weeks before: I was pulling the clothes basket out from under my father's bed to get a blouse I wanted to iron when I found Ronnie, curled up in the basket. He leaped up and started chasing me. Suddenly we were outside, running near the bushes at the end of my street. Then he jumped me, like André did when we fought, and we rolled around on the ground punching and pinching each other. I had him pinned when suddenly the skin on his neck stuck to my hand. I tried to pull my hand loose, but his skin just stretched out, still stuck to me. I couldn't get it off. Ronnie lay still, staring at me with his black eyes, his skin stretching from my hands, all yellowy brown and shiny, like molasses toffee.

I woke up the next morning sweating and nauseous. I hadn't been able to look at Ronnie since then. I made myself look at him hard now, to see what would happen. A thin shiver passed through me.

"Do you want this last egg?" I asked Joanne. "I'm not hungry anymore."

"Okay," she said, and gobbled it down.

"What if I helped pay for it with my allowance?"

My mother had just gotten back from the school in Dartmouth where she substitute taught. She took the trolley and had to transfer twice; I had been waiting for her for over an hour.

"Fifty cents a week will hardly make a difference in a coat

that costs twenty-four dollars and ninety-five cents," she said. I watched her change from her good dress into an old housedress.

"I have five dollars and sixty-five cents saved up from selling greeting cards. You could have that, too." I could feel myself getting dangerously close to throwing myself at her feet and begging.

My mother turned and looked at me strangely. Her lipstick had worn off and her nose was shiny. "You really want that coat a lot, don't you?"

On Easter morning Claude circled the dropleaf table in the living room, staring at the Easter baskets. My father had bought them from the Micmac Indian who sold them door-to-door, saying he felt sorry for him. With their wide strips of purple, yellow, pink and green straw, the little baskets shone on the table like spring bouquets. Along with penny candy from the basement, each basket held a round of maple sugar and a large foil-wrapped, store-bought chocolate bunny.

"Stay away from those baskets," André warned Claude, sounding as though he meant it. Claude, unable to resist, had eaten one of the ears off his bunny. Since he couldn't go to Holy Communion anyway, he was sneaking more bites whenever he could. He grinned at André like a cat, his face white as milk, his hair glossy black. André shoved him hard.

We were supposed to be getting ready for mass. Annette and my mother sat at the round mirror in my father's room, dabbing lipstick on their mouths.

"Claude should have to wait like the rest of us," Annette said to my mother in a low, confidential voice, as if my mother needed her advice.

My mother blotted her lipstick with a Kleenex but didn't answer. Claude was her pet. None of this bothered me, though. Over their shoulders I stared at the girl in the mirror: a girl with a blue coat, a girl with the bluest eyes. I could hardly believe that girl was me.

"Nicole must be cold," Annette remarked to no one in particular. "She's had that coat on for the last half hour." I ignored her.

"You look nice," my father said from the doorway, blinking, as if he were half-surprised.

It took us a long time to get to the church. Though it was only two and a half blocks away, we had to go up a hill and my father walked slowly. The sun warmed our faces, and we admired the yellow and purple crocus in Mrs. Pettipas's front yard. For once, my mother didn't tell my father to hurry up. I held my father's arm as we walked, and noticed how nice my mother's white hat looked against her black hair, how well the cherries on the brim matched her lipstick. By the time we got to the church all the back seats were occupied, so we had to sit near the front where we couldn't see as many people.

Overnight, the church had been transformed. The purple shrouds that had covered the statues all during Lent had disappeared, and huge pots of white lilies gleamed from the altar. Streams of rosy-gold light spilled through the stained-glass windows onto the pews, making everything look fresh and cheerful. The church teemed with people, and it seemed as though everyone was dressed in something bright or new for Easter.

Diane, sitting a few rows back on the other side with her mother, wore a pretty new spring coat. It was cream-colored, with a large collar, but not the new balloon style. As far as I could tell, no one had anything quite like mine. I glanced around again, just to be sure, when I saw Ronnie Solari looking right at me. Other people had noticed me, too. When I went to Communion I felt their eyes. I held my head up and looked straight ahead. I had never felt like that before, never in my whole life. Was this what being pretty felt like?

There was no school on Easter Monday, but on Tuesday I wore my new blue coat. On the way I slowed down to avoid having to walk near Claude and André. When I stopped at the corner to let the cars go by, I felt someone come up behind me. It was Ronnie. "Hi," he said with a smile. The black curls on his forehead jiggled. I watched his yellow neck as he crossed the street, too stunned to move. Ronnie had never spoken to me before.

Later, at recess, Joanne started telling me what her three-year-old sister, Gloria, had done with the hard-boiled eggs on Easter morning. I found it hard to pay attention. My eyes kept wandering over the schoolyard, past the little girls playing jump rope, over to the hoop where the boys were taking turns throwing a basketball. Ronnie was among them.

"What's the matter with you!" Joanne jerked my arm. "You're not even listening."

"I am." I made myself look right at her.

"Well anyway," Joanne continued, "we finally found the eggs under the bed, all squashed, so we had to eat puffed wheat for breakfast instead."

"Hmm." I nodded my head.

"Well, don't you think that's funny?"

"I heard that Ronnie Solari smokes," I said. My eyes had wandered over to the hoops again.

"Who cares! He's a creep anyway."

I studied Ronnie's face, the shadow of dark hair above his thin mouth. "You're right," I said. "He is."

When I got home André was making himself a plate of bread and molasses. The sight of it made my stomach tighten.

The following Friday, my father told me to bring out all the rest of the Easter stuff. "I'll have to sell it half price in order to get rid of it," he said.

"We'll eat it if you don't." I grinned.

"That's just the trouble. You kids already eat more candy than I sell." He took the yellow pencil from behind his ear where it hooked under an arm of his wire-rimmed glasses and started checking things off on a list.

It was cold that evening, so I borrowed a woolen hat from André and pulled it down over my ears. I buttoned up my jacket, but the space between my gloves and sleeves felt raw and bare.

I brought out an armload of duck eggs and put them in the back of the truck. When I leaned over, the left knee of my old dungarees caught on a rusted edge of the truck and tore.

"There probably won't be much business tonight," my father grumbled. "It's been bad all week."

"Oh, don't worry, Dad," I said, and gave him a hug.

Our first stop, as usual, was McDougal's on Oxford Street. As I carried in the order, I got the feeling that someone was watching me, someone who might be getting ready to grab something from the truck when I went inside. I turned to get a better look.

For a split second my eyes caught someone else's. *Ronnie!* He turned and pretended he hadn't seen me. All at once I became aware of my old jacket, my torn dungarees, the ridiculous hat. My face got red-hot, and I almost dropped the chips and ran back to the truck. Ronnie disappeared around the corner, so I hurried into the store.

"It's a good thing you've got that good little helper," Mr. McDougal said. One of his green eyes winked.

For the rest of the evening, I had a hard time concentrating. Twice, I got the orders mixed up and had to go back to the truck for something I forgot. A funny sick feeling hovered at the bottom of my stomach, and I felt alternately hot and cold. My old wool jacket felt heavy, like a dull, flat weight. I picked at the threads around the hole at my knee.

By the time we finished the evening rounds and went home, it was nearly nine o'clock. My father pulled the truck into the basement and closed the big wooden doors from inside. I handed him the iron bar he propped against the doors to keep out thieves.

I had something to tell him but I wasn't sure how.

"Dad," I said, blurting it right out. "I don't want to go in the truck with you anymore."

My father turned around and looked at me. "I thought you liked going." His big hands hung by his side.

"I did," I said, not looking at him. "But I don't want to go anymore. You can get one of the boys to help."

My father didn't say anything right away. His breathing sounded like the wind through the spruce trees, and I knew he was tired. I stared at the hole in my right sneaker. "You know how much I depend on you, Nicole," he said, finally. "I don't want to hear any more of this foolishness." He touched my shoulder.

"It's not foolishness," I said more loudly than I intended, pulling away from him and running up the stairs.

Annette and her friend Babette were in Annette's room across the hall from mine playing records. Jimmy Rodgers was singing "It's Too Wonderful," one of Annette's favorite songs. It always sounded as though he was saying *tits* too wonderful, *tits* too beautiful, something Joanne and I always giggled over. Tonight it didn't seem funny at all. I threw myself on the bed and cried.

* * *

When I came downstairs the next morning my mother had already hooked up the wringer washer to the sink and was sorting out a huge pile of dirty clothes. Annette was busy stripping the bottom sheets from the beds in the boys' room. Later she'd put the top sheets on the bottom and fresh sheets on top. My father stuck his head into the kitchen. He had on his cap with the low brim and his jacket with the raggedy sleeves.

"Hurry up, Nicole," he said. "We've got to get going soon."

"I'm not going, Dad. I told you that last night." I tried to keep my voice firm and even.

"Yes you are, damn-it-all!" he yelled.

My mother stopped sorting clothes and looked up. Annette, with her arms full of sheets, stood with her mouth open.

"No I'm not," I said, buttering my toast.

"Listen," he said. "I'm going to load the truck, and you'd better be ready to go when I'm ready or else!"

I put down my toast, went upstairs to my room and closed the door. My old work clothes lay on the floor where I had left them the night before. I kicked them under the bed and took out a clean pair of slacks and my loafers. Hanging there in my closet, all bright and new, my blue coat seemed to shimmer, making everything else look drab.

"Hey, it's me," Annette said, opening my door. "I have to get your bottom sheet. Are you really not going?"

"That's right." I went to the mirror, half-combed my hair. She whistled under her breath, took my bottom sheet and pillowcase, and left.

A few minutes later I heard my father coming up the stairs. With his hard breathing, the stairway sounded like a wind tunnel. After every few steps he stopped to rest a little, and I could hear his body rubbing the wall by the railing. My father had not come upstairs in a long time. He opened the door to my room and stood there for a moment catching his breath. Except for the fringe of white hair around his head, he looked like an enormous beet.

"Why are you doing this?" he asked. "You know I need your help." His voice was gentle, half-pleading.

"Get one of the boys to help." I heard my own voice, high and tight. "They never do anything around here."

"André and Claude are just about useless," my father said. "I have to tell them how to do every little thing. Please, Nicole, you know that Saturday is my busiest day."

"I'm too old to go with you anymore, Dad." I couldn't bear to look at him.

"Too old? Thirteen is too old?"

"Well Annette is fifteen and you don't make her go."

"Annette," my father said, shaking his head.

Annette had never gone with my father in the truck. I couldn't even imagine her carrying boxes; her big breasts would get in the way.

"Now, look, Nicole—" My father's voice was rising. "Stop this nonsense. Get your jacket on and let's go!" His voice filled the room, and a hard tight spot was forming in my chest. I turned toward the window and looked out over the trees.

My mother had tiptoed up the stairs and stood in the hallway behind my father. "I don't know what's gotten into that girl," my father said. My mother's forehead was wrinkled and her eyes were how they got when one of us was sick. No one said anything for a few moments.

"Well Charles, maybe it *is* time to start taking one of the boys," my mother said finally.

My father shook his head. "Of all days," he said. "The day I go to Spryfield."

They turned and started creaking down the stairs, one step at a time, my father holding on to the rail with one arm, and on to my mother with the other.

The thing in my chest had gotten so hard and heavy I could barely breathe. I wanted to run to my father, tell him I would go. But I was held there, as if by some invisible hand. I listened to my father's breathing, his low mutterings, felt the distance between us widening with each step.

MARGARET MCMULLAN

Lifeguarding

Three years before my father died, my mother left us to go on a thirty-day retreat at the House of Study somewhere in Ontario where we were only to call in case of emergency. I was sixteen.

That was the summer I got my first job as a lifeguard at Ravinia Green Country Club. Management was too cheap to hire more than two guards and since the other guard was a part-time caddie, I was in charge of towels, chaises, and maintaining the pool's pH level all summer long.

My mother left in June. She was already packed the day I came home from my first day of work. My nose was burnt and I couldn't stop touching the new whistle I had hanging from a tricolored string around my neck. My mother was standing in the bedroom, trying to get her wedding ring off. Retreaters weren't supposed to wear any jewelry.

She looked up, angry when she heard me whistle.

"Elizabeth," she said, putting the ring on the bureau in a dish where my father kept his spare cufflinks and his fish-oil pills. "Don't."

She gave me a list of doctors and vets, which cleaners my father preferred for his shirts, and what to tell the bridge ladies if they called.

"Just don't make it sound too Catholic," she said.

Later, my mother told me she just needed time to herself. Time to regroup.

"Regroup from what?" my father asked the night she had explained all this to us.

My mother glared at him across the dinner table and said, "Well, if that's the question, you have certainly given me good reason."

The day she left, my mother took the car my father usually used on weekends for errands. She stopped at the end of the drive near the mailbox to fasten her seat belt and I saw the outline of her in the dirty back window energetically rearranging itself in the driver's seat. The House of Study was some retreat house on the White River she could only get to by car. It was about a two-day drive. She readjusted the rearview mirror. Sister Haggels once told our homeroom that God didn't appreciate angry prayers. So I stood at the end of the drive and remained calm, hoping someone up there was taking note.

That night I made salmon and new potatoes so my father wouldn't panic. We talked about serum cholesterol and what he had for lunch. My father had flunked a stress test the year before, so we quit eating meat and eggs and started sautéing everything in olive oil. At dinner, we usually talked a lot about what we didn't miss.

After dinner someone from my mother's bridge group called during *Crime Stories*. I didn't know what to say. She's gone sounded too permanent. She left for a little while sounded as if there was a problem. What the hell was my mother doing anyway? From the phone, I watched my father watching a detective on TV.

"She went to her high school reunion," I said, and I could feel my father listening. When I hung up, he turned off the TV and everything got too quiet.

"Looks like it's beer-thirty," my father said, getting a beer from the refrigerator.

In the kitchen light, his blond hair looked grayer. He had always been a tall, thin, athletic-looking man. My cousin thought he looked like JFK. My father's brother sometimes called him Chicken Legs.

We stood at the counter listening to the water filling up in the freezer's ice maker. It was so quiet, it seemed like I should turn the TV on again. I switched the dishwasher on instead.

"Can you believe this?" he said.

He went to his room, where he called for me to come and help him pick a tie. Every night my father laid out what he would wear the next day. When I got to his room, he already had a gray suit on the chaise, a pink shirt, and two ties.

"Which one?" he asked. He stood in his stocking feet, arms crossed, his hands tucked under his armpits. My mother had told me about the pharmacy and the cleaners. She'd left her bank card number, her pesto and her vinaigrette recipes, but she hadn't shown me how to pick out my father's ties.

"That one," I said, pointing to the paisley.

He held it up next to a maroon one, nodded, put the paisley one away in his top drawer, and dropped the maroon one down on top of the shirt.

That night I lay in bed listening to the radio my father wouldn't turn off in his room. My mother liked to take long hot showers before she went to bed at night and I would often fall asleep to the sound of water and wake up with a start when she called out my father's name.

"David," she would say, still in the bathroom. "I love you poodle cat."

I had always wanted to be a lifeguard. "It's not enough to just watch," Ms. Clotfelter always told us in gym. "You've got to focus." On the last day of gym, Ms. Clotfelter challenged us. The first to save her got the certificate a week ahead of everybody else, which meant you got first crack at the coveted lifeguarding jobs around town. She put on extra sweats and sneakers and jumped into the deep end of our high school pool. Ms. Clotfelter had warned us about aggressive victims, the ones who panic and fight off people who try to save them. Ms. Clotfelter fought. Most of the girls in my class gave up and swam away. Mary Anne said she wanted to work in town at BonWits anyway, for the discounts. Mimi said the whole thing was just too gross: Clotfelter was a fat old dyke getting off on all this underwater touchy feely stuff. But I just treaded water, and waited. Waited until her Reeboks started to pull her under, waited until she came up for air less frequently and her hands didn't close into fists but spread out open trying to grab for help. That's when I took hold of Ms. Clotfelter by the jawbone, flipped her head back into the air, rested her lower back on my hip, and lugged her in.

From my chair at Ravinia Green, I watched mothers watching their sons and daughters dive from the high dive. At lunch the mothers congregated and went upstairs to the outside patio or ordered down and ate chicken salad scattered with walnuts and grapes, while the sons and daughters were allowed platters of burgers and fries. I watched young girls comb out wet knots and tangles from their hair and I tried to figure out reasons to call my mother: I was found terminally ill, she *had* to come home; Chloe bit out at a car and it ran her over. Every year in January, the day after New Year's, my father took my mother and me to a dude ranch in Arizona. My father and I played tennis and hiked around the foothills on Vulture Mine Road while my mother stayed in the casita and read. "I'm not an outdoors person," she told us once at lunch. "I'm a contemplative. I was meant to read books, eat cookies, and pray." It was a joke among the three of us. Whenever we caught her staring out the window, off into the desert, I would say, "Hey Mom. Being contemplative?" And she would say "Yeah, hand me a cookie." I liked those vacations. On the plane home, I sat between my parents, buckled up the whole way.

One morning a week later I woke up smelling sausage and eggs frying and I thought at first my mother had come home. My father was in the kitchen at the stove. Chloe stood bent over her bowl, finishing off the lentil casserole I'd made the night before.

"It's raining," he said. "You don't have to work and you know what?" He turned around and faced me. He was wearing the tie I had picked. He loosened it. "I don't either."

"Good," I said. "But let me make some oatmeal. You'll feel better."

"I'm not sick," he said. His voice was louder than either one of us had expected. He stuck a fork into one of the sausage patties, split it in the pan, and held out a piece to me. I took it off the fork.

"Hot," I said, and after I ate it I asked for more.

We went to the movies. We ate popcorn with butter and then we went shopping. He bought me a winter coat at Eddie Bauer and he got himself a cowboy hat. For Arizona, he said. We took a long drive down Lake Shore Drive and stopped at the beach. It had stopped raining but the lake was rough and when we rolled our pants up, the water was freezing and our toes turned white.

"Ever skip a rock?" my father asked, bending down to pick up a flat stone.

"You can't skip one in this lake. It's too rough."

"You think you know it all, Miss Smarty, don't you." He was kidding, but still, I was embarrassed. It had been a great day and I didn't want to blow it. He threw the rock. It sank. We looked at each other and then we laughed. He put his hand on my shoulder and together we stood there, looking out at the water.

"Well, shit," he said, joking, squeezing me closer to him.

One hot Saturday afternoon in mid-June Chloe strained on her leash while we walked and I lectured my father on beans, wheat germ, and Pritikin.

"Pritikin's dead," he said.

"I know, but when they opened his heart, it was clean as a baby's."

"Lot a good that's doing him now.

"If Mom were here, she'd be twenty yards back," he said when we reached the stop sign.

"If Mom were here, she wouldn't be here," I said, and my father laughed.

A woman walked toward us, her poodle leaning against his leash. My mother knew this woman. She had been a fat wife of a doctor when one day something came over her and she started getting up at dawn to take the train into Chicago to bake bread. She lost thirty pounds, divorced the doctor—she had money of her own—and started going to dinner parties alone. Everyone knew about her.

As we got closer, I noticed how short the woman's khakis were and that her shirt was made out of some Indian gauze which you could see right through.

"May I pet your Chessy?" the woman said.

"Beg pardon?" my father said.

"She is a Chesapeake Bay retriever, isn't she? May I pet her?" the woman said.

"Careful," I said. "Pet her the wrong way and she'll bite."

The woman laughed and bent down to pick up her dog. "Oh no," she said in a stupid coo coo voice. "Not my Little Chessy."

Her hair fell out of whatever was holding it back, and nearly tented the three of them. Chloe was beside herself, wagging her tail, and I was appalled when she jumped up and licked the woman's face.

"Whoa," my father said, taking the leash from my hand. The woman's hair grazed his knuckles as she flipped it back.

"You can bet you made her day," my father said. I called for Chloe but she was too busy with the poodle's particulars.

"I saw your wife with Father McGill just the other day," the woman said, looking up at my father.

My father looked at her and said wasn't it funny about priests. "What kind of guy marries God?" he said.

The woman laughed.

"I hadn't even realized your wife was Catholic."

"Well, *I'm* not," my father said.

I took the leash from my father. "I think she's ready to turn back now, Dad."

"Is that right?" my father said, looking at me like he was noticing me for the first time. "I guess she can just cool it."

We shopped at Janowitz that afternoon because my father didn't like the produce at Sunset. We were making vegetarian chili. My father wandered off somewhere between Pasta and Baking Needs while I picked peppers. When I went off looking for decaf, I found him standing next to the Archway cookies.

"There you are," I shouted. As I pushed my cart toward him, I saw the poodle in the woman's basket-purse.

"Elizabeth," my father said. "You remember Mrs. Fells."

"Monica," the woman said.

"We don't do Archway, Dad. They're not safe." I looked at Monica Fells. "Too high in cholesterol."

"Maybe Elizabeth would like to come along," Monica Fells said.

"Maybe," my father said, looking at me. I looked at the two of them and, wondering if this was a prearranged chance meeting, squeezed my grocery cart between them.

"Dad," I said. "Chloe's waiting."

I overcooked the chili, and afterwards my father left the table and came back with two beach towels.

"They don't allow dogs on the beach," I said.

"We're not going to the beach," he said. "We're going to the Rec Center."

The basketball court on the second floor smelled of the shoes and socks everybody was taking off. We spread out our towels at back center while my father went on and on about how great yoga was going to be for his blood pressure and his heart rate. When I looked up and saw who our instructor was I asked my father if this was some kind of a joke.

"She invited us," he said.

It was Monica Fells.

The court filled up and she instructed us on how to stretch. The man next to me wore bright red spandex bike-riding pants. They stretched over his beer gut like a girdle, and when he bent to touch his toes, gold necklaces fell out from under his sweatshirt, lacing the tip of his nose. He swung over and touched the wrong ankle, and we knocked heads.

"Excuse me," he said. "Pardon me."

Monica told us that yoga came from yug. She wrote the word on the chalkboard behind her. She pronounced it yuk. It meant yoke.

"That means joining together," she said, holding her hands pressed together. I swear she looked at my father.

"Cut it out," I said, under my breath.

"What!" my father whispered back.

We did a lot of neck rolls and leg bends while Monica spoke of centering and breathing through our stomachs. Then she taught us our first asana.

"Make like a corpse," she said. "Lie down flat."

Spandex Man burped beside me.

"Excuse me," he said. "Pardon me."

"Close your eyes," Monica said. "Concentrate. Your solar plexus is warm. You are on the beach. Picture yourself on the beach."

My father lay palms up beside me. Monica said to say Om, only if it helped. Spandex Man hummed it once and then gave up. My father began to snore. When I looked over, he twitched and then woke up with a start.

We ate nonfat frozen yogurt in the car afterwards. Peach was the flavor of the day.

"It's not exactly aerobic," I said, licking the yogurt before it could drip down the cone to my hand. "But it's a lot like those weekend retreats at St. Patrick's except that your knees don't hurt from kneeling and you don't have to listen to Sister Calhoun playing all those bad guitar songs." With my free hand I strummed an imaginary guitar and sang fast and off-key. "Allelu, allelu! Ev'rybody sing, allelu!"

"Why do they always put you on a damned beach?" my father said. "Why not the mountains or the desert?"

I got to the cone and bit in. "So go there instead."

He told me he'd fallen asleep and that he'd had a dream. There was a meeting, he said, at his firm and I was there. In his dream I stood up, shuffling through all of these notecards. I gave a speech. I was resigning from the firm. My father said he stood up and tried to convince me to stay, but he couldn't talk me out of it. He was already at his cone, which he bit into while I rolled down the window.

"Don't you just hate when you get all worked up over a really stupid dream?" he said and then he laughed and started the car.

"Don't worry, Dad," I said, buckling my seat belt. "I'm not going to resign."

I fooled myself into believing that my father was taking more interest in the asanas than he was in Monica and any time she pressed her hands together and gave him this meaningful yami yami look, I threatened my father with a resignation.

One night after class, she followed us down to the car with a plate of something.

"It's banana bread," she said. "I love to bake."

My father went on and on about how he didn't know when the last time was that he had a piece of banana bread.

I waited in the car. I watched my father with Monica, the banana bread between them. I rolled down the car window and I thought I heard her say something about the full moon and how it was shifting the water in her brain. She put her hand on his arm. He didn't move away.

When we got home, I got a knife out and asked my father if I could cut him a piece of Monica's bread.

"Na," he said. "I hate that shit."

I gave Chloe a slice and didn't stop her when she put her front paws on the counter and made off with the rest.

I caught a virus I just knew had to have come from that one

time I dove into the kiddy pool after some bubble gum a five-year-old dropped. I couldn't go to yoga.

"Are you sure you'll be all right without me?" I asked my father.

"I'm fine." He carried the one beach towel out to the car. "I just won't use a partner when we do that push-pull thing."

There wasn't anything good on TV so I went into the study and looked through my mother's journals. Her writing was nearly impossible to read. They were spiritual diaries—a lot of passages on sunlight and divine love—so I didn't feel as guilty as I would have if they had been, say, diary diaries. She kept them all on a lower bookshelf in the study, where she prayed in the early morning or late in the afternoon before she picked my father up at the train station. She always kept the door closed. A priest once told her nobody could pray with a dog in the room.

The study was the coldest room in the house and one of the walls was lined with books, history mostly, from when my mother was in graduate school. She kept all the holy titles and her journals in the lower shelves behind the sofa, out of view, because, she once told me, she didn't want anyone to get the wrong idea.

"In another life," she wrote sometime the year before, "I would have been a nun." The thought sickened me. Nuns didn't wash their hair. They ate Rice Krispies treats and always wanted you to "share" your thoughts with them. They were irrational: they'd kick you out of French class if you unplugged the projector the wrong way. I put the journal away and pulled out one with an entry dated a month before my mother left. I turned to the last page. It was blank but for two lines. Blue rug changes to yellow, it said. Consolation without cause. St. Ignatius.

Four years ago, when she was going through the spiritual exercises with a priest from Loyola, she read me excerpts from her notebook at the kitchen table every day after school.

"In this one," she said one afternoon, "you have to imagine your own funeral. What do you think we should serve?"

"But what's the point?" I asked her. "What are you trying to get to?"

"That's a good question," she said, putting away her journal. She loved when somebody took an interest in all her meditating. My father never did. "A stronger love with God. A mystical experience. Usually the strength you gain from your prayer kind of spills over in your own life."

I hated when she talked that way. She sounded like Sister Haggels in homeroom.

"What happens when you have a mystical experience?"

"I'm not sure. I haven't had one yet but there's a oneness. I've heard that you lose track of time. Things in the room can move around."

Months after that my mother thought she had a mystical experience. Right afterwards, she told me how the sofa shook, and how the books in the bookcases trembled. She said she could even hear the cups rattling together in the kitchen cabinet. All day that day she had all this energy and her face seemed luminous. She told my father at dinner that night and he laughed. That hadn't been God talking to her, he said. It was an earth tremor; it had been in the paper that afternoon.

I stared down at the passage where the rug changed color. We didn't have a blue rug. I wondered where she had been. I wanted to run and tell my father. I was so proud of my mother. I wanted to call the House of Study in Ontario and ask her things—was the rug still yellow? Consolation without cause made it sound so insignificant. Wasn't it significant? I wondered if what she told priests was very different from what she told me. I wondered if her questions were smart. I never had any good ecumenical insights. I saw Sister Haggels in the sacristy once after mass, guzzling down the rest of the wine along with a bag of marshmallows. At confession the next day, I asked Father Pickle—that's what I called him, his real name was Vlasic—how nuns hooked on junk food could lecture us on conspicuous consumption. I never did get an answer.

I tried calling the number my mother had left. A woman answered the phone and I could tell by the quiet, queer way she said, "Good Evening, House of Study," that it was a nun. I asked for my mother. She said those in retreat weren't allowed to accept calls.

"But I can take a message," she said. I thought about how greasy her hair probably was. I thought about what kind of crap she had had for dinner—a casserole most likely, with potato chips crumbled over.

"No, thanks," I said. "And please. Don't tell her I called."

In the kitchen Chloe sat near the refrigerator. I lay down beside her, my head on her belly. I could hear her heart beat. I tried to concentrate on my mother and her praying and making all of the rugs in the House of Study change color, because then maybe she would come back to us.

"O.K. now, Chloe. Focus," I said. "Picture yourself on a beach."

And I did, and I saw a starfish, and I bent over to pick it up. My toes wiggled, making little ditches in the sand. Warm, foamy waves washed over them. I held the starfish up for my mother and father to see, but when I turned around nobody, not even my father, was there.

When I woke up, my father stood over Chloe and me with a plate of bread. Chloe got up and jumped for it.

"Whole wheat," he said with a smile.

I looked at the clock on the stove. He was over two and a half hours late and when I looked at him, he looked guilty as hell.

"I don't believe this," I said.

"Mind your own business," he said, walking away.

"This is my business," I said, but then I thought about him and that woman and my mother in some cabin praying her brains out, and I felt sick.

"A month just isn't that long, Dad."

He looked down at his shoes and then up at me again.

"Is that right?"

"Goddamn," I shouted. Chloe barked. "No wonder she left. It's just no damn wonder."

"Watch your mouth," he said.

At the club, a skinny, pimply boy found out I went to an all-girls Catholic school, and in addition to shouting "Virgin!" each time he passed my chair, he took to jumping up and down on the high dive and calling me Hairy Toes.

"Hey, Hairy Toes," he shouted one afternoon. He wouldn't come down, even after I whistled. Finally his mother heard all the ruckus and started yelling for him to get the hell down from there. Then she made him come and apologize to me. I came down from my chair. The kid stared up at me, hating me.

"Sorry you're a virgin," he said and he made a grab for my breast and ran into the men's room shouting, "I touched her boob! I touched Hairy Toes' boob!"

That summer I found out what a lonely occupation lifeguarding really is. It just wasn't as glamorous as I had pictured it. I spent more time up in the chair. Some days, I only came down for lunch or for more nose cream.

The following Sunday we didn't go to class because my father felt nauseous.

"It was the sesame noodles," I said. "I put too much garlic in them."

I put Chloe up and my father fell into bed without laying out a suit or a tie.

I woke up hearing Chloe barking in the kitchen.

" 'Lizbeth?"

I thought he might be having another dream.

"It's just Chloe, Dad."

"Come in here."

The moon cast a blue-white light over my father. His sheet was wadded up next to his ankles and I was embarrassed at how thin they looked. His pajama-top collar was unbuttoned and his hand lay still there on his chest, his long fingers hidden under the fabric.

"I think this is it," he said. His voice was lower. He was breathless. He touched his brow. He was sweating. "Don't leave me. I'm so ashamed. I'm so scared. I don't know what I should do."

I ran to the kitchen to call the paramedics because I didn't want him to hear me sound urgent or rushed.

"Don't make any noise," I said to them. "And don't use all those lights."

When I came back to him, he was making his way down the hall, his hands pressed against the walls. In the moonlight, he was completely white. There were deep, dark circles under his eyes. Outside the trees cast shadows on the windows, their branches like dark arms reaching out toward my father.

"I didn't know where you were," he said.

"I'm right here, Dad," I said, putting his arm around my neck. "Hold on. Just hold on. I'm not going anywhere."

I led him into my room. I sat him on the bed. His hands were cold and clammy as though death itself were creeping into him through his fingernails. He hunched over right then and clutched at his chest.

"One to ten," I said. "How bad is it?"

"Fifteen."

He shivered and I tried to cover him with my bedspread. His whole body shook and he held my hand.

"I'm glad you're here," he said.

He shook again, uncontrollably, and with his other hand he held on to the antique prayer chair my mother and I had picked up at a house sale a few years back. I used it as a nightstand. On it lay my nose cream and my whistle.

"Tell Mom I love her," he said.

"Come on, Dad. Focus."

He was staring at my whistle. I rubbed his hand in mine, to get his solar plexus warm.

"I love you," he said.

"Picture yourself on a beach."

"Who should we be calling?" my father asked. He didn't have on a gown, because the nurse had just come in and painted a trinity of black X's on his chest, one over his heart. He was eating the Irish oatmeal and cinnamon raisin Happiness bread I had sneaked in. The kitchen always messed up and gave him scrambled eggs and full glasses of two percent.

His heart attack had weakened him and Dr. Pollard said he needed a few days' rest in ICU to get his strength up for a heart bypass.

When I called the House of Study in Ontario, the morning after my father's attack, I got the same quiet nun.

"Look," I shouted into the receiver. "Her husband's just had a heart attack."

"I can take a message," she said. My only consolation was that the Rice Krispies treat she probably held poised in front of her very thin, very chapped lips would soon clog up her chaste little arteries.

I told my father again that I just knew my mother would appear at the hospital doorway any minute.

"Any time she could sail in, and she'll call you a poodle cat in front of everybody."

My father put his spoon back down in his cereal bowl so quietly, so carefully, that I thought, right then, he was giving up.

"What should I bring you?" I asked him. "What do you want to wear when you leave?"

He looked at me. He tried to slip his finger under the plastic identification bracelet around his wrist but he couldn't. It was too tight and for a moment I had a thought that he would never leave that hospital.

I called for the nurse.

"Can we get that thing off him?" I asked when she came in. She looked at me. My voice was loud and shrieky. "They put it on way too tight," I tried to explain.

Dr. Pollard came in that night to go over the procedure.

"Show me," I said, giving him one of my father's unused napkins. He took his pen from his coat pocket and drew out a map of my father's heart. He showed us where the arterial blockage was.

"That's what's causing all the damage," he said. My father and I leaned back, looking at one another.

"How will he feel afterwards?" I asked.

"Sore," Dr. Pollard said and then he left.

"This is the pits," my father said.

"I know. They should have a radio."

A man down the hall moaned. His Gods came out Cods. "Oh Cod. Oh Cod," he said over and over, and it was so terrible my father and I laughed.

"Promise me one thing," he said. "Promise me you won't tell Mom."

I knew what he meant. I hadn't considered not telling my mother everything that had happened while she was away. I looked at my father. He hadn't shaved in two days and his beard was coming out gray and white.

"OK," I said. "But you have to make some promises too."

Early the next morning, I held my father's big toe all the way to the elevators that led to surgery. The orderly pushing him pressed the Up button and we waited. His toe was cold through the sheet and I put my hands around both his feet, hoping he could feel my warmth.

"You're doing great," I kept telling him. He was groggy from the shot they had already given him. He wasn't looking at me. He was looking at the hospital ceiling.

"Anytime you're ready," he said to the orderly. "Don't wanna be late. They're gonna cut me open this morning, then they're gonna plug me in."

The man nodded and rolled him into the elevator. "I'll see you in a little while," I said. "Mom and me both. We'll see you." He used his arm to prop his head up and I made a thumbs-up sign. He wasn't looking at me though. His eyes went past me and all around me. Focus, I thought. He wasn't focusing. I was still holding on to his toe. I was grateful that the sheet was there so that he couldn't feel how cold and clammy my hands were. I squeezed his whole foot. I didn't want to let go. The elevator doors started to close. I had to release his foot. The doors shut and then, all at once, he was gone.

The waiting room was painted with trees, squirrels, and a deer. I couldn't read any of the old magazines. I stared down at the map Dr. Pollard had drawn. I was glad I had it. I just wished Dr. Pollard hadn't drawn the clots in ink. With my thumbnail, I traced the bypass lines in the left ventricle that led away from my father's blocked artery. Focus, I thought. I took a felt-tipped pen from my purse and drew over the lines that I thought looked too thin and flimsy. I made the bypass thicker and stronger. I reinforced where the lines hooked up to the heart itself and filled in the spaces where Dr. Pollard's pen had given out. I made it so that there wasn't one kink or gap in my father's heart.

When it was time, a nurse led me into a room with old men spread out on steel tables. They looked dead. My father was one of those men and I didn't recognize him at first. He looked grayer and skeletal. His chest was painted with yellow-brown iodine and three tubes, one the size of a garden hose, the others telephone cords, were running out of his belly and chest and into a monitor that hummed near the table on which he lay.

I had to leave the room. Come on now, focus. Picture yourself on a beach. I leaned my head against the wall and when I turned around I saw my mother.

She was wearing a yellow linen dress and it wasn't even wrinkled. I had on cutoffs. When I smelled her perfume, I realized how much I smelled of hospital and chlorine. Her eyes were so clear and her skin so luminous at first, I wasn't sure at all that I wasn't looking at an airbrushed photo of an angel. Later, she would tell me that she had gotten pulled over in Racine. Bad weather had slowed her down through Michigan and she had been trying to make up the lost time. When she explained to the officer why she was speeding, he'd driven her to the hospital while she changed in the backseat. She had wanted to look good for my father. "Well," I said. "You should get his old ticker started again."

"Elizabeth," she said, putting on lipstick. "Don't be so crude."

My father didn't look so bad the second time around and I searched for his hand amid all the tubes. Yellow iodine had dribbled down from his chest to his palm and his fingers were still icy.

My mother brushed a wisp of hair away from his temple. I tried not to notice how gray and thin he looked or how old he seemed.

I watched his monitor and listened for any irregularities in his breathing. The guy on the next table looked two times my father's age but he was bigger and I wondered if that was better or worse. I wondered if my father hurt. I wondered if he was fixed.

Now, when I go through old photo albums, I hunt for pictures where my father's color looked bad. Here, I think, here's where his heart was acting up. Here's where things weren't running smoothly.

I looked at my mother. She was crying and putting on more lipstick.

"Lord, I must look awful," she said.

"Mom," I whispered and she looked up at me. I nodded toward my father. "Take his other hand."

JOHN DEVALCOURT

Indelible Mark

"You're a Catholic, ain't ya?"

How could Jaybo know that, Jimmy Babin wondered, hunching his shoulders and shrinking even farther down in his seat. He was sure it didn't show, he had never talked about this with any of the school kids, especially those who got on the bus at Hooker's Point, and he absolutely had never made the Sign of the Cross when the bus passed the Catholic church on the way to school, even though he knew he was supposed to do it and his mother would be mad at him if she found out he didn't.

Jaybo Norton had a way of embarrassing him, and he was sure his red face was showing. Jimmy remembered the day school started, less than a month ago. He had been first on the bus after it stopped near the sugar mill, and then Jaybo had been the next to get on at Hooker's Point. With plenty of seats to choose from, Jaybo had sat down beside him. Jimmy knew not to say anything first. His mother had told him that the people in Hooker's Point were common. There were also no Catholics there. He knew this himself because there were only about fifty Catholics in the whole town of Hendry and he had already met all the Catholic kids at Mass that first Sunday after they had moved. None of them lived in Hooker's Point.

Jaybo didn't say anything more for some minutes but then he leaned over and asked, "Can you say 'foolish it' real fast ten times?"

Jimmy's face turned redder, his throat tightened and he knew instantly that he was stuck. He suspected something, but if he didn't say anything, Jaybo might get mad at him. Jimmy was shy enough, but moving to Florida just before first grade started made it even worse. And Jaybo was surrounded by others who had got on with him. The bus grew silent as he compliantly choked out the words as fast as he could. After he had said it five times everyone on the bus was laughing and Jimmy still hadn't caught on.

Jimmy withdrew inside himself. He didn't know why it was so important, but it seemed that on the whole trip from Louisiana to Florida all his mother could talk about was that there wasn't a Catholic school in Hendry, or in the whole county for that matter, and that he would have to study catechism with the Sisters from Palm Beach every Saturday. Listening to her, you would think that was the most important thing about this whole move and not that his daddy had got a better job and would be home more often. If Uncle Doane, Aunt Dolie and his cousins hadn't already been in Hendry for a couple of years to make it safer for them to move, Jimmy doubted if they ever would have gone, job or no job, simply because there weren't enough Catholics there to satisfy his mother.

Jimmy hadn't known what to expect in Florida, except no Catholics, but when they drove up that hot August day in 1941 to the back door of his cousins' house and he burst out of the car, stepping barefooted into the rich black soil, he got another idea of his mother's impression of their new home.

"That isn't dirt, it's muck," she said, her first words stating clearly what the enemy was and establishing her opposition to it before she even got out of the car. Jimmy saw that same look on her face that she had in the car earlier when she talked about public schools, saying that it was a mortal sin not to send your children to a Catholic school unless there was no other choice. It was the look which came before his daddy's long silences. It was a look to which no response was possible, so no response was ever given.

The muck, it turned out, was the reason there was sugar cane in all directions, right up to the road next to the house. It was the reason the sugar mill a mile away was the largest in the

United States. It was the reason his daddy had a year-round job, unlike in Louisiana, where sugar workers had a job for only six months a year, forcing his Daddy to be a "sugar tramp," following the crops in the Caribbean every winter. But to Jimmy's mother, it was still muck. From that first day, he had known they never were going to fit in Florida. Now, sitting next to Jaybo, it was just more obvious.

"Yeah, I am," Jimmy whispered, wondering why the bus was taking so long to get to school that morning.

"You're what?" Jaybo retorted, by now having forgotten his opening question.

"A Catholic."

"Can I see your feet?" Jaybo quickly countered, before Jimmy had even finished the last word.

Jaybo's face was lit up with anticipation, of what Jimmy had no idea, but it didn't look good.

"Why do you want to see my feet? You want me to take my shoes off right here on the bus?"

"If you're a Catholic, you have cloven hoofs. It says so in the Bible."

Jimmy was pretty sure there was nothing wrong with his feet, even though he had no idea exactly what a cloven hoof was. After all, he had gone barefooted every year from the first day of spring until his birthday in October, his mother setting the dates as a way of limiting what could have gone on even longer. Florida was even hotter than Louisiana, and while it was also dirtier, his mother had reluctantly agreed to continue this practice and let him remove his shoes the moment he got off the bus after school and run barefooted the rest of the way home.

"I don't have hoofs," Jimmy said, feeling a little bolder.

"If you're a Catholic, you can never get married," Jaybo shot back.

Jaybo seemed to have a lot of ammunition, but Jimmy was beginning to feel better, because it appeared to be coming from some wild place. Didn't Jaybo know that he had parents and that they were married and they were Catholic? What could he be talking about?"

"If you're a Catholic, they're gonna cut off your hair when you get to be thirteen."

Jaybo wouldn't let up. He had swallowed a dose of something and it was all coming up now. Jimmy sat there, not saying a word. What could he say? None of it made any sense. It's true his daddy was bald, but not because somebody had cut his hair off when he was thirteen. He told everyone it was from wearing a helmet for too long in the war.

At last the bus pulled up to Hendry Elementary and Jimmy jumped off first, hoping to outrun both Jaybo and his questions.

After supper that night, Jimmy's mother told him that none of those things Jaybo had said were true, that the Catholic Bible said nothing about cloven hoofs, and if Jaybo's Bible did, then that was because Protestants didn't have the Pope to guarantee that their Bible had the right words in it.

In bed, Jimmy's eyes closed as he heard his parents talking in the next room. He heard his mother say "Muck" several times and saw in his mind the picture of the black circle in the catechism book that showed what mortal sin looked like. Venial sin was just a few little black spots on a mostly white circle, but mortal sin was all black. Mortal sin must be like muck, Jimmy thought as he fell asleep; they both brought about that same look on his mother's face.

"Sweetheart, I'm starting to worry about Jimmy. It's bad enough he runs around barefooted all day, but he's taken to scratching and pulling at himself. I'm afraid if he keeps it up he'll start playing with himself."

"Well, he can hardly help playing by himself. His cousins live a mile way and he hasn't got any other kids his age nearby."

"I didn't say by himself. I said with himself. I'm worried we made the wrong decision when we decided not to have him circumcised. I know Dr. Saucier said it wasn't necessary, but he didn't know we'd be moving to Florida. This muck just sticks to everything. Have you given Jimmy a bath lately? He's been scratching so much lately around his penis I don't know if he has a rash or if he's just made himself red all over. I think it might not be clean inside and that's why he's scratching all the time. I need help."

Jimmy's father leaned back and took a deep breath, as though he had been waiting a long time for this topic to come up. He himself was circumcised but he had never been able to think of a good reason for doing it. Most of the men he knew were not, he had never heard a single one complain, and at Jimmy's birth he had insisted there was no good reason for circumcising his son.

"I know you've been reading up on circumcision, but you know what I think? I think it's the Army. We're probably going to go to war with Japan and be fighting on tropical islands in the Pacific before too long. The Army wants soldiers to be circumcised so they won't get diseases when they can't wash for days at a time. That's why you hear doctors recommending circumcision. The Army's behind it."

"Well, that just makes me feel even more that we made a mistake. Here we are practically living in the tropics and I give Jimmy a bath every day and he's still scratching. Dolie told me both of her kids had impetigo for most of the summer. I'm going to write to Dr. Saucier and ask him what he thinks. I'm just afraid if we don't do something now it'll just get worse."

Jimmy's father didn't respond, which he knew would be taken as agreement. He didn't want to say anything because he was sure his wife was really afraid of masturbation. She had brought this up since Jimmy had started fondling himself almost as soon as he was out of diapers. He could never get anywhere when she started on this. He'd just wait and see what Dr. Saucier said. The man had agreed with him when Jimmy was born. Maybe he'd still feel the same way.

By the time he got on the bus the next morning, Jimmy had figured out how Jaybo knew he was the only Catholic in the class. It had something to do with the Lord's Prayer. He remembered how surprised he was that first morning when, after saying it, his teacher and the whole class didn't stop at the end, but kept on, adding "for Thine is the kingdom, and the power, and the glory, for ever and ever. Amen." Jimmy had never heard those words before, and when he told his mother, she called Father O'Riley, who told her that Jimmy should just bow his head and say nothing after "but deliver us from evil." Those other words were not Catholic words, and he shouldn't say them. After the Lord's Prayer, the teacher then led the class every morning in reciting the Twenty-third Psalm, "The Lord is my shepherd." Jimmy had never heard this either, and Father

O'Riley said it wasn't the Twenty-third, it was the Twenty-second, but he could say it anyway. That had to be how Jaybo found out he was a Catholic, Jimmy thought. It was when he shut his mouth after "deliver us from evil" and kept his head down.

But Jaybo didn't want to talk about Catholics today. He wanted to talk about dicks and about how Janice Barton sometimes didn't wear underpants because she was too poor. As he listened, Jimmy was glad his mother hadn't met Jaybo. If she had, she would probably want to drive him to school every day herself, and then he would not only be the one Catholic in the class, but the only boy whose mother brought him to school. Even sitting next to Jaybo was better than that.

Because it was the weekend before his sixth birthday when his mother announced that they were going to Palm Beach, Jimmy figured it was to get him that machine gun he had seen in the *Miami Herald* that was for sale at Montgomery Ward's. No store in Hendry would have it, he was sure. His mother had not been to Palm Beach since August, when they went to buy new school clothes. Because shopping was the only thing that would make her travel sixty miles on a weekend, Jimmy felt relaxed enough to doze, ignoring the look on his mother's face and his father's silence, both unbroken since they had gotten into the car.

When they jerked to a stop, Jimmy awoke to see that they were in a parking lot next to a large building in what had to be Palm Beach. He thought it was funny that although the building was large enough to be a department store, there were no toys in the windows. In fact, there were no goods at all in the windows. It wasn't until they stepped inside and he saw a nun that he realized it was not a store. This nun was not like the ones who came from Palm Beach to teach catechism on Saturdays. She wore a stiff white headdress that looked like a large paper airplane. Jimmy guessed that his mother must have somehow found a Catholic school that was worth their driving all the way to Palm Beach. They must be making up for the catechism lesson he was missing back in Hendry.

He sat quietly on a sofa with his father while his mother talked to the nun. Then they all got into an elevator, went upstairs and were led down a long corridor. After they entered an empty room with a bed in it, the nun turned and said, "This is where you'll be spending the night. You should be able to go home with your mom and dad in the morning. Everything's going to be fine." As soon as he realized she was speaking to him, Jimmy's heart started beating so fast his ears didn't seem to work, and he struggled to understand just what she meant. But it was now clear that this was not a school either. It was a hospital and he was going to be staying in it. It was just as clear that this trip had nothing to do with his birthday at all.

Jimmy's parents hadn't said anything about going to a hospital in Palm Beach. He hadn't been sick once since they moved to Florida and couldn't imagine what was wrong. His fears did not diminish when his mother turned to him and said, "Do you remember Dr. Saucier from Louisiana? He's changed his mind about something we should have done when you were born and we want to do something about it now before it gets worse. You'll feel a lot better afterwards and it won't even hurt because the doctor will put you fast asleep and you won't wake up until tomorrow morning when it's all over. Then we can go home."

The uncontrollable dread that had settled in Jimmy's stomach became even worse when his mother undressed him completely and put a thin hospital gown on his naked body. As she laid him in the bed Jimmy turned to her and asked nervously. "What's going to happen to me?"

"Don't worry. It's something that happens to most boys. It will make you feel better later on." As Jimmy's mother sat in the chair next to his bed, his father took his hand for a few seconds and then left the room without saying anything.

When he returned a few minutes later, he handed Jimmy a comic book. "I bought you this in the dime store across the street. It's the newest issue of Action Comics, with Superman on the cover."

Jimmy took it without a smile, because he knew his father hated comic books. This gift was just one more sign that something unusual was going to happen here.

Jimmy hadn't finished leafing through the comic book when a nurse wheeled a cart into the room and, while his parents watched silently, covered his nose with a rubber cup, asking him to breathe in deeply and saying he would be asleep before she got to ten. "One, two, three . . ." As Jimmy's eyes closed, he was surprised to find himself in an airplane. A young woman in uniform strapped him into his seat as they took off into the clouds.

Jimmy's mother was holding his hand when he awoke, his father looking on over her shoulder. As he opened his mouth to ask what had happened, she said, "Everything turned out fine and we'll be able to go home this afternoon. The hospital is going to let you wear the gown home because you won't be able to put your pants on until tomorrow. You can't run for a few days, but you'll be able to walk almost as soon as we get home."

Jimmy knew before he felt the first pain that something about his body had changed forever. When the pain did come, it kept him from being surprised when he went to the bathroom and saw the bandage covering what he had always seen between his legs. The pain increased when the urine, mixed with blood, began to flow from the end of the stained gauze which covered whatever Jimmy now held between his fingers. As his bare legs leaned against the cold toilet for comfort, Jimmy suddenly felt that his body was now a stranger. It made him think of Jaybo's questions, and while he knew that his legs didn't end in cloven hoofs, he wasn't sure what he'd find between them when the bandage came off. Maybe Jaybo had been right about Catholics after all.

NONA CASPARS

Stigmata

Linda Prevkey closed her eyes and her soft voice floated above the rest of our sixth-grade voices. We stood in a circle at the front of our desks, reciting our last morning Act of Contrition. I imagined I saw a halo surround Linda's thin face. She had long white hair and the veins in her lids were the same blue as the eyes they covered. I imagined if she were naked I would be able to see straight through her pale skin into her heart. It would not be sloppy with sin like my sister Shelley's heart, or like my heart. Linda Prevkey's heart would be as pure and clean and beautiful as the sand-ground ruby on the church chalice.

It was my last hour of school at St. Mary's. Next year I would graduate to the public junior high, a red-brick building a block away. The Vietnam War seemed to be ending and spring was finally seeping into winter. When the bell rang I didn't run and scream down the halls like the other sixth-graders. I didn't rip my shirttails loose from my skirt, or fling my Catechism into the trash. I walked to my desk, gathered my books, fastened my blue plastic purse over my shoulder, and followed Linda Prevkey out the door.

On the bus kids sang stupid songs and drew distorted faces in the dust on the windows. Linda sat in her front seat and stared out the dirty windows. I sat in my seat in the back, jiggling my knee against the dead radiator. I tried to think of something Linda and I could do together to become friends. This winter I'd often seen her hiking down the road early in the mornings toward the Sauk River bridge. I would wander downstairs because I missed Shelley and couldn't sleep. Linda would appear in the shadowy dawn like a ghost blurring past our living room window. She wore a long-sleeved shirt but no coat or hat and her hair was loose and flew out behind her.

She and her father had been living just outside of town down the road from my family for years, but most of the time I would only see her face pressed against the Prevkey living room window as I'd bicycle past. Linda would be staring up at the sky—like she did on the bus—or out at the barley field across the road from our houses. As far as I knew, no one from school invited Linda to their house. No one was invited inside Linda's house either. She had been marked early on as different and therefore, of course, undesirable.

I also had been marked early on—the girl who was caught with Pall Malls in her purse in the third grade, the girl who flunked gym and chorus in the fourth grade, the girl who kissed boys behind the church in the fifth grade. Now I was the girl whose fifteen-year-old sister had been secreted out of Stearns County because she was a slut. The whispers about Shelley's absence floated around the school and town like dustclouds. I would eat lunch alone, sit on the swings alone, trying to ignore the looks.

On the playground boys giggled and called out, "Hey Natalie, want to have a baby with me?" I'd laugh at them, then go home and cry, not because my feelings were hurt, but because sometimes I did want to meet them. I believed they had recognized something inside me, a desire that they could smell, a confusion. I liked kissing boys, I liked smoking, I hated singing in church and running around the football field. I hadn't thought about what this all meant until Shelley left. Since then, for four months, I had been walking around feeling like there was a hole in my stomach. I felt lonely. I also felt angry and nervous and frightened.

One day in March I was sitting on a swing on the playground. I saw Linda standing over a dead tabby cat on the ice rink where the boys were playing stick hockey. She knelt bare-kneed on the ice, folded her hands and began praying over the cat, not out loud, but I could see her lips moving. The boys yelled for her to get off the rink. They gathered around her and a few boys threw snowballs, mockingly called her "The Saint." I yelled at them to cut it out, but Linda calmly picked up the cat and held it against her chest.

I believed Linda Prevkey would be raised on a cloud above this earth where she so obviously didn't belong. I imagined that all the selfishness and desire had been burned out of her and that she hovered above the mess and confusion of growing up. She wanted things that you couldn't have.

On the bus I listened to my knee knock up against the radiator. In the front seat Linda sat perfectly still and peaceful, her silver barrette holding back her fine blond-white hair. The ten other kids who lived on our route had been dropped off one by one until Linda and I were the last two left. She pressed her face closer to the window and I tried to look at what she was looking at. The sky. I followed her eyes and the angle of her head. She was staring at the sun, not directly at the sun, but at the place where the yellow bleeds into the blue. I tried to stare at this bleeding spot but my eyes hurt and I had to look away.

"How do you do that?" I asked.

Linda glanced at me, then turned back to look out the window. I leaned forward in my seat and imagined I could smell her sweaters. Even in the beckoning heat of May she wore two thick acrylic sweaters, one green and one white. They always smelled like candle wax and church incense and her skin always smelled like cleanser. Not hand or body soap but bleach.

The bus rattled over the gravel road that led to our driveways. It slowed, then halted in front of Linda's driveway. She pulled her face from the window and gathered her books in her arms.

"Linda, I need your help this summer," I said. She dropped her head and took a step toward the door.

"I have to go," she whispered.

The bus driver was watching us in her rearview mirror. Her sunglasses glared.

"You like to walk in the morning," I said. "I could walk with you. Can I meet you at your house tomorrow?"

The bus driver touched Linda's shoulder. She turned to look out the window, then at me again.

She nodded her head. Yes.

* * *

The next morning my alarm rang just before the sun rose. I pulled on a pair of blue jeans, a sleeveless button shirt, and my gym shoes from last year. I walked quietly past my mother and father's room. Shelley's room next to theirs was empty and the bed was made up perfectly like no flesh-and-blood person had ever slept in it—especially Shelley, who rarely made a bed. Downstairs I grabbed a green apple from the kitchen and stepped outside through the mudroom. I'd never been out this early. The dawn air was moist and clean. The sky hung dark blue but where the sun rose it paled.

The Prevkey house was small and white and the back end was sagging. Linda sat in front on the top concrete step, her palms pressed together around a plastic rosary. She was staring at the sunrise. She wore her two sweaters and had wrapped a long plaid scarf around her head and chin. I felt naked in my sleeveless shirt. I looked up into her living room window to see if her father was watching us. The curtain was drawn, with no light behind it.

In the morning the bus always picked me up first and Linda second. When she left the house Mr. Prevkey watched her from the window, and after school he watched her climb off the bus and go inside the house. Her mother was dead and this was the reason, I was told by my mother, that he looked sad when he watched her. She was his only child and a living memory of his wife. He was a mechanic and worked out of his garage next to the house. He rarely spoke; he had large blue eyes like Linda and was tall and skinny. The square bones of his forehead and wrists made him look helpless and sad as he bent over the same old junkers lined up outside the garage day after day. He never seemed to fix anything. In a few years, he would close up shop and they'd move away.

I stood in front of the steps and waved my hand. "I'm here."

She stood up and started walking up her driveway, her long skinny legs in thick brown winter pants. I stuffed the apple into my jeans pocket and hurried to keep up. My legs were shorter than hers and my gym shoes pinched my toes.

We raced up her driveway and turned east on the gravel road that led to the Sauk River. I looked up at my parents' dark window as we passed my house. In another hour or two they'd wake up, turn on the TV, drink coffee. Dad would read the funnies; Mom would sew. Outside, the morning light fed the freshly planted black fields. The barley shoots reminded me of little green straws reaching out from the ground and my stomach groaned for my morning malted milk.

Linda and I passed the sand pit, the Sauk River bridge, the second bigger bridge. The sun grew hotter and I smelled the dust from the gravel road and the new manure. I had never hiked anywhere, except up and down the halls to the principal's office at St. Mary's, and my ankles and feet hurt. I wondered how often Linda went on these hikes, and what exactly she got out of them. She walked without talking; her rosary swung from her side. I watched white strands of hair slip from under her plaid scarf. Most of the time her eyes were on the sunrise, which was beautiful—it rose red, then pink, then orange and then burned away the darkest part of the sky.

We turned onto the narrow gravel road that led to the big hill. Shelley and I had bicycled in this direction a few times. We would jump off our bikes at the bottom of the hill and push them up the shallow ditch to the side. Shelley called it Death Hill. It was steep and she'd have to lie on her back in the ditch and rest halfway up, and cars often flew at high speeds over the top.

"This hill's dangerous," I told Linda.

She just leaned her weight forward and marched up the middle of the road.

A month after Shelley left I had been sitting alone at a table in the school cafeteria, which we shared with the junior high. Peggy and two other girls from the eighth and ninth grades in fever-red lipstick and blue eye shadow sat next to me. One afternoon Peggy and Shelley had taught me to blow smoke rings behind the aluminum shed in our backyard.

"Your sister pop that kid yet?" she asked. Behind me I heard a group of sixth-grade girls and their boyfriends shift their chairs. I could feel their eyes on the back of my head.

"Wouldn't know," I said. "Haven't talked to her."

I had talked to Shelley on the phone but I wanted them to leave me alone. I stared at my plate of mashed potatoes and green beans. Peggy scraped her shoe against the floor a few times, then they all stood up and sauntered away.

The girls behind me started whispering to their boyfriends. I imagined they were plotting my future—I would be like *these* girls, their whispers said, girls whose futures swelled out of their bra, girls who everyone knew would be the next generation of whores and failures.

Father Schneider said the road to peace and goodness was acting on complete faith and knowing how to suffer. One day in detention hall he'd told me, "Young lady, you are walking down a road away from God's grace toward permanent evil."

As I watched Linda's back go up the hill I imagined I was walking up one of those mountain jungle roads in Vietnam that I'd seen on TV. Boys fired guns across the road, I heard explosions. It was dark and windy. Halfway up the mountain I saw the eighth- and ninth-grade girls and Shelley, sprawled in the ditch, their faces blown off, their chests caved in, their guts strewn over their legs. I saw myself sprawled on the ground with them—a bad girl, a whore, a loser, a blowout, a slut, a no-good, a failure.

I shut my eyes and picked up my feet. The breeze rustled the leaves of trees in the pasture. Pebbles slid under my feet and inside my thongs. Halfway up I glanced over at the long grass in the ditch but I didn't stop; I didn't want to lose Linda. I heard her shoes on the gravel ahead of me. I followed the sound. Step, step, step. A bird flew over my head.

At the top of the hill I opened my eyes and breathed deeply. My tongue and throat were dry and swollen. My gym shoes were slick with sweat and the rubber sole pinched my toes. Sweat slid onto my eyelashes and into the cracks in my lips. I wiped my face on my shirt and then gazed out over the miles of green hills and trees and cows that lay ahead. Everything glowed, everything burned distinct with color.

"Look how beautiful," I breathed. "Is this why you do it? Is this what you see every day?"

Linda stood with her arms limp at her sides and her shoulders slumped. The pockets of her sweaters sagged. The veins in her eyelids and under her eyes were red but the skin of her face was moist and white.

"I don't know what you see," she said finally.

I frowned and swept my hand across the hills. "Well, this."

She followed my hand and gazed blankly over the pasture, then turned and started back down the hill.

I was still too young to understand that everything Linda saw was tainted by her belief that she was evil; every step she took was meant to push that evil away. All I knew was that I had obviously misunderstood: Linda didn't need external beauty, rewards, comfort, or people. I had known she was pure, but now I knew she was truly fearless, truly untouchable. I was afraid of both roads, but she was afraid of nothing.

That night Shelley called collect from her home for unwed mothers. I could hear girls shouting and a vacuum howling in the background. I sat at the Formica kitchen table with my feet in a bucket of warm salt water, polishing the wooden beads of the rosary I'd gotten in the first grade. Mom and Dad were watching TV in the living room in the dark.

"The whole world is a prison, Natalie," Shelley said. She said this every time she called. "I'm trapped inside this fat body and this kid is trapped inside me and kicking me every minute and we're both trapped inside this stupid house." She sighed. "I can't go out at night."

"Where do you want to go?"

"Anywhere. Saturn, Venus."

I wanted to tell her about my walk with Linda, the dawn, the big hill, the glowing pasture. After the hike I'd swept and mopped the mudroom and organized the closet in my room. I felt proud of myself, and determined. I also felt lonelier than before, not a sad lonely, but a clean lonely ache down to my bones. I wondered if I would get used to it, and if Shelley would understand this feeling.

Shelley had told the family she was pregnant right after Christmas dinner. The four of us were sitting in the living room and I stared at the string of lights and tinsel on the tree. I had eaten a bunch of Christmas candy and my stomach had started to hurt. My father glanced at the evening news, which flashed soldiers with bloody arms and legs carried off on green stretchers. He looked at his shoes, rubbed his ankle, hung his hands between his knees. My mother pulled her lips tight together and ripped a loose thread off the couch. She untied the red and green bow at her neck and let the ribbons slack. She turned up the volume on the TV. She got up and shut the curtains. She sat back down and took out her sewing.

Later I sat on Shelley's unmade bed while she picked up her hip-hugger jeans and sweaters from the floor and dropped them into a suitcase. "It's so stupid to pack all this," she said. "In two months I won't be able to fit into any of it."

Shelley had a sloppy heart. She would never sit and think about her future; she always chose the laziest path. Before she left, she didn't even say she would miss me. She went to bed and listened to her radio. My mother, my father, and I lay under our covers on the beds in our rooms, sad and lonely, our hearts blown wide open.

"If I could just have someone to kiss to break this boredom, just kiss," Shelley said into the phone over the vacuum cleaner. "There's nothing in this world like lying on the cool ground with a warm guy on your stomach."

After I hung up the phone I pulled my feet out of the bucket and let the dingy water drip to the kitchen tile. The rubber soles of the shoes had ground the top layer of skin off my toes. Puffy lavender and crimson sores blistered on the undersides of my feet. I stuck a long sewing pin into the alcohol I'd set on the table and jabbed the pin into the blister sacks. The clear fluid drained into the bucket. I swabbed the sores, pulled on clean socks, and limped into the living room.

The curtains were drawn tight and the only light came from the TV. On one side of the room my father dozed on his back in a recliner with an afghan tucked up to his chin. My mother curled in a stuffed brown armchair in the other corner. She stitched hems and he dozed as soldiers jumped out of planes and slithered on their bellies through the jungle wearing green branches strapped to their helmets.

I climbed the stairs and pressed on each wooden step until the open wounds stung. I stepped into Shelley's empty room and lay very carefully across her perfectly made-up bed. In her closet hung one fuzzy flowered sweater and a pair of white pants. I pulled the sweater off the hanger and brought it to my room. I folded the sweater over my chair by my window along with the rest of the clothes I'd prepared for the next morning's hike. My own thickest sweater and winter pants. My socks. My gym shoes.

* * *

Every morning for the next five weeks, while my parents slept, Linda Prevkey and I were the army of God marching down the gravel road past my house, over the rusty iron bridge, over the bigger steel bridge, and up the big hill. Some mornings the sun rose hot and burning and some mornings the sky hung over us iron gray and the sun was a drowning fire behind sheets of smoke. On the sunny days, Linda raced over the path. On the gray days she marched slower and squinted through the gray. The first weeks I followed a few steps behind her. The final week I caught up and we marched side by side.

On the third sunny morning we had begun praying while we walked. Linda's voice sang softly into the dawn; my voice rang low, hoarse. The wind flattened the foot-high barley, making it bow over the black fields. My sweaters soaked up my sweat and grew heavy on my shoulders. We prayed all the prayers that we'd learned at school—the Creed, the Act of Contrition—and some that Linda taught me which I would later find in old Roman Catholic prayer books. The Prayer for Lost Souls, Prayer for Wounds, Prayer for Suffering, Prayer Beseeching the Purifying Blood of Christ.

While marching up the big hill Linda and I prayed the rosary. She led with "Hail Mary full of grace . . ." and I ended with "now and at the hour of our death." The pebbles slid under our feet, our words slid together and the whole prayer moaned like one long note or plea. At the top of the hill I no longer saw the glowing green hills or pasture. I no longer imagined myself fated and broken like the eighth- and ninth-grade girls, or Shelley. I saw only the long gravel road that lay ahead. My bones and the tissue around them burned. I ached more than I ever had before, a clean, beautiful ache. My body was heavy but inside I was light; I could feel myself hover above it all with Linda. By the end of the hour hike the burning, seeping pain in my feet flowed into the rhythm of our prayers.

One Saturday morning after our fifth week of hiking I finished cleaning out the shed, and stepped into the house through the mudroom. Mom and Dad were standing in their pajamas in the kitchen. The TV was off and Mom talked in a low excited voice on the phone. Dad listened close beside her. The baby inside Shelley had finally pushed out; she could come home. Dad went outside to change the oil in the car. I sat at the table and watched Mom pack jars of cherry Kool-Aid and ham sandwiches for each of us into a picnic basket.

"What in heaven's name are you doing in all those sweaters?" she asked. "Wash your face and get some decent clothes on for the trip."

In the car I sat in the back seat and stared up at Linda's spot where the sun bled into the blue sky. We drove past her house, but I didn't see her face in the living room window. I wondered what she did inside that house all day, if she was kneeling somewhere with her rosary, if she was sleeping, what she and her father ate, if she ever watched TV or if the Prevkeys even owned a TV since the house had no antenna. The garage was open and I thought I saw her father in his long gray coveralls leaning over to fix one of his engines.

Mom and Dad talked in chirpy little voices in the front seat.

"Your sister will be home soon," my mother chirped at me. "And then we'll all drive up to Paul Bunyan Park."

It was as if they'd awakened from a thick dark sleep and had completely forgotten who Shelley was. She hated parks and family outings and would sulk at all the rest stops, restless and singing to herself. Dad would spread a blanket on the ground and fall asleep. Mom would set up a table in the shade, scratch at stains on the tablecloth, and complain that no one knew how to have good plain fun. I would sit and feed half my ham sandwich to the squirrels and birds. But in the car, I wanted to believe in their gracious, wholesome Shelley, and not the faceless gutted one lying at the side of Father Schneider's road. My father drove and my mother hummed something that sounded like "Jingle Bells."

At the hospital Shelley was propped up on pillows and asleep. Her black hair straggled over her hospital gown and into her face. I said her name and she opened her eyes. She swept her hair back from her face and smiled at me. She was pale and tired but she giggled and looked me up and down. Mom and Dad stood nervously in the doorway. I walked up to the bed.

"You're limping, kiddo," Shelley said.

She pushed herself up and pointed to the green plastic chair next to the bed. I sat and she reached down and grabbed my knee. I slid down the chair and laughed and she pulled my leg up into the air. She pulled off my shoe, and then my sock. My swollen ankle hung in the air and my toes and the bottom of my feet were thick with old scabs and new yellow calluses. She frowned at me with her mouth open. She looked over at Mom and Dad, who still stood side by side in the doorway, wide-eyed, looking wounded and helpless. "What in the hell has she been doing to her feet?' she asked them.

"So what'd you do while I was gone?" Shelley asked. We were playing Crazy Eights in my room. Shelley had snuck up a bottle and was sipping brandy out of a hospital juice cup. My feet were raised on pillows.

"Nothing," I said. "Does the, you know, hurt?"

Shelley adjusted my pillows and offered me her cup but I shook my head.

"First it feels like someone's ripping you in half," she said. "Later, it's just like you've been burned down there."

My mother and father took turns carrying trays of cereal and graham crackers up and down the stairs. The days were long and gray. I started to feel restless.

I didn't tell Shelley or my parents about my walks with Linda. I started worrying, thinking about whether she hiked without me, or waited for me on her front steps. Whether she even realized I wasn't behind her or marching beside her. Every day I lay at home I grew heavier. My mouth ached for a sip of Shelley's brandy, or a cigarette, or anything that would make me feel forgetful and light.

On the fourth morning before Shelley awakened I heard a sound outside my open bedroom window. I sat up and heard Linda's pure soft voice float up through the curtains.

"Natalie," she said. "Get up. I have something beautiful to show you."

I got up and looked out the window. She was standing in our front yard in her green and white sweaters and plaid scarf. She was staring up at me and her face seemed thinner and paler than before. She seemed excited about something.

"Please," she said.

I pulled on my sweater and grabbed my shoes. Outside the July sun was gathering full force. She smiled at me and started walking toward her house. I limped behind her. At her front door I waited on the bottom step but she motioned me inside. I followed her into their living room. The Prevkey living room was immaculate. The walls were white and bare. In one corner were two plastic kitchen chairs that looked like they'd never been sat on. The house smelled of bleach like Linda.

We walked down a hallway past a closed door and then her bedroom. The door was open and I saw two sweaters spread out neatly on her perfectly made-up bed, and pictures from our Catechism taped on the walls. In the hallway outside her door hung a picture of a woman holding a baby and kneeling on the wine-red carpet at the front of St. Mary's Church.

"Follow me," she repeated.

I followed her farther down the hall into her bathroom. It was clean and small. Linda pulled her soiled white sweater over her head, and her green sweater. She stood before me naked. Her bones pushed up against her skin. I saw a pattern of feverish welts on her chest, scratched up her shoulders and sides as if she had tried to scrape off her skin. I saw scabs and half-healed cuts on her forearms. She had carved fresh letters into the skin above her wrist: LINDA.

"Who did all that to you?" I asked.

"It doesn't hurt," she said. She smiled at me and told me to wait, there was more.

She stood in front of the sink. She tilted her head back, opened her palms over the porcelain bowl, and stared up at the fluorescent light above the mirror. She stared just below the bulb, where the yellow shone on the blue ceramic tiles. On the wall above the light hung a picture of Jesus and I realized she was holding her hands like his, open to the world, expectant, hopeful. I heard her breath go in and out and my breath go in and out. I hoped some miracle was going to happen; that she was going to show me her secret. One of the cuts of her name had opened and I saw a drop of blood weep out and trail down the bone of her arm. She caught it in her palm.

"See?" she said. "Stigmata."

I saw the blood trickle down from the cut on her arm and Linda saw it grow like a long-awaited sign out of her palm. Her pale blue eyes lit up. I stared in the mirror at the place where her heart was. Her chest was covered with dark red scabs and messy scratches. At the moment I was confused, and sorry for her, but later I felt angry and betrayed. I had imagined that inside Linda's heart was God's grace. I had imagined that this grace was something you could earn, like a gold star on a paper, that once you had it you were safe.

She was looking at me. I couldn't look back. Later that summer, and throughout junior high before she and her father moved away, I would mostly remember how she had looked at me—like she needed me. And this disgusted me most, that Linda was as dark and cold and messy inside as everyone else. But in the bathroom that morning I still wanted to believe in her completely. I stared at the blood in her palm and convinced myself, the way a sixth-grader can, that something had happened, that this blood was a mystery blessing all our work, marking our futures.

"I saw it," I told her.

She put on her sweaters and walked me to the front door. The sun had risen above the barley. I walked down the road past my house, then cut through the ditch and over to the middle of the field. I sat down in the dirt between the rows. My stomach felt sick; my ankle hurt. Across the road I could see Shelley's dark head sticking out her bedroom window. She was leaning on her elbows with a cigarette in her hand, blowing smoke rings and gazing over the field. As I watched she leaned farther out the window, until it looked like she was balancing only on her hips. Suddenly I felt afraid, not just for Shelley, but for myself, for Linda, for all of us. The fear was thick in my stomach and rose like a pain up my chest. Shelley waved her arms and called across the road to me. I held my breath, lifted both my arms, and waved back.

BRENDA BANKHEAD

The Other Path

for the Catholic girls before us

The moon was pale and washed out in the late-afternoon sky. The coolness of autumn was coming on and Ruby Thoreau wondered what it would be like to reach up and tilt that sickle-shaped crescent so that its warm luminance spilled out across October. She walked briskly down a path worn out in the woods. The air was just short of chilling her. She had no coat. Her arms hung down at her sides, her hands poking out of the thin wool sweater she wore open over her gray plaid uniform. Her hands were large naturally and made larger still by the seasonal picking she and her family did every year. She was a raw-boned twelve-year-old, small for her age and skinny. Her skin was very, very light, high yella as they called it in Louisiana, and her thin coarse hair stuck out in two braids on the back of her head. Ruby brought her gaze from the sight of the moon moving through the arch of branches over her head and back down to the black, heavy boots she wore on her feet. They were men's boots, rough and unpolished. There was a gaping space between her shins and the top of the leather. The shoes squished as she walked along, head down. Her good oxfords were tied together at the shoelaces and slung over her shoulder to save them wear.

Mushrooms were beginning to sprout among the tall blades of grass. It had rained the night before and the leaves did not crackle under her footsteps. Ruby liked to watch her feet as she walked. Their rhythmic pacing caused her mind to float free. In school that day the teacher had accused her of daydreaming and told her to stop. She was one of the oldest in the tiny one-room school. Sitting like a lump and staring cross-eyed into space wouldn't get her very far, Sister Agnes said. If she wanted to waste her parents' money, she might as well go to public school. Ruby knew that going to public school meant not going to school at all. The nearest one was ten miles away and no colored children went there. The Louisiana school district of 1949 didn't send school buses to her part of the county, which was made up mostly of Creoles. The "French Negroes" the people in town called them, because so many of their bloodlines were mixed up with those of the white French immigrants who had settled the area. If it hadn't been for St. Luke's Catholic Church setting up an auxiliary school for the Creole converts of that parish she wouldn't have had a chance to go at all. But Ruby couldn't help herself. The patter of rain on the roof or the sight of a crow circling the fields outside brought her to a place in herself where she no longer controlled her thoughts and they moved like clouds, immense and varied, across her mind. Sister Agnes swooped down on Ruby during mathematics, her black habit forming a dark ripple behind her.

"Wasting your parents' money is a sin," the nun hissed. "So is your disobedience."

She pushed Ruby toward her immense desk, which dominated the room. With Ruby's small hips pushed against the ledge of the desktop, Sister Agnes sat behind her and positioned a math book so that they could both see the group of word problems of the math lesson. The nun made Ruby recite each problem out loud and solve it without benefit of pencil and paper. She also made a fist of her hand, allowing her index finger to curl up against the thumb and stick out until the first joint became a point. Each time Ruby gave the wrong answer Sister Agnes jabbed this point sharply into the small of her back, causing her front hip bones to collide against the hard wood of the desk. Ruby's face was wet with unwiped tears when she was finally allowed to go back to her seat. Sister Agnes looked at these tears, her own pale blue irises like hard marbles in her eyes.

"Your mother has sacrificed a great deal for you. This will remind you of the pain she bore to bring you into this world. Think on that as you write these problems out after class."

Ruby sniffed a little as she walked down her special path home. At least none of the other children were tagging along after her. Although few of the others cared to come this way. It was too overgrown. The other children preferred the wide main swath of a road cut out on the east end of the woods.

A jay flew overhead giving a warning call, and Ruby heard twigs breaking to the left of her. She heard voices too. One of them sounded like her pa. She made her way around a thicket and came upon two men squatting over a set of snares set underneath bushes. One of them was her father, his battered old hat shoved down to his brows. The other was Mr. Zeke, a neighbor man. He was spitting tobacco juice every few minutes onto the ground. Ruby remained in the bushes, watching them. They were busy disentangling the bodies of rabbits from the ropes of their snares.

"The girl's got to quit school," her father was saying. "We can't afford to keep sending her and we sho can't buy her books. 'Specially with the new baby comin'. Her ma'll need her help. And with Jim gone, well, she's been a help to me in the fields before. She's got a bit of strength for one so small."

Mr. Zeke nodded. "I don't see the point on it. She'll get babies soon enough. They all get hot to marry after a while. Nothin' on Jim?"

"Naw. We thinkin' maybe he cut on out to La Salle."

The two men were silent, their hands busily working. Ruby hoped her brother, Jim, was in La Salle. He was the second from the oldest. The oldest had run off a year ago to jump freight trains. It was the boots of this brother that Ruby wore. Her mother had saved the shoes for a long time figuring her son would come back, but the family had heard nothing. Finally, sadly, the woman passed the boots on to Ruby. Now Jim was gone, too. Ruby and Jim were favorites of each other. Jim taught Ruby how to whistle. He whittled little stick animals for her out of willow branches.

Mr. Zeke stood up. He held the bodies of three rabbits by the ears in his gnarled hands. "I sho 'preciate what he tried to do but you can't keep white folks from gettin' what they covet." Brown juice dripped down his chin. He caught it with his tongue, then spit again.

Her father grunted. "He don't understand. You got to choose the battles you fight. This one'll get him killed."

He walked to a square of cloth with the body of a rabbit hanging like a dishrag in his hands. He placed the body on top of others that lay on the cloth; then he brought the four corners of the material together and slung the bundle over his shoulder. "A good haul," he said. "Be meat for a coupla days."

"What you wanna do wi' this un?" Mr. Zeke held up a tiny limp body.

"Too small t' eat. Just toss it over in them bushes. The ants'll get it soon enough."

After the men left Ruby went over to the bushes where they had squatted. She found the body of the small rabbit they had thrown back and knelt beside it.

"Poor thing, poor little thing," Ruby crooned. She stroked the body with her hands. She riffled the fur and saw the dark brown undercoat under the tan hairs. The hairs crackled under her fingers. Ruby laid her hands still on the body and waited. Her hands became very warm, almost hot. She watched the rabbit intensely. Its feet began to twitch. A high-pitched squeal escaped its tiny mouth and Ruby knew to release it. She watched as it struggled to its feet and hobbled away from her to sit under some bushes. It sat in a little ball, very still, looking dazed. Ruby sat back on her haunches and tilted her head to catch the flitting of the birds in the tree branches. She mused on Jim. Her brother was the only one who had ever seen her heal a thing with her hands before. They'd gone fishing and had come upon the drowned cat on the edge of the pond. Ruby had put her fishing gear aside and had laid her hands on the cat's chest of wet, matted fur. After a moment the cat sputtered awake, hacking, then spit up water. They left it sitting up in the sun. They walked in silence together until Jim asked quietly,

"That cat was dead, wasn't it?"

"Near dead," Ruby replied. "I can bring 'em back if they ain't quite gone. I never tried it on a real dead, dead thing before."

"How long you been doing this?"

"Since I was little."

"Nobody else knows?"

"Just you, Jim." And Ruby smiled up at him.

That was the summer before Jim went up north to New York

City to stay with some cousins and finish high school. He was different when he came back. Not so much with Ruby and his family as within himself. He was quiet. His eyes were more intense. And he looked white men in the eye. When a white man got the best piece of Mr. Zeke's land through a legal trick, Jim tried to get the colored folk to organize. He also turned to any sympathetic white person who would listen. He talked about bringing a lawyer up from New York to try to win Mr. Zeke's land back. The whole district began to talk. Some people labeled Jim an agitator, a radical sent in from New York by those Jew communist reds. His father took a strap to Jim when he heard that. Both father and son knew he was too old for it. Jim left that night. That had been three days ago. No one had heard a word from him since then.

Ruby brought her gaze back down to the rabbit. It suddenly became aware of her presence. It bounded off, kicking up the brown leaves under its hind legs. Ruby stood up and wiped the dirt from her hands, clapping them together.

When she got home her father was out back in the shed cleaning rabbits.

"Hi, Pa."

"Ruby." His hands pulled the skin back from a rabbit in long strips. "You a little late, ain't you?"

"Little." She watched him for a minute. "Rabbit stew. Mmmmm." She turned to go into the house, then turned back. "Pa, y'all still going over to Hendersons' place tomorrow to clear the brush?"

Her father grabbed a cleaver and came down on the joint of the rabbit's thigh. "Yup," he said.

"Can I come with?"

"You got to finish your work here first."

"I will, Pa."

Ruby walked into the small wooden house. Her mother was changing the baby. The rank smell of the diaper filled the kitchen. Her mother was pregnant with her sixth child. Her face was bloated and the bun pulled back severely from it only accentuated its puffiness. She moved as if it hurt to walk, her swollen feet wrapped up in rags because she could no longer bear to put shoes on them.

"Ruby, where you been, girl? I got wash out back waiting for you."

Ruby did not answer immediately. She walked to the pantry, grabbed a knife, hunked off a piece of bread and smeared butter on it.

"Yes, ma'am," she said between chews.

"Take Nathan and the baby out there with you. I got to get these beans canned before the end of today and Lord, it's been a day."

Her mother finished diapering the baby and put him down from the sink. He toddled across the floor to Ruby. He grabbed her by the legs.

"Be be be be be," he gurgled up at her. His face was red with rash.

Ruby looked down at him, still chewing her bread. She pushed the tip of his nose with her finger. "Ma, Pa said I can help him at the Hendersons' when he goes."

"They going to pay you, Ruby? Don't go out there hauling tree limbs if they don't pay you."

Ruby nodded. She took the baby by the hand and led him outside with her to the washtub. She sat him down and turned to the wash before her. John toddled away toward the bushes. Ruby trotted after him. She put him down on the patch of grass again. She gave him a rag doll. John put it in his mouth.

"Nathan!" Ruby yelled.

Her ten-year-old brother slid out from under the house.

"What you doing?" Ruby asked.

"Huntin'," he sneered at her. He backed his body back under the house.

Ruby proceeded to do the wash. Every few minutes she had to chase John, who seemed determined to hurt himself. When she filled the tub and brought him with her, he pounded his head against the pump, then wailed at the top of his lungs. Ruby soothed him. As she worked scrubbing clothes against the washboard, he leaned his body over the edge of the tub, threatening to tip headfirst into the water. When she placed the wrung-out wash on a piece of tarp she had to constantly dance around it to keep him from putting the soapy ends of it in his mouth. It was only when Ruby began to hang the heavy, dripping laundry on the clothesline that the baby grew tired. Ruby spread a blanket out for him. He lay down on it and played with his toes before drifting into sleep. Ruby wished she could join him. She felt frazzled. She pushed strands of hair out of her face. Her hands worked quickly, throwing dripping sheets over the line, then straightening them out. But gradually her rhythm slowed. She began to enjoy the coolness of the air around her. She looked up at the white clouds in the sky. She felt as though she had not seen them for a long time. Her face relaxed. She moved among the sheets, letting their wet ends wrap around her legs in the breeze. She pressed her face against one of them and tasted the coolness of the water soaking it. She closed her eyes. Her feet were planted solidly on the ground and she began to hum a Latin hymn she knew from church. The timbre of her voice vibrating in her chest and the smell of the wet wash enveloping her made Ruby tremble. She felt poised to take off like a bird. Where, she didn't know. Water soaked through the thin material of her dress. Ruby's nipples hardened as the cold water reached them. She opened her eyes and looked down at her chest. Her breasts were two small mounds, hard and pointed. Water formed a dark stain across her front. Ruby laughed. She stepped out into the sunshine. She crouched down and stared at the baby. She had been the one to help deliver John. She'd gripped her mother's hand as she groaned in pain. She'd willed her healing power to ease her mother's suffering. But it hadn't seemed to work. Her mother had continued to cry out fiercely. Her father's words in the woods came back to her. A rush of sympathy flooded in on Ruby. Her mother did need her help. She sacrificed so much for them and she often seemed so sad. The priest at church talked about sacrifice, especially about Christ's sacrifice on the cross for all the sinners of the world. Couldn't she, Ruby, sacrifice just a little of herself? The sky and the woods and the green grass would always be there for her. She could go to them whenever she needed them but right now her mother and her family needed her. Her duty was to them first, not books. And book-learning had never come easy to her. Still, when she'd heard her father that afternoon fear had tugged deep at her insides at the thought of leaving school. She knew that door, once closed, would never open again. She had not dared to think of her father's words again until her mind was ready for some kind of acceptance of them. Now she felt resistance in herself giving way. She imagined Jesus looking down from His cross and smiling at her. She felt saintly.

There was a sudden movement in the bushes. Ruby started. Then she saw Jim between the green leaves. She rushed to him. His face was haggard, his clothes dirty. There was an ugly red mark going down his cheek. Ruby threw herself at her brother. Jim hugged her, then pushed her off.

"I came to say bye," he said.

"Where are you going?" Ruby asked. Her insides felt tight again.

"I'm heading back up to New York. If anybody asks you, you haven't seen me. They're after me, Ruby."

"Who's after you?"

"The white bosses of this district. I've been too uppity for them. That night I left here? There were some of them out waiting for me. I don't know how they figured I'd be walking down the road. Maybe they were sitting there working up the guts to come pull me out. But I stumbled right into them. There weren't that many. About three or four. And I fought. That surprised them." Jim laughed dryly.

Ruby watched his eyes as he laughed and the sparkle that was usually there was not there now. She became more frightened at how hard her brother's eyes looked.

"I ran off into the woods," Jim continued. "They chased me but they didn't have any dogs with them. I headed straight for the water and been laying low ever since. I need you to get my clothes for me. They're in a suitcase under my bed. I was ready to leave, anyway, see. I was all packed. I knew I couldn't stay here any longer."

Jim rubbed his hands over his face in great fatigue. He seemed to forget Ruby was there. "Why can't people fight for themselves? I can't do it alone."

Ruby reached out to him. Jim looked at her again.

"Listen, I need food, too," he said. "Think you can get me some?"

Ruby went into the house and came out after a time with a cloth sack. She knelt down beside Jim.

"There's eggs in there and bread and butter and some ham, too," she said. "Your suitcase is out by the side of the house under the window. Be careful. Nat's under the house playin' but he's over on the other side, I think."

Jim smiled at her. "Thanks, Ruby. You're my girl. Lay your hands on me now. Lay them on me for some kind of luck. I need it if I'm going to make it out of here."

Ruby laid her hands against Jim's chest. "It don't work unless you're sick," she said weakly. Tears blurred her vision. "When I'm going to see you again?"

"Don't cry, sugar. You'll see me. Come up north. I'm hopping trains to get back to Cousin Lea. I'll write but you come on up and finish school."

Ruby sobbed. "Pa says I'm not to go to school anymore. Ma needs me here."

Jim shook her gently but his eyes and his voice were fierce. "Fight them," he said. "Don't let them take that from you. You keep going to school. Finish it. It's the only way you'll escape." He took her hands in his own and placed them over her own chest. "You've got the power in you, Ruby. Use it." He kissed her on the cheek. "For luck," he said. Then he was gone.

Ruby continued kneeling like a penitent, her arms crossed around her chest, her whole body racked by her silent sobbing. After a few minutes she stood up and went back over to the sleeping baby. She wiped her nose and face on the ends of the blanket, then picked the baby up and walked back into the house. The sight of her mother standing over the stove made Ruby afraid because she knew that was where her path lay. Her mother had married at fifteen. She'd never had any schooling to speak of, her parents thinking an education for a girl was wasteful and silly. As a result, her mother could not spell her own name. Ruby had caught her mother once staring at her wistfully as she did her homework.

"Maybe you can teach me someday," her mother had said. But there had never seemed to be enough time. If it wasn't a new baby occupying her time it was the canning like now. Her mother's face and hands were red and chapped from the steam rising out of huge pots. The rags on her feet were beginning to shred. And as Ruby watched the gray tatters of them trailing behind her mother, she felt something besides fear well up inside herself. She felt a firm resolve to take the other path, the one her mother had not been able to choose. Jim was right. She would never allow herself to become like her mother. She would read her books over and over and over again.

Her mother looked up from the boiling water and noticed Ruby's tear-stained face. "What's happened?" she asked, alarmed. She hurried over to Ruby and took the baby from her arms, scrutinizing him.

"I'm not quitting school," Ruby said clearly.

Her mother looked up sharply. "Who's been talking?"

"Don't matter. I'm not quitting. I'll do my work here and do outside work to help pay but I'm going."

Her mother stared at her. Ruby turned on her heels and walked down the hall to the boys' room. She shut the door behind her.

"Child, what you doing?" she heard her mother say.

"Fighting," Ruby said. And she threw herself on Jim's bed.

PATRICE VECCHIONE

Anger's Gift

Grandmother who kept her own teeth
all eighty-nine years of her life
kept her anger longer, has it even now
in the company of angels and lambs.
She wore her anger
like spit behind the ear, used it
to make the family move, the screen door
shaking on its hinge.
She used it to bend my mother's back
and then to make her hair
fall out, every last stitch. Without losing
any of it she gave it away to her daughters,
the way some women pass on
tatted doilies or remedies to sooth stiff feet.
And my mother used her inheritance
well and long, when she called me "fat pig"
in front of my school-girl friend
and when she chased my sister
all the around the circle house
with a knife in one hand.
Early on she passed it to me,
the fire stick I will juggle all of my life.
During the day I wear it
in my dress pocket, try to keep it down,

tamed a little. At night sometimes
it comes out and I don't sleep.
I watch it get big in the room
and surround me so that God
and all the good angels have to come
save me from the family heirloom.
They sing the Gloria and Ave Maria
to shrink the anger until it is only
one brick-hard loaf of bread
that I don't know who would eat.

PART THREE

Wild Heart

Wild as I was, all my beautiful sins.
—Cecilia Woloch

MAUREEN M. FITZGERALD

Sister Cool

My parents were the thriftiest people in America. Officially, I mean. It's been documented.

Promenade, a magazine that sat on coffee tables in hundreds of thousands of homes across America, sponsored a nationwide search for the *Thrift Family, America, 1968*. The prize for the family judged "the thriftiest in America" was two thousand dollars. My parents won the contest and we become celebrities. They unveiled the secrets of their thrifty lifestyle in a feature article in the February 1968 issue. My dad told how he built our house with his own hands. How he bought food from a school hot lunch supply warehouse. Barrels of creamed corn and towers of canned sauerkraut filled our pantry. Dad gave tips about saving slivers of soap, scraps of tin foil, and plastic containers, and how to turn them into useful items like dish soap and Christmas ornaments. He announced proudly that he "gave" us library books as Christmas and birthday presents. And worst of all, he said he and my mother combed through out neighbors' garbage on trash day to rescue used toys and household items.

"We encourage Mary and Betty to come along," he's quoted. "We call these our 'treasure hunts.' "

My mother told America she loved to sew but it was hard to keep up a wardrobe for two growing girls. That was why she bought our clothes at garage sales, a couple of sizes too big, so we would *always* have clothes to fit us as we grew. She didn't stop there. Then she blabbed, in print, that the dresses my sister and I wore in the family picture in the magazine used to be purple velvet curtains in the rectory at Immaculate Conception. The caption to the picture read "Mary Margaret, age 10 (L), and Elizabeth Beatrice, 13, wear dresses hand-made by Mrs. Thrift from fabric donated by a local church."

If only they'd left out "donated by a local church." It made us sound like refugees. The dresses were identical—empire-waisted and bell-sleeved, short enough to be mod, long enough to be modest. They were warm and dusty and smelled like incense. In the picture, I am round and grape-colored. Betty, a head taller, looks straight into the camera and the world, daring anyone to make fun of her.

Dad told how Betty and I were learning thrift from his example. We collected pop bottles and returned them to the store for the nickel refund. Betty baby-sat. I raked leaves. Any money we made went to our savings account for college tuition. It was our job to collect paper clips, pieces of paper, and the rubber bands that came around bunches of vegetables. We also had to cut up the net onion and potato bags for scouring rags. Everything in our house was used, used, and reused.

After the article came out, the playground became a hostile planet ruled by alien children. The meanest kids would run up to me, poke my arm, and then chase others on the playground, yelling: "Keller's cooties! Keller's fleas!"

"Rag-picker Keller! Dress in the dark again today?"

The boys in my class formed a line and shouted: "Mary Keller, two by four, can't get through the kitchen door!"

One day, Kiki Lang, the meanest girl in my class, pointed to my hand-me-down black-and-white saddle shoes. My mother had scooped them up at a yard sale. Going to school barefoot would have been better than wearing those corny shoes. I longed for white patent-leather go-go boots like Kiki's.

"Where'd you get those shoes, Keller? The dump?" Other kids laughed when she said things like that.

"Garbage man! Your dad's a garbage man!"

The teasing spread like a rash—in the lunchroom, on the playground, and in gym class. I prayed for someone else to take over my position as the school reject. Someone with head lice, or a new pagan kid who transferred from a public school.

My teacher, Sister Carleen, was too absorbed in preparing us to be soldiers of Christ to notice how my classmates tortured me because of my sudden fame as the child of people who went through other people's garbage. She made it even worse one day, a day when my mom made me wear the purple dress to school:

"Mary Keller, tell the class what you do in your free time. Is it true you read the encyclopedia for fun?"

I froze in my seat. I could hear my heart thumping. Sister Carleen knew the awful truth from reading the article: my parents had retrieved an almost complete set of 1945 World Book encyclopedias from someone else's trash. In the article, there was a picture of me on the floor, staring intently at an encyclopedia unfolded in front of me. Dad said I was disappointed the D volume was missing because I liked to read about dogs. World Book sent us a D volume—1968 version—a few days later.

I stared at an ancient spill of ink on my desk. Scratched a scab of glue on my hand. I could feel myself turning red. I was sweating because I kept my coat on all day that day. My stomach spun and did flips.

"Um, er, er, er . . . ," I choked. I wanted to say: "That's a lie! I build forts! Steal cars! Smoke cigarettes!"

"Just *National Geographic,*" I mumbled.

"Well, I hope everyone in this room will follow your example, Mary."

I was a social outcast, but my sister was more popular than she had been before. Boys liked her. Cheerleaders wanted to be her friend. And somehow, the secondhand clothes my mom found for her looked *stylish* on Betty. She looked chic and Parisian wearing pedal-pushers from 1962, while I just looked chubby. And the *Promenade* article came out at the same time that Betty began her career as a junior-high disc jockey.

It started out as a joke. Betty took over the record player, the story goes, at Judy Bauer's slumber party. She threw a towel over her head and started to call herself Sister B. Bea Cool, "spinning the coolest tunes on the planet." Betty always made fun of Sister Beatrice, the history teacher who said any girl who got her ears pierced was destined to unwed motherhood by the age of sixteen. It helped that Betty's middle name is Beatrice. Everyone laughed and Betty made an amazing discovery: she liked the sound of her own voice. She had a low, melodic voice, and sometimes she sounded like a boy.

"Let's listen to a song about someone with pierced ears," Betty would say, starting off a set with "Lady Madonna." With Judy's record collection and her own ultra-cool patter, Betty was asked to play records at more parties. Judy Bauer became "Judy in disguise" after the hit song by John Fred and His Playboy Band. Judy flipped the records.

We didn't have any cool records—just a bunch of old 78's my parents had retrieved from a condemned house. Bing Crosby singing love songs—very uncool. Betty saved her baby-sitting money to buy albums by the Doors and the Beatles, and slowly amassed her own record collection. But she had to hide the albums at Judy's house because my dad thought it was wasteful, sinful, even, to spend money on rock 'n' roll records.

Betty also began to buy Yardley lipstick and Chantilly perfume. I watched her before the mirror as she twisted the frosted pink wand, smacked her lips, and adjusted the beaded Indian headband with a bright blue feather, which became her D.J. trademark. Later, she would wear love beads and paint daisies and peace symbols on her face in the girls' bathroom at St. Jude's High.

"I don't know, Mary," she said, filling in her lips. "Something comes over me when I get near a mike."

She told me she had as much personality as Petula Clark, and then broke into a chorus of "Downtown."

Betty was cool. She was *born* cool. If anyone in her class teased her about being part of "The Thriftiest Family in America," all she had to do was glare and look away in disgust. I asked her why nobody bugged her, the way kids bugged me.

"I don't know, Doughgirl," she said, poking my arm. She knew I hated it when she called me Doughgirl. "Maybe it's just because I am Sister Cool." We both looked at her smiling at herself in the mirror. Then I heard Judy Bauer's mom honking in the driveway. Betty and Judy were going to a dance at Teen Town. "Sister B. Bea Cool" was going to play *The Association's Greatest Hits,* and it would be the first time anyone in her class slow-danced to "Cherish."

* * *

Our house was nice, and *new.* My mom had seen a picture of one like it in a magazine. She'd sent away for the plans. My parents built the house themselves. They borrowed a bulldozer, mixed their own cement, and poured the foundation themselves. The house took shape from remnants, discounts at lumberyards, and closeouts at hardware stores. The handmade house they finished in just one summer looked surprisingly a lot like the one in the glossy magazine picture, except for the shimmering turquoise swimming pool in the back yard. I wished for a pool I could dive into from my bedroom window. I liked the house. It always smelled like fresh laundry.

My father worked at the library. He started a program called "Books for Buses," so people could read while they were on the bus. My mother gave knitting lessons at a craft shop. They had a steady income. I think people viewed my parents' knack for thrift with a mix of respect, scorn, and amusement.

" 'Few men realize how great a revenue is thrift'—*Cicero,*" my father would say when questioned about his penny-pinching zeal. When I got older, I wondered if my dad wasn't just really pathologically stingy, and he knew it, but tried to elevate his tightfistedness by quoting Jesus, Benjamin Franklin, and other great thinkers of Western civilization.

Our neighbors would stand on their porches on trash day, shaking their heads, hands on hips, smiling a little as they watched my parents sift through the cast-off household goods and toys left on the curb.

My parents peered. They poked and probed. When I read about the Leakeys in *National Geographic,* I made believe my parents were really famous archaeologists searching for fragments of primitive man on our block. My parents were as busy as ants, scurrying from neighbors' curbs to our house, hauling things on their backs or in sacks made from old pillowcases. When my parents asked if they could take things from other people's garbage, I would walk up the block and pretend I belonged to a different family.

A few of our neighbors were considerate enough to bring junk over for my dad to revive before they curbed it. I felt like I was living in a Goodwill store: stacks of clothes that smelled like cedar chests, old toasters, and irons with thick, frayed cords, and a chair or two splitting cotton stuffing all sat in our living room.

"Do you mind if I take this bicycle?" My father pointed one day at an ancient heap with embarrassingly fat tires and pedal breaks in front of Mrs. Wilson's house. It was a dirty white clunker with two purple stripes down the fenders. He brought the bike home for me.

I couldn't believe it. I dreamed of riding to school on a gleaming new Schwinn three-speed bicycle, flashing electric-blue chrome and a headlight that really worked, and my dad expected me to ride an old heap with balloon tires. A bike with a weight problem.

"Some bike, huh Mary? I'll just grease up that old chain and you'll be ready to roll!" said my dad.

"But Dad, can't I ever have anything new?" This time, he'd just gone too far. If I had any chance of breaking out of the mold of nerd-dom so solidly cast for me, it would be lost forever if I rode that bike in public.

My father sighed, looked heavenward, and said: "Far be it from the life of the humble Nazarene . . ."

The bike was ugly. It smelled of old rubber and a stranger's basement. I refused to ride it. It sat in the garage for days after my dad polished it and tuned it up. But slowly, I began to feel sorry for the bike. It was like me: chubby, neglected, and out of style.

I named the bike Gloria, and I began to ride it on my solo trips around the neighborhood. It was spring, there was a smell of new grass in the air, and I liked the fresh breeze that blew around me when I rode Gloria.

The article and the bicycle established my place as the reject of Immaculate Conception Grade School. I sought refuge at the library, where I read fairy tales from around the world. I dreamed of a magic wand that would change history: make the article disappear, make me like my sister. I wished for my own personal fairy who would play tricks on kids like Kiki Lang. I looked at all the pictures in the *National Geographic* magazines. I wished I could jump into the pictures, especially the ones of Tahiti and Argentina. I wanted to wade in the warm clear blue water of a Polynesian reef, ride my bike into the sunset on the Pampas.

When I got tired of that, I would go to the basement of the J. C. Penney store. I wandered among bolts of gingham, poplin, and wool plaid, under flickering tubes of fluorescent light. The cool air smelled of new fabric and the colognes of women who got dressed up to shop on Saturdays—Jean Naté, Muguet des Bois. I would look in the mail-order catalog at the clothes my parents would buy for me if only they weren't so thrifty. I picked out new wardrobes of school clothes, play clothes, and fancy dresses for the parties that I would be invited to in my fantasy life.

Before I went to sleep at night, I prayed for divine intervention, for me and the pagan babies.

I asked Betty again what to do about my problem at school.

"Just ignore the little brats," she said, and shrugged her shoulders. As if it was that easy.

I tried to explain; maybe she didn't understand. Someone, probably Kiki Lang, had changed the lyrics of the song "Georgy Girl" to "Garbage Girl," and even the first-graders would sing it when I walked by.

"Look, it can't last forever. After all, you are my sister. That's gotta do *something* for you."

"Maybe if they saw me with you? Maybe if you walked me to school? Maybe if you let me hang around with you and your friends? I don't think anyone *knows* I'm your sister . . ."

She looked up in horror from the piece of paper where she was practicing writing her name in different ways: "Sister B. B. Cool," she wrote, making the "S" into a music staff, and "Bette," with a tail on the "e" that reversed direction to underline her name. Then she looked out the window.

"Hey, gotta go now, chubs." Judy Bauer was walking up our drive. Betty and Judy were going to a party, to dance with boys from the public junior high, and my parents weren't supposed to know.

My parents talked all that spring about the prize we had won. "Isn't it wonderful we had our picture in a national newspaper?" said my mom, as she admired photographs of us in the magazine. She sent copies of the article to everyone she had ever met.

"Mary, I think you look so cute in that purple dress that I made for you!" She pointed to the picture where I looked like a grape with anklet socks. "This picture is just darling! Why don't you wear that dress more often, honey?"

"Umm . . . can't find it, Mom."

One night at dinner my dad surprised us.

"Kids, you've been doing so well in school, and we have a little extra money now, so I think I'm going to go ahead and put in a little natatorium in the back yard."

I looked up from my macaroni and cheese. Betty jabbed the air with her fork.

"Oh, no, Dad." She looked scared. "You're not going to put something weird in the back yard again, are you? A bomb shelter or something?"

"A swimming pool, Betty! He means a swimming pool!" I almost choked on my milk, I was so excited.

"Mary's right," said my dad, winking.

"Sure," said Betty, piercing her green beans. "I'll believe it when I see it."

"Wow! When will we have it?" For a minute, there was no doubt in my mind that my dad was talking about a beautiful chlorine-blue pool with a diving board and a deep end.

"How about the day after school gets out, when you all come home with straight A's?" Dad leaned back and smiled in his best imitation of Ward Cleaver.

"That's a nice idea, dear," Mom murmured from her position at the sink.

The next day, I wore the purple dress to school. I didn't keep my coat on all day.

"Hey, there, Garbage Girl!" It was Kiki Lang again, singing that horrible song. "Keller! If your parents are so rich now, why don't they buy you some new clothes?"

"My parents are so rich they're putting in a swimming pool, Kiki!"

"Oh yeah? Big deal."

"How big a swimming pool?" asked Cindy Taylor, Kiki's best friend and shadow. Somehow, Cindy got blamed when it was really Kiki who stole the communion hosts—blessed ones, no less—from the tabernacle and passed them out to first-graders on the playground during recess one day.

"You've seen the Olympics, haven't you?"

Kiki and Cindy raised their eyebrows and tilted their heads.

"Yeah, so," they said at the same time.

"You've seen the U.S. Olympic Swim Team on TV training in Mission Viejo, right?"

I knew this was true because everyone had a crush on Mark Spitz and Don Schollander. Kiki and Cindy raised their eyebrows again but didn't say anything.

"Well, it's about *that* big!" I spread my arms out.

"Oh yeah?" Kiki and Cindy said, again in tandem.

"Yeah! And it'll be heated! And in the winter we'll freeze it over and go ice-skating!"

What a difference a pool made.

At the next recess, Kiki told me to come over and play foursquare. Later in the week, she asked me to be her partner at tetherball. And finally, in May, as the end of the school year approached, she invited me to play at her house after school.

The whole class looked on me with new eyes. Until the end of the year, I drew a crowd at every recess, describing our new pool. I threw in other embellishments as well. The other kids suddenly liked me, I thought, because they liked my stories.

"Yes, we do drink coconut milk for breakfast," I said one day. "In fact, the only coconut tree in Wisconsin is growing in our back yard." The next day: "We once had a pet lion but it was hit by a car. Our house is so big we ride our bicycles in the hallways."

I became almost as cool as Sister B. Bea Cool. I even started to feel thin. "We'll import dolphins from Florida on the Fourth of July for a dolphin show! I already know how to feed dolphins! You know, there isn't just one Flipper, there are a bunch of dolphins on the TV show, but they call them all Flipper, and, you know there isn't just one Lassie, there are about ten of them . . . and, and—Mark Spitz is going to come and train in our pool this summer!" As I chattered, I followed Sister Carleen's revolution around the playground. She saw and heard all, black habit swinging around her like a bell. My neck burned when she stopped to talk to Father Grace. I knew he would recognize my voice through the crossed slats of the confessional.

* * *

On the last day of school, I invited Kiki and Cindy over to my house for the grand opening of our new pool, which my dad promised for the next day.

"How high is the diving board?" asked Cindy, doubt in her eyes, a suspicious lift to her voice. She really believed me, I realized. She believed in the pool.

"I'm not sure . . . ," I said, avoiding her eyes. I was beginning to worry.

"There better be a pool in your back yard, Keller," said Kiki, narrowing the menacing green beads of her eyes.

"Are you kidding?" I said, holding my palms up. I spoke to the space over their heads. "You guys won't believe this pool . . ."

That night my dad was late for dinner.

"Your dad has a few things to do tonight, kids," said my mother. "He's out getting the pool."

"*Getting* the pool? Doesn't he have to build it?" I was still in denial, hoping for a miracle.

Mom laughed. "It's not the kind of pool you build, silly!"

"It's the kind you blow up," said Betty. She crossed her eyes at me.

I ignored them both. The image of a shimmering Olympic-sized swimming pool was so deep in my mind I thought I could conjure it up, if I just concentrated hard enough. I ate all of my sauerkraut without gagging. I hated sauerkraut.

Although I knew my dad was not really going to construct an Olympic pool in our back yard, I avoided thinking about how Kiki and Cindy would react when they discovered the truth. We had gotten to be such good friends, I figured we would all just laugh about it. "You mean you can't see it?" I would say, pretending it was a magic pool, visible only to me. "Oh, Keller, you're such a spaz," Kiki would say, punching my shoulder affectionately. Cindy would laugh along with us.

That night I dreamed the Holy Family was in my back yard. Their halos guided them like the bulbs of miners' hats as they transformed the lawn into a beautiful turquoise pool. When it was done, the Blessed Virgin filled the pool with holy water from a glowing clay pitcher. The pitcher, too, had a halo.

Betty's radio woke me up the next morning. I heard the Rascals singing a song about a beautiful morning. I couldn't get excited about it being the first day of summer vacation. I avoided looking out the windows facing the back yard.

At eleven, Kiki and Cindy rolled up our drive on their shiny bicycles, all bright chrome and colored streamers. They were wearing new swimming suits I had seen in the J. C. Penney catalog. My suit was a hand-me-down from my cousin who lived in Florida—a white one-piece covered with red and blue seahorses. The suit was too big, and the straps kept sliding off my shoulders. My chest was not hard and flat like Kiki's, and I blushed. I had grown since the last time I put on a swimming suit, the summer before.

My mother wouldn't let us go in the back yard until after we'd finished the pizza she hand-tossed just for us. I saw Kiki and Cindy looking at each other and I knew they thought my mom was weird. I wasn't sure if that was good or bad. It was a hot clear blue day in June, perfect for the first swim of the summer. We were waiting for the signal from my dad.

"O.K., Eileen," I heard him holler. "Bring the kids out!"

I ran through the screen door with Kiki and Cindy on my heels. Betty was already in the yard, with a funny look on her face.

There, in the middle of our weed-free green lawn, was a large plastic wading pool. It was about ten feet long and five feet wide. The bottom was painted with large hot-pink tropical fish, and rest of the pool was bright yellow. It was the silliest, ugliest thing I had ever seen in my entire life.

"That's fifty square feet of fun, kids!" called my dad from the garage, where he was changing the oil on the station wagon. Betty stood by the plastic puddle and rolled her eyes.

My stomach began to swing inside me. My heart seemed to swell and I could hear it pounding in my ears. I felt my face getting hot. Kiki and Cindy started to giggle.

"Some Olympic pool, Garbage Girl! Hey, where's Mark Spitz? What about the time trials?" said Kiki.

"Where's the high dive?" Cindy squealed.

I smiled dumbly and blinked back tears.

Kiki laughed. "Keller, I could have more fun in my bathtub!"

"Aw, why don't you both go play on the railroad tracks," said my sister, in a voice like a growl. Betty didn't get mad very often, but when she did, it was scary.

Kiki and Cindy looked at each other, ran down the driveway, and hopped on their gleaming Schwinn three-speed bicycles.

"Thanks for the pizza, Mrs. Keller," called Kiki, as she rode past the kitchen window. My mother waved. She was boiling the twenty-four mason jars she'd found at a yard sale.

My dad sang like Bing Crosby, a tuneless "ba-ba-ba-boo," as he inspected the dandelions popping up through the asphalt in the driveway. "ba-ba-ba-boo . . ."

I couldn't move. I looked at my sister, the pool, the house, my dad, and I burst into tears.

Betty, who never touched me, put her arm around my shoulders and made me turn so my dad couldn't see I was crying. "You can hang out with me this summer, Mary. You don't need those snotty girls. You'll be cool with me." And then she hugged me.

We went back to the pool. We splashed around. Betty ran inside the house and came back wearing my mother's cat-eye sunglasses and the smart red two-piece bathing suit she had also inherited from a cousin. Betty tested the water of the pool, swirling the grass clippings that floated in the tepid water with her toes. The yellow and hot-pink wading pool looked different with Betty, Sister Cool herself, lounging in it like a model in a Coppertone ad. I got in too, and turned my face up to the sun just like she did.

JOHN LOGAN

The Relic

When I was younger I was very devoted to a saint. His name was Silvestris and he kept a garden back in Roman times and nobody knew he was a Christian. He kept it to himself. It wasn't that he felt "every man to his own religion, more or less, so why make an issue of it." The reason he kept quiet was because it was dangerous to yourself and your family if others knew you were a Christian. For example, you might be made into a living torch, or sent to the Circus and the wife and kids along with you.

St. Silvestris wasn't worried about repercussion on his family, because it happened that he was a bachelor, but somebody had convinced him he should think of his own safety—why be so presumptuous as to suppose you were a St. Ignatius, born to be martyred, impatient to be made into wheat for holy bread within the mill of the lion's maw? Silvestris was not so sure a man, and so he stayed quiet and kept his garden, content to bring up the rear in heaven.

I am telling you something about this saint because I loved him once, and that was why my friend sent me the relic of him. One day's end, when Silvestris was minding his own business in his small garden, a lady and her very beautiful daughter, whose name is not recorded, turned off the road and came toward him. It was getting dark and Silvestris thought the beautiful young one in particular was quite mistakenly away from home and was approaching with impropriety. Furthermore, her mother stepped on some of the tomatoes he was setting out, and he became righteously angry. He shouted at them to get the heaven out of his rows and go home where the two of them belonged at this hour.

The women left without a word, but they later took Silvestris' sharp language to court—it seemed they were innocently looking for someplace to buy garlic sets—and so Silvestris was called before the magistrate. His habit of not showing up for sacrifice became known through the questioning, he was revealed a Christian, his garden was trampled and he was eaten either by a lion or by a large leopard.

Something about him made me love him and think of him as a special patron. Possibly, I thought, because he loved to garden: so did I. There are many saints who used to garden, but most on a huge monastic scale for gain or penance. Silvestris just seemed to like to do it for himself, as I did. And one needs saints that could possibly take an interest in one, I thought, so I made my needs known to him and he seemed to help me. Soon I came to think of him as a kind of father.

My own father hated gardening and was only interested in baseball in the spring. Baseball bored me. My older brother played ball too, beginning in January and continuing until October, and from November through January he used an electrical machine to play baseball in the house. Once he was running backward to catch a fly my father had thrown him and, instead, he got caught himself in one of my fresh rows and fell backward hitting his head, or rather the soft back of his neck, against a stake that carried a sign for "peas." It cracked some of his vertebrae and put him in the hospital flat on his back for many weeks. I went to visit him and found complicated traction machinery holding his head in a vise the way he used to hold me in fights, which I always lost if they were fair. Once in a not-fair fight I had hit him on the head with one of his baseball bats.

I thought my brother was going to die in the hospital, and I went to visit him almost every day, but he got completely well. However, he played ball in a lot around the side of the house the next spring and didn't come near my garden. That happened to be the first year I had a genuine Silvestrine Garden.

I had told my friend Doug O'Dell about Father Silvestris, as

I called him, and Doug also became interested. Together we read everything we could to find out about Father S., and I wrote a poem on his life based on a research paper Doug did for an English class. The poem was published in the high school paper, of which Doug was editor. We started the Silvestine Garden Club and offered a money prize, kindly put up by our principal H. O. LeMars, for the best spring garden. The prize was given on May 31, Father Silvestris' feast day.

There were no girls allowed in the club. Let them join the Future Farmers of America, we said. We followers of Father Silvestris (we all called him this, though the parish priest said he was merely a lay saint) weren't planning to be married and we weren't planning to be farmers, selling food to people and transporting it in huge trucks and raising animals. We were gardeners because we loved gardening and were going to have it always as a hobby.

Some of the Silvestrines also played baseball avidly, but Doug and I played only under pressure. The last year in high school he and I sometimes talked about learning tennis. It looked to me like the uniforms were a lot more comfortable and also it was just you and the other person, or you and him and another couple.

However, that last summer I was more interested in gardening than ever, had the biggest one yet, and even extended it around the side of the house where my brother had practiced since his fall. Sometimes that summer I also played catch with my dad. He tried to teach me how to catch right-handed. I had always caught and batted with my left and I felt funny, especially about the latter, standing on the wrong side of home plate and making the pitcher uncomfortable. I had some success learning to catch with my right hand, because I owned a right-hand mitt of my father's, which he had given me. It seemed to me like the huge hand of a man, and it helped me, though it was awkward to use. I think I could still find it someplace.

I prayed to Father Silvestris a lot that summer. I was trying to decide whether to join the air force in the fall or take a job or go to college. I thought I might work in a greenhouse, or study botany. I didn't really know what the hell to do because I didn't know who I might be and I used to talk to my father about it while we played catch. I thought I wanted to fly more than anything and often dreamed of it. I used to stand in the garden, after cleaning the weeds all out in the evening and making the thing orderly, and look up at the sky—watching the quiet, turning birds and trying to imagine the ecstasy of freedom, the intense inner relaxation they felt. I associated it somehow in my mind with Father Silvestris' freedom, the freedom of the saint.

One day I stayed out in the yard long after dark and lay in the grass, watching the airplane beacon twenty miles away as it swept across the bottom of the sky. I followed it with longing and began to anticipate in myself the appearance and disappearance of the cycling light until I began to feel that somehow the beacon lagged. The repeated inner motion and the sharpness of the inner light made me a little sick, and I found myself calling Father Silvestris' name softly in the recurring dark and hearing him answer with the coming of the changing light across the sky. It was like an obscure conversation.

The next morning I discovered I had made up my mind—no more problem. I was going to college to study botany. After that I supposed I could always depend on Father Silvestris.

Doug O'Dell joined the navy and went to Italy on a cruise late the following year, my third term in college. We corresponded often and one day he told me he had visited the church where Father Silvestris was buried and had started negotiations to obtain a relic of him—a piece of bone he hoped. I wrote that I was very glad for him and very envious. I sent him a poem about the rising of the bit of bone to form the spiritualized limbs of Father Silvestris, moving about in the gardens of light beyond the airplanes and in the places where no one ever trampled. The last stanza began:

Perhaps the beautiful girl
Who came to his garden and
Sent him to the lion
Now walks with him as sister
In the rows of Eden upon the
Mount of Zion.

The poem ended with the idea that the poet hoped some day to join the two of them in their ecstasy.

One day I got a letter from Doug saying he had met a girl on leave in Rome and had fallen head over heels in love. The letter was completely about the girl, Ida. I wrote back that he was the first to break our Silvestrine pact against women, for we had agreed not to marry even if it led to lions or something of the kind. I tried to introduce a tone of levity into my warning that the phrase "head over heels" reminded me of what happened to my brother in my garden. (Doug of course knew the story of my brother's accident.) I told him I had no time for girls anyway, being too busy studying, and that I had plans for the largest garden of my entire career that summer, in which I intended to carry out some experiments for a course in plant physiology. I said the experiments struck me as necessary because otherwise a garden of the size I was interested in would produce so much I would probably have to sell some to get rid of it, which would mean I also had broken the pact.

Doug replied to the effect the pact be damned, that he found out he wasn't at all interested in bachelorhood and that when he told his girl about my letter she got huffy and asked him to let me know she had not the slightest intention of breaking his neck. On the contrary, she said. Doug added a rather vulgar remark about his "girl's garden."

The letter made me depressed because I was afraid I had made him mad and that we wouldn't be friends any longer.

It's easy to understand, therefore, how completely overwhelmed I was when a few weeks later I received from Doug not only a letter but a gift—he sent me the relic of Father Silvestris he had applied for! The letter of presentation struck me at the time as both touching and witty—the latter a quality I hadn't been sure Doug had. His concluding sentences were elaborated into rhymed verse, perhaps in exchange for the poem I had sent him:

> And thus I send you, dear old dog and brother,
> A bone from your bachelor father.
> May it bring you comfort through the years of burden
> And be buried with you in your beloved garden.

ROBERT CLARK YOUNG

Impurity

1. Hot Dog Day

I'm six years old, in the first grade at St. Jerome's School, and I'm standing in the wrong line. I don't know it yet. It's Hot Dog Day; instead of bringing our lunches, we've brought a nickel, a dime, and a quarter, which we've exchanged for the corresponding school tokens, black rubber coins chewed out of shape by three generations of neurotic Catholic kids standing in lines like these. With these tokens, we're supposed to buy milk, a cupcake, and a hot dog. We're standing single file, arm's distance, in half a dozen lines in the parish hall. The black-hooded nuns dish out the food like medieval mess sergeants.

"You! You in the green sweater!"

I don't turn around. Nobody does. There are three hundred kids in the parish hall, all in green sweaters. We have the SJS monogram over our left pockets.

"You, boy! You're in the wrong line!"

The hall becomes quiet. We've recognized the strident, accusatory voice: it's Sister Claire Patrice, the principal, the most powerful person on Earth. God has left her in charge of his planet while he confers with the Saints, the Pope, and other important Italians.

Sister Claire Patrice marches toward my line. "You!" Her finger, white as bone, sticks out from the black folds of her habit—at me! I stop chewing on my five-cent token, paralyzed, my head hot and heavy, as though the ceiling and walls are pressing down on it.

"What are you *doing* standing *there*?"

I have no answer. It's as though God has descended to Earth in an angry black cloud and demanded to know what I'm doing in North America. *You there, you miserable misplaced thing in a green sweater!* But I'm more afraid of Sister Claire Patrice than of God. We were in God's house this morning, practicing for Ash Wednesday mass. We had to kneel and get up, kneel and get up, over and over. The kneelers kept sticking to our knees, then falling to the floor, causing Sister Claire Patrice to cover the ear-spots on her black hood with both hands.

"You're offending God!" she yelled in the church. "Stop bouncing His kneelers! You there, in the green sweater, and you!"

As Sister Claire Patrice approaches me, her face an angry blob of too-white dough protruding from its black prison, the entire school is watching.

The pointing finger has been joined by the rest of her fingers, a white claw—it closes around my upper arm. It keeps closing, and closing. I wince as her nails slice through my green sweater and white shirt, into my skin, into the bone. She grips me hard, harder—nobody watching knows how hard she's twisting her nails into my arm; it's a private communication of hatred.

"You're in the—wrong—*line*!" She yanks me physically off my feet, and I start crying. As she drags me across the parish hall, my ankles feel like they're going to collapse; my head swims in the white light from the neon tubes overhead.

She thrusts me into the proper line, but still doesn't let go.

"Please," I say through my tears, "it hurts."

"Christ had nails through His flesh. Do you understand? They stuck thorns in His flesh because of *you* and *your sins*. Your pain is nothing next to His on the cross."

"My arm," I sob.

"Your arm belongs to God. Do you understand me? Every sinning little piece of you belongs to Him. If a piece of your body causes you to sin, you should cut it off and offer it back up to God. The human body is a dirty, sinning thing."

But then she notices something else, across the room. "You

there!" she says, releasing me. "You there, in the green sweater. You go to the milk line *before* the cupcake line. You there!"

I rub my arm. It stings for an hour.

2. *One Hundred Forty-Seven Tongues*

I'm ten years old, an altar boy. The human body is a dirty, sinning thing. It's my job to help Father McGill restore the dirty, sinning bodies of St. Jerome's Parish. Only Christ's body is clean. The people must take Christ's body into their own bodies, to make them clean. But they won't stay clean for long—the process must be repeated every day. This is true of everyone, including me. I'm a dirty impure thing with a cursed body, as wicked and corrupt—somehow—as the fallen bodies of Adam and Eve.

I wear a white robe over a red tunic. I kneel behind the priest and ring, at the appropriate moments in the liturgy, a golden musical bell so shiny I can see myself in it—in the curve of the bell, I'm warped, misshapen, not worthy of touching it. Before the moment of consecration, I bring water and wine to the priest. The liquids sit in thick glass decanters with big stoppers, so that my hands won't soil the pure fluids which will become the blood of my Savior.

My greatest responsibility comes during communion. I must accompany the priest as he moves down the railing where the people are kneeling. At the end of a handle, I hold an oval golden plate. I put it beneath the chin of each communicant—this is in the case the body of Christ should fall off the tongue; if I allow the host to fall to the floor, the curtain in the temple will rend, the sky will open with a black rain of death, the universe will double on itself and erupt in cosmic flame. God is testing me. If I let Him fall to the floor—the dirty floor where sinners' feet have been—the world will end, we will all go to Hell, and it'll be my fault.

I watch my work carefully. I don't like watching it. The first time I served as altar boy, I was sickened by what I saw. The human tongue, thrust forward and laid out flat, is not an attractive thing. Each tongue was repulsive in its own way, this one coated in white, this one too red and veiny, this one almost brown and curled back on itself. The tongues of the old are the worst—sick dying anemic spotted tongues, all of them wicked and diseased, hideous, unworthy of the pure white host the priest must dispense with his purified hands.

I'm not allowed to look away from the horrid tongues. If I do, a host might fall. And with it a universe. To distract myself, I count the tongues (though I know this is also a sin—my mind must be on God's work). I count one hundred and forty-seven tongues. Evil, fleshy, twisted, fat, and gnarled. Unholy.

I will never look at mine in the mirror.

3. Miss Mazur's Dirty Little Secret

I'm eleven years old. It's the first day of sixth grade. Sister Maureen, my homeroom teacher, overweight and wearing thick brown glasses, is introducing the new science teacher, Miss Mazur. We've had lay teachers before (not enough women are becoming nuns these days), so there's nothing special about Miss Mazur—except for a quality I can't name.

She's young, with blond hair, with legs that are moving . . . crossing and uncrossing, nervously, under a knee-length skirt. She has pointed little breasts, larger than, but reminding me of, the alluring protobosoms of the seventh- and eighth-grade girls. I enjoy looking at Miss Mazur. I've never enjoyed looking at a teacher before.

"Miss Mazur has something to tell you," says Sister Maureen, slurping a Tab. She's always carrying a soda. "After she's told it to you, I don't want anyone to treat her any differently. You must love her and respect her as though she were—any other teacher. These are difficult days for God's Church."

Miss Mazur stands up. I enjoy watching her stand up. Her body is interesting. I'm troubled by this, and anxious to hear the revelation.

"Boys and girls," she begins. She bites her lower lip in a shy attractive way. Then she opens her mouth and I see her tongue poised for speech—her tongue is small, pink, beautiful. After a moment she says, "Sister Maureen thinks it best that I should—" Another pause. Her eyes flutter. "That I should tell you that I'm a Methodist."

We're so quiet, you could hear a communion wafer drop. We're sitting rigidly, looking down at our desks.

"There aren't enough Catholics in the world," Sister Maureen says. She slurps her Tab. "At least, not enough who are willing to teach or become nuns." She sighs. She burps. She looks embarrassed and leaves the room.

Throughout the science lesson—plants, photosynthesis—I watch Miss Mazur. I love to watch her move. Her blond hair bounces, her legs suggest themselves beneath her skirt, her bottom shifts from side to side. I can tell already she's going to be my favorite teacher, this exhilarating sprite, this exotic Methodist. I feel a delicious stirring in my crotch.

Is everyone as intrigued as I am? Apparently not. At the end of class, a girl in the front row clutches her books, runs to the door, turns, and looks straight at the new teacher. The girl's face erupts in tears. "We don't care if you're a Methodist, Miss Mazur—we still like you!" The girl escapes before Miss Mazur can respond.

I continue to feel stimulated in this odd, new way. It's exciting and strangely depressing. I cannot name this thing. But I already know it's a sin.

4. *The Boner that Went to Hell*

I'm in eighth grade. The class is preparing for confirmation. The boys have been separated from the girls. This is confusing, since we won't be playing sports. Father Flanagan, a special priest sent by the Archdiocese, will be instructing us. Sister Maureen has announced the title of his presentation: "Keeping a Pure Manly Body in a World of Sin."

At two o'clock sharp, Father Flanagan comes bouncing into the room. He's a small man, built like a frog, bowlegged and barrel-chested, with a warty reptilian head wider than it is long. The effect is exaggerated by his ear-to-ear smile.

"My name is Lloyd Flanagan," he says, "and I'm a new kind of priest. I'm the kind of priest young men can talk to about their problems. Bishop Delaney has asked me to talk to you about being a man." He pulls out a little stack of business cards and begins handing them out. "This is my private telephone number at the diocesan office, boys. I want you to call me whenever you have a question about being a man. Remember, I'm a new kind of priest, so you can tell me anything that's on your minds, in the words you'd normally say. Does anyone have any questions about being a man?"

Nobody raises a hand. We're all reading the cards:

Lloyd G. Flanagan, S.J.
"A Priest You Can Talk to"
Call this number when you're tempted to act impurely:
555-4GOD
(Collect Calls Accepted)

"I'm going to talk to you straight, boys. I'm going to use the words you would use. Do you know what I'm here to talk about? I'm here to talk about boners. A boner is something known as a hard-on or a woody."

We look away from his smiling toadlike face. We couldn't be more shocked or puzzled if he confessed to being a Methodist.

"A boner," says the priest, shoving his hands into his hip pockets and strutting across the front of the room, "is nothing to play with. God created boners for marriage, so you can bring more souls into His Holy Church. Most of you, of course, have already experienced a boner. Listen to me, boys, this is very important: having a boner is *not* a sin. At your age, involuntary boners may occur at any time, unaccompanied by impure thoughts. However, if you *touch* that boner in a way that is pleasurable to you, a venial sin has been committed. Who can tell me the punishment for a venial sin?"

Every hand goes up. All students at St. Jerome's, even those who don't know the word "boner," have been able to define "venial" since first-grade catechism.

"A venial sin," one of the boys answers, "gets punished by Purgatory. Purgatory can last forever, unless your parents or some cloistered nuns are praying for your dead soul."

"Correct," says Father Flanagan. "Now listen to me carefully, boys. If you touch that boner and continue to touch it until a sticky white substance shoots out from the tip, you have committed a *mortal* sin. What is the punishment for a mortal sin?"

"Eternity in Hell," several boys respond.

"Very good."

"But—" somebody says, and we all turn around. It's Wally Rickman, a skinny guy with glasses. Last week, he won first prize in the science fair for a pinewood rocket, powered by propellers and rubber bands, that went flying over the rectory. Now, like Galileo, he must challenge the Church: "But Father Flanagan, are you saying that—that playing with yourself—is the same as murder? A mortal sin is like killing someone."

"That's *exactly* what I'm saying," says the priest. "Boners and ejaculations are reserved for marriage, for the conception of children. If you masturbate, you're killing your own children."

"That doesn't make any sense," says Wally.

"Whether it makes any sense to you or not, the important thing is that you never, ever touch yourself *down there*."

That night I lie rigid—vertically and horizontally—in bed, unable to sleep. The pup tent in my pajamas confirms what I've always known: my body is a dirty, sinning thing that will take me to Hell. I go partway to sleep, suffering half-dreams, a replay of the priest's lecture, Miss Mazur's thighs moving beneath her skirt, slick pages cut from *Penthouse* and passed furtively in gym class, a cartoon from another sex magazine—Moses standing on Mt. Sinai, a stone tablet in each hand, talking to the cloud which contains God—"Now let me get this straight, you want us to cut the tops of our *dicks* off?"

I'd rather have my entire penis cut off than suffer this half-sleep which can be relieved by only one thing, the thing which will take me to Hell, the release of my impure fluids . . . only the fluids of Christ, the water and wine sitting in clear decanters in the sacristy, are pure . . . all other fluids are tainted with sin . . .

I give in—my boner will go to Hell and take me with it; I touch myself *down there*.

5. *Father Flanagan's Trailer*

Two years have gone by. I'm in high school, masturbating two or three times a day, going to Hell, confessing it on Saturdays, giving in again on Saturday night, living the doubly hellish, Catholic version of *Portnoy's Complaint.*

In biology lab, Wally Rickman hands me a newspaper clipping that's been circulating among the guys. He watches me grimly as I read:

CATHOLIC PRIEST SUED BY WOMAN'S HEIRS

A Roman Catholic priest is being sued by the daughters of a Los Angeles widow.

Alice O'Brien and Rebecca Magniola charge that the priest, Lloyd Flanagan, 52, used his position in the church to influence their mother, Mrs. Fred Habersham, to change her will. Mrs. Habersham, who died March 19, willed the priest $3,000, a 1976 Chevy Nova, and a 54-foot mobile home.

O'Brien and Magniola claim that Father Flanagan had a six-month sexual relationship with the 83-year-old widow, whom he met at a bingo game at St. Jerome's parish in West Los Angeles. The sexual relationship allegedly developed after Sunday dinners in the woman's Santa Monica trailer.

The children of at least three other west side widows are alleging that Father Flanagan met their mothers at bingo games, had dinner with them, then took advantage of their loneliness in order to obtain sex, cash, automobiles, and mobile homes. . . .

"It's not as bad as it could be," I say through my shock.

Wally knows what I mean. "That's right. At least he didn't touch himself *down there.*"

6. *The C-Word*

I'm a senior in high school. I've just taken over as editor of our school paper, *The Jeromian*. I'm developing into quite an anti-sports, anti-dancing, compulsively masturbating intellectual. I'm no fun. I've written an editorial condemning the unhygienic conditions I've discovered at the sophomore bake sale.

Sister Katha is the faculty moderator for the paper. She's young, twenty-three. She's a "modern" nun, the Church's grudging nod to contemporary culture. She plays folk guitar at mass. She has a McGovern sticker on her Volkswagen. She wears a blue veil that doesn't completely cover her hair and a blue skirt that doesn't completely cover her knees. She's a California nun with a tan.

Sister Katha doesn't like me. I keep returning her memos with spelling and grammar corrections.

She asks me to stay after journalism class. I stand before her desk. "Why do you hate people?" she says.

"I don't hate anyone," I say. I despise her; I despise all stupid people. I'm seventeen and already smarter than half the faculty. Several prominent Catholic universities have offered me four-year scholarships. I'm no longer afraid of nuns.

"This is unacceptable," she says, throwing my editorial on the desk. "We can't publish it."

"Why not?"

"You put down those sophomore girls. You make them look like ninnies. You insult them—I got mad when I saw the C-word."

Horrified, I rummage frantically through memory. I was up till two A.M. writing the editorial—in my bleary, condescending frustration, how many four-letter words did I allow my typing fingers to stray over? Next to the mortal sin which my body commits almost naturally, a four-letter word seems like nothing. Still . . .

I pick up the editorial. "Where? Where's the C-word?"

"Paragraph five."

I'm surprised she knows what a paragraph is, this folk-singing, beach-bumming, hippie-hugging nun. I read the paragraph:

> Most disturbing of all, perhaps, is the propensity toward anti-intellectual activities at an institution whose focus is ostensibly academic. How many classes must be interrupted for pep rallies, club meetings, sports announcements—and now for cookie sales?

I toss the editorial back at her. I know my writing is better than that of any seventeen-year-old in the school, the city, the state—possibly the world. "I don't see anything wrong with this," I say.

"You can't use the C-word."

"It's not there."

"Cookie," she whispers in disgust. "You can't use that word! It makes the Baking Club sound small-time and stupid."

"The Baking Club *is* small-time and stupid. *All* the clubs and sports teams are small-time and stupid. This *school* is small-time and stupid."

She looks at me with the puzzled shock of a five-year-old. I expect her to begin sobbing and to choke out the words: "I'm gonna tell my mommy!" Instead, like a drill sergeant, like a dock foreman, like Hitler—like a nun—she says, "You're on report, sir!"

"Scratch a folk-singing nun," I say, bolting from the room, "and you get the same old Nazi nun."

Later that afternoon, in the principal's office, I'm fired as editor and given ten demerits for calling a teacher a Nazi. "Do you have anything to say," asks Sister Magdalen, the black-hooded, traditional nun who runs the school, "in your own defense?"

"I would've called her a brown shirt, but the allusion might be over her head."

I'm given ten more demerits.

I work off three of the demerits by washing chalkboards. Skeeter Kelly, a football player who's always in trouble, wants to know why a "poindexter" like me has to stay after school. I tell him.

His pronouncement, as he rinses out a sponge, is what you might expect: "Aw, man, that Sister Katha needs a good fuck."

7. *Love Among the Seminary Boys*

I'm nineteen. For the past two years, I've been attending one of the top Catholic universities in the country, majoring in English. I've come to accept my body—or at least my genitals. I no longer believe I'll go to Hell. I no longer believe in Hell. In fact, I no longer believe in God.

I've become an atheistic novelist. In place of Roman Catholicism, I have a new set of delusions to torture myself with: I'll become one of the greatest novelists known to Western literature . . . I'll receive a six-figure advance . . . I'll win the love of the world's most beautiful women . . .

Being a swinging writer, I soon find out, is just as hard as being a "good Catholic boy." My stories come back from New York with rejection slips as severe as any penance doled out in the confessional. Nor am I becoming a ladies' man—the coeds I meet are either frigid from years of modeling themselves on statues of the Virgin Mary, or, if they've rebelled against the Church, they've rebelled in the only way possible, *completely*—if you want to date *them,* you've got to be a Protestant guy from State.

The months of sexual frustration drag on. Rejections from publishers keep pace with rejections from women. In the midst of this, scandalous headlines appear in the papers:

HOMOSEXUALS THROWN OUT OF SEMINARY
SEMINARIANS DENY ORGY RUMORS
CHURCH DELIVERS BLOW TO GAYS

It turns out somebody *has* been getting laid at this school—in the seminary dorm, night after night, young men have been cuddling, kissing, blowing each other, fucking each other in the ass, and falling asleep in each other's arms. Some of the priests have become involved. The scandal breaks when the monsignor's jilted lover goes to the newspapers.

The bishop acts quickly: the students involved are expelled; the priests are transferred. But it's too late. Gay activists from as far away as Provincetown and San Francisco picket the university. Campus security arrives in squad cars that are yellow and white—Vatican colors—with crosses painted on the hoods. The cops plead vainly for the crowds to disperse.

The bishop arrives with a megaphone. "We love you," he tells the protesters, "we just hate your sins."

A group is mooning him: dirty sinning asses, right in his face.

8. In Open Defiance of Rome

I start looking for women off-campus. I meet Janis, a Protestant girl with big breasts. We fall in love. We have sex all the time. She meets me after my Latin class and we make love behind the thick bushes outside the classroom. This is the best experience I've had in sixteen years of Catholic education.

Over Christmas, we go to Europe for three weeks. England, France, Italy. We visit the Vatican. In the Sistine Chapel, I see the only penis recognized pictorially by the Roman Catholic Church—Adam's pre-fall cock on the ceiling.

In the basilica, Janis is intrigued by the big wooden confessionals. "They're neat," she says. "They're like God's telephone booths."

I'm comfortable. "Not exactly," I say.

"I think it's so neat you can go inside there and get things straight with God. If you want to go in, I'll hold your camera."

"I don't want to."

"Why not? I can't imagine not wanting to go. If I were Catholic, I'd go every day."

"No you wouldn't. There's a priest in there who'd give you nine different reasons in nine different languages why you'd have to stop seeing me. Our whole relationship is a sin. I'm not even supposed to be bringing you here—Lutherans were excommunicated five hundred years ago. Come on, let's get the hell out."

Janis is hurt and confused. I'm moody and withdrawn the rest of the day. I remember a bumper sticker I saw many years ago in the church parking lot: THERE'S NO SUCH THING AS AN EX-CATHOLIC. My depression deepens.

The next day is Christmas. We awake in Papa Germano's Pensione in the heart of Rome. Down the hall, Papa Germano and his three dozen children by his four mistresses, the forty children of all his children's mistresses, and his fat happy wife are singing Italian songs, cooking wonderfully redolent food, and drinking good red Italian wine before noon. If you've lived in the shadow of the Vatican for two thousand years, you learn to adapt.

Janis and I make love in the huge sagging Roman bed. Five kilometers to the west, half a million people fill St. Peter's Square. They've come to hear the Pope tell them what they can and cannot do with their impure, sinful bodies. He will decry abortion, birth control, eroticism. Though I can't hear him, I'm aware of every word he's uttering as Janis and I explore one another, putting fingers and mouths where no Catholic fingers or mouths should go; unrolling a condom, that vulcanized murder weapon produced by an atheistic high-tech America; uncapping the hundred million mortal sins in a tube of spermicidal cream; fornicating, fornicating, fornicating; cumming together, panting, gasping, murdering a hundred million would-be souls; and finally, holding each other in satisfied silence as the party next door dips and bubbles and explodes, echoing our defiance of Rome.

GRACE FLANNERY

Sister Consolata of the Brassieres

Sister Consolata was small. Petite. Her wire-framed glasses and black veil left only patches of pale skin showing on her fierce face. Her posture was rigid, her back was tense. She moved swiftly, with no swinging, no swaying, no wasted motion. She kept a handkerchief in her hand, or up her sleeve, and used it to blot her forehead, complaining about the heat on even the coldest days.

Sister ruled over my sixth-grade class at St. Bernard's School. The room was bursting with fifty-three boys and girls on the verge of hormonal madness, barely contained by Sister's determined focus on the Church. Under the girls' navy-blue jumpers (mine was proudly dry-cleaned once a year, otherwise tossed in a corner of my room when not in use) and white, round-collared blouses, small pink breasts were budding on soft white or tan skin. Pubic hair sprouted, underarms became tangled forests, menses began to flow.

In our hearts as well as our bodies, strange unknown yearnings moved us. We entered into a fog of confused thinking, half-girls, half-teenagers. Our parents wondered what to do with us. We did, too. I felt miserably out of place, different and uncomfortable lots of times, then suddenly I'd be okay again, riding my bike or hanging around with friends.

My own body hadn't offered much evidence that I was changing, yet, but a few of the girls had definitely developed breasts. Some proudly carried spare Kotex in little shiny pink plastic envelopes in their new purses. Now I understood why women carried purses. Some, like Suzie Mahon, were as flat-chested as me except at parties, which were another new thing in sixth grade, because boys were invited too, and the parties were on Friday nights instead of Saturday afternoons. Suzie would show up wearing a fancy dress with a bra underneath, stuffed with toilet paper. Much to the disbelief of the rest of us girls, the boys fell for it every time. How could they be so stupid? Not just the boys, but Suzie too.

I began sixth grade as a child. No breasts, no blood, no pubic hair, unless you counted a few new wispy strands down there and under my arms. I did notice that my pubic bone seemed to have inexplicably gotten larger. In October, I started bleeding. I choked and stuttered as I tried to tell my mother what was happening. She took me up to the bathroom, sat on the edge of the tub with me, gave me an elastic strap with metal hooks hanging off it—she called it a belt—and some thick paper "napkins" that were fat in the middle and had long thin ends hanging off. She showed me how to hook the napkin onto the belt, and how to wrap it up in toilet paper before I threw it away.

Mother told me I was growing up, I should be happy that my body was getting ready to be able to make babies. She talked about my uterus, that it was growing a thick bloody lining where babies could grow. When the lining got old, it came out as my "period," and then my body made a new lining that would come out the next month. Unless I got pregnant, which of course I wouldn't be doing for years and years. Finally I got it that she wasn't talking about school periods. Now I knew that Beth-Ann had been telling me the truth back in third grade when she said her sister bled from her bottom every month and was old enough to have babies. The blood was called a period.

Sitting there on the edge of the tub with my mother talking to me like I was a real person, I felt different. I was getting closer to adulthood and the bright red blood on my panties was going to help me reach that place of freedom. My mother kept emphasizing things like cramps and bad odors and how to wash the blood spots out of my clothes and bed sheets before they became permanent. I dreamed about being a grown up, having my own life instead of trying to fit in to the childhood I didn't feel at home in anymore. A couple of months later I found out that cramps meant not just stomach cramps but backaches, leg aches, stomach pain, diarrhea, constipation, blood clots, and headaches. My mother wasn't very sympathetic—she just told me to take some aspirin and stop moping around. I'd feel better if I'd get moving, she'd say.

Once I understood what cramps were, I thought it was a gyp to have to have a period at all. And this was going to go on every month for years, farther ahead than I could imagine! At least I could hide it from the boys, not like poor Cecie whose breasts had been very large even in fifth grade. She got teased all the time, and that strange kid named Roger who went to public school used to punch her right in those tender breasts whenever he thought he could get away with it. I dreaded getting breasts even while I examined my flat chest every day for signs of growth.

God only knows what horrifying changes were happening under the boys' uniforms. I certainly hadn't a clue. Although Sister complained about the stale sweat-filled air that fouled the classroom after their gym class, she didn't divulge any male secrets to us girls, if indeed she knew any.

Sister did, however, take advantage of the opportunity to speak with us girls alone, while the boys sweated under Mr. Angelino's nasal drone. "The next exercise is the neck exercise! One! Two! Three! Four!" He must have been the most boring teacher in the world. We did those same stupid neck exercises every week for years. But while the boys had their turn, Sister lectured us relentlessly about our gossiping, laziness, flirtatiousness, and the impending doom we were headed toward, which we could still avoid by heeding her words.

I let my mind wander, fixing my eyes on Sister and acting attentive while I waited for her to wind down. I was fascinated by how the air around her turned black when she was angry. Sister had a habit of speaking through clenched teeth. The overhead lights reflected off her glasses. Her eyes were tiny slits behind the glare. Hardly a muscle in her body moved, but the effect on the classroom was masterful.

Sister threatened to put a chart on the blackboard with all the girls' names and a check mark—yes or no—to indicated who was wearing a "brassiere" that day. Nobody else but my mother ever called a bra by that name. Sister said she'd run her hand up each of our backs as we came in every day, and feel for the band. Then she'd put a mark in the appropriate column. That way, we wouldn't have to gossip, we could pay attention to her. We sat in uncomfortable, squirming, disbelieving silence. I felt helpless, imagining the torment of walking into class every morning and having my flat chest announced to the whole class. Maybe I could sneak into my older sister Katherine's room and find one of her old bras to wear.

Sister's attitude, the part that made it through my haze and into my brain, made me mad. No, I wasn't *only* interested in who wore a bra and who didn't. No, I didn't *necessarily* know who had started to bleed, who had kissed whom, who wore falsies. Yes, I did *too* sometimes read things besides teen magazines and romantic novels. So what if I sometimes daydreamed about being stuck for weeks in a bomb shelter during an attack from the Russians with my deskmate Danny. I also was smart and responsible and always did my homework. Besides, I was polite and careful because I wanted all my teachers to like me.

I tried to believe Sister Consolata made sense. She had to, she was a nun. My parents firmly believed, and I was taught, that nuns and priests are Christ's representatives in this world. In my father's eyes, children should always treat priests, nuns, parents, and other adults with deep respect. They were always right. My mother, always practical, was less concerned about respect and more determined that we should be obedient. Nuns, priests, and parents were always to be obeyed.

My older brother, Johnny, seemed to have found a way to balance all this. He charmed the nuns and priests, and at home he held the place of honor as my parents' firstborn son. Daddy wanted him to be a politician, thought he had just the right charismatic personality. Johnny could get away with being a bit superior, with making a joke of anything that made him uncomfortable. He moved through life magically, always a year older, always graceful, always welcome wherever he went.

Meanwhile, Daddy told me if I was a good girl and turned out to be real pretty, I could grow up to marry a prince like Grace Kelly. Mother expected my future to hold a lot of cooking and sewing and cleaning, and she wanted me to do it right. I would grow up to be a good mother. I wandered through my life aimlessly, unfocused. Of course I would need something to fall back on, like teaching. It was taken for granted that I would get good grades and be a "good" girl, although it seemed to me that nobody much liked "good" girls, that they were considered boring and were never popular.

Johnny had always been the best. He and I were "Irish twins": we had the same birthday, a year apart. When we were little he had helped me get ready for kindergarten by teaching me how to spell all the colors. And he stood up for me with the other kids. But now it was getting harder to talk to him about things. We were growing apart. These days it was like we were from different planets; I guessed it was because he was a boy. I was too embarrassed about the whole idea of bras to be able to tell him what was happening in school. He hadn't liked Sister Consolata when she'd been his teacher the year before, but he'd never told me she was this weird. I felt really alone.

The day of the big disaster, when I was crying my way back to school, I had to admit to myself that this year had begun all wrong, and I had no idea why. On the first day of school, Sister had said she wanted us all to get a fresh start with each other. She thought we'd probably all heard stories about her from the older kids, and maybe we had some preconceptions, were predisposed not to like her. Just like she had about us. For instance she didn't know anything to like about Mary Grace Flannery except maybe her penmanship.

That was me she was talking about! The good girl, the model student, the responsible one who always got good grades. My mouth dropped open. The room seemed to close in on me. All the other kids turned and looked at me, while I frantically wondered what to do. The room got very hot. I felt paralyzed. My mouth shut, then opened again, then shut. Nothing came out, not even any air. I had stopped breathing. I couldn't imagine Sister even knew who I was! I'd only been in that school one year! Why did she dislike me?

But on she talked. And then, magnanimously, said she was willing to bury the hatchet, and hoped all of us would too. She was willing to give me another chance. I sat in a state of stunned disbelief. I was mortified. Slowly, shallowly, I started to breathe again. Why was this happening to me?

I wanted desperately to forget what Sister had said so I could pretend it hadn't happened. After school, I couldn't find Johnny to tell him about it. Maybe that was better—if I told him, it would be more real. Besides, maybe she hadn't liked him either, maybe that's why she didn't like me. He used to make fun of how she wasn't as smart as him, he knew more about science than she did.

I didn't tell my mother about it either; I felt ashamed, like somehow I deserved what Sister had said. I was afraid Mother would say it was my fault Sister didn't like me. I just didn't get it.

And then, that night, I remembered that incident the year before with the ice cream machine. I had forgotten about it, but now it all came back to me in a sickening rush. It hadn't been my idea to try to make nickels out of cardboard. How was I to know they would get stuck in the machine and break it? Why did I always get blamed? After all, that had been Terry's idea. Why didn't Sister say there was nothing to like about Terry?

I never said another word about Sister's opening-day speech, to anyone. In class, I acted like nothing had happened. I didn't want the whole ice cream machine incident to come back up again. But I knew this whole year was doomed.

After I told Mother about the chart Sister was going to put on the blackboard, Mother coughed and choked a little, then changed the subject. Every so often she would ask, "Anything new with Sister Consolata and the brassieres?" One night at dinner she further humiliated me by telling Daddy the story. How they laughed! I stopped telling them anything about what happened at school.

In the meantime, Johnny had a problem at school that my dad got real upset about. The seventh-grade teacher, Sister Magdalene, treated Johnny horribly. He had been badly hurt in a car accident and his recuperation was slow. Sister Magdalene shamed him and called him a sissy. My dad went to parents' night—which he'd never done before, as far as I knew—and told her she should be ashamed of her behavior, she wasn't even Christian. Sister was indignant, but treated Johnny better. Johnny was embarrassed. I was jealous.

By November, I felt desperate. Mother went in the hospital when Julie was born. Yet another baby sister. Now I was the fourth of ten kids, though my family was still behind the McMurphys with their twelve. Being fourth was miserable in an invisible sort of way, but at least it was the same as Robby McMurphy was in his family. Robby was cute and tough and smart and distant and I'd had a crush on him ever since I first came to St. Bernard's School the year before.

I missed Mother, wanted her to come home so badly that I

cleaned the house in anticipation. I imagined she'd walk in the door, turn to me, and say she knew it must be her Mary Grace who had taken so much care to make her homecoming so pleasant!

When she did come home, it was only for a day, and then she went right back in. Both my grandmothers came to take care of the new baby. They contradicted each other continually and used us kids as go-betweens. One afternoon Grandma Flannery told me to put her casserole in the oven at 325 degrees at four o'clock. Then Grandma Lesperance said to brown the meringue on her lemon pie at four-thirty for fifteen minutes at 375 degrees, and the oven had to be preheated just right before I put the pie in. I started to tell her about the casserole but she said to shush, to just do as I was told. I burnt the casserole and got lectured by my dad for being so stupid.

Another day, I overheard my grandmothers talking about kidneys and veins and how women weren't built to have so many children. They were worn out with taking care of us, they said they would have to tell my dad they were too old for this. Really, I think we were too much for either of them to handle alone; they didn't get along well enough to want to try to make it work between them, and they both wanted to get back to their homes for Christmas.

Soon, Agnes appeared, an Irish woman with a wonderful brogue and red hair. She was to take care of us kids so that when Mother came home we wouldn't send her right back to the hospital. The grandmothers left. I fantasized that Agnes would adopt me and take me away with her, treat me special and never have any other children but me.

I felt scared, lonely, needy, and responsible for everything that went wrong. I had nightmares that the new baby was crying and I was the only one home. I had to sterilize the bottles, mix the formula, feed her, change her diaper. I couldn't find the empty bottles, and I didn't know how to mix the formula right. I was sure if I did it wrong the baby would get sick and die!

After school and in the evening I did the dishes and my homework and lurked around the grown-ups, hoping for some information about what was going on. I followed Agnes around, admired her clothes, and hoped she would treat me as a grown-up, and let me in to her secrets.

My father roared at us to keep us in line. He was determined to maintain control, not wanting to look ineffective even though he was only left in charge every two years or so, when Mother had no choice but to stay in the hospital with the latest baby. Agnes fed us and sent us off to school on time. No one explained what was happening in the hospital, why Mother was there so long, when she'd be coming home.

At school, Sister Consolata raged on. One day, while everything was so scary and hard at home, something happened that made everything just so much worse that I thought maybe I should just run away. I wished I would be magically adopted by another family and move far, far away, maybe to another country.

Sister wanted our total attention, and she was tired of working hard to get it. She threatened that the next one to talk (unless called on by her) would lose twenty-five points off their score on the history test, which she was just about to hand back to us. She wasn't at all pleased with our performance on it, but I knew I'd get an A. Maybe that's what she wasn't pleased about.

Her threats had started to seem hollow after the bra chart failed to appear on the blackboard, and her control of the class was slipping. The class settled down some after this latest tirade, but was nowhere near silent.

I wasn't the only one who talked out of turn. Danny, my deskmate and the object of many fantasies, made a joke, and I answered him, I don't remember what about. Cinda and Mary-Lou were talking, too. Suddenly, I sensed immediate danger. Sister descended on me in full fury. I was to be made an example of, for the whole class. This must have been the moment of her dreams. I still didn't believe she would follow through. I wasn't the only one to disobey!

At the height of her outburst, Sister stopped dramatically, picked up our papers, and began handing them out to us, one at a time. She paused when mine came up, crossed out the "A—100%" and wrote "C—75%" in dark red ink. Gone was my perfect score. I glumly stared at my first C grade. My heart sank to my stomach, which seemed to be trying to get into my throat. My mind was full of panicky voices, protesting, appealing for justice, all the while knowing Sister would never relent.

Slowly, my head cleared. My heart filled with righteous anger. If it hadn't been me, she would have merely yelled at us, given us another warning. She'd never done this to anyone else! What about Cinda and Mary-Lou and Danny? She was only too happy to slash my grade. Logically, I reasoned that it would have been okay to cut my grade in behavior. That would have been appropriate. But this was all wrong. I knew that history, and my test was perfect. Surely my parents would back me on this one. I wasn't going to sit still and take it.

I scowled, created my own black cloud around me, hoped Sister would suffer for what she'd done to me. At lunchtime, I calmly collected all my belongings from my desk—including my lunch—and quietly walked past Sister on my way out the door. I didn't look at anyone, or say anything. My dignity was intact, because I was going to stand up for myself. Sister looked at my face, then down at my lunch bag and the books I carried, then back to my face. I ignored her. I carried my things all the way home.

Home, where Agnes awaited, an avenging Irish angel, flames of righteousness around her head. Sister's phone call had beaten me there, and I never got the chance to tell my story. Suddenly I was listening to my father, on the phone, telling me in no uncertain terms that I was to turn around, go back to school, and apologize to Sister for my bad behavior. Now! He'd have more to say to me when he got home.

How could Agnes betray me? I'd expected her to take my side! She didn't even give me a chance to talk! Simply shut me in the kitchen, like I was a brainless little kid, to eat my lunch, what I could of it, then sent me out the back door. She and my father expected me to willingly walk back into that classroom and apologize. There was no justice in the world.

Tears of rage and frustration streamed down my face as I stumbled the six blocks back to school. I walked as slowly as I could, commiserating with myself about what an awful year this had been. I couldn't imagine going back into Sister Consolata's classroom, but I also couldn't imagine doing anything else than what I'd been ordered to do. How could the world be so wrong? I should have known Daddy would never take my side! Gone were my dreams of being rescued by Agnes. Where was Mother? She was the only one who could ever change Daddy's mind.

Too soon, I found myself back at the school building. I didn't know how I could go through with this. I vowed to stand up for myself. I went in through the side door, wiped my face on my uniform, and crept through the empty halls, scared and quiet, to my classroom. The other kids were already back from lunch. Sister met me at the door. Silence. All eyes were on me.

With squared shoulders, I looked at Sister, told her my father wanted me to apologize. Then told her I knew she was wrong, and God did too. I told her she was unfair, had singled me out for no good reason. I don't remember what else I said, but I went on for a while, then ran out of words and courage, and fell silent. My classmates stared at me, watching solemnly, just like I had watched other kids in trouble so many times before. This time it was me. Some of them smirked, some fidgeted, most showed nothing on their faces. I wondered if I had any friends left. I'd never deliberately spoken out against a nun before.

Sister hissed at me through those tiny clenched teeth. Her black cloud filled the classroom. I didn't flinch. She told me she'd talk to my mother about it when she got home from the hospital, that I was especially bad to be causing my parents more worry at a time like this. I should be praying for my mother's safe return, and helping to take care of that new little sister, not misbehaving like this.

Conscious that the trembling in my lips was barely controlled, I focused my eyes on a spot two feet above the other kids' heads, walked past Sister, across the room, and back through the rows of kids to my desk. I sat there, humiliated, staring straight ahead and fighting to keep from crying. I bit my lip and flared my nostrils, hardly breathing. I couldn't really see or hear anything going on around me. I was afraid to look at Danny, sure he'd sneer or look away.

Not knowing how to get by as anything but a good girl, I was sure I had just taken my first step down the path of evil. There would be no turning back. My life was doomed. How ironic to find out years later that Danny and Robby and lots of other kids had seen me as a heroine, holding on to my honor, standing up to what was wrong in the world.

Much to my surprise, life went on. Grounded for two weeks, I vacuumed and polished and welcomed Mother home expectantly. She was pale and stern and weak and didn't understand the importance of it all. I had been disobedient, and I had to pay the price. Johnny was uninterested in me—the year's difference in ages between us was suddenly monumental.

At school I was sullen and burned with resentment. I didn't know who to trust, who to talk to, who to turn to as a friend, so I shunned all the kids. They thought I was cold and tough. I thought they would reject me if I gave them a chance.

I began to get into trouble more often, at school, with the few friends I still trusted, and eventually even at home. I dyed my hair red, using a fiery mixture from the dime store. Mother hated it and forbade me ever to do it again because it turned the towels and my pillowcase pinkish orange for weeks afterwards. I loved it. I learned to flirt, and I wanted the boys to flirt back, even though I still thought they were useless. Who'd ever seen one of them stand up to a nun? I started to enjoy my new rebellious self-image.

My handwriting deteriorated, purposefully. I didn't want Sister to have anything to like about me. I wanted to send her a message with my wild, unruly scratchings. I still earned straight A's, except for a B-minus in penmanship and a C in behavior. I survived that year and the next.

But late in seventh grade I learned Sister Consolata was to be made principal of St. Bernard's School, and would now be teaching eighth grade. This couldn't be. I started working on my mother, relentlessly pleading for mercy. The public schools were better academically. We didn't have the money to pay for Catholic high school anyway, so I might as well make the switch now. Miraculously, she assented.

Mother went to the school office to tell them I'd be leaving. Sister Consolata was there, as fate would have it, and asked why. She asked if it was because of her. She told my mother that it had been a really difficult year for her, and that she was afraid she might have taken it out on me, might have been rough on me. I really was a good child, but somehow she was afraid she might have been hard on me.

Mother came home, told me what Sister had said. I longed, in my new tough, angry way, for her to say, "Daddy and I were wrong not to trust you, not to back you up, not to know you were a wonderful child." I couldn't help sulking that she didn't. A year later, Mother pulled all my younger brothers and sisters out of those classrooms and sent them to the public schools. It was a hollow victory. By that time I didn't want to look back.

THOMAS CENTOLELLA

Humility

Humility is what they liked to teach you,
those peaches-and-cream-cheeked nuns,
but not by the golden rule. With a ruler
the sisters rapped your tender knuckles
in front of everyone, or bare ass in the cloakroom,
while the rest of the class, as guilty or not,
gloated in safety behind their desks.

In high school, the men known as brothers
forced you to stand on your own two feet
for half an hour, arms spread as in a crucifixion.
Your parents gave them the power to make you balance
on the back of one thin-wristed hand
the weight of the Old Testament. On the other,
History of Western Civilization.
Drop either one and a hammerlike fist would nail you.

But the old parish priest . . . Not sadistic. Sad.
His windblown hair aglow, he called it
his "disheveled halo." The advancing senility
your parents mentioned was not apparent to you.
At a parish breakfast once in wartime, lost
among the pillars of the community, he wandered

up to you and murmured, "If you ever
come across the word *Pyrrhic,* remember:
it means victory at a terrible cost."

And because you were greedy for perfection
every Saturday after lunch you'd eat humble pie
and go down to confession, and slip into your side
of the dark. You'd say, "Bless me, Father, for I have sinned,"
a Christian thrown daily to the Christians.
He knew you'd been mauled and believed in you,
raising his right hand to make the sign
that means *freedom from fear.* A little humility,
he'd say, can keep us healthy. "Pride goeth before a fall."

JOHN SKOYLES

The Brothers

When someone in our neighborhood had a troublesome child, a relative would almost always say, "Wait till he gets the Brothers." The nuns' verbal abuses and twisted psychologizings ended. The Brothers just threw kids around. This happened in the seventh grade, when the boys moved over to a separate building.

The Franciscans' brown, hooded robes were tied at the waist by a cord bearing three knots, representing the vows of poverty, chastity, and obedience. The principal of St. Bartholomew's, Brother Paul, in his late sixties, wore a stained and dusty robe cinched by a cord whose knots always unraveled. He served as substitute to all classes and, no matter what the subject, he read either "The Highwayman" or another poem whose climax came when he waved the pointer out the window and yelled in a frothy pitch, "The Duke!" Other times he let us put our heads on our desks while he told his life story, which included his writing a poem on the wall of the San Francisco coffee house The Hungry I.

On our first day, Brother Mark's pockmarked face leaned close to McCormack's. McCormack stood on his toes, brought to that height by Mark's yanking fist around his tie. McCormack's whole face was distorted to the left, and you could tell McCormack wanted it to go right, back to his desk, which was the way Mark's fist encouraged him to feel.

McCormack, the son of the school janitor, had eight sisters and brothers at St. Barth's. On Christmas and Easter, a special collection was taken for them. We knew Mr. McCormack from his scattering green absorbent on the floor, as well as from watching him receive communion before everyone else on Sundays, off to the side of the altar, so he could get back to his chores of sponging and filling the holy water fonts, straightening the leaflets in the back, and passing the long collection basket.

McCormack read a dirty book in the back row during Mark's review of each of our new texts, and Mark had correctly suspected that McCormack read too intently. McCormack had been dragged out of his seat by his tie and now hung from Mark's wrist in front of the class.

"Why do you read that stuff, McCormack?" Mark said. "To get hot under the pants?"

Mark was in his twenties, a huge, muscular man who wore round, horn-rimmed glasses. At six feet four, he looked like a student athlete past his prime. When his pockmarked face flushed, the redness skipped places here and there, giving a gridlike look to his cheeks. Books seemed tiny in his hands, and sticks of chalk like aspirins.

Mark dropped McCormack, who straightened his school tie angrily and smoothed out his very worn shirt with the great indignity of a stage drunkard. He turned to go back to his seat, but rolled his eyes the second he faced the class. As if with second sight, Mark gave him a parting shot, a slap from his huge hand against the base of McCormack's skull, which popped out his eyes.

In this first hour of our first day, McCormack must have wanted to make his offense seem an exception, and not the rule it had been during his previous six years with the nuns. And so he turned another hurt look at Mark, who was already leaning over his desk, back to his book.

Mark taught all subjects to our class of forty. We started each day with religion, then moved to math and science. After lunch we studied English and history. Each day was the same. We had no breaks, except for a trip to the bathroom. There was no exercise class, and so lunch hour filled the schoolyard with games of punchball and slap, whirling yo-yos, card games, tag, fighting, kissing, and copying of homework. I could hear the rising roar when I ate lunch at home, two blocks away.

Mark recognized we needed a break from routine, and started a "Current Events" period. Our first topic was the recent sanitation workers' strike, or "the garbage strike" as it was called. The boys, mostly sons of civil servants, argued over which service was most valuable to the city.

My friend Michael said, "Without police, you'd all be robbed on your way to school." His father, the police commissioner, had imparted some political sense to Michael; he had already learned to make his point personal.

Plonsky, whose father was a garbage man, said with a heavy lisp, "If garbage men stay home, plagues will be breaking out all over the city."

Garbarino's father was a subway conductor and he argued that no one could get to work without him.

Sensing the heat, Mark decided to expand the debate: each of us had to stand and tell the class the importance of his father's occupation. At the end, we would vote on the top three professions.

I wanted to win this competition, and by the time I formed my arguments, I was sure my father had a chance.

Orlando drew big applause for his father's work as cartoonist for *Mad* magazine. A respectful silence followed Avery's account of how his father, a doctor, cured a little boy who might have died. Chico's father repaired televisions and he said that if people had to stay home because of plagues, crooks, or lack of transportation, then his father made it possible for them to watch television. The dentist's son got Bronx cheers, as did the teacher's. McCormack made a joke about his father's broom closet and everyone laughed. My turn was approaching as we went through the alphabet: Segreto's father sold life insurance, and Sisti's father pushed a cart of rags and newspapers through the neighborhood. I decided to use a technique I had read in *The National Enquirer's* column called "Melodramas." Week in and week out, the writer's strategy was to depict the humble story of a Hollywood star, revealing the identity in the final sentence: "And that used-car salesman today: Charlton Heston!"

I said that if it weren't for my father's job, there would be no mail for the mailmen to deliver, and there would be no way of getting the other workers paid.

Then, in grand style, I said, "My father is an envelope salesman."

When the votes were counted, Avery, the doctor's son, came in first. Second place went to Keller, whose father was an usher at Yankee Stadium, and Charlie Lewis' father, chauffeur to Clancy, the borough president of Queens, came in third.

I blamed myself, because my father also sold paper, which I had failed to mention.

Little by little Mark's preoccupations surfaced. The first was his intolerance of "babies"—boys who cried or complained when he punished them. The second was his terror of loud noises.

He lectured us on "Momism," a too great reliance on our mothers. Mark seemed as upset by whining as by violence or vandalism, and punished all with equal strength.

Many mothers gathered outside the school to walk their children home, something not necessary for me since I lived close to the school. They formed a noisy and colorful group, standing around their strollers and chatting, fanning themselves in summer, stamping their boots on the ground in winter. Other teachers stopped to talk as they left the building, but Mark put his chin to his chest and dashed past them on his way to the friary. He spoke openly about our mothers, whom he called "old washerwomen," and reddened at the thought, swinging his pointer through the air, as if lopping off the heads of mothers.

When garbage trucks collected trash from the apartment building next to the school, Mark flew at the windows that ran the entire length of the room, slamming them shut. If anyone dropped a book or binder from a desk, Mark sat straight up or whipped around as if stung. He wandered out of the room hunching his shoulders when the intercom squeaked feedback.

At school ceremonies, he paced the aisle, and put his fingers to his lips if the slightest rustle or whisper came from one of our rows. This childish gesture, so unlike the broad man it came from, contrasted eerily with his burliness.

* * *

In late November, the class begged for a Christmas tree, since every classroom had one. Mark finally relented when Tony Price said his mother would deliver it and set it up. Mrs. Price was a tall and beautiful woman. She wore her blond hair back so that she looked businesslike, but she had a smile of such warmth that the combination created a tension in every boy. We had known her throughout the earlier grades, as she always provided us with Dixie cups of ice cream after plays, tiny Easter baskets, and mesh Christmas stockings of hard candy. Even the nuns seemed drawn to her, and Sister Helaine, an ornery third-grade teacher, had us all write a card of thanks which we signed "With love," an unusual closing for Helaine.

Mark had the class's full attention this afternoon. He was discussing the torture and martyrdom of two Jesuits, St. Isaac Jogues and his assistant René Martin, by the Iroquois. The descriptions in the textbook were exact: pulled-out fingernails, skin peeled off in strips, burning reeds put into their eyes. He came to the end of the passage, reading aloud: "The two martyrs showed such strength that the Iroquois tore their hearts out while they were still alive, and ate them for courage."

As he closed the text, D'Amico immediately called, "Brother!" from his seat closest to the door. Mark turned, full of annoyance at having the effect of his reading spoiled, when D'Amico continued, "Mrs. Price is here with the tree."

At this, Mrs. Price poked her head in, and smiled. Mark, head down, walked over to meet her. He summoned Flemm and Hattera, two of the biggest boys, to bring the tree up from her trunk.

Mrs. Price walked in after the tree, carrying a stand. She looked elegant in her white suit, her blond hair pulled into a bun. Mark's hands looked larger than ever as they dangled in front of him. Mrs. Price sent the two boys back to her car, and they returned with boxes of ornaments and lights. Sent out again, they carried bags of cookies and a case of milk.

Mrs. Price whispered to Mark, then turned to the class, saying, "Brother and I will decorate the tree while you have your snack."

"First," Mark said to the class, "I think we should thank Mrs. Price."

"Thank you, Mrs. Price," we chimed in an exaggerated way.

"You're more than welcome, boys," she replied.

Looking at Brother Mark, Mrs. Price casually said, "Oh, Brother, please call me Linda."

We jumped at this innocent request, in what I now know is called "projecting."

"Whoa!" we yelled in unison, dragging it out significantly.

Mark had blushed at the remark, and now flushed further, turning and holding his finger up to his lips and mouthing, "Shsssh." Next to his prim and posed companion, his hulking, robed shape looked ridiculous and macabre and we kept laughing, knowing we were safe as long as Mrs. Price was present.

Mrs. Price knelt down, handing the ornaments to Mark, which he placed attractively around the tree. Finished, they both stepped back, and Mark plugged in the lights. The multicolored lights looked beautiful, and gave a lovely glow to the classroom. We applauded and whistled as Mark and Mrs. Price smiled and shook hands. She wished us all a Merry Christmas, and since it was the end of the day, she called Tony, and they left together.

It had been a wonderful afternoon, but Mark scowled and ordered D'Amico to the janitor's closet for a drum for the milk containers. The bell for dismissal rang, but Mark held us, and gave us more homework than we had had all year.

The tree became Mark's third obsession. The next morning Michael Dono rubbed against a branch as he walked past, and some of the lead tinsel fell to the ground. Mark ran down the aisle, spun him around, and drew him close via his tie. "Careful, numbskull," he whispered.

Walking to the front of the class, he said, "You have the tree. It's a nice tree, but I didn't want it, you did. I don't want it to cause any problems, any distraction. I want you to be very careful around it. Those ornaments do not belong to us, they belong to Mrs. Price. I don't want anyone near it. D'Amico, you're in charge of plugging it in in the morning and unplugging it at night."

A half hour later, as the first row was leaving for the bathroom, two boys began sticking their fingers down the backs of each other's collars and, as they twisted away from each other, they whirled into the tree. The whole thing shook for a minute, and Mark and the rest of the class froze as the tree gyrated, then vibrated slowly to a standstill. Not a ball fell, but Mark jumped from his desk, grabbing them from behind by their necks and cracking their heads and shoulders together until they fell into a heap of arms and legs scrambling after the others down the hall.

Delicately, Mark adjusted a ball here and there, checked to see the lights had not come unplugged, and returned to his desk.

The tree terrified us. It was a chore to come in and out of the classroom; it was easy to forget and run right into it. It also seemed to leap out and grab certain students. Dono hit it again with his shoulder, although he entered the classroom a good four feet from it. It seemed to draw him into its vortex, but in spite of this, not an ornament shattered to the floor.

When Mark was sick one day, Duke Weber walked to the front of the room and flicked his cigarette lighter at it a few times, at the high and low branches, and we all rose up in our seats, leaning forward, breathless.

On his return, Mark lectured for most of the day on religion, which brought him to the subject of eternity, and he became passionate about it. The answer to the question "Where did God come from?", posed by the catechism of our earlier grades, was: "He always was and He always will be." This notion continued to make my head spin, just as it did in the lower grades. When I became sufficiently bewildered and nauseous, I was sure that I had made a true prayer.

We had to come up with our own definitions, and then Mark pointed out their flaws. The best of these came from O'Connor, who defined it as the time it would take a girl's hair to grow long enough to reach from one end of the country to another. Inspired, Orlando said, "The time it takes a pebble to become a rock."

"Do rocks grow?" asked Mark.

"How do you think you got mountains," Orlando replied.

Mark called a halt and then gave his definition.

"Suppose the earth is made of solid steel. And the moon, the moon is also made of solid steel. Eternity is the time it would take a sparrow to fly from the earth to the moon," and here he became excited with his further thought, pacing back and forth, "and then to land his tiny feet on the moon, and then to fly all the way back to the earth. By the time it takes the sparrow to have completely worn away the whole earth and moon, by just touching them with his feet—that's eternity!"

My head was starting to spin again, and the class seemed transfixed as well, when Mark turned directly into the Christmas tree, fully entangling himself in it for a split second. As he reached for a branch from the toppling trunk, a sharp twig lurched at his eye. Mark grimaced and squinted; he was unable to grasp it, and it crashed to the floor in an instant, brash and musical. Ornaments shattered, and the lights became unplugged, but most of the noise came from the class which roared with relief. Mark wheeled, red with anger and embarrassment, and yelled, "Nobody laugh, nobody laugh!" as he crunched on broken ornaments. I immediately put my head down under my seat, pretending to get books from the shelf there. Those who were seen laughing were hauled out of their desks and pitched to the front, as Mark called, "Clean it up," to each of them.

Ten boys stood around, righting the tree and sweeping up the glass. By the time the lights were plugged in again, it had a gap in design here and there, but looked fairly decent. Mark did not move from his desk and no one said a word. At the end of the day we filed out, relieved. The tree's aura had been broken, and everyone walked loosely past it.

Across the hall, the other section of the seventh grade was taught by Brother Christian, a dapper man who wore a straw fedora in the summer and a bowler in the winter. His overcoats were chesterfields and his thin mustache gave him an English look. I often saw him on the subway, or walking about the neighborhood with his little Pekingese, Poncie Ponce. My friends in that class said he told stories for most of the day, and they never had homework.

How we envied that class, particularly since Mark kept up his punishing style throughout the year. The lectures on being a "Momma's boy" continued, as did his twisting of ties and slapping of faces and heads. When he found a homemade tattoo on the arm of Ellie Smith, the class's only black, he chopped a brutal judo punch to the side of his neck, crumpling him quickly to the floor.

We were silent all day and Mark went from subject to subject without a smile. In science, Mark's explanations amazed us. Discussing physics, he said, "To hit something very hard, hold the hammer by the very end," and he tapped a hammer against his palm. In chemistry, he told Chris Colombo, our science whiz, that distilled water was simply melted ice cubes, causing the experiment Colombo entered in a citywide contest to fail. He said appendicitis was caused by swallowing watermelon seeds, and that when they filled up a little pocket in the body, the appendix burst. Birthmarks, he explained, came from a scare given a pregnant mother: wherever the startled mother grabbed herself in fright, that's where the child would have a mark. He assigned one row the project of "growing an amoeba," and began by saying, "Take some sewer water. . . ." To Colombo, whose thirst for experiment was great, he advised putting horsehairs in a bottle of water to grow snakes. This took us aback because in our religion lessons with the nuns, we were told that there was no such thing as spontaneous regeneration, that maggots were not born from a piece of decaying meat. "Only God can create life," Sister Helaine told us. "Man would be God if he could create Ford automobiles that produced little Fords." These words had stayed with me, and now Mark was assigning a heresy as a science project. More practically, Colombo held his palms skyward and asked, "Where can I get horsehairs?"

The current events class was interesting, even if it focused mostly on unions and strikes. We learned that Mark's father had been a "longshoreman." My mother spoke with great admiration of the strength of two professions, longshoremen and steamfitters. My mother often pointed out men in the neighborhood, saying with a knowing look, "He's a steamfitter," or "Look, a longshoreman," and while I couldn't define either, I was captivated by the names, and by my mother's awe.

During a longshoreman's strike, Mark posted photos of acres of crates of food spoiling on the docks. It gave us an interest in the newspapers to see the photographs of brawls, and men holding ice picks and sickles facing off with the police.

Mark drew New York's harbor on the blackboard. He loved using the board, even though the chalk slipped and broke in his hefty fingers, and it was almost impossible to read his words or understand his diagrams. Still, while it looked like a struggle, it seemed a pleasure to him.

He made an outline of lower Manhattan, which looked like an enormous W. Then he drew a long oval shape protruding from it while he talked about the routes the ships would take. Standing in front of his drawing, he rambled on, about schedules, cargoes, crews, and captains. The class tried to suppress its giddiness: his illustration looked exactly like a huge cock and balls. Heads in every aisle snapped over at neighboring rows. Boys in the front squirmed backward looks at their classmates.

Mark talked passionately about union bosses, and then unions in general. He gave us the tonnage the longshoremen unloaded each day and numbered the docks on the waterfront, to show us how many there were. At this, he went back to the board and drew short lines jutting from the W, adding the final realistic touch to his sketch, stroke by stroke: small lines looking exactly like pubic hair. As if in a dream, the entire class began laughing. The drawing was too perfect, too exact, and pubic hair too touchy a subject with us at age twelve. It was as if he were playing a trick or testing us. Whatever it was, there was no holding back, and we howled.

Mark stood dumbstruck. Then, realizing his sketch had caused the uproar, he walked to the side and stared at the board. In a flash he smashed his chalk to the floor, pointing and yelling at the forty students, "You're babies, you're all babies!"

Instantly silent, we knew there could be no retribution since all were guilty. I hadn't even thought of bending over my desk to hide. This laughter was too spontaneous, too universal for disguise.

Mark wildly erased the board and sat down, his brown robe trimmed with chalk dust from the defunct cock and balls.

He looked straight at us; his lips quivered, his cheeks flushed their checkerboard grid, and his tongue stuck. Taking a deep breath before what we were sure would be a long speech, he simply gave us some rote work until the lunch bell rang.

Out in the schoolyard, no one mentioned Mark's lecture, and when we returned, the boards had been wet down, dissolving the sketch into a series of streaks and drips that pooled into the chalky ledge.

LEN ROBERTS

Emma

Ronny Michaels would go blind,
Richie Fremont grow hair on his palms,
Maureen Risteau's and Sylvia Ryan's
bellies grow big as beach balls
if we did not heed the Messenger
of the Lord,
his wings outstretched in that seventh-
grade classroom
where Sister Ann Zita drew testicles
and vaginas on the board,
the condom passed from desk to desk
to show us what it was like,
Ann Harding holding it at arm's length,
Donald Wilcox trying to blow it up
while the rest of us stared at the outlined
man and woman
on the wall-sized print, the dotted lines
of the penis inside the dotted lines of the *cunt,*
word Johnny Dumas whispered from the back,
making us look up, making us laugh.
This is not funny, Sister said, whacking
the thick pointer in her palm,
staring at Ronny and Donald, at easy Emma
who spread her knees at lunch and showed her

underpants,
Emma, the girl the high school boys took
to the Cliff,
the Cohoes Drive-In, to the after-midnight
parties at Charrette's,
lovely Emma who wore a black bra beneath the
white blouse,
who never tucked in her legs or hitched up
her skirt,
who dyed her hair blond,
then red, then
streaked
it silver and brown, who wore a heavy gold
heart
between her breasts and smeared gold specks on her lips
that Father Mulqueen always wiped off at the Front
Street entrance. Emma,
who raised her hand that day to ask Sister
how she knew about love
and was made to stay after school for a month
in detention,
writing a thousand times, *I am sassy and bold*
in red ink,
then having to do it all over again in blue,
Emma, who walked in one day with giant wings
tied to her arms and declared she was our angel,
Emma, whose cheeks flared with the flames
of Sister's fingers,
whose hands bled from welts ridged by Sister's
triangular ruler,
who was made to sit on a stool in front of the class
while we learned about syphilis and crabs and gonorrhea,
how a virgin bled, how a woman bled every month,
Emma's heart-shaped face white as the chalked words
drifting
in blurred clouds on the board behind her,
love, abortion, marriage, sex
as she wet her lips with her pink, pink tongue.

MARIA BRUNO

Wild Heart

I had just finished junior high the summer after President Kennedy died. It was the time of big hair and wild hearts. At least I had big hair. The biggest. I made it into a dime-store ritual, buying steel ratting combs, large velvet bows, three-inch bobby pins, steel clips to hold my peroxided spit-curls in place. I stood in front of the mirror for hours ratting, smoothing, pinning, spraying my hive into a mound of perfection. I ratted it high until I looked like a shaman or an Egyptian goddess, pinning the velvet bow onto my bangs as a final touch. Oh, I had heard stories: once a girl from Long Island had found a rat in her hair with a litter of nursing babies; another out west housed killer bees, and still another in New Jersey had provided a much-needed home to a vampire bat which was displaced when the girl's father reroofed the house. But in junior high we never listened too much to the rumors. And we didn't care too much about the environment then, either. Ozone layer be damned—we lived for Aqua Net. Big cans of it. We filled the school halls with a sweet sticky mist, making our hair stiff like day-old meringue.

Boys were a mystery to me then. All the songs on the radio by the Shangri-Las and Shirelles told me I needed one to be complete. I was determined to have a boyfriend so I wore tight straight miniskirts, mohair sweaters, and white fringed go-go boots. I bought a bullet bra for $1.29 at the dime store. My neighbor, Johnny Marino, told me bullet bras drove boys crazy even though they pinched and left circles on my breasts like the rings of an old tree. I bought packs of Lucky Strikes and blew smoke rings to the cruisers on Woodward Avenue. I practiced French-kissing bottles of Nehi Grape. I outlined my eyes in black like Liz Taylor in *Cleopatra* and painted my lips with Maybelline's "White Lotus." I was pale, ghostly, cool—the coolest.

Johnny Marino was two years older than me. He was what we used to call a greaser, an auto-shop kid. He was a loner who smoked Pall Malls and wore leather, who found solace in the debris of old Plymouths, music in the shaky hums of rebuilt engines. He didn't have the jock's butch cut, but longer dark hair that curled around his ears. And dark dark eyes. I never admitted it to anyone but I found him handsome.

He had always been a loner. In elementary school he never played kickball or basketball; he would just stand to one side, as if he wished he were someplace else, as if there were some cosmic folly that was associated with our behavior that only he was privy to. You could like any of the boys back then, announce it to the lunchroom, have one of your giggly friends go over and make a "going steady" deal. But no one, to my knowledge, ever announced their intentions for Johnny. By junior high he was considered dangerous. He listened to the Rolling Stones and smoked marijuana. Grew his own in the back seat of his Fury. That's not all that happened in the back seat of his car, they'd say. No decent girl would or should go out with him.

By the time high school rolled around, I decided to seek popularity and defy the traditional stereotype of the Italian girls at the Shrine of Perpetual Guilt. It was rumored we were fast, dark, and exotic. By the time we were sixteen we were expected to peroxide our spit-curls, wiggle our hips like Marilyn Monroe, and know in the biblical sense the back seat of every Fairlane in suburban Detroit. But I wanted higher ground. I had become enamored with the popular boys, the ones who looked squeaky-clean, the ones who wore madras shirts and chinos and Bass Weejun loafers. I took down my uninhabited beehive and traded in my bullet bra for a plain white cotton one, the kind a novice nun might wear. For the first day of high school, I spent the night before sleeping on empty Minute Maid orange juice cans to make my kinky hair straight. I then reset it at four a.m. on brush rollers into what was going to be a perfect flip. For the next two hours I slept with the scratchy knowledge that I would be beautiful for my high school debut. In the morning, after an hour's ritual in front of the mirror, I sprayed my flip with half a can of Aqua Net Super Hold, making it point toward the heavens. My crown of ratted hair forever gone, I stood before the mirror staring, wondering who it was.

My mother had further orchestrated my debut, all the while calling me her "good little girl." She bought me a white blouse with a Peter Pan collar, which I secured with my brand-new monogrammed circle pin. I talked her into buying me an outfit like the popular girls wore—a plaid skirt, a plaid vest, and matching plaid Capezios. I traded those little blue bottles of Evening in Paris for the free samples of Shalimar I got at Hudson's. I put a plaid ribbon in my hair—I was ready.

But it was a typical first day of high school. I forgot my locker combination and I was late for algebra. I had to pee but all the bathrooms were locked to thwart smokers, something I'd never had to deal with in junior high. It was Indian-summer hot; my circle pin was choking me, and I wanted to rip it from my throat. By eleven-thirty my perfect flip had fizzled, gone kinky, one side hanging lower than the other. I stood in the lunchroom holding a tray of Pizza Surprise and Tater Tots, my warm half-pint of milk curdling. My matching Capezios pinched my toes, and I could swear Muffy De Vries and Boo Egan, their blond flips still flipping, were sniggering at me. I had nowhere to sit.

Johnny Marino sat alone in the corner. There was nothing on his tray, but he was drinking something; it looked like coffee. He must have swiped it from the teachers' lounge, I thought. He looked up and stared. I thought if I sat with him it might skew the direction of my entire high school career. But I knew he wouldn't say much, and I wouldn't have to say much to him, so I sat down.

"Hey, Rosie," Johnny said, "having a bad day?"

"You can't call me Rosie anymore," I snapped. "I want to be called Rosalie." I didn't tell him I planned to dot the "i" with a big heart.

"Whaja do to your hair?" he asked. "I liked it better the other way."

"That was the old me," I said, struggling with my carton of

milk, trying to get it open. I lopped the sleeve of my blouse into the Pizza Surprise. I started to cry.

"You wanna blow this popstand?" he asked softly. "Come on, let's go."

I knew if I went with Johnny my whole high school career could be threatened. I'd be picked last for the teams in gym, doomed to date the audiovisual boys, the greasers, or the guys in butch cuts and army fatigues who shot birds from trees. Rumors would run rampant, all fueled by Muffy and Boo: I went all the way—I did it—you could score a home run off of me. No decent dates, no prom, even low SAT scores. My future loomed before me like a B movie: I'd have a two-year stint at a community college majoring in cosmetology or travel and tourism. I'd marry someone named Lance who had a ducktail. We'd move into a trailer park in Livonia; I'd be watching *Another World* while presoaking Tiffany's and Lance, Jr.'s diapers in my Hoover portable washer. My big night out would be bowling at Yorba Linda Lanes. Lance would start calling me Rose. I'd wear a pink chenille bathrobe, and suddenly I'd look like Shirley Booth in *Come Back, Little Sheba.*

"Come on," he said, and reached for my hand. We didn't clear our trays. I was sure everybody noticed. Outside I took off my shoes and unfastened my circle pin.

"This way," he said, leading me toward the path.

I was completely indoctrinated with the movie-like scenario planted in every adolescent girl's brain that the Prince, the gorgeous Prince, would arrive someday and save me from a grim existence of blind dates with boys who ate their boogers, lit their farts with butane torches, or tried to unsnap my bra during the intermission. In the fantasy, I envisioned myself at a formal dance unescorted.

Muffy and Boo are there in their pastel organzas, their silky hair framing their faces like golden auras. A tall blond tuxedoed boy, looking straight out of Hitler Youth, arrives; he's new in town. His name is Skip. He takes one look at me, walks past Muffy and Boo and even Wanda "Jugs" DelFlorio, who, it's rumored, lets all the boys unsnap her bra and go "down there," and stands in front of me. I look up and almost swoon because his shoulders are so square, his jaw is so strong, his hand is so forceful. We glide onto the dance floor and the rest is history. No trailer park in Livonia for me. No ducktails or a Lance wanting his meatloaf and mashed potatoes. It's Ivy League for both of us; our composite SATs so astound our principal, Sister Immaculata, in fact, that she erects a mini-shrine to us, complete with votive candles and holy water, and an inscription, sketched in gold, which reads "MR. AND MRS. SKIP KIRBY." The fantasy doesn't end there. Muffy and Boo go to community college and become keypunch operators and Wanda DelFlorio takes a home-study course and replaces Sister Immaculata as principal at the Shrine of Perpetual Guilt. Skip becomes a corporate lawyer and I become a famous novelist or a backup singer for Ray Charles.

"This way," Johnny said again as we finally found the path. He gripped my hand gently.

"Johnny, I have to get back," I said. "I'll miss algebra. Math is my worst subject."

"Come on," he said, moving quickly. "I have something to show you."

I suppose I should have been scared, considering the rumors and all. Some people said Johnny could unsnap a bra in exactly three seconds, that he could French-kiss and make you see God, that he carried ribbed condoms in his pack of Pall Malls, that he could recite all the lyrics to the Stones' "King Bee"—I'm a King Bee, baby, buzzin' around your hive—while he removed your panties. But I was more worried about the nights of detention stretching before me; the call to my parents which would send my mother straight to the backyard to lay a flower at the Holy Virgin's feet; my reputation, which could be destroyed instantly, so that suddenly tough boys with names like Carmine and Rocco would be asking for my phone number. Guys who would say things like "I want to live fast, die young, and leave a beautiful corpse."

Johnny stopped, and knelt, and pointed to a mayapple. It was already purpling, getting ready for fall.

"There's a trillium," he said, "and a jack-in-the-pulpit." We moved farther into the brush and stopped at a bare patch of earth.

"You know what this is?" he asked, looking up.

"No," I answered, feeling warmer. I unbuttoned the top button of my blouse.

"Bucks scratch here. Then they urinate all over it. Then they wait for the does."

"Wait for the does to do what?" I asked. I had no idea.

"To mate. To come for the males."

"Oh," I said, watching Johnny carefully. Was I in trouble here? I asked myself. Was he going to start hoofing his stiletto-toed shoes into the dirt? Was he going to unzip, pull *it* out? Would I then be his forever? Would there be no Skip, no waltz across the dance floor, no Ivy League?

"C-can we go now, J-Johnny?" I stammered. "I'm going to get detention." It was then that he kissed me. Nothing dangerous. No Rolling Stones. No tongue. No nirvana. He had more than three seconds and he didn't even reach for the snaps on my nun's bra. But I did feel my bare toes in the wet grass, the warm sun streaking the back of my neck, his hands around my waist. I could hear the clucking of red-winged blackbirds in the low brush. His leather jacket felt hot next to my fingers. My heart raced.

"Johnny, I . . ."

"I know, I better get you back."

I looked into his eyes. He kissed me again. I smiled.

I wish I didn't have to tell the end of this story.

For some reason I never really spoke much to Johnny Marino after that day. Perhaps I felt it was too risky; maybe I just wanted to be accepted a little too much. Two months after my first kiss, Johnny quit school and enlisted. I began growing my hair long after that, ironing it straight with my mom's Steam 'N Press. I bought a guitar and started to think less about Muffy and Boo and more about the world. I thought about Johnny on and off during my senior year until the day I heard he had died somewhere in the jungles of Vietnam. I often wondered if he was alone when it happened, separated from his platoon, off somewhere looking at the wildflowers.

Sometimes I wonder what he would think of the world today. He'd be forty-four now. Tabloid TV says President Kennedy used to sneak his mistresses into the back door of the White House; trilliums are on the endangered species list and there's a hole in the ozone layer. Sister Immaculata is still at the Shrine of Perpetual Guilt worried about hymens and the Madonna/Whore dichotomy; my daughter, Francie, attends public schools. She always wears black, and is noted for her tortured artist's clothing, powdered Kabuki cheeks, and maroon lips. She treasures her thick brown hair, which leaps from her head like live wires. She never fusses with it. She questions everything and I love her for it. My mother, a widow now, spends a lot of time in the backyard with the ceramic Holy Virgin, planting red and orange poppies for my nephew, who is stationed in Saudi Arabia, where no wildflowers grow. I have gray hair and the natural curls flow to my shoulders. I'm on my second divorce. I never found Skip or even a close replica. I saw Wanda DelFlorio the other day working at the 7-Eleven. She's married now and sends her children to Catholic school. She seemed bigger and more powerful than I remember. Her red hair flowed to her shoulders free from the ratting comb; she had Sophia Loren lips, and those large breasts, the objects of perpetual fascination long ago, were hardly noticeable under her uniform. After her shift, I bought her a Big Gulp and a chili dog and we sat on the curb waving at the cars going by.

"Remember how we used to do this all the time in elementary school?" she asked, sucking on the plastic straw. "You know, at Wesley's drugstore?"

"Yeah," I said, watching her, thinking she was so beautiful now.

"What happened? Why didn't we talk anymore?"

"I'm sorry," I answered. There was a silence.

"You believed everything they said about me, didn't you?"

"I guess so," I stammered. I felt fifteen again.

"A lot of it was true," she said, smiling. "I have no regrets." She began to laugh. Her eyes were as large and round as moons, her mouth opened to gasps of laughter. I followed suit. And there we sat, arms entwined, howling into the air. For a moment, I thought I saw Sister Immaculata drive by in her black car, looking to see if our legs were properly crossed at the ankles. I flashed her the peace sign and hugged Wanda tighter.

Wanda and the 7-Eleven got me thinking about how I got Saturday detention after that day with Johnny, and how my mother and father both headed for the ceramic Holy Virgin and buried some peeled plum tomatoes beneath her rose-covered toes. Johnny was suspended for three days; he rebuilt an engine in his driveway. Sometimes when I can't think of the world anymore, I think of Johnny Marino and the woods and the sun and the song of the redwinged blackbirds in the brush. I think of the trillium, the way his mouth tasted, how the heat of his jacket felt between my fingers. I remember my wild heart.

LEROY V. QUINTANA

Susanna

Susanna suddenly became a neighbor
one summer next door.
Instantly all the boys liked her, as did I,
but from afar, and long after the rest.
I was also in love with Susan Hayward:
that color photo of her in my mother's movie magazine.
Her red hair on fire.
Sister Ruth explained to us once the torment
of the fires of hell. It was the soul, not the flesh,
that burned, and forever. Forever.
I was only twelve or so and bursting into flames.

ROBIN BEEMAN

Burning Joan

Joan of Arc stood in her cart on the way to her pyre, her eyes on the jeering crowd. They'd taken away her armor. They'd made her wear a gown. They weren't going to let her save them after all. It never occurred to either Isabel or me as we stared at the bright screen in the dark auditorium of Holy Redeemer School that Joan was anything but the kind of person we would want to be. We'd each donated a can of food for a benefit movie for the poor of our parish. I brought beets and Isabel brought spinach, and we were getting every ounce's worth of beauty, bravery, and martyrdom.

"I wonder what I'd look like if I cut my hair," Isabel said as we blinked in the afternoon sun, startled not to be in France after all, but in Marigny, Louisiana, beside the rectory parking lot.

"No, not your hair," I said. My hair was dark and curly and my mother insisted that I keep it short. Isabel's hair was long ropy blond, the kind of hair only one person in a thousand gets. Isabel didn't look much like Joan. She had a tipped-up nose and an overbite, but the fact that she would even consider cutting her hair seemed like a step on a road somewhere. Everyone knew that cutting hair was the first stage to renunciation of the world. Nuns cut their hair.

"You could do it while my mother's at work."

"Think about it a little first," I said. Isabel's mother had beautiful hair, too. I didn't think she'd understand if I cut her daughter's. She wasn't the saintly type.

"I'm still thinking," Isabel said the next day as we stretched out on the sandy strip of beach by the lake. There Phillip Duvall sat, with the kind of egalitarianism we admired him for, not on the high chair for lifeguards but with his back against one of the supports of the chair. He was surrounded by everyone important in our world. There was talk that he'd get a football scholarship to LSU. He'd just broken up with someone, and now four senior girls lay on towels beside him. They were all shapely and beautiful and wise and wonderful enough to be kind to me and Isabel. I was eleven and Isabel almost twelve. They considered us pets.

It was flattering to have them know our names, but when I sat beside them I felt hopeless and unformed, like a lump of dough. The problem was, however, that I wasn't even lumpy and neither was Isabel. We were tube-shaped, completely without bumps or curves or mysterious shaded regions.

"Isabel's thinking of cutting her hair," I told them.

"Oh, no," one of them said. She had black hair that curled under at the ends and perfect teeth. The others echoed her.

"I won't marry you if you cut your hair," Phillip Duvall said.

"Do you believe he's actually thought of marrying me?" Isabel asked. We were sitting in her bedroom with the fan on playing gin rummy.

"He said it."

"But he was joking, wasn't he?"

"He wouldn't have said it if it hadn't crossed his mind."

"He's the most beautiful man in the world," she said. "I could be Mrs. Phillip Duvall—after he gets out of LSU."

"He's seven years older than you are."

"He'll wait if he loves me."

"Suppose he wants to kiss you. Will you let him?"

"Oh, Holy Mary," she said and put down the cards. "I don't know how to kiss. I don't want him to kiss me until I know how. We have to practice, Kate." She leaned over the cards, her mouth puckered, her eyes on me.

"Girls don't kiss girls."

"How do we learn then? Think about it."

"It's weird—girls kissing."

"What's weirder, kissing a girl, or not knowing how to kiss at all?"

As usual, Isabel made her point. I shrugged and closed my eyes, but I wasn't prepared for the aggressiveness of her mouth, for the muscular properties of lips. "Kiss back," she said, taking a breath. I didn't know whether to tighten or loosen. "You're terrible." We tried again, I relaxed this time and let her mouth take over, letting my lips do what hers did. We fell over backwards onto the pillows. "It's okay," she said. "We're girls."

That same afternoon we burned Bo Peep. In second grade, when we'd become friends, I'd been impressed by Isabel's collection of Storybook Dolls. She had a row of them lined up on a bookshelf with their full-skirted stiff dresses, wide-open eyes, and swirls of hair. Her aunt sent them to her. Isabel wasn't particularly interested in dolls, but she knew these were enviable. Their arms were jointed, but not their legs. They weren't made to be played with.

We stripped Bo Peep of her finery and dressed her in a tunic we made from an old sheet. When we'd bound the dress with a piece of dark twine, it was not unlike what Joan had worn. We borrowed a small red wagon from the driveway of the house next door and put Joan into it and jounced her behind the shed, where we assembled a pyre from fallen pine branches. We placed a fairly straight branch in the center for a stake and tied the doll to it.

The dried pine needles caught fire immediately. Flames lost no time licking Joan's feet and igniting her dress. The doll, celluloid, flared briefly, then caved in on itself, the small glass eyes bulging before they dripped away from the head. The hair smoldered at first, then shot into sparks and soon also disappeared into ashes. The whole event probably lasted no more than five minutes. We sat back on our heels amazed at what we had done.

"What's that smell?" Isabel's grandmother called from the back door. She was supposed to watch us, but she almost never left her room, where she sat each day reading novels.

"We're getting ready to roast marshmallows," Isabel answered, rolling her eyes at me.

"Don't set anything on fire!" The screen door slammed shut.

"Let's go to the store and get marshmallows," said Isabel.

"And Coke," I said. My throat was dry. I felt as if I had a fever.

We had the world to ourselves that summer. My own family faded into a benign pallor as Isabel's mostly absent family became mine. Her mother, who looked like an older, more assured version of Isabel, was divorced—a distinction of some kind in those days. She worked as a legal secretary for the district attorney and rarely appeared when I was there. Isabel's brother, Nick, who was rumored to be the smartest boy in school, was gone for most of the summer visiting cousins in New Orleans. When Isabel's grandmother made a foray from her room, it was usually only to leave money on the table for Isabel to do the family shopping. She always left enough for us to buy Cokes and candy and a magazine—usually a *True Confessions* or a *Photoplay.*

Each afternoon Isabel and I rode our bikes to the beach, and, after swimming, rode back to her house waving away the yellow-jackets that followed our wet hair. We played cards, talked, and kissed occasionally. We were practicing for boys. We also burned Little Miss Muffet, Sleeping Beauty, Little Red Riding Hood, the Queen of Hearts, and Snow White.

On the day Nick got back, his friend Charlie came over. Nick had changed. He'd put on a little weight, maybe even muscle. He'd been quiet before, interested only in the chemistry lab he'd set up in his bedroom, trying to frighten us with stories about how he was about to make nitroglycerine and blow us up. Now he swaggered and wanted to talk. As he and Charlie and Isabel and I sat in the kitchen eating tuna sandwiches, I watched Nick chew and wondered whether he was good-looking or not. He and Charlie were going to be sophomores at St. Ignatius High in the fall.

"I went on Bourbon Street with my cousins," he told Charlie as we listened. "They're at Tulane. They knew a guy at the door and they got me in to see a stripper. Her name was Tempest and she took off all her clothes but two little stars on her nipples and a tiny G-string. They said that sometimes she takes off everything and sits on guys' laps."

"What do you do to get to see her take off everything?" Charlie asked, pulling off his glasses and rubbing the lenses with the bottom of his T-shirt. His fingers were long and moved constantly like insect antennae.

"What were the stars on her nipples made of?" asked Isabel.

"How the hell do I know?" said Nick. "They were shiny. She had big tits and her skin was really white. She probably sleeps all day."

"Like a bat," I said.

Charlie laughed and Nick scowled at him.

"I'd like to see a stripper," said Isabel.

Later that afternoon Nick pushed open Isabel's door while we were lying together on the bed.

"Don't you know about knocking?" said Isabel.

"I have this present from Aunt Inez that I'm supposed to give you. Besides, you're my sister."

"Probably another dumb doll." Isabel took the gift-wrapped box from him. "Thanks."

"Drop dead," he said and slammed the door.

"Cinderella," she said after tearing off the paper. "Wouldn't you know?"

"Poor Cinderella." I started to laugh and then Isabel laughed too. We rolled around on the floor and held our stomachs when they began to hurt.

They had been smoking cigarettes that night and they had a bottle of rum. Isabel's mother was at a meeting. "We're making Cuba Libres," said Nick. He and Charlie stood in front of the refrigerator putting ice in a couple of glasses. "That's what everyone at Tulane drinks."

"Make me and Kate one," said Isabel.

"No way," said Nick.

"Aw, don't be so hard on them," said Charlie.

"They're just kids." Nick handed Charlie a glass.

"Just one drink," Isabel said.

"Why not?" said Charlie. "Let them have fun, too."

Nick frowned and looked from me to Isabel and then back to me. "Do you really want a drink?"

"Sure," I said. Isabel nodded.

"Okay," Nick said, "but you have to drink in my room and promise not to tell."

"We're not going to tell," said Isabel.

The drinks weren't bad. They were mostly Coke with rum and a little bit of lemon juice. Nick had twin beds in his room. He sat on one and Charlie on the other. Isabel and I sat on the floor beneath a table loaded with glass tubes and vials. Nick and Charlie kept leaning over and whispering while we drank. We finished the first, and Nick made us each a second. When we were about halfway done with those, Nick leaned back on his pillow. "Charlie thinks you two ought to do a striptease for us. Charlie thinks you two are cute."

"Hey wait!" said Charlie, spitting out some of his drink. "You were the one talking about getting girls to strip."

"Yeah, okay," said Nick. "Who cares whose idea it is?" He turned to us. "It's not just taking off your clothes. It's dancing, too."

"What do we wear?" asked Isabel.

"I don't know," said Nick. "Get something out of Mother's room. Use your imagination."

"How much do we have to take off?" I asked. I was a little uneasy about how quickly Isabel seemed willing to go along, but the idea was intriguing. It seemed to belong with drinking, to be a buoyant and spinning thing to do.

"As much as you want," said Nick.

My mother had utility white underwear. Isabel's mother had lace and colors, but everything was too big for me. When I put on a black bra, the cups crumpled over my chest.

"Stuff it with something," Isabel said.

"No. Then when I take it off the stuffing will fall out. That'll look dumb."

"Are you really going to do this, Kate?" Her question surprised me. I thought she'd been all for it.

"Sure," I said. Now that I was getting dressed, I wanted to—but not by myself. I took another swallow of the drink and noticed that Isabel's was almost finished.

"Her drawers are going to be too big for you."

I had on a pair of black panties trimmed with lace. When I let go, they slid down over my hips. My own were cotton with tiny flowers. "I'll use a ribbon and scrunch mine up on the sides to make them littler." I wanted to ask her how far she would go, but I was feeling bolder than I'd ever felt, adventurous, and I didn't want to give her an excuse to back out.

Isabel had on pink panties and a pink bra. She pulled out a black slip and handed it to me. "You look good in black. Black's sexy." The slip was silky. It came almost to my ankles. I looked in the mirror and took a lipstick from the dresser and put it on. I smeared some on my cheeks. I drew darker eyebrows. I lined my eyes. I gave my chin a beauty mark. I didn't look like myself at all.

Nick and Charlie had been busy, too. Nick had brought in the phonograph from the living room. They'd turned off the lights except for two gooseneck lamps that shot beams onto a cleared patch of floor.

As soon as Isabel and I got into the room, I felt different. Charlie and Nick sat behind the lights, their faces in shadow. Nick put on a record—Louis Armstrong. "They always strip to trumpets," he said.

"Let's do it together," I said. Isabel looked relieved.

Neither of the boys objected to our not going singly. They were probably as surprised by all of this as we were.

When the music began, both Isabel and I giggled. Instead of feeling sexy, I felt dazed. I couldn't remember why I was standing there, but it seemed as if we'd made a pact and had to go through with it. Isabel put her hands up in the air and wiggled her bottom and turned around. I recognized it as part of the hokey-pokey and did it, too. It seemed like a good way to begin. We did a little bit of hula too, although the rhythm wasn't right.

"Take it off," said Nick. Charlie joined in and they both chanted.

I don't know who went first, but as soon as I'd tossed the slip to the floor, I looked over at Isabel and she was in bra and panties, too. I decided not to watch her anymore. I closed my eyes and listened only to the trumpet. I slid the bra off my shoulders and let it fall down around my hips. I felt like a snake wriggling out of its skin. I sneaked a look through half-shut eyes and saw that the lights had turned my body white. I stared down at my nipples, flat and hard as coins, my feet moving on the scarred wood floor, as distant as stars. I reached for my panties and pulled them down. It was awkward, but I knew it had to be done.

When the overhead light went on, I opened my eyes and saw that we were both naked, stepping up and down on two small islands of abandoned underwear. Isabel's mother stood in the doorway.

She gave us time to get dressed, then came into Isabel's room and sat beside us on the bed. I could tell that she'd been drinking, too. Her breath was sour. Her beautiful hair was messy and her lipstick was almost gone except for a thin outline. She looked at Isabel first, then me, then sighed and fixed her eyes on a spot across the room.

"God wants you to stay pure," she said. "Girls should be pure." She looked tired and I could tell right away that she had no heart for this, but that she believed she had to do it. "Boys don't understand that you're really pure inside. If you do things like you did tonight, they'll take advantage of your innocence. You should learn to pray for the strength to resist."

Neither Isabel nor I looked at each other while she spoke. I turned my eyes down to the bedspread. It was white chenille. I plucked at the tufts and rolled the threads that came out into little balls.

She left us alone and went to her own bedroom. I was supposed to spend the night with Isabel, but as we undressed—for the second time that evening—I felt a pain like a buzz saw sounds right behind my forehead. "I have to go home," I said. "I have a headache."

"You probably need glasses," said Isabel. She sat in her pink shortie pj's examining her face in a hand mirror. She hadn't managed to get off all the mascara and her eyes had a smudgy, old–movie star look.

"I'm going home," I said and began pulling on my T-shirt.

"Just take two aspirin." She'd put down the mirror and was glaring at me. It wasn't hard to tell that she was annoyed.

I broke the cardinal rule of constant contact the next morning by not calling Isabel as soon as I'd eaten breakfast, but I was ready when her call came. "Come on over after lunch," she said. "We're not finished."

Isabel's mother was at work as usual and Nick was off, probably shooting baskets. In the drowsy summer stillness, we dressed Cinderella as Joan, then rattled her along the driveway in her cart and tied her to a stake made from a piece of broken lattice. We were driven by a sense of urgency, a need for haste. We built a pyre higher than any before and stood back while the first young flames sprang up. I looked over them to Isabel and our eyes met. Neither of us could control our smiles and I knew that her heart was pounding, too. The fire raced up to the larger twigs. We backed away as the doll's tunic turned first brown, then black, and the tiny figure became a torch that burst open to reveal flames licking inside. The blond hair ignited into a joyously bright crown as sparks shot into the air and sappy twigs burst like firecrackers.

"We loved Joan," I said when it was over and we stood staring down at the charred circle in the grass. "Why did we want to burn her?"

"She asked for it," said Isabel.

My glee was gone. I felt old, older even than the girls on the beach. As I pedaled home into the breezeless afternoon, I wanted only to outdistance the smell of smoke that clung to my hair and clothes.

A little later, lying in the tub with a tower of lather on my head, I decided that no matter what my mother said, I'd let my hair grow and grow. I closed my eyes and, for a moment, I could already feel it brushing my shoulders.

MARY HELEN STEFANIAK

Voyeurs

The first time Judy and I saw the naked man, it was by accident. We were thirteen, and we were crossing the Walnut Street bridge over the railroad tracks, talking about whether we would ever get an abortion or would we have the baby no matter what. It was 1964. I said I would have the baby no matter what. So right away Judy asked me if I'd seen the movie *The Cardinal,* which, I knew, had been rated B by the Catholic Legion of Decency. It was playing at the Avalon at the time. I reminded her that my mother wouldn't let me see movies that were rated B by the Legion of Decency. Well, said Judy (whose mother played the saxophone in a three-piece band and didn't give a hoot for the Legion of Decency), in the movie the Cardinal's sister gets pregnant. They all know it's a risky business for her, but of course she goes ahead and has the baby anyway—no matter what. "But then," Judy said, "in the middle of being born, the kid gets stuck somehow and the doctors say the only way to save the Cardinal's sister is to crush the baby's head and yank it out of her."

"Jeez, Judy," I said. "That's not *abortion.*"

Anyway, Judy told me, the Cardinal has to make the decision—either save his sister's life by killing the baby or let them both die naturally according to God's will. Years later, when I saw the movie on TV with my mother, I remember I got so angry at her for being on the side of God and the Cardinal that I refused to stay for supper. Judy, however, didn't get a chance to tell me what the Cardinal decided because it was at that moment, as we reached the highest point of the bridge, that we saw the naked man.

He was in a fourth-floor window in one of the new-brick apartment buildings next to the tracks. We decided later that he probably thought people on the street couldn't see him up on the fourth floor, but because of the little hill we were on and the hollow the building was in and the angle of the street and other fortunate features of the terrain, his window was a bit below our eye level and not more than ten or twelve yards from where we stood, rooted to the spot on the crest of the bridge.

Judy said, "Holy moly!" I said, "Oh my."

We could only see part of him—the important part—from below the shoulders to right above the knees. He had a lot of hair (red hair, like my cello teacher, Mr. Krumpf, I thought with alarm). It covered his chest and inched down his belly in a thick, curly triangle, diminishing to a copper-color line that pointed—as Judy told Pam later—all the way to Texas. The naked man was thin (unlike Mr. Krumpf, I noted with relief). We could see from the bridge the shape of his ribs and hipbones. Of course, we were not much interested in ribs and hipbones. Judy took advantage of the opportunity to use one of her favorite words.

"Look at his cock," she whispered.

Judy and I had been best friends since first grade, but by the time we were thirteen, certain differences had developed between us, and "cock" was one of them. Judy teased me for saying "penis," a word she considered old-fashioned, anatomical, and lame. She would repeat it after me in a wheedly voice, drawing out the long "eeee" and the "ssss"—as in *sissy*—but I still couldn't bring myself to use her alternative. Not only because I believed that my mother would wash my mouth out with soap if she ever heard that somebody heard me say it, but also because of all the other cocks I was afraid I'd ruin by association. Once I started using "cock" to mean *cock,* then what would I do in school, or in ordinary conversation—maybe with my mother!—when somebody and something was cock-eyed? Cock-eyed. Think about that. What about stopcocks and peacocks and shuttlecocks?

Eleven-year-old Pam, who was the junior member of our best friendship, solved the problem by calling it a "thing"—which Judy said was better than "penis"—but I wasn't about to compromise "thing" either, and I had a cousin named Dick, so most of the time I tried to avoid calling it anything at all. Now, however, watching the naked man walk past the window with his penis/cock/thing swinging to and fro in full view, I knew I had to say something. I whispered vaguely, "You'd think it would get in your way."

"What?" Judy whispered back.

"You *know* what," I said. "Hanging down like that."

The naked man had stopped in front of the window. He was flexing his arm muscles, such as they were, this way and that as if he were using the window as a mirror, while, down below, his penis adjusted itself to every change of posture.

"You probably get used to it after a while," Judy said.

We watched in silence for another moment—the naked man went on flexing and adjusting—and then the second worst possible thing that I could have imagined happening happened.

"Here comes a car!" I cried.

There was no place to hide on the top of the bridge. I would have run for it—foolishly calling attention to myself, Judy pointed out later—if she hadn't taken me by the arm and hauled me back to the railing, out of the path of the approaching headlights. There we leaned, with our backs to the tracks and the apartment building, just as if we had stopped to chat on the bridge, where—Judy also pointed out—we had every right to be at nine o'clock on a warm spring night. When the car passed—my heart was pounding so hard in my ears that I barely heard Judy say, "Coast is clear!"—we turned to look again. The naked man walked past the window wearing pants.

"Shoot," said Judy.

"Show's over," I said, my knees weak with relief.

We were both pretty quiet the rest of the way home. I was still trembling and thanking our lucky stars for what I considered a narrow escape. Judy—I found out when we reached my back porch—was thinking about something else. She sat down on the bottom step, avoiding the patches of light from the kitchen windows, and, tossing her long, blond hair over her shoulder, she said into the night, "We could charge admission."

I sat down beside her. At a window behind us my cat appeared, casting a monstrous shadow at our feet.

"Admission for what?" I said warily.

"For the *show,*" she said.

"What do you mean?"

"Hey—you're the one who said it," she said.

"What did I say?"

"Show's over!" she quoted me.

"Jeez, Judy, *that's* not what I meant."

She slapped me on the back and the cat shadow vanished. "So you're a genius and you don't even know it."

"But, Judy," I said, "what if we got caught?"

She stood up and started pacing in front of me. "Doing what?" she said. "Standing on the bridge? I mean, it's not like we used binoculars, is it? There's no law against standing on a bridge."

There were flaws in this reasoning, I was sure of it. Unfortunately, I didn't know what they were.

"But, Judy," I tried again, "what makes you think we'll ever see the guy naked again? Maybe he just forgot to pull his shade, you know?"

There was a moment of silence. Judy stopped pacing and sat down beside me again.

"Well?" I said, thinking my point had been well taken.

"Well," she said slowly. "Actually, I've seen him naked before."

"What?" I gasped. "Where?"

"What do you mean, where? In the window, of course. Same place, same *time,* same station—get it?" She leaned into me. "Look, Mary. It's simple. All we have to do is blindfold people and lead them all around, through the bushes and over the tracks and everything, to the right spot at the right time! For a price," she hastened to add. "*Now* do you get it?"

"Judy," I asked her, "how many times have you seen this naked man?"

She tugged on her bangs. "Oh, once or twice." She fidgeted. "Well, actually, twice. Not counting tonight."

"And you never told me?" I was not only shocked but hurt. A naked man seemed like the sort of thing best friends should share.

Judy rolled her eyes. "I just *did* tell you," she said. "Now, are you with me or not?"

The next night we took Pam, who had five older brothers and knew about these things, to see the show free of charge. We stopped in the middle of the bridge, where Judy and I had been the night before, but I was so extremely nervous about waiting there, in full view of the occasional passing car, that we moved into the lilac bushes where they made a leafy cave at the end of the bridge and found that we could see the window even better from there. After about five minutes of swatting mosquitoes and thinking I heard footsteps coming over the bridge, I tried to make a case for going home.

"Come on," I whispered. "This guy isn't going to parade around in his birthday suit every night for our benefit. Let's go."

Judy and Pam ignored me.

"The mosquitoes are eating me alive," I said, slapping a big, bloody one on my arm and conspicuously failing to mention what was really bothering me. Last night, after all, I had seen the naked man more or less by accident, even if I did hang around and watch for a while. Tonight we had come looking for him. I was trying to think of a way to point out this fine ethical distinction to my friends, when Judy grabbed both my arm and Pam's and said, "Look!"

Holding on to one another in the lilacs, we looked. There he was—same time, same place, and as naked as he'd been the night before.

"What do you think of *that*?" Judy asked Pam.

"You can see his thing, all right," Pam said. She turned to me in the darkness to see what I thought. Now was the time to share my reservations about window-peeping. Now or never. They both looked at me in the darkness. My two best friends.

"You can see it all right," I said.

The following night I found myself in the alley blindfolding Carrie Tuttle, who'd risked her very life to sneak out of the house after nine o'clock, and also Helen Mahoney, who'd come along only because she happened to be spending the night at Carrie's (and who was—I felt, knowing Helen—making a big mistake). Judy did the same to Leah Fischer and Heather Wisniewski, while Pam took care of the twins, Lenore and Linda. Then we led the six of them, stumbling and giggling, around the block, through a couple of yards, down over the railroad tracks, and back up to the spot. When we took the blindfolds off, they were understandably annoyed to find that they had paid a quarter each to be led to the end of the Walnut Street bridge, and there was a lot of grumbling in the lilac bushes for a while. To make matters worse, the naked man's light was off.

"You see?" I whispered fiercely, taking Judy aside and leaving Pam to ride herd on our dissatisfied customers, one of whom had scared me half to death by shrieking when a cricket landed on her. "What did I tell you?" I hissed. "Just because a guy is naked three nights in a row doesn't mean we can *count* on him—"

I stopped in mid-sentence. This time Judy didn't even have to say "Look!" Her eyebrows told me to turn around. The light was on in the window. Seconds later, our friend appeared from about the neck down, shedding garments where he stood.

Everyone was impressed. Carrie and the twins agreed that the guy's thing (I noticed they all said "thing") was easily the longest one any of them had ever seen before (as if any of them had ever seen one). Heather, an only child who always got the highest scores in the class on her California Basics, admitted that this was the first penis she had ever seen. "A handy thing to have on a picnic," she mused. Leah Fischer wondered if red-haired men had freckles *everywhere* (we couldn't quite tell from the bridge), and poor Helen Mahoney, whose glasses reflected the streetlight, giving her an astonished, alien look, said nothing.

Nobody asked for her money back.

When, after a few minutes, the naked man disappeared from the window, I had another quiet but heated argument with Judy about whether or not it was time to go. Even she had to agree that the nine of us made a pretty conspicuous crowd in the lilac bushes, and I think we might have left right then if the naked man hadn't chosen that moment to reappear with a towel thrown over his shoulder and, it soon became clear to us, something strange happening down below. I don't know what he was looking at or thinking about, but one minute his penis was hanging there, like always, and the next minute—

"Ho!" said Linda. "Look at that!" said Lenore.

"His cock looks like a diving board," Judy whispered, giving Pam an attack of giggles so severe that we practically had to suffocate her to keep her quiet. It didn't help matters that the others were giggling, too, all except for Helen, who would have been looking shamefacedly at her shoes if she could have seen them down there in the dark. By the time we had composed ourselves enough to look again, the penis was pointing straight up. It seemed to be trying to get a look at what it was attached to.

"*That's* an erection," Pam of the five brothers said authoritatively.

"It looks like a little person," whispered Heather, in something like awe.

The next night Judy had so many customers she had to take them in two shifts. She warned both new and returning ones—all of whom seemed willing to pay rather than venture to the spot on their own—that she couldn't *guarantee* what they would see on any one night and that they might have to spend more than a quarter to get their money's worth. For several nights in a row, she and Pam had the lilac bushes filled to capacity. Each of those nights, Judy reported, the naked man obliged them by turning on his light, right on schedule, although his fantasy life, from all appearances, seemed to be in something of a slump.

I didn't go back to the bridge again. I told Judy it was because my cat had run away, which was true. She had. She was a clawless indoor cat unacquainted with the dangers of automobile traffic, and for days after she disappeared I approached with dread all crumpled bags and piles of leaves or garbage in the street. I even examined a freshly flattened squirrel to make sure it wasn't a cat. I spent my evenings on the back porch waiting, hoping, with milk and tuna fish, and Judy helped me post my Lost Cat signs everywhere, but Nancydrew never came back.

In the meantime, the end of May turned into the beginning of June, the lilacs faded, and I couldn't believe, as more and more girls found out about Judy's little operation, that nobody had blown the whistle on her yet. When she told me she and Pam were thinking about extending their word-of-mouth advertising to Hoover Junior High, I told her she was nuts.

"You don't even know half those kids," I said "What if one of them turns out to be a wimp and tells her mother?"

"Helen Mahoney didn't tell," Judy countered. "Who could be more of a wimp than Helen Mahoney?"

I had the feeling it was not a rhetorical question.

The first week of June was also the last week of school, when, according to tradition, a priest took the eighth-grade boys into one room and a nun took the girls into another for a last-minute session in sex education. I don't know what the priest told the boys, but Sister Lucinda was not too explicit. She showed us a couple of pictures—cross-sections of pertinent male and female anatomy—briefly discussing the "deposit" of sperm in a prim, precise way that made me think of bank tellers and pneumatic tubes, and then she went straight to the Ninth Commandment, where she lingered for some time.

Thou shalt not covet they neighbor's wife covered a great deal more territory than it spelled out, she emphasized. It covered impure thoughts, dirty magazines, B-rated movies, and more, she said, as she looked with knowing eyes from one of us to the next. I remember glancing at Judy to see if she was taking this in. She met my eye for only a second, but it was long enough to tell me that she didn't need Sister Lucinda's list of sins any more than I did. We both knew what the commandment covered; it covered the naked man.

Later, I clutched Judy's arm. "She knows!" I said.

"Oh, she does not."

By this time I realized that Judy and Pam were going to be in big trouble sooner or later if I didn't do something to stop them. Unable to convince them of the danger they were in, I racked my brain for a way to eliminate what Sister Lucinda would have called the occasion of sin. Somehow, for the sake of my friends (and, I believed, for decency's sake as well), I had to get the naked man himself to close the show.

There seemed to be no safe way to contact him. I didn't know his apartment number (there were sixteen all together, I learned from checking the mailboxes of an identical building on Locust Street), and I was not going to throw a rock through his window or otherwise seek him out face to face. For one whole catless, friendless evening I pondered. Then I thought of writing the notes.

I used the nice pink notecards with matching envelopes that Aunt Frances gave me for my birthday every year. After fiddling with the wording for a long time, I settled on this:

Dear Sir,

People can see you naked from the street. Please pull your shade or something.

Signed,
A concerned neighbor

Needless to say, I omitted the return address. I also took the precaution of riding my bike down to the Post Office instead of using the box at the end of our block to mail the pile of pink envelopes, each addressed to the "Occupant" of a different apartment from 1 to 16.

When I told Judy what I'd done, she was furious. She said I had no business ruining everything for everybody else. She said why don't I go hang around with Helen Mahoney then. She said the Ninth Commandment was about coveting your neighbor's *wife,* for God's sake, and they weren't coveting anybody anyway. They were only looking at him.

"But, Judy," I tried to defend myself, "how would you feel if he was looking at you?"

Judy narrowed her eyes at me. To this day I remember the way she narrowed her eyes at me. She said, "Whose side are you on, anyway?"

KERRY DOLAN

A Perfect Day at Riis Park

Theresa and I are waiting at our usual spot—the Belt Parkway entrance on Sixty-sixth Street—but it's a slow morning. We share a seat on her duffel bag, feet out toward the road, too tired to stand up for a ride. Earlier we passed up two cars of weirdo guys, then ripped a slice of pizza in half and finished it. Theresa threw the whole cheese blob down her throat at once, then squished the crust with her foot—into the road.

"Fuck—those guys down there got one," she says. Guys with Frisbees and towels. They pile in looking free and on the go. Usually we get the rides first—we're girls and Theresa's tall and beautiful and looks at least nineteen.

"Do you want another slice?" she says. Vinnie's is across the street.

"No." I'm thinking about how I shouldn't have eaten the first slice. I hate pizza in the summer, but she talked me into it. When I don't eat in the morning, my stomach's flat at the beach—a valley with hip bones for mountains—but now it'll be a round little hill and I won't be able to see past it to my toes.

"We're gonna miss the best beach time," I say. It's ten-thirty and we've been here for nearly an hour. "I know," she says. We lie flat out on the road with towels under our heads so we don't miss any rays. Our legs are tan—brown—in cutoff shorts, but mine look eight inches shorter, like baby legs. Cars roll by, give breeze after breeze, but they don't stop. We do this every day:

meet in front of Dominic's Deli, pick up suntan lotion and iced tea, then hitch a ride to Riis Park. It's the only way to get there without a car. There's no train or bus; every day it's like an adventure, like a place we might not ever get to.

A red car slows down. Some kind of sportscar. We hop up, grab our bags in a daze. It's a woman—what luck. "Where you headed?" she says. The tape deck's blaring.

"Riis," says Theresa. Theresa leans her elbow on the window and her hair falls into the car—I'm startled by how pretty she is.

"Riis Park," I add. The woman doesn't look like a local. "The beach. It's one stop past the Flatbush Avenue exit. You have to cross a bridge—there's a toll but we can pay it, if you want."

"She *knows* it," says Theresa. "Everyone knows it. You going that far?" she says to the woman. She's older, in her twenties.

"Yeah maybe," she says. She lowers the volume, considers us. "Sure, get in."

Theresa shrugs her eyebrows at me, but this looks like a better ride than most.

I get in the back. I always get the back. Usually I keep the conversation rolling—boom out questions with the wind hitting my face—while some dumb guy watches Theresa's legs. Theresa checks out: rolls down the window, flips the radio dial for the right song. That's her part, to let her hair fall in her face and her turquoise bracelet glitter.

The woman, the driver, has an Elvis Costello tape on, but she shuts it off. "Do you girls like Springsteen?" She has a lazy California way of talking—the way she says like is like li-i-ike.

"Yeah," we both say.

She laughs. "Yeah, I figured." This woman—she's like a chick really, some cool spy chick—has chopped-off dark blond hair and a purple tank top. Her arms are lean and muscular, casual; real set at the wheel. She leans one arm out like it's meant to be there. She's got a good jaw. I never think of that—jaws—but she's got one.

"*Darkness?*" she says. "Or *Born to Run*?"

"*Darkness,*" says Theresa.

"No-o—ugh—please—*Born to Run,*" I say. We have this argument all the time. *Darkness* has just come out, and I feel betrayed. "He's lost it," I argue with Theresa. "He got famous and he lost it." The whole subject just upsets me.

"Or *Greetings,*" I say. "Do you have *Greetings from Asbury Park*? That's my favorite." It has that line "Crawl into my ambulance, your pulse is getting weak." I think it's the most romantic line I've ever heard. I think of crawling into Bruce's ambulance, revealing myself while I've still got the strength to speak.

"No. Sorry," she says. "That is a good album, though." She slips in *Born to Run.* She pulls onto the highway, accelerates. I wonder what her favorite Bruce song is.

"Air-conditioning?" she says.

"No," we both say. We like the wind blowing. By the time we get to the beach our hair's always tangled and in our face.

"That's a cool shirt," I say.

"Thanks."

"You from around here?" I ask. She can't be.

"I'm from New Mexico, Santa Fe, originally, but I've lived a lot of places."

"Oh," I say. "Like where—where have you lived?"

Theresa's leaning her head against the window with her eyes closed, humming.

"Oh . . . Boston, and California." She tosses it off like it's no big deal—a whole list of no big deals. "And Colorado—I lived there for a while." Her voice is husky and dry, totally cool.

"In Denver?"

"No. Colorado Springs. I went to school there."

I haven't heard of it. "Is that near the Rockies?" The only thing I know about Colorado is "Rocky Mountain High."

"Yeah. Kind of."

"It must be beautiful, huh?" I say, though I never think about beautiful landscape—if that's something you're supposed to look for. Every year in grammar school we used to take a class trip to Bear Mountain—it was the closest nature deal. We took the same dumb ferry and the same dumb bear trail, and everyone said God, isn't this so beautiful, but I don't know—I just don't get it.

"Yes, it's great," she says. "I'm Daphne, by the way." She turns to look at me.

"I'm Allie," I say. *Daphne.* "That's short for Alice."

"Theresa," Theresa says with her eyes still closed.

"I live in Brooklyn now, though," Daphne says.

"Where, the Heights?" I lean forward on the seat cushion. I've never met anyone from the Heights.

"No, Park Slope, actually." That would've been my second guess.

"It's pretty there," I say.

Daphne turns the volume up on "Tenth Avenue Freeze-out," and I wonder if I'm asking too many questions. I meant to ask her what radio station she listens to—probably NEW. I have to tell her about FUV, the one in South Orange; you can only get it really late at night if it's raining and you turn the volume all the way up.

It's a great day. The sun's shining blue, there's no traffic, we're driving by water. We're—the whole car's—streaked in sun. It's Tuesday. I've got my peach yogurt in my pack and Theresa said she had three joints left. We don't need anything else in summer. It's just perfect day after perfect day. I try to catch myself in the rearview mirror. I look almost pretty, like another person, with a tan. I can never get over the change, but I'm afraid Daphne will see me so I cut it out.

"Are you two sisters?" says Daphne. "You could be sisters." We both have long straight hair parted in the middle.

"No," I say. I'm flattered but I know Theresa hates this. She thinks she's much prettier and anytime anyone notices me first—which is like once in a million—she gets pissed. Last week two guys stopped by our blanket, stood right at the edge, and stared. For a while they didn't say anything. Then one said, "Ssss . . . I don't know which one-a you is prettier." Then the other said, "Greenie. Hey Greenie." I was wearing a green bikini. "You ain't beautiful now, but you will be. You're gonna be prettier than your momma here." Theresa didn't talk to me for the rest of the afternoon.

"So how old are you guys?" says Daphne.

"Fourteen," says Theresa.

"Almost fifteen," I add. "Our birthdays are in the fall."

"Huh," she says. "You look older," she says to Theresa.

"How old?" says Theresa.

"Oh . . . about seventeen. But you don't," she says to me. "Do you go to school around here?" I wonder if she's interested or just making dumb conversation.

"I go to FDR, and she goes to Catholic school," says Theresa. "Our Lady of Roses."

"Our Lady of *Lourdes*. I used to go to FDR," I say, apologetically. "But my mother made me switch after eighth grade." She was afraid I'd get into trouble, hanging out with Theresa and Karen Messina and the gang on Fifty-sixth Street. Every night she'd pull me by the hair, smell my breath, cry, say What am I going to do with you. "I'm still a virgin, Ma," I'd say. She was worried I'd end up like Diane McGill, busting beer bottles on the sidewalk, getting knocked up, heading off to reform school. When I was out she'd look through my drawers, my diary, my record albums—once she found some rolling paper in an Eagles cover. I had to keep one trick ahead of her.

So she transferred me. But it's a liberal school and the Catholic girls are wilder than the public ones. Father Bill lets us smoke in his office. This girl Elaine's fucking the gym coach, Oscar, in the locker room after school. In religion I have to write letters to Jesus as though he's my friend. "Dear Jesus," I always start off. "How are you?" I make up a bunch of bullshit, then end it with "Hope you are well. Your friend, Allie." It's retarded.

"Where are you driving now?" I ask Daphne. "I mean, is Riis on your way?"

"Well, I was thinking of heading to the beach for a few hours. Coney Island, but I've never been there. But Riis is nicer?"

"Oh yeah, Coney sucks," says Theresa. "The waves stink."

"Brighton sucks, too," I say.

"Oh God, Brighton's worse," Theresa says.

"But Manhattan's the worst," I say.

"Oh God, yeah," says Theresa. "You have to swim through puke at Manhattan."

Daphne laughs. "Well, thanks, it's nice to know all this. It's like having a tour guide. I've only lived in Brooklyn three months and I don't know my way around at all."

"I bet you spend a lot of time in the city, huh," I say. She must have all sorts of friends and hang out in cafes.

"Yes. My friends are there, and last year I was living downtown—but it got too expensive." She pauses, thumps the steering wheel. "But I just love Brooklyn. It's got that neighborhood feel."

"Yeah. There are a lot of neighborhoods here," I say.

"Where I picked you up is near *Saturday Night Fever,* right?"

"Kind of," I say. Theresa and I hate this topic. "The disco's around the corner from my house. It used to be a bowling alley."

"Oh really," she says.

"Yeah. And we saw John Travolta when they were filming it. He was eating a knish . . . you have to turn here," I say. We're heading over the Marine Parkway bridge. This is the best part of the ride—almost being there. The water looks rough and clean.

"What do you do?" I say. "Do you have a job?" I'm wondering why she's not at work, in an office somewhere.

"I'm a photographer."

"Wow, *really*?"

"Yes."

"Theresa, did you hear that?"

Theresa had her head out the window, trying to get an early start on her tan. "Yeah."

"Where do you work?" I say. "Do you have a big office?"

"Oh, here and there. I freelance."

"What does that mean—you have your own agency?"

"No, not exactly. I work on assignment." She looks at me. "You're very curious, aren't you?"

I feel embarrassed, shrug.

"No, that's good. You should be a reporter."

I like this idea—a reporter.

"What do you take pictures of? Do they tell you, or you just come up with it yourself?"

"You have a general assignment, and then you work from there."

I can't believe how much we've lucked out with this ride. Last week we got stuck in a Hell's Angels van. They were moving their cycles all the way to the West Coast, and we had to sit in the back with the bikes. There were plastic spiders, Day-Glo and New Riders posters. The back window was shaped like a heart. I had to sit on some guy Dickie's lap. Theresa made out with one of them all the way to the beach. But a photographer—now she really seems like a spy chick. Sunglasses, short hair, camera lenses sticking out of her pocket. "Have you been to London?" I say.

She laughs. "Yes. I spent my junior year there."

We see the sign for Riis Park Gateway Recreational Area. Daphne pulls into the parking lot; the sun's out, the pavement looks hot and dusty.

"Which bay should we go to?" Daphne says.

"Fourteen," says Theresa. We always go to fourteen.

"Can't we go to a different bay today? It's a special day," I say.

"I told Mooney we'd be there." Mooney's the guy she likes. He has a mustache and a beer belly and is stoned around the clock. He's nineteen and just lost his job at Fayva—it took him too long to lace up the shoes. When I tell her she could do better, get a better crush, she says, "But he needs my help." Yeah, with his diet, I say.

"I know, but we can see Mooney any day." What I mean is we can't see Daphne.

"Tell you what," says Daphne. "Why don't we go to Bay Eight for a couple of hours—I can only stay for a little while anyway—then I'll drop you off at Fourteen and you can see your friends."

"Okay. Sounds good," I say. "Theresa?"

"Yeah, all right." She's annoyed. "But I told Mooney."

Theresa's my best friend, but sometimes I don't even like her; though I know she likes me even less. But I've had my best times with her, especially in summer. Walking barefoot and stoned in cutoff shorts in the rain, all the way along Seventh Avenue till the end—till you could see Staten Island. We saw the whole rain together. On the way back we bought bagels.

Then, in seventh grade, going to Kings Plaza, the shopping mall, with her. It took me two weeks to ask her: she was boppy and pretty and got lousy grades. She chomped on pistachio nuts in Miss Bartinelli's class. She made funny noises and said it was Joey Brown. Probably everyone wanted to go to the mall with her.

But she agreed to go and we went. It took an hour and a half—three buses—to get there. I hated the preparation time; I wanted to just be having the experience. I was wearing my favorite blue shirt, bunched up around the chest and ending at my naval. Once we got there we didn't buy anything. We went into the record store, the shoe store, Alexander's. We tried things on, asked salesgirls questions, spat from the top floor to the ground. We yelled hey at strange guys. We were bumping and giddy—we were lighting up the place. I thought it was the best day I'd ever had, wearing my shirt, being out with Theresa.

We get to Bay Eight and it's empty. I think a clear stretch of sand is about as beautiful as things get. We follow Daphne till she stops in a spot no different from the others, but maybe she has a feeling about it. I get that way, too, follow my intuition. I pull out my Indian bedspread beach blanket and we lie down, feet facing the water. It's after eleven and the sun's right in the center of the sky.

"Do you wanna smoke?" Theresa asks Daphne. She waves a joint.

"Sure," says Daphne. Daphne pulls off her shirt and there's nothing underneath. On the bottom she's wearing boys' black underwear. We're both in bikinis. Theresa gives me a look, but I try to act nonchalant, rise above her. I can't believe it either, though—this is like—this woman I wanna be.

Daphne lies down as though there's nothing between her and the air. We both stare. Her breasts are small and round, cute; so that it doesn't even seem like she's naked. I wouldn't mind having breasts like that. They'd never get in the way or weigh you down. You could just pull on a tank top and no bra and be free—they'd be good breasts for a spy.

Theresa passes the joint to me and I pass it to Daphne.

"How old are you?" I ask her.

"Twenty-five." I don't know anyone who's twenty-five; my sister Shari's twenty-three, but she's married and dull.

"Do you have a boyfriend?" I ask.

She smirks, takes a toke from the joint; she's enjoying this.

"Sort of. I don't know."

Sort of. You have a boyfriend, or you don't, or you get married—that's the way it works. I want to grow up to be a woman who has all these sort-of boyfriends.

We finish the joint and Theresa turns on NEW. Daphne curls one arm under her head and lights a Newport 100. I take out my peach yogurt and an orange. I try to peel the orange, but it's so hard at the beach; not to get sand. It makes me mad every day, but I still bring it. I'm on a diet and I don't want to die. It makes me feel better, knowing I have a little orange in me.

"Do you want some?" I ask Daphne.

"No thanks."

"Are you thirsty? I could get you a Coke." I'm afraid she'll get bored and leave us.

"No thanks."

"You can get me a Coke," says Theresa.

"Fuck you. Get it yourself." I used to do favors for her all the time, and now it makes me mad thinking about it. Once she stole my earrings, my favorite silver hoop earrings. They were in my jewelry box one night, and then they weren't. Then I saw her walking down Fifty-sixth Street with them hanging out of her ears. "Those look like my earrings," I said. "Oh yeah?" she said. She seemed a little embarrassed, but not too. "I guess not, though," I said. I felt it was my fault, for some reason.

From then on I saw them in her ears, but I didn't say anything. I forgave her. I tried to look at it a new way: her father was dead and her mother spoke Polish. Maybe she needed them more than I did. Maybe I was meant to give them up, like a sacrifice. I don't know.

Theresa lights a Marlboro and turns up NEW. That was eighth grade. Now sometimes I wish I had them back. She doesn't even wear them anymore. She could've just borrowed them.

"So do you know what you want to be when you grow up?" says Daphne.

Theresa rolls her eyes at me. "Nope," she says. I know for a fact she wants to be a flight attendant.

"'What about you?" Daphne says.

Now I think maybe I want to be a photographer—I always sort of wanted to, but I never met one before—but I'm embarrassed to say it 'cause Daphne'll think I don't have my own ideas.

"Maybe I'd like to be in a band," I say. I play guitar, a little.

"Hah," says Theresa.

"My voice isn't great, but I think, maybe, I have some talent." I can't believe I'm continuing but I feel so free, all of a sudden. "Sometimes songs come to me—you know, lyrics. And the melodies too. They just come in my head."

Or maybe, I tell her, I want to be a disc jockey. "It bothers me, the way they never play the right songs back to back." I have a lot of ideas in this direction.

Daphne looks at me seriously. "It's a pretty unstable life, songwriting. Disc jockeying, too. It's like photography."

I like this idea: having an unstable life, like Daphne. Driving a sportscar with the windows down. It might suit me.

"I would just really hate that, says Theresa.

"Yeah well, like they say," says Daphne, "you don't choose it, it chooses you." She ends the sentence with a drag on her cigarette.

I like this idea, too: of being chosen. But I wonder when you know. Like are you just supposed to decide you're chosen, or is someone—your mother—supposed to tell you. Once my mother told me my hair was a mess and I looked like a slob. "I'm ashamed of you," she said. "You used to be pretty, like Shari, but now you look like a disgrace. I can't believe you're my daughter."

I wished she hadn't said it. Now the words were out there, permanent. "What, should I look like you?" I said. She was a secretary, wore high heels and lipstick.

She put on that injured martyr look. I stormed out and locked my bedroom door. I kicked the wall, knocked down my Todd Rundgren poster. Fuck her. She insulted me first. Just fuck her.

In a minute I was out there, crying like crazy. "I'm sorry, I didn't mean it." I thought I'd never cried so much in my whole life—it felt good, like being washed over; all my sins being washed out, even though I didn't believe in sin anymore.

An hour passes, maybe less. The sun feels good, like it's drying up all the bad stuff. Daphne gets up out of nowhere and heads for the water. I can't believe her ass—it twitches, but not in a stupid way. "She is so cool," I say to Theresa. "Yeah, she's okay." Okay? Sometimes I think Theresa's the biggest moron in the world—she has no sense of anything. "But I don't see why you're chasing her," she says. "She's a snob. She's just making fun of you."

"No she's not."

"Oh really—a *reporter*, a *songwriter*—God. You're so stupid."

I don't believe it. Daphne must see something in me—that's it, she sees something. I wonder if I can call her up, talk about things.

"She likes me," I say. "She likes to converse with me."

"Oh, give me a break. Why would she want to hang out with *us*. She wanted tips on a good sun spot. We gave her some free grass. She flashes her tits. She's happy."

"Oh, shut up," I say. I get up and the sand surprises me—it's so hot I can't walk. I sort of hop toward the water. My high's leveling off and I'm feeling—great. Just great.

I see Daphne dive and swim out far—I'm a lousy swimmer, but I think I'll follow her anyway. The waves are rough. I get knocked down and my mouth's in sand. Maybe I'm more stoned than I thought. I come up, start to dog-paddle. Daphne sees me and smiles. She's out there where it's brighter, past the waves.

I keep paddling, but another wave—a high green wall I'll never climb over—smashes me. I can't get up. I feel this rush in my ears like the ocean's pulling me to something. Then Daphne grabs me, takes my hand. I hug her skin—it feels better than anything I've ever felt—and we just float like that.

BRUCE WEIGL

What Saves Us

We are wrapped around each other
in the back of my father's car parked
in the empty lot of the high school
of our failures, sweat on her neck
like oil. The next morning I would leave
for the war and I thought I had something
coming for that, I thought to myself
that I would not die never having
been inside her body. I lifted
her skirt above her waist like an umbrella
blown inside out by the storm. I pulled
her cotton panties up as high
as she could stand. I was on fire. Heaven
was in sight. We were drowning
on our tongues and I tried
to tear my pants off when she stopped
so suddenly we were surrounded
only by my shuddering
and by the school bells
grinding in the empty halls.
She reached to find something,
a silver crucifix on a silver chain,
the tiny savior's head
hanging, and stakes through his hands and his feet.

She put it around my neck and held me
so long my heart's black wings were calmed.
We are not always right
about what we think will save us.
I thought that dragging the angel down that night
would save me, but I carried the crucifix in my pocket
and rubbed it on my face and lips
nights the rockets roared in.
People die sometimes so near you,
you feel them struggling to cross over,
the deep untangling, of one body from another.

THOMAS BURKE

The Beauty of the Stations

As the end of August came I savored each last day of it, all the while dreading September's inevitable arrival. September would bring a start to my high school career. The cousins, the dreaded Murray cousins, would be there at the St. Alban's Abbey School for Boys at Poolesville. Full of boys from Boston, New York, Philadelphia, and Washington, Poolesville Abbey was not my choice. These cousin-like boys with lawyer-banker-doctor dads were not of my ilk.

My own father, Richard Slowinski, died two months before I was born. He is only a name to me, but his name is a great deal. It is all that is allowed me of the father who never held me or heard my voice. Richard Slowinski abandoned me in an automobile accident on Christmas Eve. Skidding on a patch of ice, his car leapt off the Francis Scott Key Bridge into the frozen Potomac River. I sometimes wonder if there were Christmas presents in his trunk.

There is no way out of this; my grandmother is paying for me to go away to the Abbey. That's what she always calls it, "The Abbey." Like it is the only one in the world. My Grandfather Murray went to school there, all the Murray uncles and cousins have gone, and now it is my turn. But I am not a Murray. Murray is my middle name. My mother's family, these Murrays, have a hard time getting their tongues around my last name. I have always been called John Murray, John Murray Slowinski,

". . . just like Henry Cabot Lodge," my Aunt Mary Murray says when introducing me.

As Mom and I drove into the town of Poolesville, the Abbey grounds were immediately visible. The front fields of the Abbey became a golf course some time in the 1920s. Close-clipped grass lay taut over the rolling hills—as if green velvet had been stretched on a Christmas train set. A driveway poked through a small valley; inset on a brick gatepost was a plaque:

SAINT ALBAN'S ABBEY SCHOOL FOR BOYS
POOLESVILLE, MARYLAND
ESTABLISHED 1763

POSTED
NO HUNTING—NO TRESPASSING
CAUTION: LOW FLYING BALLS NEXT 500 YARDS

A wood-paneled station wagon pulled into the driveway just ahead of us; its Pennsylvania license plate read, "BOOFEY."

"What do you think that means," I asked my mother, pointing at the license plate.

"Oh my God." My mother smiled. "That's Mercedes McCann Geoghegan, she used to go with your Uncle Bob. I can't believe she has that name on her tags."

"What does it mean?"

"It's her nickname," Mom said. "She actually prefers it to Mercedes. Old Boofey McCann, I wonder how she looks."

Mom pulled the Falcon up near the front of a red-brick Georgian building with a great white-pillared portico. Carved into the portico frieze were the words "Gift of the Class of 1869." A robed monk stood holding a clipboard. After waving on the Boofey-mobile, he motioned for us to pull forward.

"Your name please," the monk said.

"Slowinski," my mother said, "John Murray Slowinski."

"Ah, a new boy." The monk looked up and smiled. "You'll be in Gunlocke Hall, it's around the back, just follow the lane here. Your roommate arrived last night. Welcome to the Abbey."

"Roommate," I said to my mother. "I never really thought

about that. I'm going to have a roommate. I don't know about this."

"Too late." Mom continued to drive. "You're paid up through May, you'll have to make do."

Gunlocke Hall was a smaller version of the Gift of the Class of 1869. The ivy creeping up its red brick reached the first-floor windowsills. My room was on the top floor. It looked out over an amphitheater at the back of the building and beyond to the pointy Victorian steeples of the new Abbey church. I was hoping for bunk beds, but two identical beds stood on either side of the room. Behind the beds were desks, also identical, pushed against opposite walls. A long-torsoed blond-haired boy was seated at one of the desks. As he turned to get up, I thought about turning to run. My cousin Bradley Murray—the fourteen-year-old football, golf, and swimming champion of Greater Washington—was staring at me. I was to be confined in this reform school with big, blond, stupid Bradley.

"Aunt Margaret, so nice to see you." He walked over to kiss my mother on the cheek. "And John Murray, isn't this great, Dad asked the school if we could be roommates."

"Great," I mumbled.

"Well, isn't this a nice treat." My mother clapped her hands and beamed at the two of us. "I think I'll leave you two alone and let you get on with things. You don't need your old mother and aunt hanging around."

With that Mom was out the door.

"Listen," Bradley began as soon as Mom's footsteps were no longer audible, "this wasn't my idea. I'm not so crazy about it. But we have to stay together at least until Christmas. I already checked into it."

"I'm not so crazy about this whole thing." I couldn't believe the words were coming out of my mouth. Bradley usually intimidated me. "I didn't want to come to this school anyway."

"Ungrateful little shit," Bradley continued. "Gram is paying a lot of money so you can come here."

"Nobody asked me if I wanted to come here."

"Just don't be a jerk, O.K? You can be such a fag, you know. Just don't embarrass me. Everyone's gonna know were related, so just be cool."

"Yes, your highness."

"Don't be an ass," Bradley sneered. "Let's go down to dinner. I hope we don't get put at the same table."

The first week of school I tried not to pay too much attention to life as it happened around me. The Abbey school day seemed to have been designed by sergeants of the Third Reich. We were awakened by a honking electric bell at 6:35 A.M. Showers and "morning ablutions" were to be completed by 6:55 A.M. Morning prayer was at 7:05 A.M., except Wednesdays, when we had Mass beginning at 7:15 A.M. Breakfast was at 7:30 A.M., except of course on Wednesdays, and the first academic class began at 8:10 A.M. We were counseled frequently by Dom Anselm, the prefect of discipline, "not to tarry unnecessarily in the showers." Any free period in our schedule was filled with a physical education class; eight phys ed periods showed up in my first-semester schedule. I got the idea this was somehow connected with tarrying in the shower.

Most of the boys spoke in the same dialect. It was a shorthand understood to all of them, and though I recognized parts of their talk, much of it eluded me. It seemed to consist of a lot of geography.

"Where did you say you're from?" one would ask another.

"New York," the other would begin, "well, actually Greenwich."

"Country Day or Saint Ed's?" would come the question.

"Saint Ed's," the other would answer with vague superiority, "and you?"

"Washington, we live in Chevy Chase."

"Oh, you must have gone to Mater Dei?"

"Yeah, how'd you guess?" A little sarcastic chuckle would emerge. "Maybe you know my cousins, the Harringtons, they live in Rye, one of them went to Saint Ed's."

"Of course, we see them in the summer at Rehoboth, Fluffy Harrington was the first girl I ever kissed."

And so it went. They all knew one another and their brothers and sisters and mothers and fathers. They were so sure of themselves within this world. I was fascinated and repelled at the same time.

While I was eavesdropping on an after-dinner where-do-you-summer conversation one night, a boy from my Latin class came over to me and asked, "Do you understand any of this? All these people seem to know each other and be related to each other. My name is Phil Lilienthal, you're in my Latin class."

Phil put his hand out to shake. It was natural, not forced and awkward like my cousin Bradley when he put out his hand. I had noticed Phil the first day of Latin class. He had obviously taken Latin before, he answered questions easily and knew how to pronounce things. The Latin monk was pleased with Phil.

"So you don't have to go to Mass tomorrow either, huh." Phil continued, smiling.

"What?" I asked. "Of course I do, they know where we are at all times. You'll get in trouble if you're not there."

"Nope. I don't have to go. My parents arranged it. You should get yours to do the same."

"How'd you do that?"

"Aren't you Jewish?" Phil screwed up his eyebrows as he asked. "Your name is Slowinski, I thought—"

"Oh, no. Are you?" This was great, someone out of the St. Country Day Racquet Club loop.

"Well, yeah. Why don't you tell them you are too, and then we could—"

"What," I interrupted, "and have another period of phys ed, no thanks."

"No, I get to go to the library for a study hall with Abdullah the Kuwaiti prince, the Korean brothers, Wan Hun Loi and Wan Han Loi, and the three other token Jews. You have to prove you're not a Christian to get out of the Mass thing."

Phil, like me, was not particularly interested in athletics. Since we were required to play a sport, he suggested we go out for the cross-country team. All we had to do was walk to the Field House, change into our running clothes, then run until we were out of sight of the buildings. We were then free to walk or sit or do anything until our alotted phys ed period had ended. In the warmer months we went to the swimming hole of the creek. It was down a ravine and well hidden from any monk's view; we could stay there for an hour or more. In winter, we huddled by the old brick barn that had been turned into the campus powerhouse. Its rough red walls were always warmed by the steam of heating pipes.

"We gotta get out of here. I'm sick of this place," Phil said as we practiced our cross-country style, lying down near the creek shore. "If your cousin Bradley Murray calls me a fag one more time, I swear." When Phil lifted his head from my stomach, it stayed warm with the heat of him for a few moments.

"Didn't you hear his latest," I broke in, "we're now Latin Men—get it, homos. Such a clever dumb ass, my cousin and dearest roommate." I slapped Phil's butt slightly with my foot as he rolled over to look me in the eyes.

"Yeah, well I've had it with all of them," Phil said, turning to skip a stone across the creek's surface. "You want to go to that dance over at the Leesburg Convent School on Saturday night? There's gonna be a bus to take us."

"I don't know, Bradley and all his friends are going. His sisters Maureen and Mary Virginia go to school over there and I don't especially want to see them."

"Oh come on, let's go," Phil said and began to tickle me. "I've got some friends there. My friend Penny Hochschild said she could get some pot if we came."

"Shh." I hugged him close to me to make him stop the tickling. "Oh, I guess no one can hear us." I held on to him in a leg lock, almost shouting, "Wow, pot, have you ever tried it?"

"No, but Penny said all the girls at Leesburg are doing it. Come on, let's go."

Bradley found out I was going to the dance. I made the mistake of telling my mother, who told Gram. Then Gram told my Aunt Mary, Bradley's mother. Aunt Mary told Maureen and Mary Virginia when she dropped off their weekly supply of goodies at Leesburg. Maureen told Bradley when she came over to the Abbey to watch a lacrosse game one afternoon.

"So, you and your little boyfriend are gonna go to the dance at Leesburg tonight," Bradley said to me as he came back into our room from the shower. "That's cool. I'm going too. It should be fun. Those girls are so horny they'll be hanging out the windows when we drive in."

As was his habit, Bradley dropped his robe on the floor and stood looking at his naked self in the mirror. "They're all gonna want to get a hold of some of this," he said, grabbing his dick and waving it at me. "You'd like some too, huh, I see you looking at me all the time."

"That's not exactly difficult since you're always prancing around without anything on," I said, looking anywhere but at him.

"I'm hot-blooded, O.K?"

"Do we have to wear a tie?" I looked at his eyes.

"Yeah, you have to wear a jacket and tie. Sister Berchmans, the headmistress, stands at the door. You have to shake hands with her and everything. It's so no one will be drunk or stoned. She looks you in the eye and smells your breath. Mary Virginia told me all about it."

I pulled my favorite outfit out of the closet. The last time it had been worn was at my going-away party.

"Nice." Bradley smiled. "The green leisure suit." As he came over to touch the suit his dick brushed against my robe. I moved away quickly. "That's great," he continued, "the girls will love that."

Bradley pulled out his blue blazer and madras pants. All his friends at Poolesville wore madras pants on Sunday, when we could wear what we liked.

"Are you gonna wear your platform shoes, they're really great, they make you look even taller, the girls will love you," Bradley said, still naked and applying polish to his brown Bass Weejun loafers.

"Yeah, I am," I said, looking through the closet, "and I'm looking for that green vinyl belt, have you seen it?"

"No, but I did wear it last Sunday."

"Really." I was strangely pleased that Bradley would have worn some of my clothes. Though I didn't remember seeing the belt on him. "Oh, here it is. I got it."

"Hey, you look really sharp," Bradley said and smiled. "The girls are going to be all over you."

Maybe being his roommate wasn't such a bad thing after all.

Dom Helwig drove the bus to the dance. I loved Dom Helwig. He was retired from teaching, and unlike the younger monks, he was concerned that we should be happy and not too worried about our schoolwork. "Lads, there are other things in life," he said frequently.

We drove out the gate, through town and down to White's Ferry, which crossed the Potomac River between Poolesville and Leesburg, Virginia. There was much Abbey and Convent lore about lovers swimming across the torrents of the Potomac. That night, the fierce Potomac was little more than a broad creek. I sat in the back of the bus with Phil; Bradley and his friends sat up front. They talked and laughed the whole way. We reached the ferry as it was just departing with its full load of six cars, so we had to wait for the next run.

Looking out the window and across the river, I was excited about my first dance, about being away from the Abbey and being out with my friend. Phil was saying something, but I wasn't really paying attention. Even though I wasn't trying to hear what was going on with Bradley and his friends up front, I heard one of them say, ". . . and your little Pollack cousin John Murray is real cool, the lime-green leisure suit is nice, where did you find him, Bradley. He is such a jerk."

"Yeah, and those platform shoes," someone else said, "I guess they'll figure he and the Jew boy are locals from the public high school trying to crash. . . ."

So that's why Bradley had been so nice.

"Don't worry about them," Phil said, "they all look alike. Who cares? Remember, my friend Penny will be there and we're going to smoke some pot. Who gives a shit about your cousin and his asshole friends."

As we drove into the Convent of the Sacred Heart at Leesburg I felt sick to my stomach. I didn't want to be on the bus, at the dance, or anywhere near Bradley and his friends. My cousins Maureen and Mary Virginia would be there; it was too horrible to imagine.

The bus pulled up to the Oval. Most schools would have called it the quadrangle, but not Leesburg Convent. An oval drive cut through a flat expanse of lawn between two opposing dormitories. A matching brick and limestone Federal dining hall guarded the south end of the Oval. Bradley's friends had said over and over, "They'll be hanging out the windows."

So far, the windows were empty. Pulling to a stop in front of the dining hall, Dom Helwig turned around and said, "All right, lads, have a grand time. I'll go in with you. I have to introduce you to Sister Berchmans or she won't let you through. Then you're on your own. I leave at eleven-thirty sharp, so be back to the bus on time."

We filed off the bus and formed a line. "I've never met a nun before," Phil whispered to me.

"I haven't met many either," I said, "but I think it should be easy. You can't see very much of them. They're all covered up, except for their faces, and I don't think they're real comfortable around men. You know, like how the monks get when someone's mother comes to school, and they're real nice to them, but they're backing away from the woman the whole time they're talking to them."

"Yeah, I've noticed that."

Sister Berchmans wasn't all that bad. When Dom Helwig introduced me, she said something about knowing my mother and then nodded to let me know it was time to move on. Our entire conversation lasted less than twenty seconds.

Across the room was another doorway. The girls were entering through that one. As they came into the room, each girl made a small curtsy to a thronelike chair. In the chair sat an ancient woman dressed in the same black habit as Sister Berchmans. The fabric seemed to be swallowing her. A small white face foundered in her wimple. Tiny clawlike hands peeked from under her half-cape. She didn't say anything to the girls, but each one performed the little ceremony to her as they entered.

"What's that?" Phil said, pointing at the old nun.

"I don't know, she must be the head nun, huh?"

"I thought the one we just shook hands with was the head nun," Phil said.

"Maybe she's dead and they're just being polite," I said. "I don't know, let's find your friend Penny, come on."

"No, she's not dead, I can see her sort of shaking." Phil kept staring at the old woman. "O.K., there." He pointed. "I can see Penny, she just did her curtsy thing, let's go."

We met Penny and her roommate. They asked us to dance, which was a very good idea, because we would never have thought to ask them. When the band took a break, Phil and I went to get some sodas for the girls. Bradley and his friends were standing by themselves in a corner. They watched as we came over.

"Hey," one of them called, "aren't you gonna introduce us to your friends?"

"Oh, I don't think you'd like this little Jew boy's friends," Phil came back.

Returning with the drinks, Phil got down to business with Penny. "So, did you get the pot?" he asked. "Can we go try some?"

"Yeah, it's good stuff," Penny said. "We had some before we came over."

"Really?" I asked in true amazement at the fourteen-year-old sophistication I was witnessing. "Are you high right now?"

"Of course," Penny said in an offhand manner. "Listen, you'll have to wait until the music starts again, then you can slip out."

"Aren't you guys coming with us?" Phil asked.

"No, we'd be missed," Penny said, "that's why we had some before the dance started, but you guys can go out the door behind where old Mother de Sales is sitting, she'll never notice you."

"So that's who the old one is." Phil seemed greatly satisfied to know who the crone was.

As the band began to play, Phil and I sneaked out the back door. Penny had passed a small purple velvet drawstring bag to Phil. In it was a finger-sized brass pipe along with a cellophane bag containing brown and green leaves. The leaves looked like oregano.

"Come on," I said to Phil, "we'll go to the chapel. I know where it is and no one will be there right now."

The whitewashed clapboard Gothic chapel stood at an angle to the Oval. I pulled Phil into one of the fabric-smoothed oaken pews.

"Do you think we should smoke in here?" Phil asked. "I mean, it's a church."

"I know." I was suddenly thrilled with the naughtiness of it all. "Let's do it, come on."

Even though Phil said he had never tried pot before, he seemed to know what to do. I spent a lot of time coughing at first. Eventually I mastered enough smoking skill to hold some of the smoke in my lungs before exhaling. I think I got high.

Conversation flowed forth from me and I lay down in the pew and put my head in Phil's lap.

"Wow," I said, "this is really great."

"I know," Phil said.

He leaned down and kissed me on the lips. I was startled, but it felt good. I kissed back. He lay down in the pew and kissed me again. We kissed and talked and kissed some more. We both seemed to be naturals at this kissing business. After what could have been hours or minutes, I said, "We should go back to the dance, they might come looking for us."

"Yeah, you're right, but why don't you come back to my room when we get to the Abbey?" Phil asked. "My roommate is away for the weekend."

"O.K., great."

As we walked back toward the Oval, I noticed that there were no lights in the dining hall. The dorms were also dark.

"Oh my God," we said at the same time.

"The dance must be over," Phil said.

"What are we gonna do? We're stuck here on the Virginia side of the river," I said. "How are we gonna get back to the Abbey?"

"We're not," Phil said. "We're dead. What are we gonna do?"

"It's starting to rain. Come on, let's get out of the rain."

"Where to?" Phil asked.

"Back to the chapel. We know no one is there."

Hitchhiking back to the Abbey at daybreak, we concocted our alibi. To the monks we told *the truth*—that I was showing Phil the chapel since he was thinking of converting. We lost all track of time while I was explaining what each Station of the Cross meant.

"Oh, they do have a lovely chapel at Leesburg," Dom Anselm said.

"I was very moved by the beauty of the stations," Phil responded. "Jesus was a Jew, just like me. It's all so fascinating."

To the boys at school we intimated that we had spent the night with Penny and her roommate. We did not say those exact words; didn't have to say them.

Discovered

She feared his eyes.
She feared the priest would know
that under the stars, while the village slept,
her young lover unbuttoned her dress
and warmed her blood.

She feared his eyes.
She feared the priest would shake his head
and say, "No white wedding dress."
And her mother's eyes would close.
And her father's eyes would burn.
And her lover's eyes would unbutton
her dress again.

RITA WILLIAMS

The Mathematics of the Moon

Mt. St. Gertrude's Academy for Girls sits on the butte like a penitentiary for the criminally female. A black iron fence confines the parched crabgrass lawn, which is bruised by blowing sand. Thickets of cholla cactus flourish just outside the school, providing sanctuary to pale green scorpions and the roadrunners that feed on them.

Before the Jesuits erected this fortress above the desert floor, this land was a lookout for Geronimo. The gold moon has risen early this evening and hangs in the salsa sky, full and round as a burnished whole note. Elf owls nesting in the belfry murmur to each other as they loft their feathers for this evening's hunt. In the far distance, the eighteen-wheelers rumbling up the interstate provide a steady, bass hum accompaniment to Mass and Vespers.

I still wonder whether the holy water that sanctifies their rituals contains the spore of leprosy for this halfbreed. Still, when the nuns scrutinize me now, my skin no longer feels so stained. Like a diamondback, I have molted. I will do anything to stay here. Including study.

It's not for Jesus' sake. The sisters are right to be suspicious of my contriteness. I am guilty. My sin springs from that most original of Original Sins. I covet their knowledge. I want to understand why they flourish while my family, descendants of

Geronimo and the black pioneers, die meekly, like roadkill on the interstate.

I don't know what to study. I only know it must be outside their web. Maybe I should examine the vectors of the moon, which brings me to heat and puts me to sleep within the logic of its own mysterious circuitry.

I have beseeched the earnest plaster face of La Virgen to make me pure, yet I still bleed and yearn twelve times a year. La Luna they call me—moon crazy. I have asked for guidance. Who knows? Maybe it was those very prayers that led me to the metal-skinned trailer of Kayitah.

But crazy or not, after class, I race to a corner desk at the back of the library and immerse myself in the day's lessons—redraw the pistils and stamens of the lilies, make the translations of Julius Caesar clean in my spiral notebook. I submerge myself in the healing powers of fractals and logarithms. The snowflake-intricacy of the world I almost missed makes me lightheaded. I grieve when the prayer bell summons me. The library has become my chapel—dour Sister Mary Richard the truest saint who replaces these treasures in their berths on the dusty shelves.

Last year, my stomach ached all the time. I was like a coyote that had eaten the poison bait, skulking just outside the light of the campfire hoping this time would be different. I hung back, doing the absolute minimum. It was a point of honor not to let them break my spirit.

Once I found out how easy it was to slip through the fence, my one consistent goal was to sneak into town for a half pint of Old Crow. It's curious I wasn't caught the first time. I wasn't hard to miss with my hands shaking in fear. Most of the girls were white; the other Indian children, docile as lambs.

Before Vespers I crouched in the phone booth jamming sticks of Juicy Fruit in my mouth to conceal the cigarettes and whiskey on my breath. In the quietest part of the Mass when the priest was about to consecrate the Host, Maggie Travis loved to whisper loudly, "Sally Ann, you been out partying again?" Of course everyone looked at me instead of her.

I was ashamed to admit I could never really keep up in her crowd. She always stood on solid ground, as I was drifting out to sea on some mysterious riptide invisible to girls like her. Although Maggie looked sweet, she could chug a quart of Coors like a bullrider. Last spring, I went home with her for a visit. Her brother's friends got a jug of sweet white wine and took us racing in his Mustang 125 miles an hour down a hilly dirt road. Each time we crested a rise, the car took flight. Not only did it scare me spitless, the wine made me sick. At least I made it out of the car before I got sick.

When we got to the party, I put on a stoic face and continued to drink with the group until I passed out. I never found out which one of those guys made me pregnant that night. I just know when I came to, my clothes were in a wad in one corner and I was in a wad in another. I was too ashamed to ask anyone what had happened. But Maggie assured me I had had a great time.

Then my body began to swell. First the ankles puffed. Then it spread up my thighs. It felt like my body was encasing itself in a bag of water. The ligaments of my pelvis stretched to accommodate this new presence. My belly became distended. Finally, when my breasts exploded at such a rate that it scarred the skin, I admitted to my innermost self that I was indeed pregnant. Luckily there was only one month of morning sickness to get through before summer break.

With the same bony frame as my mother had, I started showing right away. She had had a scholarship to New Mexico U. which she gave up for a black soldier from the base. When she died, her four daughters were scattered all over New Mexico in foster homes. I could not imagine what I would do when fall came and it was time to return to the Academy.

I knew I would be completely unlike Karma Tyler. When I was a sophomore in my first term at the Academy, she went to class the entire term burgeoning quietly. Just kept stuffing herself with bread and chocolate, publicly worrying about her weight, pinning her uniform skirt lower and wearing the white blouse outside. No one knew she was pregnant until that gray Saturday afternoon when we were all in the auditorium stuffing the Christmas piñata.

Like a cat, Karma delivered her baby in her alcove alone. Then she wrapped it in the bloody sheets and stuffed it down the laundry chute.

When Sister Mary Augustine came by our alcove and heard

the six of us whispering about Karma, she said we must turn our eyes to the ink of Original Sin blackening our own souls. Stupidly, I asked what happened to the baby. Sister replied that Eve was the root of the word evil and that she and Adam were cast out of Paradise because she insisted on knowledge. Karma and her baby vanished by Vespers.

There was no possibility I could take the baby home. When I got expelled from the school before this, my aunt told me she was fed up, that my next stop would be the reformatory. Her last effort on my behalf was to get me into the Academy. Somehow, she had convinced the nuns that I truly wanted to become a novice.

But when she dropped me off, her final words to me were, "Don't even be thinking about bringin' no brats home. You let them hot pants get you in trouble, you are on your own."

Somehow, I made it through my junior year, morning sickness and all. When I got home to Albuquerque for the summer, I was terrified my aunt would realize I was pregnant.

She didn't, but when I started work waiting tables, Betty, whom I had known since childhood, recognized the symptoms immediately. She had dropped out of school to raise two toddlers and she envied my chance to finish school. She told me about the abortionist. I went to spend an innocent weekend at her house and arranged to meet him at midnight.

He was late. While I waited, I sipped whiskey and tried not to worry about the squeaks coming from the Dumpster behind the restaurant. I had always been warned never to go into the District. Then his car drove up. At first, it wasn't clear to me that he was actually going to do it in Joe's Rib Shack.

First, he took the sock full of money I had been saving from my mother's death. Then he ushered me into the back of the restaurant, where a sheet-covered butcher block was jammed against the wall. Huge steel pots hung on hooks over the crusty black stove. On the drainboard by the sink, a cigarette coated in pasty lipstick had been left in a shot glass.

I took off my coat. It was a minute before I realized he was waiting for me to strip completely. Betty had never actually met this man. She just knew someone who had been here.

"My name is Duane," he said. "I know this looks kind of casual, but we won't be bothered here. You just relax and take a sip of this." He handed me a glass. I expected it to be medicine. But when I smelled it, it was rye whiskey. I drank it gratefully.

When I began to unbutton my shirt, he stared at me until I stopped and stared back. Then he started bustling about arranging various small surgical knives on a white towel.

He handed me a little gown with strings at the neck. Then he pointed to the butcher block against the wall.

"Let's get going."

The steel bowls stacked underneath clattered when I hoisted myself onto the table. The aroma of a bag of yellow onions almost crowded out the smell of disinfectant. I watched the second hand of the grease-spattered clock spasm from second to second. It was such deep night that I could actually hear the freight trains at the switching yard five miles away.

His hair was like strands of black syrup across a pink scalp. When he saw me looking at the water boiling on the stove, he said cheerfully, "Got to keep that steel sterile, know what I'm saying?"

His white coat was frayed at the cuffs. As he rolled the instrument tray over to the block, my legs clamped together.

When Duane grinned, I could see that his gums had receded.

"Now I just want you to relax, take a deep breath and drop your legs open."

I contemplated lying there, wide open as a slit salmon, inhaling the ammonia from the mops soaking under the sink. Duane couldn't stop chatting.

"Why don't you tell me about yourself. What's your favorite subject? You are in school, right? This will all be over in a jiffy. Keep in mind, I won't actually be cutting on *you*." Then he patted my knee with a hand covered in cream-colored rubber.

He moved to put a mask over my face; I started to wonder seriously why he should cut on me at all. It didn't make sense. Suddenly I wished I hadn't been drinking. I sat up.

"Wait a minute," I said.

Duane's smile evaporated.

"We got one hour to get this thing done and get out of here."

"I can't do it."

"What do you mean *you* can't do it. I'm the one has to do it."

"Are you a real doctor?"

He waited too long before he nodded.

"Just give me my clothes and let me get out of here."

"Fine, little lady, but I'm keeping the money. I had to get the keys to this place. Still got to pay off the night watchman so nobody knows. Come here in the middle of the night at great risk to my personal self and you get cold feet?"

I climbed down, shivering with relief in spite of his tirade. I needed some privacy to dress, but as I moved toward the swinging doors that led out into the dark dining room, he became incensed.

"Where do you think you're going? Dress right here. I ain't taking my eyes off your scrawny ass till you are out that door." It was the word "scrawny" that did it. Stark naked, I walked over to the butcher block and grabbed a scalpel.

"Know something, Duane," I said. "I intend to leave here with my money."

He blanched.

"Now wait a minute," he said, edging around the drainboard. I could see he was trying to decide whether or not to rush me. I rushed him.

"Give me my money, or I will cut your liver out and fry it up with one of these onions." Then I started laughing.

Keeping his eyes on me, he reached into his pocket and tossed the sock of money on the block. My hands were shaking so badly I got my underpants caught in the zipper of my jeans. When I was dressed, I headed for the door, shoes clutched in one hand, scalpel in the other.

Then I slipped outside. The scratching noises in the Dumpster were quiet. I was very relieved not to be lying at the bottom of it covered in coffee grounds and rib bones. I started to laugh, then weep, then laugh. In the distance, dogs barked.

I started running. Finally, when I got to the highway, my hysteria subsided; I had to consider the practical question of where I was running to.

I walked briskly until I heard a rattle. Then I remembered it was dangerous to walk the desert highway in the dark because of rattlesnakes trying to absorb the heat from the still-warm asphalt. I walked a mile on the median until a pickup truck loaded with hay climbed the hill. I stuck out my thumb. When it pulled over, a friendly black and white shepherd stuck its head out the window.

At the wheel was an old man with a face the color of clay tile. He had the high wide cheekbones of the Mescolero Apache of my mother's clan. When I saw the gentleness in his eyes, I burst into fresh tears.

"Was it something we said?" he asked, snapping his fingers for the dog to move over.

He let out the clutch and guided the truck back onto the highway. The floor of the cab was littered with bridles and tools, the seat covered with a horse blanket. His faded flannel shirt smelled of sunshine. He was completely at ease with my sadness. The sheer ordinariness of the ride was a gift. In the moonlight, the desert floor seemed bright as steel dust.

When we came to a railroad crossing, I looked over at him. "Where are you headed?" he asked without looking at me. "By the way, my name's Kayitah."

"I don't know. I'm still pregnant," I said.

"If you don't mind me asking, what has that got to do with you being out here in the middle of the night?"

I realized there would be no reason to lie to him, so I told him the whole story. He didn't respond for so long that I wondered if he had even been listening.

"Where are we?" I asked, as he turned up a dirt road.

"About a mile from my trailer. If you want to sleep on the couch, you're welcome."

The old fear gripped me. I grabbed the door handle.

"I promise not to bother you," he said. "In the morning, I'll take you to meet my daughter Lupé. She went to that school too. She's a doctor now."

When he pulled into the driveway and turned off the motor, a gray mare with a colt whinnied. The trailer, nestled against a bluff, was an old silver Slipstream.

Inside, the trailer was remarkably small and immaculate. I sat on the couch at the end and leaned against a saddle that formed a perfect pillow, while he opened a can of pork and beans and set it on the burner.

"Hungry?" he asked, taking a roll of bologna out of the refrigerator. I nodded. He unsnapped a knife from his belt and sliced off chunks of meat and put it on rumpled white bread. I had never smelled anything so delicious.

"Got to go feed the ponies," he said. I followed him outside to the corral, where he began unloading the hay.

"I wish I had stayed in the reservation school. The Catholics ran that one too. Preach the virtue of poverty, but somehow they have it figured so they own everything that used to belong to the *Diné*. They're a funny, constipated people." He chuckled as he cut the twine on a bale of fresh hay.

"With those soft shoes, you need to mind where you put your feet," he said. It seemed odd that Kayitah should know about Mt. St. Gertrude's. The school, Maggie Travis and the abortionist all seemed like a distant dream from someone else's life.

"Me and the wife only had two kids that lived and they both had a time with whiskey. Juan's a big muckymuck priest back east. It looked like Lupé was heading for the pen sure as hell. She's a fighter just like you. But she found a way to beat them at their own game. You ought to think about that."

When we went back inside, he made a sandwich for himself. Occasionally a gust of wind whipped sand against the trailer. I had no idea when he stopped talking. The last thought I remember having was that he knew what to do.

I woke up to the sound of Kayitah working outside and coffee percolating on the stove. I was covered with a blanket. The dog was watching close by, stamping her paws to be outside. When I turned to stretch, she came over and licked my hand. She smelled like pheasants, which cleaned themselves with dust. I was on my second cup of coffee before I noticed the time. It was five-thirty, but even with only a few hours' sleep, I was deeply rested.

"Glad you're up," Kayitah said when he came back in. "We got a long drive."

There was one word over the door. "Clinica."

It was a corrugated tin shed thrown up on a long concrete slab. He said it used to be a feed store. Mustard-colored strips of insulation as lurid as nerve ends had been thrown up casually and left exposed.

There was a jukebox in the waiting room. Kayitah said he

had found it at the city dump, thrown it in the truck and brought it out. He said he had fished a couple of bullets out of its selection display. Now rescued and taped together, it wheezed and hummed electrically until it conjured somebody to feed it quarters.

"She bought this place with oil money from her mother's relatives in Stillwater," Kayitah said.

Lupé came out wearing a western shirt with pearl snaps, oxblood leather pants and a stethoscope. She had hips that flared like a tulip and a blue star tattooed beneath her right eye. She looked tired. When she saw Kayitah, she smiled. They spoke to each other warmly in a language I did not understand.

"Got another one, eh," she said in English.

When she turned her attention to me, I was suddenly terrified. Her gaze was as direct and searching as a hawk's. We went inside to an examination room.

"So, how far along are you?" she asked me. I told her I didn't know.

"How did you know I'm pregnant?" I asked.

"The same way I can tell you drink too much," she replied.

"And how is that?" I asked, stung.

"Sweetie, your skin is yellow. And what's making your stomach big isn't only the pregnancy. At least half of it's your liver."

"I don't drink that much," I said. Everybody I knew wanted to give me a lecture.

"If you hadn't been drinking you wouldn't have gotten pregnant. If you hadn't gotten pregnant, you wouldn't be in trouble at school. If you don't stop drinking, we'll do this procedure and three months from now, you'll be pregnant again and out of school. Without even hearing your story, I know that it will be the same as your mother's." She took the stethoscope off and sat down.

"I won't perform the abortion unless you come here for the rest of the summer for treatment for alcoholism."

"Look," I said, pulling out my money. "I can pay."

"So you can. But I don't need your money. Try it for a month. If it doesn't make sense, I'll buy you a bus ticket and a case of fine rye."

I really had no choice. I nodded.

"Know what, Sally Ann? In the spring, I pitch my teepee on

the mesa some nights. Others I sleep under stars. I cook in the Dutch oven and stay there as long as it pleases me."

She warmed the stethoscope in her hands. "It's no good, you know, living in square houses. A woman particularly needs to live in a circle. I bought the mesa so I could put my teepee on the place where I can inhale the spirit. Breathe deep."

All the women I knew—things just happened to them. I didn't know any women who made things happen.

"Do you know Sister Mary Richard?" she asked me.

"You mean that old nag in the library?"

"You read that one wrong, Sally. She owns the key to the whole place. I don't know if you noticed, but beyond the black dresses and rosary beads, that place is a ticket to the very world it wants to hide from you. In the fall you must return there to study. Come on, let's get started on this procedure."

MARY DALY

Early Moments: My Taboo-Breaking Quest—To Be a Philosopher

As a student in a small, working-class catholic high school in Schenectady, New York, I was a voice crying in the wilderness when I declared that I wanted to study philosophy. Even the sensitive and generous Sister who was always encouraging me to write for publication had no way of empathizing with such an outrageous urge.[1] Moreover, the school library had no books on the subject. Yet this Lust of my adolescent mind was such that I spun my own philosophies at home. I have no idea where I picked up that Strange propensity.

As a result of help from my parents plus winning the Bishop Gibbons scholarship (awarded on the basis of a competitive exam in religion) plus saving money from my supermarket check-out job, I managed to go to a small nearby catholic college for women. Being an inhabitant of the catholic ghetto, I had never even heard of such schools as Vassar, Radcliffe, or Smith. Even if I had heard of them, they would not have been accessible—nor would they have appeared desirable. I wanted to study "*Catholic philosophy,*" and the path of my Questing Journey led logically and realistically to The College of Saint Rose in Albany, New York.

Ironically, the college did not offer a major in philosophy, although a required minor consisting of eighteen credit hours in that subject was imposed upon all students. The difference in my case was that I loved the subject. This love persisted, despite the boringness of priest professors who opined that women could never learn philosophy, and whose lectures consisted of sitting in front of the class and reading aloud from the textbook, thereby demonstrating their ability to read English. They appeared to be thoroughly mystified by my interest, and the mystification was no doubt associated with the fact that they had never experienced enthusiasm for this pursuit in themselves. While they sat and droned, I sat and wondered at the incongruity of the situation. This wondering itself became incorporated into my own philosophical questioning. I did not yet understand that for a woman to strive to become a philosopher was to break a Terrible Taboo.[2]

Although those professors contributed little to the furtherance of my philosophical Quest, my own experiences contributed a great deal. There had been shimmering Moments in early childhood. For example, there was the Time, when I was about five or six, that I discovered the big gleaming block of ice in the snow. There were no words for the experience. The air was crisp and it was late afternoon. There was a certain winter light and a certain winter smell when I came upon the block of ice—probably in our back yard. I was all of a sudden in touch with something awesome—which I would later call Elemental. It was a shock that awakened in me some knowing of an Other dimension and I felt within me one of the first stirrings that I can remember of the Call of the Wild. I know that my capacity for meeting ice in the snow in that way has never totally gone away, because recently, while working on this book, I went for a walk on a winter evening and it happened again. This encounter was Strangely familiar.

The shimmering Moments occurred with great intensity in early adolescence. There was the Moment, for example, when one particular clover blossom Announced its be-ing to me. It Said starkly, clearly, with utmost simplicity: "I am." It gave me an intuition of be-ing. Years later, studying the philosophy of Jacques Maritain, I knew that I was not alone with this intuition.[3]

Yet, of course, I was unspeakably Alone with it. It was always calling me somewhere that no one else could tell me about. It would eventually lead me to cross the Atlantic, basically without any money, to obtain doctorates in theology and philosophy in a strange, medieval university where courses were taught in Latin and where my "fellow students" were catholic priests and seminarians.

The encounter with that clover blossom had a great deal to do with my becoming a Radical Feminist Philosopher. If a clover blossom could say "I am," then why couldn't I?

Spiraling Back: Early Grades and Private Junkets

It would be difficult to convey the foreground dreariness of the forties and fifties in America, particularly for a potential Radical Feminist Philosopher with a Passion for forbidden theological and philosophical learning—it *would be* difficult if the patriarchal State of Boredom had not managed to repeat itself by belching forth the insufferable eighties and nineties, reproducing a time of dulled-out brains, souls, and passions. So I need not ask the reader to imagine or try to remember such a time; she need only look around.*

In those decades, however, there was no point of comparison, no possibility of nostalgia. There was only the self-legitimating facticity of Boredom, with no apparent way out. For me, however, there was the Call of the Clover Blossom. Propelled by the idea that *I Am*, I made exploratory journeys by way of warming up for my Outercourse, which is, of course, the Direction my life has taken.

But I must Spiral back a bit, because before the Time of that existential encounter, there was "elementary school."

Let me assure the reader that I have always, that is, spasmodically, made abortive efforts to conform. For example, in the first grade at Saint John the Evangelist School in Schenectady, when I perceived that many of my classmates had dirty, second-hand readers, I spat and slobbered over the pages of my own

*There is a difference, however. In the course of the last two decades of this millennium it has been and continues to be possible to Re-member the early Moments of this Wave of the women's movement in the sixties and seventies—either directly or through the writings and stories of Other women who were there. It is also possible to Re-Call Feminists of earlier Times.

brand-new one to make it appear used. When my teacher, Sister Mary Edmund, asked for an explanation, I was speechless. I have no idea whether she understood my motivation for the slobbering, but I do think that I myself had some idea of attempting to "fit in."

One of my classmates in the first grade, whose name was Rosemary, was hit and killed by a trolley car when she was crossing the street in front of her house. There was some confusing story about her not looking both ways and not hearing the sound of the oncoming trolley because the one she just stepped off had started to move. The whole class had to go with Sister Mary Edmund to see Rosemary "laid out." She was wearing a white dress. I did not like being there. The experience did not fit in with anything. It was like a white blob that hung there. It was impossible to understand and was worse than a nightmare.

My second grade teacher was Sister Mary Clare of the Passion, who droned a lot—too much, I thought—about "God's poor." I did not understand why the poor were God's. I had her again in the fifth grade, and I remember a feeling of deep shock when she made fun of a boy in our class who was really poor and whose name was Abram Spoor. She assaulted him with a jingle which went something like "Abram Spoor . . . and he *is* poor."

Upon reflection, I have come to the conclusion that this shocking behavior was inspired not by malice but by a passion for jingles, puns, and wordplay in general. I remember that it was Sister Mary Clare of the Passion who more than once wrote on the tops of papers I handed in to her the title of the (then) popular hymn "Daily, Daily, Sing to Mary." These words would be crossed off with a very light scribbly line—as if to indicate that she had written them there by mistake. I understood that this was meant as a game or a joke, but I did not see anything very funny about it at the time.[4]

Upon further reflection, I Now realize that this woman had a strong creative streak. One day when I was in the fifth grade she told us all to bring in some toy that we had become sick of. The idea was that we would exchange our old toys and everyone would get something new. I brought in a tin monkey with a drum who obligingly banged this instrument when you turned the key. I was ready to discard this because it seemed much too childish for a person in the fifth grade. I remember that Abram Spoor's face lit up with sheer joy when he saw my mechanical monkey and said, "I'd like *that*!"

No doubt this woman had an interesting time watching all of our transactions and reactions. Personally I was delighted with my own acquisition of two oddly shaped books about "Our Gang." But the truly memorable experience of the day was the look on Abram's face and the sound of his voice when he got my monkey. Obviously he had never owned such a wondrous toy in his whole life. I am struck by the accuracy of Sister's insensitive and unfortunate pun. I Now wonder if her puns popped out uncontrollably without consideration of the consequences. Perhaps her weird and lugubrious name—which in all probability she did not freely choose—inspired her to be rather reckless and satirical with words.[5]

Sister Mary Arthur, who was my teacher in the third and sixth grades, was a handsome young woman with shaggy black eyebrows who stormed up and down the aisles hitting the boys—only the boys—with her ruler. She had my unflagging loyalty and admiration.

These Sisters all belonged to a congregation called "Sisters of the Holy Names." Their coifs had stiff white material extending out along the sides of their faces. This headgear must have seriously affected their peripheral vision. So they had to swivel their heads quite a lot, but I didn't think of this phenomenon as too unusual, since that's how it was at Saint John the Evangelist School and I didn't know any other nuns who could serve as a point of comparison.

I missed quite a few days of school during those first six years of my formal education. Even a slight cold was an excuse for staying home in bed and reading my favorite books, such as *The Call of the Wild,* the "Raggedy Ann" stories, and the "Children of All Lands" stories by Madeline Frank Brandeis. It just seemed right to me that I could break the routine and sail off into my own private world sometimes. The special ambrosia served to me by my mother during these outer space voyages was chilled "Junket," which came in three exquisite flavors: chocolate, vanilla, and strawberry. Maybe it also came in raspberry.

The price extorted by my teachers for these blissful free days was lowering of my grade average, which reduced me to being ranked second highest in the class at the end of some weeks. The way they managed to do this was by averaging in "zeros" for tests missed on my excursion days. I thought that this was very unfair, especially because my rival, Sarah Behan, who never missed a day of school, then got to be first, even though her grades were lower. But those Times of flying free, which gave me an enduring Taste for escaping imposed routines, were worth it. I think that my mother, co-conspirator that she was, knew this.

The World of Glowing Books and the Call of the Wild

Well, the years of elementary school skipped along in this fashion. My passion for the intellectual life burst forth at puberty, in the seventh grade to be precise. Since Saint John the Evangelist School ended with the sixth grade, I had moved on to Saint Joseph's Academy. This catholic school was attached to a working-class German parish and provided education for pupils from the first grade through high school. It was staffed by the Sisters of Saint Joseph of Carondelet. Saint Joseph's Academy no longer even exists. But for me that poor little school was the scene of Metamorphic Moments that can be Re-Called and Re-membered. For many of their hundreds of pupils, some of the Sisters who taught there, who were often unappreciated, created rich Memories of the Future. They formed/transformed our Future, which, of course, is Now.

I was an extremely willing scholar. Few understood my true motivation when I followed the high school students around worshipfully, ogling their armloads of textbooks, especially tomes of chemistry, math, and physics. What was really going on was that I was drooling with admiration and envy because they had access to these learned, fascinating books. It never crossed my mind that their attitudes toward these tomes ranged from indifference to loathing. In my own indomitable innocence I saw these as portals to paradise, as magical and infinitely enticing.

Even though, years later, I found out the less than magical qualities of many of those books, this Dis-covery was not an experience of disillusionment. My preoccupation with the high schoolers' tomes of wisdom had been grounded in a Background intuition/Realization of the Radiant Realm of Books, which was not an illusion. Therefore, there was nothing at all to be disillusioned about. Later on I did find out about the foreground level of most books, but that took nothing away from my knowledge of the Thisworldly/Otherworldly Reality of Books.[6]

My parents had always given me many beautiful books as presents, especially on holidays. So the World of Glowing Books somehow entered the realm of my imagination very early and became a central focus of the Quest to be a philosopher. More than once in high school I had dreams of wondrous worlds—of being in rooms filled with colorful glowing books. I would wake up in a state of great ecstasy and knowing that this was *my* World, where I belonged.

During that early adolescent time I also Dis-covered the "celestial gleam" of nature. Since my father was a traveling salesman who sold ice cream freezers, I sometimes went with him on drives into the country when he visited his customers' ice cream stands. My awakening to the transcendental glowing light over meadows and trees happened on some of these trips.[7] Other Moments of contact with Nature involved knowing the Call of the Wild from the mountains and purple skies and the sweet fresh smell of snow.

These invitations from Nature to my adolescent spirit were somehow intimately connected with the Call of the World of Glowing Books. My life was suffused with the desire for a kind of Great Adventure that would involve touching and exploring these strange worlds that had allowed me to glimpse their wonders and Lust for more.

Taboo-Breaking: "The Convent" as Flyswatter

I was reasonably well equipped to follow this seemingly improbable, not fully articulated, yet crystal clear Call. For one thing I was endowed with insufferable stubbornness—a quality which never failed me. I also had the gift of being at least fifty per cent oblivious of society's expectations of me as a "normal" young woman and one hundred per cent resistant to whatever expectations I did not manage to avoid noticing. For example, I never had the slightest desire to get married and have children. Even in elementary school and in the absence of any Feminist movement I had felt that it would be intolerable to give up my own name and become "Mrs." something or other. It would obviously be a violation of mySelf. Besides, I have always really *liked* my name. I wouldn't sell it for anything. A third asset was a rock bottom self-confidence and Sense of Direction which, even in the bleakest periods, have never entirely deserted me.

Looking back, I recognize that all of these assets were gifts from my extraordinary mother. For one thing, she had always made it clear to me that she had desired only one child, and that one a daughter. I was exactly what she wanted, and all she wanted. How she managed to arrange this I was never told. At any rate my father seemed to have no serious objection. For another thing, I cannot recall that she ever once—even once—tried to promote the idea that I should marry and have a family, although she often said that she was very happily married, and indeed this seemed to be the case. She was hardly one to promote the convent either. I was the one who tossed around that threat, chiefly as a weapon against well-meaning relatives and "friends of the family" who intoned that "some day the right man would come along." I never followed through on my threat of joining the convent, but it worked well enough as a defense against society at large.[8]

This is not to say that I never seriously considered entering the convent. I was not exactly insincere in proclaiming this as a goal. It just seemed indefinitely postponable. Perhaps if the Sisters had had the possibility of becoming great scholars, as I supposed monks did, I would have been more seriously tempted. However, I saw something of the constraints imposed upon their lives. They were deprived of the leisure to study and travel and think creatively to their fullest capacity. Even those who taught in college were confined to somewhat narrow perspectives. The Sisters were in fact assigned to be the drudges of the church.* So

*This was perfectly in keeping with the drudge role to which all women were/are assigned by the church and by patriarchal society in general.

I couldn't exactly identify with the convent as a goal and just kept moving on in my own way. Later on I read an article in which someone referred to old maidhood as a sort of "budget religious vocation" which was accorded some modicum of respect in the church, especially during the forties and fifties, and especially if the old maid in question was dedicated to her work. I am sure that message had entered my brain and seemed a pretty good deal to me. I know that some women tried to escape "love and marriage" by joining the convent—a strategy that would have worked better in the Middle Ages when many monasteries were Wild places. But I did not see it as a real Way Out. For me, to be an Old Maid/Spinster was the way to be free. Yet I could not fully articulate that idea, even to myself, because even that idea was Taboo. So I just logically acted on it, while waving the banner of "the convent" like a flyswatter when necessary.

---

1. This was Sister Athanasia Gurry, C.S.J., who taught me English throughout my four years of high school at St. Joseph's Academy in Schenectady.

2. There was and still is a taboo against women studying philosophy seriously and becoming teachers and scholars in the "field" of philosophy. Even mere uncritical teaching and writing of scholarly articles about male philosophers was and to some extent still is taboo. But this is not what I am referring to in this passage. I am referring to breaking the *Terrible Taboo* against a woman's striving to become a philosopher in her own right. I already knew that my Quest was *to be* a philosopher, and—although I did not have the words for it—I knew that this was an Elemental Quest, implying Intimacy/Ultimacy. See Mary Daly, *Pure Lust: Elemental Feminist Philosophy* (1984; San Francisco: HarperSanFrancisco, 1992; London: The Women's Press Ltd, 1984), pp. 243–53.

3. See Chapter Four. My dissertation, subsequently published in Rome, entitled *Natural Knowledge of God in the Philosophy of Jacques Maritain*, was written for the doctorate in philosophy at the University of Fribourg, Switzerland, in the mid-sixties. Although it centers on the meaning and implications of the "intuition of being" in Maritain's philosophy, on a subliminal level I was really trying to understand the meaning and implications of my own intuition of be-ing for my own philosophical Quest—for my own be-ing. I did not spell this word (*be-ing*) with a hyphen then but that was the sense of it. I later developed my own philosophy of be-ing as a verb (not a noun). See Mary Daly, *Beyond God the Father: Toward a Philosophy of Women's Liberation* (1973; reissued with an "Orig-

inal Reintroduction by the Author," Boston: Beacon Press, 1985; London: The Women's Press Ltd, 1986). See also my subsequent books.

4. I would see it as ineffably funny years later. For further details on "Daily (Daly), Daily, Sing to Mary," see Chapter Five.

5. The Sisters usually could not choose their names in those days. Many were "stuck" with men's names, which must have felt alienating and bizarre to the recipients. Of course, some feminine names were also weird and could have been devastating to a woman's self-image.

6. Seeing through the fraudulence of elementary caricatures need not dilute one's appreciation of the wondrous Reality that is simulated. Discovering the unreality of donald duck and disneyworld need not diminish but can enhance by way of contrast one's appreciation of Real Ducks and the Real World. The same principle of distinction between Background Otherness and foreground fraudulence applies also to Books.

7. I hope it is clear that by *transcendental* I do not mean "beyond" natural knowledge and experience. I use this word to Name a Supremely Natural Knowledge and Experience which should be ordinary but which, in a dulled-out society, is, unfortunately, extraordinary.

8. Nor did any of the Sisters urge me to "enter." I suppose that they were perceptive enough to foresee that I would not last long in that austere environment. Besides, it was clear in high school that I was hell-bent on going directly to college, and in college it was obvious that I was dead set on graduate school.

Contributors

Rudolfo Anaya is the author of *Alburquerque,* which won the 1993 PEN/West award for fiction. He has also written *Bless Me Ultima, Heart of Aztlan,* and *Tortuga.*

A. Manette Ansay has published stories and poems in more than thirty journals, including *North American Review, Story,* and *Quarterly West.* Her first novel, *Vinegar Hill,* was published by Viking in 1994. She is an assistant professor of English at Vanderbilt University.

Tony Ardizzone is the author of *Larabi's Ox: Stories of Morocco* and *The Evening News,* which received the Flannery O'Connor Award. He has also published two novels, *In the Name of the Father* and *Heart of the Order,* from which "Baseball Fever" is excerpted. He attended Catholic grammar school and four years of all-boys high school, taught by the Christian Brothers, in Chicago.

John Azrak is chairperson of a high school English department in New York. His book on secondary education, *The Learning Community,* was published by Paulist Press, and his stories have appeared in *Apalachee Quarterly, Fine Madness,* and other journals.

Brenda Bankhead has recently completed a collection of short fiction about African-American women and children and their survival in America. Her work has appeared in *Obsidian II, Black Literature in Review, Love's Shadow,* and *The Time of Our Lives: Women Write on Sex after 40.* She lives in Los Angeles.

Patricia Barone is the author of *Handmade Paper* and *The Wind* (New Rivers Press). She graduated from Marquette University, after sixteen years of Catholic education, right in the middle of the Vatican II changes. One change was the new practice of holding hands in a circle after communion, which she disliked. For many others these changes amounted to a revolution of the soul.

Robin Beeman grew up in Louisiana and now lives in Northern California. Her fiction has appeared in *North American Review, Crazyhorse,* and *Fiction Network.* Her collection *A Parallel Life and Other Stories* was published by Chronicle Books in 1992.

Maria Bruno is an assistant professor of women's studies and writing at Michigan State University. Her fiction has appeared in *Ms., Earth's Daughters, New Directions for Woman,* and the anthologies *Eating Our Hearts Out, Women's Friendships,* and *Breaking Up Is Hard to Do.*

Christopher Buckley grew up in Santa Barbara and attended Catholic grammar school, high school, and college. His sixth book of poems, *Dark Matter,* was published in 1993. He is co-editor of *What Will Suffice: The Ars Poetica in Contemporary American Poetry* and has recently completed a volume of creative nonfiction, *Golden State.*

Thomas Burke has published in *The Chiron Review* and *Evergreen Chronicles.* Thirteen years of bead squeezing have rendered him a Catholic boy in perpetuity. He remembers the monks and priests who taught him with affection and carries a boundless appreciation for human eccentricity as well as for the sound education he received.

Giovanna (Janet) Capone is a working-class Italian-American writer. She recently learned that her roots on her father's side are Sephardic Jewish, an interesting revelation given her Catholic upbringing. She identifies as a pagan lesbian. "Gramma and

Mrs. Carmichael" is from her novel in progress, *Olive and Lavendar.*

Nona Caspars has published fiction and poetry in *Calyx, Negative Capability, Word of Mouth,* and *Women on Women Volume* 2. Her novel, *The Blessed,* published in 1990 by Silverleaf Press, explored salvation and personal ghosts. She lives in San Francisco.

Thomas Centolella lives and teaches in San Francisco. His first book of poetry, *Terra Firma,* published by Copper Canyon Press, was a winner in the National Poetry Series and also won a Before Columbus Foundation American Book Award.

Lucille Clifton is Distinguished Professor of Humanities at St. Mary's College of Maryland. Her collections of poetry include *The Book of Light, Good Woman,* and *Next.*

Geraldine Connolly is the author of *The Red Room* (Heatherstone Press, 1988) and *Food for the Winter* (Purdue University Press, 1990). She teaches at the Writers Center in Bethesda, Maryland.

Mary Daly is the author of six radical feminist books, including *Outercourse, Pure Lust, Gyn/Ecology,* and *Beyond God the Father.* She disturbs the peace by lecturing to audiences in the United States and Europe, and by teaching feminist ethics at Boston College.

John deValcourt grew up in the South and was a member of the Christian Brothers for twenty years. He now lives in Santa Cruz, teaching mathematics at the University of California at Santa Cruz and at Cabrillo College.

Kerry Dolan grew up in Brooklyn, where she attended Catholic schools for twelve years. Her stories have appeared in *Quarterly West, Greensboro Review,* and *The Next Parish Over: A Collection of Irish-American Writing.* She now lives and teaches in San Francisco.

Michael Dorris is the author of *Paper Trail* (essays), *A Yellow Raft in Blue Water* (a novel), *Working Men* (stories), *Morning*

Girl (a children's book), and *The Broken Cord,* winner of the 1989 National Book Critics Circle award for nonfiction.

Mary Ellis was born and raised in northern Wisconsin and currently lives in Minneapolis. Her fiction has appeared in *Bellingham Review, Wisconsin Academy Review*, and the anthology *Uncommon Waters: Women Write About Fishing.*

Louise Erdrich is the author of the novels *Love Medicine, The Beet Queen,* and *Tracks* and two collections of poetry, *Baptism of Desire* and *Jacklight.*

Maureen M. Fitzgerald lives in Madison, Wisconsin. She spent hours as a Catholic girl exercising her imagination during morning Mass at St. Mary's in Wausau and believes this has helped her become a writer. She recently started to collect holy cards and is working on a collection of short stories.

Grace Flannery works and lives in San Francisco with her partner, JoAnne Churchill, and her cats, Rose and Brigit. She looks back on her Catholic upbringing with mixed feelings, a sense of humor, and no regrets.

Linda Nemee Foster has been published in *The Georgia Review, Indiana Review,* and *Nimrod.* She is the director of literature programming for the Urban Institute for Contemporary Arts in Grand Rapids, Michigan. A contributor to *Catholic Girls,* she says, "From my firm belief as a child to my reverent skepticism as an adult—once a Catholic girl, always a Catholic girl."

Kay Hogan has been published in *Catholic Girls, Columbia Pacific Review, Long Pond Review,* and *North Country Anthology.* Her Irish Catholic and New York background provides a continuous source of material for writing.

Maureen Howard is the author of the novels *Natural History, Bridgeport Bus,* and *Facts of Life.* She lives in New York City.

David Kowalczyk was born in Batavia, New York, where he is currently living. He has taught English at various colleges, including Arizona State, and has published in *Albany Review, Maryland Review,* and other literary journals.

John Logan was poetry editor for *The Nation* and *Critic Magazine.* He published poetry, critical essays, and fiction. His last two books of poetry were *Only the Dreamer Can Change the Dream* and *Bridge of Change.*

Gigi Marino and her grandmother appeared previously in *Catholic Girls.* A poet and freelance writer, Marino lives in Pennsylvania, where she teaches at Penn State and Rockview Correctional Institute.

Kristina McGrath has published fiction and poetry in *The American Voice, The Paris Review, Harper's, The Pushcart Prize XIV,* and *Catholic Girls.* She received *The Kenyon Review* Award for Literary Excellence in Fiction. Her story "Under the Table" is an excerpt from the novel *Housework.*

Margaret McMullan was educated by the Madames of the Sacred Heart in Illinois. In college she rebelled by studying Buddhism and Judaism. She recently did the unthinkable by marrying an Irish Catholic boy. Her novel, *When Warhol Was Still Alive,* was published in 1993 by The Crossing Press. She teaches creative writing at the University of Evansville in Indiana.

Pat Mora is a native of El Paso, Texas, and the author of *Nepantla: Essays from the Land in the Middle* (University of New Mexico Press), three collections of poetry, titled *Chants, Borders,* and *Communion* (Arte Publico Press), and several children's books, including *A Birthday Basket for Tia* (Macmillan).

Simone Poirier-Bures grew up in Halifax, Nova Scotia, in a French Acadian family. She teaches in the English department at Virginia Tech University and has published award-winning fiction in many literary magazines. Her novel, *Candyman,* of which "Blue Coat" is a part, was published in 1994 by Oberon Press in Canada.

Birute Putrius-Serota lives in Santa Monica and teaches disabled high school children. She has completed a novel about a family in nineteenth-century Lithuania, where the fabulous was an everyday occurrence. What she misses most about her Catholic childhood is the possibility of miracles always being present.

Leroy V. Quintana is the author of *The History of Home* and *Sangre,* both award-winning collections of poetry. He grew up in New Mexico and has taught writing in public schools, colleges, and the prison system. He is currently as associate professor of English at San Diego Mesa College.

Viki Radden has published fiction and essays in *Sage: A Scholarly Journal on Black Women, Off Our Backs,* and *Connexions Quarterly.* She is contemplating her second novel and is making a film titled *Black Girls Don't Swim.* She lives in Forest Knolls, California, and is desperately seeking a patron saint. Or just a patron.

Alberto Ríos is a professor of English at Arizona State University. His most recent collection of poetry is *Teodoro Luna's Two Kisses* (W. W. Norton, 1990).

Len Roberts has written dozens of Catholic poems, some of which have appeared in *The Iowa Review, New England Review, Poetry,* and *The Paris Review.* He is the author of two collections of poetry, *Counting the Black Angels* (University of Illinois Press, 1994) and *Dangerous Angels* (Copper Beech Press, 1993).

Maureen Seaton is the author of two award-winning collections of poetry, *The Sea Among the Cupboards* (New Rivers, 1992) and *Fear of Subways* (Eighth Mountain, 1991). She lives in Chicago and is continually transforming the faith of her fathers.

Bettianne Shoney Sien is the radical eighth daughter in a family of thirteen children. Her work has appeared in numerous feminist journals, and a collection of her stories, *Lizards/Los Padres,* is available from Her Books. She believes the devil, if he exists, invented Catholicism.

John Skoyles is the executive director of the Fine Arts Work Center in Provincetown, Massahusetts. He has published two books of poems with Carnegie-Mellon University Press, *A Little Faith* and *Permanent Change,* and has recently completed a memoir.

Gary Soto is the author of five poetry collections, including *Who Will Know Us* and *Home Course in Religion,* both published by Chronicle Books. He edited the anthology *California Childhood* and has published in *The New Yorker, The Nation,* and *Poetry,* among others.

Maura Stanton teaches at Indiana University and is the author of a collection of stories, *The Country I Come From* (Milkweed Editions), and three collections of poetry. Her work has appeared in *Ploughshares, Quarterly West,* and *Michigan Quarterly Review* and in the anthologies *Love's Shadow, Lovers,* and *Catholic Girls.*

Mary Helen Stefaniak was born in Milwaukee, where she attended St. Veronica's, St. Mary's Academy, and Marquette University. Later, she graduated from the nondenominational Iowa Writers Workshop. She considers herself a recovering Catholic.

Amber Coverdale Sumrall taught second grade for two years at Holy Family in Los Angeles, the school she attended fifteen years earlier. She was responsible for preparing her fifty-plus students for First Holy Communion and, when asked one day why *she* never received, decided to find her vocation elsewhere. She has edited or co-edited ten collections of writings by women.

Thom Tammaro, the grandson of Italian immigrants, was raised in the heart of the steel valley of western Pennsylvania, where he graduated from Purification of the Blessed Virgin Mary elementary school. He is co-editor of *Inheriting the Land: Contemporary Voices from the Midwest* and is professor of multidisciplinary studies at Moorhead State University in Minnesota.

Ellen Treen knits up her non-Catholic life in Santa Cruz. She has published in the anthologies *Catholic Girls, Sexual Harassment: Women Speak Out,* and *Women of the 14th Moon: Writings on Menopause.* She believes the Church's belief in hell is based on its ability to create hell on earth.

John Van Kirk teaches writing at Marshall University in West Virginia. He is an O. Henry Prize–winning writer and has published stories and essays in *The Hudson Review, The New York Times,* and *Paragraph.*

Mary Grace Vazquez was born in Bayamón, Puerto Rico, and now lives in Northampton, Massachusetts, where she works for City Hall. In addition to writing, she is a photographer and deejay for the women's community.

Patrice Vecchione tried hard throughout her childhood to believe in the afterlife. She imagined gold-paved streets and all the candy she could eat and prayed to be good enough to get there. She is fairly certain now that this life is the only one but if there is another time around she'd like to come back as a hummingbird.

Bruce Weigl is the author of six collections of poetry, including *What Saves Us* and *Song of Napalm.* He is the editor or co-editor of three collections of critical essays, and his collection of poems co-translated from the Vietnamese with Nguyen Thanh, *Poems from Captured Documents,* was published in 1994. He teaches in the writing program at Pennsylvania State University.

Rita Williams is a recovering Catholic who is working hard to attain a spiritual life in Los Angeles. She is a freelance writer of op-ed pieces and book and theater reviews for *LA Weekly.* Her work has appeared in the anthologies *Lovers* and *Catholic Girls.* She is working on a novel, *Wild Woman of the West,* about her family of African-American hunting guides in the Rocky Mountains.

Robert Clark Young has published work in *Black Warrior Review, ZYZZYVA, Buffalo Press,* and *The Houston Post.* He attended Catholic school with one of the contributors to *Catholic Girls,* who suggested he submit to *Bless Me, Father.* He currently lives in Ohio.

Yvonne is a poet, essayist, filmmaker, and former poetry editor of *Ms.* She has written two collections of poetry, *IWilla/Soil* and *IWilla/Scourge,* both published by Chameleon. She spent sixteen years in the Catholic school system and is currently working on a book about black Catholics.

Permissions

(This constitutes an extension of the copyright page.)

An excerpt from *Bless Me Ultima* by Rudolfo Anaya © 1972 (Quinto Sol) is reprinted by permission of the author.

"Blue Light Special" by A. Manette Ansay originally appeared in *The Madison Review*, Fall 1991.

"Baseball Fever" by Tony Ardizzone is reprinted by permission of the author from *Heart of the Order* © 1986.

"Sister Barbara" by John Azrak originally appeared in *Artful Dodge*, #14/15.

"Burning Joan" by Robin Beeman is reprinted by permission of the author and Chronicle Books from *A Parallel Life and Other Stories* © 1992.

"Wild Heart" by Maria Bruno originally appeared in *Italian Americana*, Spring/Summer 1992.

"Days of Black & White" by Christopher Buckley originally appeared in *Black Warrior Review* and is included in *Dark Matter* (Copper Beech Press,© 1993).

"Humility" by Thomas Centolella is reprinted by permission of the author from *Terra Firma* (Copper Canyon Press,© 1990).

"Far Memory" (Parts 1 & 2) by Lucille Clifton is reprinted by permission of the author and Copper Canyon Press from *The Book of Light*© 1993.

"The Linens of the Sisters of St. Vincent" by Geraldine Connolly is reprinted by permission of the author from *Food for the Winter* (Purdue University Press,© 1990).

"Early Moments" by Mary Daly is reprinted by permission of the author and HarperCollins from *Outercourse*© 1993.

"A Perfect Day at Riis Park" by Kerry Dolan originally appeared in *Quarterly West,* Summer/Fall 1990.

"Fooling God" by Louise Erdrich is reprinted by permission of the author and HarperCollins from *Baptism of Desire*© 1990.

"Wings" by Mary Ellis originally appeared in *Glimmer Train,* Fall 1992.

"The El Train" by Kay Hogan originally appeared in *Descant.*

"Role Model" by Maureen Howard is reprinted by permission of the author from *Facts of Life.*

"Sinner" by David Kowalczyk originally appeared in *Oxalis,* Fall 1990.

"Relic" by John Logan is reprinted by permission of BOA Editions from *John Logan: The Collected Fiction*© 1991.

"Lifeguarding" by Margaret McMullan originally appeared in *The Greensboro Review,* #47.

"Discovered" by Pat Mora is reprinted by permission of the author and Arte Publico Press from *Chants*© 1985.

"Susanna" by Leroy V. Quintana is reprinted by permission of the author and Bilingual Press from *The History of Home*© 1993.

"Emma" by Len Roberts is reprinted by permission of the author from *Counting the Black Angels,* (University of Illinois Press,© 1994).

"The Purpose of Altar Boys" by Alberto Ríos is reprinted by permission of Sheep Meadow Press from *Whispering to Fool the Wind*© 1982.

"An Ordinary Mass" by Maureen Seaton originally appeared in *Indiana Review.*

"The Cold War" by Bettianne Shoney Sien originally appeared in *Sinister Wisdom* #51.

"The Music at Home" by Gary Soto is reprinted by permission of the author and Chronicle Books from *Home Course in Religion*© 1991.

"John McCormack" by Maura Stanton is reprinted by permission of the author from *The Country I Come From* (Milkweed Editions,© 1988).

"Voyeurs" by Mary Helen Stefaniak originally appeared in *The North American Review,* May/June 1992.

"First Day of School, 1951" by Amber Coverdale Sumrall originally appeared in *IKON: The Nineties,* #12/13.

"Eternity" by Thom Tammaro originally appeared in *North Dakota Quarterly,* Fall 1990.

"What Saves Us" by Bruce Weigl is reprinted by permission of the author from *What Saves Us* (TriQuarterly Books© 1992).

"Impurity" by Robert Clark Young originally appeared in *Pikestaff Forum* #12 under the title "Catholic Boy."

"Evangeline, #8" by Yvonne is reprinted by permission of the author from *IWilla/Scourge* (Chameleon,© 1986).